"KOLYA! WHAT'S HAPPENING TO H

Stasov stared down at the dolphin, which was now swimming frantically around the tank. As long as Kestrel was in no immediate physical danger...what was the dolphin hearing now? What went on in his mysterious head?

The dolphin rose out of the water with a long, ululating cry. Then it spoke: "*Let me die!*"

A
DEEPER
SEA

"Intriguing...Harrowing...Bizarre... A lyrical and eerie tale"
Booklist

"Thoroughly believable... Strangely humbling"
New York Review of Science Fiction

"A quirky, intelligent novel, full of surprises... Definitely an author to watch"
The Thirteenth Moon

"Jablokov is a craftsman of the first water"
Michael Swanwick, author of *Stations Of The Tide*

Other Avon Books by
Alexander Jablokov

CARVE THE SKY
NIMBUS

A DEEPER SEA

ALEXANDER JABLOKOV

AVONOVA
AVON BOOKS • NEW YORK

A DEEPER SEA is an original publication of Avon Books. This work is a novel. Any similarity to actual persons or events is purely coincidental.

AVON BOOKS
A division of
The Hearst Corporation
1350 Avenue of the Americas
New York, New York 10019

Copyright © 1992 by Alexander Jablokow
Cover illustration by Eric Peterson
Published by arrangement with the author
Library of Congress Catalog Card Number: 92-12916
ISBN: 0-380-71709-3

First AvoNova Printing: December 1993
First Morrow/AvoNova Hardcover Printing: November 1992

AVONOVA TRADEMARK REG. U.S. PAT. OFF. AND IN OTHER COUNTRIES, MARCA REGISTRADA. HECHO EN U.S.A.

Printed in the U.S.A.

RA 10 9 8 7 6 5 4 3 2 1

To Alla and Victor Jablokow,
who did all they could to raise a decent child,
got a writer instead,
and have learned to live with it.

Acknowledgments

Particular thanks go to David Smith, Dee Meaney, Sarah Smith, and William Green for editorial advice far beyond the call of any reasonable duty.

Thanks also go to Steve Popkes, Jon Burrowes, Joc Carrabis, Steve Caine, and the Cambridge Science Fiction Workshop. Paul Olkhovsky, Marilyn Tessier, Janet Lockhart, and Val Smith provided additional editorial help.

It is unfortunate that a good editor only gets his reward by being mentioned in tiny print in a writer's acknowledgments, but that is all I can give. So I want to note the efforts of David Hartwell, under difficult and thankless circumstances, in making this a better book.

CHAPTER ONE

2015

BY THE TIME THE FISHING BOAT ROUNDED THE HEADLAND most of the sea lions had stopped screaming. The scene revealed in the rocky bay was chaotic. Struggling shapes shredded the water, sending spume into the misty air. Dorsal fins cut the water like black sailboats.

"They're here," Colonel Ilya Stasov said exultantly. He pounded his fists on the wooden rail. "I *did* hear them planning it. There!" He pointed a long finger toward the torn waves. Georgios Theodoros followed with his eyes.

A desperate male sea lion, six hundred pounds of insulated muscle, struggled across wave-washed rocks. The ocean foam around it was already pink with the blood of its fellows. It hunched, trying to gain a purchase on the smooth cliff face that curved above. Obdurate, the land refused it and it slid back. It turned and, with astonishing speed for a creature so large, bounded across the rocks and into the water, its ancient salvation. In an instant it would find that the sea had turned traitor.

A smooth black shape shadowed beneath the waves. Its high dorsal fin sliced toward the sea lion. The killer whale rose up out of the water, showing the white spot behind its eye and its white belly. Its form was liquid grace. The sea lion had time for one last bellow of fear or defiance and then the orca was on it. Teeth flashed and penetrated flesh.

"My God!" Theodoros said. Both shapes disappeared beneath the water. The boat yawed sickeningly as the pilot turned sharply at the bay's shallow entrance and Theodoros grabbed for the railing. "How many orcas? I can't even tell."

"Twelve," Stasov said. "Most of the pod. Margaret and Ram are off gallivanting somewhere."

"All right. So why did you haul me all the way out here to see it?" Stasov had heard the calls late the previous night and had been insistent that his guest witness the orcas' hunt.

Stasov kept his hands on the railing but looked sideward at Theodoros. He had a strong and severe face, with high forehead and cheekbones, but his lips were surprisingly full and sensuous. He pursed them, disappointed by his guest's ill humor. "I thought you'd be interested in observing some orca behavior first hand. You don't have killer whales in the Aegean, do you? All you have are stories. Here are the real creatures right in front of you. What do you think?"

Theodoros looked out toward the bay and tugged at his ecclesiastical beard. The violence of the past few moments had settled and the water was calmer. The dirty wool sky pressed down onto the dark gray rocks, which in turn seemed but solid waves escaped from the ever-gray sea. The dorsal fins of the orcas cut a complex dance pattern. They had clustered at the bay's shallow end, a stretch of water leading up to a gravel beach.

Stasov's scrutiny made him feel ungrateful for not appreciating a four-hour boat ride in rough weather to watch killer whales massacre sea lions, even though he suspected the main purpose of the expedition was to prove that Stasov could understand some rudiments of orca dialect.

"I think I preferred the Aegean, Colonel." Theodoros shivered and tried to pull his rain jacket closer around him. He missed Thera with an almost physical longing. "But this doesn't have anything to do with what we were talking about. It's just a textbook example of predation."

Stasov grinned. The third large star on his officer's shoulder boards was new enough that he still enjoyed the novelty of the salutation, even from a foreign civilian. Theodoros used this fact, judiciously, to calm the sometimes touchy Russian down.

"You've been reading the wrong textbooks." Stasov was cheerfully blunt. "Watch. See those little spots there on the beach? Those are the pups. The parents tried to protect them. But the parents are dead."

Theodoros peered into the bay. Small sea lion pups moved aimlessly on the gravel beach. They rolled and bounced in what could have been joy but was clearly terror.

"Surely the orcas are sated by now."

"Their bodies may be sated. I'm not so sure about their souls. Watch."

As if in response to his command, an orca slid into the shallow water and delicately nipped a pup from the beach. The orca did not swallow but flung its head back. The pup went flying into the air with a squeal, faint over the sound of the waves and the boat's engine.

Before the pup could hit the water another orca slid inshore, caught the little sea lion on its flukes, and threw it back skyward. Several of the other orcas joined in. They captured the pups and threw them back and forth, tearing the water as they rolled in the shallows. The orcas were stunningly beautiful creatures, sleek and elemental. They rolled on their white stomachs in the surf and flipped the tiny pups into the air, occasionally jostling each other good-naturedly. Eventually the pups ceased their wailing and their silent bodies, mere lumps of flesh now, were thrown into the water and allowed to wash up on shore.

The tide rose and one by one the orcas were lifted free of the shallows and made their way back into deeper water.

The boat thrummed as the pilot backed engines to keep off the rocks as the tide rose, then slewed sideways. Theodoros glanced nervously over the stern. Colonel Stasov's associate Grisha Panin actually seemed to be paying attention, though he was now slumped languidly over the engines, half-smoked cigarette hanging from his lips. Stasov had picked Panin because he was the only one at the base who could handle the craft's balky engines, not because he was a particularly good pilot. Panin grinned at Theodoros, waved, and returned his attention to the throttles.

In a moment of idle fancy, Theodoros had asked for a wooden boat for the trip, trying to recapture what he remembered of the fishing boats of his youth. He had not expected the efforts Stasov went through to satisfy his visitor's request. The carbon composite launches of the Uglegorsk Research Station stayed at their moorings, and a retired fisherman made some unexpected money renting his obsolete hulk. The smell of generations of salmon seemed to be the only thing holding its weathered planks together.

The starboard engine choked and backfired. Panin leaned over it, his limp blond hair hanging over his face. He did something mysterious with a screwdriver. The engine ran smoothly once more.

"Orcas sometimes kill whales solely to eat the tongue," Stasov said musingly. Theodoros, stunned, stared toward the now-placid beach. The few pups still living keened in abandonment among the motionless bodies of their siblings. The water that foamed around them was regaining its clean whiteness, the blood of their parents quickly mixing with the cold Pacific. "They'll pursue the whale for days but leave the body floating in the water. Just the tongue."

The killer whales had gathered in a dense group and were heading back out to the open ocean.

Theodoros took a deep breath. "All right. So why do orcas eat only the whale's tongue?"

"I have no idea. A delicacy? Spite? A trophy? Maybe it's some ritual. Or just for sport." Stasov leaned pensively forward on the railing. "Those things are aliens. Not cute animals with big teeth and not men in fish suits. Alien creatures. I try to understand them but I don't expect to succeed, even though they're sitting right there in front of me."

Theodoros felt as if he was making a prison visit. He'd stopped at a cell and was staring at someone through an iron grating. Ilya Sergeiivich Stasov was a brilliant man trapped in a dead end. He commanded a futile, underfunded dolphin research effort here on the Far Eastern island of Sakhalin while the rest of the world moved on. No one in the delphine research community paid attention to their work which, in any case, was devoid of results.

"That was your specialty before, wasn't it? Alien communication. . . ." Theodoros stopped himself.

"Don't worry, Georgios." Stasov was melancholically amused. "I won't throw a tantrum if you bring it up. Who's to say if I would have been any more success-ful at that?" He pushed himself off the railing and walked to the center of the boat, balancing easily on the rocking deck. As men in prison often did, Stasov had become obsessed with his physical self. Early some mornings Theodoros had seen him running into the hills, the mist of his breath adding to that already veiling the landscape.

"Before . . ." Stasov mused. "Before the Soviet Repub-lics gave up on space. Before we decided that it didn't matter if there was life in Jupiter's atmosphere or not. A Soviet tropospheric probe detected the first intelligent signals, as I think I've already told you a dozen times." He grimaced at his own obsessions.

As far as Theodoros understood from his reading, Stasov was making an immense leap of faith from some seemingly nonrandom electrical impulses in the Jovian atmosphere, but held his peace. He was about to state some platitude about the rewarding challenges of communicating with cetaceans when Stasov spoke again.

"But before we can conquer the planets we first have to pacify the Central Asian republics. Isn't that right, Grisha? The universe can wait."

Panin looked up from his engines. "I spent a year in an engine-repair depot near Tashkent during the reconquest of Uzbekistan. I did see Samarkand once. From a distance. Those minarets could have been an old oil refinery or factory though. The tanks kicked up so much dust it was hard to see anything."

Stasov shook his head sadly at Panin. " 'Reconquest', Grisha? The correct word is 'stabilization'." He turned back to Theodoros apologetically. "It's a problem translating from Russian to English. You lose some of the subtleties. But look!"

The orcas spouted together and vanished smoothly under the waves. The sound of their voices, a series of loud pulses, rumbled through the wooden hull. The men could feel the vibration in their feet. Suddenly one of the orcas bumped the bottom of the boat hard enough to rock it. Theodoros grabbed for the railing. The orca bumped the bottom again, less savagely this time, and then was gone.

"Let's go home, Grisha," Stasov said. He hunched down in his coat, his small victory at having predicted the orcas' behavior now in the past.

Panin lugubriously rattled some engine fittings. "I wish you'd given me more time with this thing before we left. It'll quit halfway there."

"If I'd waited, all we'd have found here would have been empty rock." Stasov spread his hands in apology. "I'm sorry. But I knew you'd keep it going." He smiled up at his engineer, almost shyly, Theodoros thought.

Panin smiled wearily. "Sure." He turned the boat around and headed it back toward Uglegorsk. The stinking exhaust blew over them. They churned past the sloping rocks of the Sakhalin coast.

"Was that bump a message, do you suppose?" Theodoros said. "The first bump was malicious but the second seemed thoughtful." He looked after the orcas but they had vanished, only the dissipating steam of their last spout marking their passing.

"I think that was the one the local fishermen call Bottom-Thumper," Stasov replied. "He was just giving us a reminder to let us know they're still down there. And that we still don't understand them."

"ARE YOU REALLY THAT INTERESTED IN OLD STORIES, COLO-nel?" Theodoros stumbled up the wet stone steps, his long coat inadequate protection against the wind blowing off the Tatar Strait.

Stasov paced easily up the wide stairs. His greatcoat swung open to reveal his uniform, as if he welcomed the wind in. Binoculars bounced on his chest. "Is there a reason why I shouldn't be?" His clear gray eyes examined Theodoros quizzically.

Theodoros winced, wary of giving offense. He was far from home and these Russians, who could hug you tearily in the evening and threaten you insolently the next morning, made him uncomfortable. Stasov himself was a man who obviously believed himself to be easy, with a mind as open as his coat, but Theodoros found him impossible to read. "My stories don't have anything to do with what you're studying. You seem too practical a man."

"That's what I thought at first too." Stasov had greeted Theodoros's visit, arranged by some unknown administrator at the Vladivostok Oceanographic Insti-tute, with the pained expression of a man who already had too many pointless tasks to perform. "I thought you were a bad joke, but I've come to realize otherwise. You have something for me, Georgios." He smiled. "We just have to figure out what it is."

Theodoros had read Stasov's dossier while sitting on the beach at Perissa and watching his children play in the shallows, purple-and-green inflated sea monsters hugging their sun-browned middles. Its terse account of ambitions frustrated and dreams deferred had oppressed him even there. Stasov, near the top of his class at the University of St. Petersburg, had been ready to join the Jupiter research effort when war broke out and sent the Red Army into Kazakhstan and Uzbekistan, independent for two decades. After the successful reincorporation of those corrupt emirates into what was now known as the United Soviet Republics, an unsympathetic army administration had sent Stasov here, to rot in the dampness at the empire's edge.

"I wish I knew what it could be." Theodoros had grown to like this man. He tried not to pity him. "The stories have been passed from mouth to ear for millennia. All the meaning's been worn out of them."

"Maybe. But I suspect no one knew there was any meaning to be gotten from them. Until you got hold of them."

For some reason the praise embarrassed Theodoros. He thought Stasov was grasping at straws, trying to find anything at all that would give meaning to his otherwise pointless work. Some other ridiculous theory might have done just as well.

"It's dangerous to look for meaning in anything that old." Theodoros contradicted his own position to see what the other would say. It was a habit that annoyed his children.

It annoyed Stasov. "Of course it's dangerous. I know that. Russians love giving stories morals. Like my mother. She claimed that the story of Circe turning Odysseus's men into swine was an allegory of Soviet politics in the 1930s. I didn't believe her. My mother had an odd sense of humor."

Theodoros could imagine the young Ilya, romantic, myth-ridden, exasperated by his mother's capricious jokes. Youthful romanticism, raised on old legends, is notoriously serious. To the Greek, Stasov lacked that broad good nature that was the essence of humor. He did have a dry, dominating wit, and even that Russian laugh which in its boisterousness implied melancholy, but not what Theodoros recognized as humor.

"That's it," Theodoros said suddenly. "I didn't mean to say that you were a practical man, before. I meant romantic."

"An interesting mistake." Stasov was thoughtful. "I wish I knew what led you to make it."

"I make a lot of them. It's how I learn."

Theodoros stopped on one of the landings, affecting to enjoy the view, but actually to rest. There was little enough to look at. The sea before him was gray, with sharp-toothed waves. The thick clouds lowering over it obscured the boundary between sea and sky. This was nothing like the warm, dark Aegean where he did his delphine research. The island Sakhalin was a rough, hard place, filled with the remains of both Tsarist and Soviet prison camps.

"Then give me the opportunity to make my own," Stasov said. While Theodoros gasped, his breath was constant. Whether Stasov was resting or climbing didn't seem to make much difference. "I see some of your stories as evidence that what we are trying to do has actually been done before."

"A farfetched interpretation."

"Perhaps. But I want to shake those stories until something falls out of them."

"Colonel Stasov—"

Stasov raised a hand. "If you were a Russian, you would call me Ilya Sergeiivich. Since we are both speaking English, just call me Ilya. That is how Americans do it, isn't it?"

"All the ones I've met do," Theodoros said. At a gesture from Stasov, they turned and climbed another flight of stairs. These stairs, heavy granite, smoothly planed, were the best-constructed things Theodoros had seen on the entire island. They seemed ancient, paradoxically older than the mellow ruins of Greece. "Be careful of using myths to gain practical results. Particularly when they are yanked from their original context." And laid out for dissection on a cold island on the wrong side of Asia, he added to himself.

"Practical results? Or romantic ones?" Stasov grinned. "Myths contain more than we know."

Theodoros rolled his eyes in amusement and exasperation. "That may have been true in the nineteenth century. After two centuries of philological and anthropological investigation . . . stories are not necessarily myths, no matter how old they are. They might be philosophical allegories, etiological explanations, remnants of political propaganda, history vaguely remembered and embroidered—"

"Or just stories. Something heard by the fireside. I know. Odysseus's men might just have turned into pigs for the entertainment of the listener. But still, your stories seem to hold something inside of them."

"A romantic vision, Ilya."

"Nonsense. Purely practical."

They stopped on another landing. Theodoros looked out over the sea again. It looked no different from their higher elevation. The research station at Uglegorsk sprawled out beneath them. Beauty being pointless against the cold rocks of Sakhalin, the station had seemingly striven for extreme ugliness, and succeeded in the Soviet manner. The metal huts, some of WWII Lend-Lease vintage, were rusted and patched. Captive dolphins splashed and leaped in the holding pens that crowded the shoreline. The base was dominated by the concrete vault of the dolphin laboratory, built with more recent American aid.

"What humans and dolphins did during the reign of the Cretan Thalassocracy is significant to us here," Stasov said. "I thought it was nonsense when you came here, Georgios. Now I'm convinced otherwise. Thirty-five hundred years ago the Minoans knew how to talk to dolphins. I believe that you have brought hints and fragments of that knowledge with you to Uglegorsk." He tugged at the binoculars around his neck.

"They did *claim* to speak to dolphins," Theodoros murmured. "Perhaps they did." For years no one had listened to his theories, mostly because they were vague and unbelievable. Now that someone was willing to listen, even adamant, he found himself reluctant, uncertain of the consequences. Stasov wasn't interested in mere theories. He meant to act.

"They did," Stasov said. "I'm sure they did. But how? How did they learn it? And why did they forget it?" He paced the platform.

Theodoros watched him. Perhaps the climate and the place gave Stasov his intensity. The cold rocks, dense forests, and insect-infested swamps of Sakhalin did not invite repose. Theodoros remembered Crete with its limestone hills, springs flowing out through secret systems of caves and conduits. That was the land where satyrs had run in ancient forests. Zeus himself was raised in a cave at Mount Ida. A god raised on Sakhalin would surely be quite a different matter: dark, wrathful, and guilt-ridden, with none of the superficial charm of the Greek god. Such a Sakhalin god might have given Zeus pause.

The cold wind cut at him. He was tired. He'd come to Uglegorsk expecting a somnolent research facility with bad food, to which he would contribute several sparsely attended seminars. The food was indeed atrocious, but nothing else matched expectations. The research station was frantic with activity, and he had not been allowed a moment's rest since Stasov had met him at the military airfield a week before, despite Stasov's initial lack of cordiality.

Theodoros had come, reluctantly, as a gesture of politeness toward the unrespectable Russian research efforts, which were a matter of humorous scorn among the world dolphin research community. Theodoros himself was far from respectable. His specialty was human-dolphin interactions during the second millennium BCE. Available information centered around the Bronze Age Minoan civilization of Crete, what some people called the Cretan Thalassocracy. Delphine researchers found this subject bizarre and vague, while classicists and mythologists found it suspiciously practical. The official invitation from the Vladivostok Oceanographic Institute had come as a surprise. The intent curiosity he'd found at Uglegorsk had been a shock.

Stasov sat down on a stone wall and stared off toward the sea. The wall was made out of carefully dressed blocks of granite. "Could you tell me the story, Georgios? Never mind how insignificant it seems."

Had the man really climbed up all this way for a view of various shades of gray? Through binoculars yet? Theodoros shivered and sat down next to Stasov.

"First you tell *me* something. Why are these stairs here? They seem like a triumphal staircase to some temple, but I don't see one." The stairway vanished into rough brush a few flights above them, near the crest of the hill. Far beyond rose densely forested mountains, cloaked in mist.

Stasov chuckled. "They are well made, aren't they? That should tell you something. They were put down by laboring German POWs after the Great Patriotic War, in 1950."

Theodoros ran his fingers across the smoothed rock. The hours of labor in these pointless stairs was incredible. "That was five years after the war. You really kept them that long?"

"I'm sure they would have been kept longer if possible. Regimes change in our nation but some things remain constant. If one has Germans to do the work, one is loath to part with them." Stasov snorted. "I think they *were* laboring toward a temple here. To the Coryphaeus, the Plowman, the Master: Josif Stalin. Like all great heroes, he had many names."

Theodoros was startled by the bitterness in the man's tone. Russians took their history seriously. Stalin was over sixty years in his grave.

"Now your story, Georgios."

Theodoros leaned toward Stasov, the way he did when he told stories to his children. "It took place on Delos, long enough ago that the Egyptians had no Pharaoh and built with reeds. A singer lived on this island, a lyre player who had dedicated his life to Apollo and played to the sky and the sea. After a storm, the singer went down to the sandy shore to see what the sea had tossed up. On the beach lay a whale, sighing at the knowledge of his certain death. He cried thick, bitter tears."

He looked down at the complex, curved sandbars off the research base. "I once saw three right whales on a beach in Cape Cod in America. The sea was still, the tide had been high the night before. They had beached themselves deliberately. Two were still alive when I saw them, but they ignored me, waiting for the end they sought. Bulldozers came and cleared them away.

" 'Why are you here, brother?' the lyre player called. 'Why are you not off tossing the sea over your back, as is the natural duty of whales?'

" 'I have come to hear your songs,' the whale replied. 'Sing to me while I die.' "

Theodoros found himself in the rhythm of the story, changing the cadences for the different voices. He wished he could tell the version in old Greek verse so that Stasov could hear the syllables clashing against each other.

"The singer sang to the whale for three days, while the birds wheeled and cried overhead and the sun rose and set and the whale's flesh began to stink. At the end of the third day the whale died. The man wept and sprinkled water on the whale's head, since dust seemed improper. He wished him good hunting in the world to which whales go, for he did not think that Hades had a place for him.

"He looked out into the sea and saw a dolphin dancing. The dolphin leaped and gamboled. When he saw the man on the shore he first ignored him, then slid up onto the sand.

" 'Do you wish to sing to your dead brother?' the lyre player asked. The dolphin said nothing. 'His soul needs your songs to speed him to the dark sea where he now swims.' Still the dolphin said nothing. 'He cries for the sound of your voice.' The dolphin remained silent. In a rage the singer raised up his lyre and broke it over the dolphin's head. 'Speak not then, dumb beast, and go to your death unknown.'

"Blood came from the dolphin's blowhole and he cried out. 'Why do you torment me so?'

" 'To teach you the responsibilities of death and the songs that it calls for,' the singer said.

" 'I will hear you, then,' the dolphin said. 'Teach me the songs, if you will not let me be silent.'

"And so the man taught the dolphin to sing the rhythmic songs of the ancients, those sung by shepherds at first light, by fishermen pulling in full nets, by priests to the brow of the impending storm. The dolphin took the songs and made them his own, adding the sounds of the sea.

"Apollo, hearing the songs, came down laughing, though his hands smelled of blood and corruption. He was an Asian god then, from Lycia, but was on his way to lead the Greeks."

Stasov frowned at this unnecessary analytical intrusion into the story and Theodoros hurried on.

" 'I have slain the monster, Typhaon, at Crisa beneath snowy Parnassus,' he told them. 'My Temple and wooded grove are to be there. Now that you are able to sing, friend dolphin, you will aid me. Find me my priests.'

" 'The sea moves,' the dolphin said. 'The land is solid. I will search.'

"The dolphin swam the seas until he saw a ship of Cretan priests bound for Pylos. He sang to them from the sea and they followed him, to that place beneath Parnassus that was forever afterward to be called Delphi, after the dolphin who had led them. Men and dolphins spoke from that time afterward."

Theodoros felt the warm light of the Aegean island die, and found himself again sitting on a cold stone wall above hammered-metal waves of the Tatar Strait.

"It's there." Stasov paced back and forth in front of Theodoros. "I know it is. So he broke a lyre over the dolphin's head and it spoke. But why did they then stop talking?" He stared at Theodoros as if suspecting a deliberate refusal to reveal information.

Theodoros sighed. "I have found nothing that even hints at why. Remember, the stories are told by men, not dolphins."

"Are they? The dolphins must have stories too, if we could understand them. Myths. Things that tell about themselves."

"If they talk, they might have such stories," Theodoros said. "But you have to talk to them first."

Stasov smiled. "That is a problem, isn't it? Why do you suppose communication ended?"

"If it existed at all." Theodoros tried to maintain some sense of objectivity. "It may have ended when Crete fell, some decades after the eruption of the volcano Strogyle, on the island of Thera."

"Crete fell, but men still spoke to each other. Why not to dolphins?"

"Ilya, we've reached the end of my knowledge. Actually, we've gone far past it."

Stasov shook his head. "No. I'm convinced that your stories tell more than you know. That we don't see it is a scotoma, a blind spot in our vision." He stood up and put the binoculars to his eyes, staring out at the featureless gray of the horizon. Theodoros wondered what he was looking at. "Perhaps the dolphins refused to talk. Did they feel betrayed when men's civilization fell? Have they spitefully refused to talk since, no matter how beseeching we are? Perhaps the volcano . . ." He stopped and sucked in a breath.

"What is it?" Theodoros asked. "What do you see?"

"What the Trojans saw: the black ships of the destroyers." Stasov handed Theodoros the binoculars and helped direct his look. After a minute he found what Stasov had seen: a sleek dark ship calmly cutting the water at the horizon. Seeing in her an Achaean warship seemed a bit extreme, the natural consequence of too much immersion in ancient stories.

"A Japanese vessel," Stasov said, just as Theodoros spotted the Rising Sun flapping at its stern. "A Mogao class heavy cruiser."

Theodoros suddenly remembered that the man standing next to him wore, under his greatcoat, a military tunic with the epaulets of a Colonel in the Red Army. When he looked at a ship, he saw something other than what Theodoros saw. What did he see when he looked at a dolphin?

"The Americans should be more cautious." Stasov took the binoculars back from Theodoros and examined the Japanese cruiser further. "As long as they provide all of the armed strength in their alliance, they can decide when war occurs and with whom. But they say they can't afford it, and let the Japanese build warships. A mistake. The Japanese claim the southern half of Sakhalin, you know."

Theodoros had no idea why anyone would want the place. "I don't think the Japanese are interested in war."

Stasov studied him obliquely, still holding the binoculars pointed at the Japanese ship. Theodoros felt uncomfortable, as if he had just said something truly foolish rather than a mere commonplace. Stasov finally turned his eyes away. "I would feel more comfortable if the decision were left up to the Americans. They prefer to fight small nations on the edges of continents. The Japanese know to go for the heart. The Americans may find themselves pulled into a war they did not ask for."

He watched the Japanese ship out of sight, then dropped the binoculars back to his chest. "Do the dolphins have a religion, do you suppose?"

Theodoros smiled, relieved at the return to the previous topic, safely theoretical. "That's even harder to answer than questions about their myths. We have to learn to talk with them first. Then we can worry about those other things."

"That's what everyone tells me," Stasov replied. "I don't think it's true at all. In order to talk to them, we have to figure out why they are silent." He roused himself. "Let's go back down. We have some time. Grisha wants to have a party so that you can drink with us one more time before you leave."

Theodoros, his stomach churning at the thought of another of the massive drinking bouts which, besides arguing, seemed to be the only form of entertainment at Uglegorsk, followed Stasov back down the stairs.

CHAPTER TWO

2015

THE VAULTED DOLPHIN RESEARCH CENTER WAS AS HUGE inside as an aircraft hangar. The floor was always wet and the air smelled of seaweed and iodine. Cables snaked across the floor with no attention to safety. Theodoros tripped over them constantly, even sober, while the Russians had no trouble roaring drunk. The arrangement of tanks and equipment was nonsensical, the result of several changes of plan, and it was almost impossible to find anything. Even the dolphin tanks were connected by a virtual maze of conduits, frequent dead ends indicating where funding had not been sufficient to continue.

Theodoros was not surprised to discover that Colonel Stasov had been in charge of requisitioning personnel for the past year and a half. Those moved to Uglegorsk before that time tended to the sullen incom-

petence that Theodoros associated with large-scale
Soviet projects. Those who had come during Stasov's
tenure were superficially similar: hard-drinking, gab-
by, somewhat boorish. They had an odd quality about
them however, a sort of hardheaded mysticism, like
experienced monks. This was as true of the women
as of the men. Some of them even had that essential
ability to make do with shoddy equipment. Without
such 'fitters', no project in the newly baptized Soviet
Republics would ever have gotten anywhere. And they
all loved to argue.

An argument was going on when Stasov and Theodoros came in. It was taking place in the main seminar
room, an oddity, since arguments were usually sponta-
neous affairs, occurring during dinner, or over a piece
of equipment disassembled for repair, or even in the
middle of the night at the latrine door.

On the seminar room's wall hung a map of the eastern
Mediterranean as it had been in the middle of the 2nd
millennium BCE. Crete was covered with notations of
Minoan cities, the island of Thera marked with a big
star. Today the island was a ring, a lagoon in the center,
but the Russians had scribbled it in solid, since the
volcano Strogyle had not yet exploded. The Hittites
ruled Asia Minor, the Mycenaeans southern Greece,
their kingdoms drawn in over the modern political
divisions. The major cities of that time: Knossos,
Mycenae, Thebes, Troy, Hattusa. A half-dozen eager
researchers were gathered in front of the map arguing
in their loud Russian, their arms waving. It seemed to
Theodoros that everyone's voice was louder here, as
if to assert some existence against the barren world
around.

Larissa Sadnikova saw them and smiled. She was a
small, exact woman with tiny, pearllike teeth. "Thank

goodness you've come," she said in English. "This isn't something that can be solved from first principles. We're disputing the date of the Hyksos invasion of Egypt. Grisha thinks the eruption of Strogyle was just a minor contributory cause, that the fall of Crete was due to invasion. Were the Hyksos Mycenaeans, do you think? He's yelling something about ash deposits and tree rings in building beams."

Theodoros shook his head in amazement. While none of the Russians had known the precise chronology of events in the eastern Mediterranean from 2000 to 1500 BCE, they were familiar with the *Iliad*, Mycenae, the Hittites, and the fall of the Egyptian Middle Kingdom, and had been able to put all of his remarks into context. And these were technicians, computer programmers, and delphinologists, not classicists. When asked about this, Stasov had shrugged and said: "We're not uneducated peasants, you know." As Russia had declined in international power, it had turned its attentions inward. A decent education was apparently one of the fruits of introspection.

It was Grisha Panin, the pilot on their expedition to see the orcas, who had the most to say. Like most engineers, he had a view of history as a mess of gears and lever arms. Push here and something calculable happened *there.*

"No one is sure who the Hyksos were," Theodoros said. "Josephus thought they were Israelites. There have been weirder theories. But they definitely were *not* Mycenaeans."

Panin pouted. He was a floppy man, with floppy blond hair, floppy lips, floppy belly. "That's just a scotoma," he said, using one of his favorite words, picked up from Stasov. "A blind spot in your understanding. Just because the Hyksos were supposed to be Semites. . . ."

And they were off, Panin coming up with a ludicrous position and maintaining it skillfully, Theodoros patiently dismantling it.

As the argument continued, Stasov drifted through the crowd toward the map. He was interrupted twice to make procedural decisions. Theodoros could see him disposing of issues like toilet paper supply and pump maintenance irritably but efficiently. At last Stasov was able to make his way over to the map of the eastern Mediterranean. The sea was marked with estimates of its depths in the second millennium BCE. He put his finger atop the filled-in island of Thera and pushed as if wanting to force it completely into the sea. He turned away from the map to look at the poster of two dolphins, taken from a wall painting at Knossos, which graced the opposite wall. Theodoros kept half an eye on him. His host's behavior was sometimes as hard to figure out as a dolphin's.

The argument, through some unspoken agreement, quickly became a farewell party for Georgios Theodoros and spread among the dolphin tanks, as if the researchers wanted to include their charges in the festivities. Bottles of vodka appeared, and plates of food. Someone strummed a balalaika, an archaic instrument lately popular among the most recent generations of Russians.

Stasov jerked his head at Theodoros. They found a quiet corner to finish their discussion. Stasov balanced a bottle of vodka on a signal processing box and handed the other a pickle out of an unlabeled jar. It seemed to the Greek that everything was pickled here: the cucumbers, the cabbage, the peppers, the fish, and the researchers. He tossed back a shot of vodka, took a bite of pickle, and grimaced.

Stasov chuckled. "You've learned to do it like a real Russian. The trick is never to look as though you enjoy it."

"I *don't* enjoy it."

"Ha. You *are* a real Russian."

They sat next to a wide, circular tank, opalescent in the overhead lights. Light pushed its way into the swirling depths but found no solid shape to rest on, and so hung loosely down into the darkness. Suddenly a sleek form pushed its way through the light, its shadow plunging below it. The dolphin surfaced with a clearing of its blowhole and swam around the tank's perimeter. Stasov stared pensively at it, like a father contemplating a favorite but wayward child. He picked up a yellow ball and threw it into the tank. The dolphin nudged it dutifully, but without enthusiasm. His name was Kestrel.

Kestrel was of the species *Delphinus delphis*, the Common Dolphin. His back was black, his belly white, and his sides were patterned with waves of blue-gray and yellow. He was quite unlike the light-gray Bottlenose Dolphin that Americans liked to use in their shows and spectacles.

"It's amazing how vivid-looking they are," Theodoros observed. "They seem made to be put into wall paintings as decoration."

"Perhaps that's the only reason the Minoans painted them," Stasov said moodily. "That could have been the origin of their fascination. Pure aesthetics. Why should we think that dolphins are at all intelligent?"

Theodoros was taken aback by this sudden pessimistic bitterness. "People have been studying them for years—"

"And not proved a damn thing." Stasov swung away

from the dolphin, as if irritated at the creature for not being more forthcoming. "After all, they follow tuna schools and die by the hundreds in tuna fishermen's nets. Over and over. They never seem to learn. Is this the action of an intelligent creature?"

"Perhaps they have some deeper reason," Theodoros suggested. "Or it's something they can't help."

Stasov looked thoughtful. "Perhaps. Also, we're ignoring the fact that someone can be intelligent and stupid at the same time." Seeing that Theodoros's glass was empty, Stasov refilled it. The Greek had been trying to hide it under a junction box. "Their thoughts, if any, are alien to us. Perhaps it is absurd to search for life in the depths of Jupiter while we don't have any understanding of what goes on just beyond the beach where we sun ourselves."

Theodoros tried sipping at his vodka. Useless, horrible. He missed raki. He downed the glass and groped for pickled herring. "True enough, Ilya. History is full of intelligent men who were astounding fools."

"Many were my own countrymen in this past century, slaughtering each other in the name of a political economic theory created by linking Hegelian logic to wishful thinking." He poured vodka over his tongue to get rid of the taste of his words. "Millions dead. And I don't think we're through yet. That makes getting caught in a tuna net seem like an honest error."

Kestrel leapt up and, with a flick of his snout, hit Stasov in the head with the yellow ball. With a huge splash, he dove back into the water and swam underneath to another tank. Stasov looked off after him until the swirling water settled back to a glassy smoothness.

"Though ancient, the story you told me is probably hundreds of years newer than the events it describes."

Enthusiastic a few hours before, he now sounded doubtful.

"More like a thousand years newer. And a story told by Greeks, to boot. The events, if anything like them happened, took place in pre-Hellenic Crete. You have to keep reminding yourself that the Minoans were not Greeks."

"Greeks never talked to dolphins," Stasov said.

Theodoros yanked frantically at his beard. "I don't know, Ilya! I don't know. Did anyone talk to dolphins? None of us has any idea. It's possible that that's one thing the Greeks did not learn from the Minoans."

The huge form of General Anatoly Ogurtsov loomed over them, a pair of reading glasses around his neck. "More of these damn foreign computers for you, Ilya?" He waved a stack of requisition sheets at Stasov. "How can our budget support this?"

Stasov shrugged. "Sit down, Tolya." He poured the General a glass of vodka. "I need sophisticated array processors. Who else makes them but the Japanese?"

"Damn their yellow souls," Ogurtsov said, in ceremonial anathema. "They do make good gadgets. I hope we can buy enough now to defeat them when we finally go to war." He sighed hugely. "That's all image processing gear. Why do you need it?" His sharp blue eyes were tiny against the vastness of his face.

"I have some ideas," Stasov said.

Ogurtsov's jowly face expressed a familiar irritation. "Some ideas, Ilya?"

"What, isn't that enough for you?" Stasov looked challenging.

"It's not a matter of being enough for me. I can't requisition a hideously expensive load of military-grade computing equipment simply because Ilya Stasov has 'some ideas'."

"Damn it!" Stasov jumped to his feet. "How am I supposed to get anything done? If it were up to the central financial administration we'd be trying to communicate with dolphins by blowing ocarinas."

Ogurtsov was unimpressed. "If it were up to the central financial administration we wouldn't even exist. Sit down, Ilya. It's not me you have to convince."

Stasov sat. "You don't understand! We might have a way, a new way, to communicate. We could break through whatever it is that restrains them."

"What do you mean?" Theodoros was startled by the conclusions Stasov had managed to squeeze out of his stories.

"I mean that we've been making a mistake in communicating with the dolphins linearly." Stasov leaned toward him. "I think we need to hit them with complete aural images. We have no equipment to handle such a thing."

"An interesting thought," Theodoros said. "What sort of images?"

Stasov looked at him thoughtfully. "Images they might have encountered in Aegean times . . . Minoan vessels, the ancient coast of Thera before it erupted . . . but I need the equipment to do the work. Understand that, Tolya?"

"That's all very well." Ogurtsov tapped the papers on a pump housing, aligning the edges. "But I need something more than your persuasive voice before I can forward these."

"Like what?" Stasov looked beseeching.

"Come on, Ilya. You've been in the Red Army long enough to know how things get done. How about we trespass on Navy territory? Particularly since, as the senior service, we've been doing it all along. Could your oral images—"

"Aural, Tolya. Your English is atrocious."

Ogurtsov forged onward. "Could they be used to distract antisubmarine-warfare sonar detectors? Or even passive-pressure detectors?"

Stasov raised his eyebrows. "I doubt it. But it wouldn't be hard to come up with some halfway plausible rationale. Hmm. If we can create an aural image to fool a dolphin, no reason why it couldn't fool an ASW vessel. . . ."

"That's a good boy." Ogurtsov beamed. He glanced at Theodoros. "See the keen intelligence. I predict that in less than a decade Ilya Sergeiivich will be able to file a leave request with fewer than three errors in it."

"Don't bet your dinner on it." Stasov scratched his head. "This is going to take some work—work in addition to everything that already has to get done."

Ogurtsov shrugged massively. "Come up with a military reason I can cite and I'll forward these. Be sure to mention the Japanese at least once per paragraph."

"You are implacable, Tolya."

"Not at all," Ogurtsov protested. "If I didn't take care of this stuff, who—"

Stasov smiled and squeezed his hand, a most unmilitary gesture, Theodoros thought. "I know, I know. And someday, I suppose, I'll thank you for it. Not yet, though." Stasov turned to Theodoros. "If this is going to work, I'll need your help."

"How can I help you here?" Theodoros asked. He looked around the damp, vaulted space that gave the feeling that the experiments were being carried out far underground rather than on the shores of an ocean. The damp had penetrated his bones and he sometimes woke shivering at night, having dreamed that the sun had fallen hissing into the sea and vanished like a wet cinder.

"By coming back." Stasov hunched his wide shoulders forward, resting his elbows on his knees. His gray eyes pleaded with Theodoros. "I don't have the expertise I need, even yet."

"Coming back . . ." Theodoros was leaving in the morning for Alaska and California. From there he planned to fly to Woods Hole and then back to Europe. "I'm spending a week at Ketchikan. They're doing some interesting work with orcas there."

"Overly sentimental," Stasov said crisply. "But useful. Weiss is their best man."

"After that, it's down to Santa Cruz. Mike Taylor and Anna Calderone, there. And San Diego. Margaret Landseer's work—"

"Is utter fantasy. She thinks dolphins can be convinced to communicate through a common interest in the focusing of cosmic energies. I read her last paper. She's a confidence trickster. Or the reincarnation of an ancient Hindu saint. Or both." His voice got higher, as it did when he was excited.

"Please, Ilya," Ogurtsov broke in. "Do you think you can convince Georgios to stay by showing him all other dolphin researchers are fools?"

Stasov sighed. "No, of course not." He sat back. "But I need your work, Georgios. You go to those places. Talk to them. Pay attention to whether they hear what you say. Then think about what I need here." He poured himself another glass of vodka.

Theodoros watched him as if Stasov was performing some delicate chemical titration. "How can you people make decisions when you drink so much?"

"According to Herodotus, the ancient Persians would reconsider all decisions made sober by getting drunk and deciding again."

Theodoros threw up his hands in defeat. "You are

too eloquent. I will consider your offer. Sober, I'm afraid." He felt like a child in a custody fight, the fact that he was desperately wanted by someone giving him no comfort.

"At any rate, there are still some things you can give us whatever you decide. To begin with, I'll need good sonic maps of the Aegean and best guesses from oceanographic archaeologists on the conformation of the sea bottom in about 1500 BCE. Can you do that, at least?"

"I think so." Theodoros was startled once again, as he had been continually startled on his visit. When he had come here, to find the crude pens of inferior concrete already cracking, the drunken technicians, the obsolete foreign electronic equipment cadged or stolen from other research projects, he had been sure that he was wasting his time. Compared with the clean redwood boards and earnest college students of Santa Barbara or the elegant institutes at Monaco, this place was a hellhole. He'd been looking forward to leaving and getting to the United States where research facilities looked like serious business, not shady dealings in abandoned warehouses. But his attention had been caught here. He could feel the motion and was starting to worry about being left behind.

"We'll do it, you know," Ogurtsov rumbled. "Ilya will make sure that we do."

"General," Theodoros said, "I have no doubt that you're right."

ILYA SERGEIIVICH STASOV PUT DOWN HIS COPY OF PRZHE-valsky's *From Zaysan via Hami to Tibet and the Upper Reaches of the Yellow River*. It was the original leather-bound 1883 volume and had come from the library of Stasov's father. Sergei Stasov made a small hobby of collecting books about Russian explorers of Central Asia and the East. The collection had awed Ilya in his youth. Borrowing this one volume from Sergei had taken weeks of pleading. But it was printed under Przhevalsky's supervision while he planned his next expedition and had his signature on the flyleaf.

Przhevalsky and his men were wandering the Tibetan plateau, a place as bleak as Sakhalin and seemingly as little worth visiting. Stasov was tired of wrestling with the text's minuscule printing, dense with the gravestonelike letters of pre-Revolutionary typography.

He looked out over the sloshing tanks and Grisha Panin's plump back. The engineer knelt by a frightening tangle of multicolored wires, sorting them with nimble fingers. A strong overhead light left Panin an oasis of light in the damp darkness.

Panin sensed a change in the silence behind him and looked up. Blond hair flopped down over his forehead. "Not long now. I'm just getting the main connections."

"You are a wonder, Grisha. I don't know what we'd do without you."

"What would we do without any of us? Without you, for example."

"True enough," Stasov said. "We're a historical accident here. A chance-met group. If that's what we have to depend on in this country, it's a wonder anything ever gets done."

"Hmph." Panin sat back on his haunches. "Did chance requisition me from my little place in Yekaterinburg? I was using the base electronics shop to repair stereo and video equipment. I was getting rich. And now look at me. Kneeling in puddles and playing with rainbow spaghetti."

"Would you rather be back in Yekaterinburg, garden spot of the Urals?"

"It's not so bad as you Petersburgers think," Panin said aggrievedly. "We had an opera. And a good soccer team. No one bothered me."

Stasov remembered the long evenings he had spent going through the many contradictory and poorly maintained databases available on the All-United Republic Military Network, finding those lost souls who would be most useful to him. Since many of the skills he sought were irrelevant or even actively irritating to the Red Army, it had been surprisingly easy to detach most of the group from their duties and bring them to Uglegorsk. Among other things, it had brought him people who had become good friends. Like Grisha Panin.

He looked at Panin, suddenly dismayed. "Are you unhappy that you came here, Grisha?"

Panin regarded Stasov from under his brows. "A bit late for a question like that, isn't it?" He waved his hand dismissively. "Don't worry about it. Might as well rot here as anywhere else in our gloriously resurrected Soviet Union." Panin deliberately used the old, twentieth century name of the recently reunited nation.

This was less than the ringing endorsement Stasov sought. But, indeed, why should anyone be happy about being asked to share his own melancholy fate? He slumped back and thought about going to find a drink.

"You know," Panin said meditatively, "you really should be doing something else."

"Like what?" Stasov asked. "Working for the Moscow Circus?"

Panin refused to be amused. "I don't know. Something that works, I guess."

Stasov stood up. "That's nothing you have to tell me about. But this is what I've got, and I'm going to *make* it work." He hoped his voice had the right note of resolve. He'd learned it from watching old movies from the 1930s and '40s, with their dedicated workers and soldiers, their obstacles encountered and over-come by will and dedication. He'd always found the movies absurd, even as a child, but their patently false bright-eyed optimism had stuck with him. It seemed that there must be a time and place where such an emotion was appropriate.

"Sure, sure." Panin, clearly having been brought up on some less self-consciously inspired fare, returned resentfully to his task.

"Don't be so grumpy."

"I'm not grumpy," Panin said, unbending a little. "I'm just tired."

"You're not the only one." Stasov walked off into the darkness of the vaulted research center, leaving Panin in his circle of light. It was an old habit. Even as a boy, he had walked for miles at night among the residential apartment buildings of his neighborhood, as identical as encyclopedia volumes. At night the traffic lessened and he could smell the dry odor of Russian fields. His mother had always worried over what her only child was doing out on the featureless streets of their residential zone. On his return his father would ask for some odd observation: the altitude of Orion, the number of migrating skeins of geese, the loudness of certain street bars. He encouraged his son to find the remnants of old villages absorbed by the spread of modern St. Petersburg. Otherwise he showed no concern, responding to his wife's entreaties to "talk to your son about this" by puffing furiously on his suddenly hard-to-light pipe.

Stasov's footsteps echoed off the vault. He wondered if his father would have requested a sonic analysis based on the way the echo sounded in different parts of the research center. It was the sort of information his father had liked to file away and remember, for no useful reason. And a dolphin would have known the shape of the vault immediately from the sound. He felt the leather spine of Przhevalsky's book. Books had always been Sergei's defense against a shrunken world that made almost everyone superfluous. Stasov's father's prime years had been those when the ramshackle Soviet Union of the late-twentieth century fell in on itself like an abandoned peasant's hut. Like most thoughtful citizens, he had pulled away, the same way he fled into his study when his wife Ada was throwing a party.

Sergei would often claim to be getting something. He would bring up some obscure subject, get someone else to express some interest in it, and then say: "Well, then, I do have something you might want to take a look at. Quite a find, actually. I bought it at one of those stalls along Nevski Prospekt. An old book, but in great shape. Just a second, I'll pop off and get it." And he would wander into the back bedroom, away from the loud music his wife played on the stereo, the bright lights, the tables of food and vodka, and the endlessly gabbing guests, and disappear.

Ilya remembered sneaking back there to escape his own onerous duties of lying in tangled sheets, catching only fragments of the conversations going on outside his door. The bedroom served as his father's study, piled with dusty books. He found his father, one tiny light over his shoulder shining on a book as he peered intently at it. He read all books that way, as if each had some mysterious secret concealed in the mundane text, a puzzle from the author that he was supposed to figure out. The puzzles the world had given him were insoluble.

When Ilya crept in, pillow clutched under one arm, he would look up without surprise and say something like, "Still awake? Look at some of these Japanese prints. They show heroic actions of soldiers during the Russo-Japanese War of 1904." And Ilya gazed in wonder at the colorful designs showing fiercely scowling samurai in military dress being blown up by land mines, swimming rivers, and firing salvos at pale-faced opponents in Russian army uniforms. They made the war seem like a romantic folly of some sort, dramatic and gaudy. There was even one fireworks display of the exploding *Admiral Nakhimov*, sunk at the Battle of Tsushima. The image implied that the ship had been created only to provide a display of its destruction, like some sort of cardboard model burned at Mardi Gras.

And Ilya settled down at his father's feet, curled around the pillow, and watched his father read, waiting to be tossed the occasional interesting tidbit: an odd historical fact, a curious illustration, a ridiculous false statement by the author. All these nights had blended together into one in his memory, the strongest and clearest image of his father that he had.

Once Sergei had shown his son an old engraving of Novgorod's destruction at the hands of Ivan the Terrible. It showed screaming people being fried in griddles over open fires. "Tsar Ivan Vasilievich, being a Russian, kept his sense of humor under all circumstances," his father said. "And, like all Russians, his sense of humor was of the crudest sort. Frying pans! And our tortures have been the same from that day to this, makeshift and ludicrous."

Some of the books, left near an open window during a thunderstorm, smelled of mildew. That odor, combined with the aroma of stale pipe tobacco, strong tea, and dust, was what Stasov smelled when he remembered his father. And he always heard the party in the other room, muffled, punctuated with loud laughs. The study was dark, the light over his father's shoulder picking out spines without revealing titles. His memories of his father outside this room were vague and confused: a day at the zoo, a long afternoon at some elderly relative's, a streetcar ride. His father seemed real only here.

Eventually Ada would find them. She would appear at the door, face flushed, an elegant party dress clinging to her slender shape, rings and earrings glinting in the hall light that silhouetted her against the darkness of the study, and lean against the doorjamb, looking at her two men. Both of them would start guiltily, as if she had no idea of where that room was and it wasn't even connected to the rest of the apartment, floating somewhere high above the canals of St. Petersburg, a colored festival balloon, the two of them aboard it, sailing to some romantic destination. But she could bring out a jeweled pin and bring them back down to earth.

"Ilya, back to bed, this instant." Without a backward glance at his father the boy put the pillow over his head as if protecting himself from rain and padded quickly to his room, there to make a tent of his blankets and crouch expectantly, awaiting some illumination that never quite came. His dog, Graf, peered at him with his black bead eyes, making sure that the same boy had returned as had left, wagged his tail in elaborate salute, and fell back asleep under the bureau. With weary amusement, Sergei put the book back on the shelf and followed his wife back out to the party. Soon Ilya heard his father's low, fluid voice among the rest, discussing some dark issue like official corruption or starvation in Central Asia, for these were the topics that the late night was consecrated to, once the vodka had been consumed and the more mundane personal problems discussed and dispensed with. The boy fell asleep then, to be pursued by colorful Japanese soldiers armed with fry pans.

Somewhere in the darkness a dolphin rose out of the water, cleared its blowhole, took a breath, and dove again. Stasov could feel a sequence of ranging clicks vibrate the side of the tank.

Stasov's quiet father, his life dogged by an obscure sadness, vanished. How in the world were they ever going to understand dolphins? Stasov was piling up an immense amount of equipment in pursuit of a guess, as if he were marshalling tank columns for the invasion of an unknown country. It was folly. His reputation . . . He smiled to himself. Abroad, Soviet delphine researchers were considered boorish primitives who probably ate their charges for dinner after investigating their pain reflexes. Within the Red Army, the Uglegorsk group was classified as a transport-machinery repair depot, there being no closer category. Stasov was a prophet with honor nowhere.

But he would know what went on in those dolphin heads. He would.

CHAPTER THREE

2015

Kelp tangled around Anna Calderone, moving gently in response to the waves just overhead. A young sea otter, no more than a meter long, skimmed past her, the tentacles of an octopus dangling from its mouth. Calderone rarely saw octopus swimming, but the otters had no trouble finding them.

Her head broke the surface. In the distance she could see the brown, house-covered hills of Santa Cruz. "Meg!" she called. "Are you up?"

"Behind you. You'd make a terrible dolphin."

"I think that's part of the problem."

Anna Calderone's friend Meg Tritek floated just behind her, not far from the small sailing skiff they had taken from the Santa Cruz Oceanographic Institute for their day's expedition.

"Don't be so down, Anna."

"Why shouldn't I be?" Calderone stroked powerfully toward Tritek. She'd been a swimming star in college and still held the Institute's unofficial long-distance championship. She sometimes thought that it made her upper body too bulky but she enjoyed swimming too much to stop for the sake of her looks.

"Because the creatures we study never do what we want them to." Tritek, a plump, round-faced blonde, dimpled. "Even men, and they're much simpler than sea otters or dolphins."

But today even Tritek's calculated cynicism about the male half of the species couldn't cheer Calderone up. Besides Calderone's problems with her dolphins, her lover Martin was, as Tritek had more than once pointed out, all too predictable.

"It's not a question of what I want them to do. It's a question of what they are. If they're just animals, why are we spending so much time with them? If they're intelligent, why can't we figure it out?"

"Maybe they're just smarter than you are." Tritek refused to take the problem seriously. "Maybe they think you're boring."

Meg Tritek studied the bay's sea otter population. Frustrated with the performance of her dolphins, Calderone had decided to play hooky and spend the day with Tritek's sea otters, cheerful and clever animals that accepted her presence without surprise.

"Sea otters could be intelligent, if they wanted to," Tritek said. "Hell, I bet they could take over the earth if human beings ever knocked themselves off. If they wanted to." A sea otter drifted by, stomach up, breaking clam shells on the rock it balanced there. It glanced at them, its whiskered face giving it the look of some bunco artist inviting them to a game of three-card monte on its belly table, then stroked away.

"But you don't think they want to." Calderone had been intensively indoctrinated during her post-doc at Woods Hole not to attribute human motivations to even the most intelligent-seeming of animals, preparation for her dolphin studies. It was a rule constantly violated, not too surprising in view of the fact that most people attributed intelligent volition to such things as automobiles and toasters.

"Why should they?" The well-rounded Tritek made Calderone feel long and raw-boned. The two of them had formed an alliance against the men of the Institute, to the dismay of some of the other women. "They can get all the food they want in a couple of hours of work and spend the rest of their time playing. What a life." An otter popped its head up next to her and she patted it. "What use do they have for intelligence?"

"To play in a more interesting way? I mean, when you've got food and sex taken care of, everything else is just a way of passing the time."

"Those dolphins *are* driving you crazy, aren't they, Anna?"

"You know they are."

"I think it's the fault of that monk of yours. He takes everything too seriously."

Calderone grinned. "Georgios Theodoros? He's no monk. He's married and has three children. He's shown me pictures of his family. They're all cute."

"Well, he *looks* like a monk. Is he enjoying himself?"

"I don't think so." Calderone realized she hadn't really thought about it. She ran her hand down her side and adjusted the balance of her buoyancy harness so that it pumped air down to her legs. She floated on her back as easily as a sea otter and looked up at the sky. "He tells us we have amazing technology, then tells absurd stories about ancient Crete. 'Amazing technology'." She snorted, suddenly annoyed at the Greek's misplaced praise. "He makes us sound like children playing with toys we don't understand."

"He's leaving in a couple of days, though. You won't have him to worry about anymore."

"No, I won't."

Despite the dislocation their visitor had caused to her schedule, Calderone found herself sorry to see Theodoros go. He was a formidable eccentric and a relief from the eager boys with whom she spent her days.

Tritek, inspired by the thought of Theodoros, was telling an anecdote about a man she was seeing, a divinity professor at Santa Cruz State. "He's always talking miracle this, miracle that. Sunrise. The veal piccata at dinner. My breasts." She laughed. " 'Miracle?' I said. 'I've had 'em for years.' " She laughed again.

"Do you like him?" Calderone asked absently. She turned and looked westward toward the horizon. Uglegorsk lay an incomprehensible distance in that direction, half the world away. There were people there crazy enough to believe Theodoros's stories, or so he would have her believe.

"Like him? Yeah, sure, I guess so. Quit probing. It's not fair."

"Sorry." Calderone shook herself like a sea otter. "Let's see what's going on. Where are your kids?" Tritek was raising two orphaned sea otters, testing the limits of their behavior.

"Hunting clams. I like them, so they like them too. They're better at finding them than I am, though." Tritek flipped her goggles on. "Let's go look for them."

*   *   *

IT WAS NIGHT BY THE TIME THEY RETURNED. TRITEK MOORED the sailboat, waved cheerily, and headed off for a date with her divinity professor. Fog had rolled in off Monterey Bay, turning the lights of the bayside walk into fuzzy spheres. Anna Calderone walked slowly along the water toward the lights of the Santa Cruz Oceanographic Institute. A California Sea Lion barked in the darkness, but was not answered. Fall had not yet arrived but he had already migrated up from the sea lions' summer haunts in Southern California. Calderone wondered what had brought him back north so absurdly early.

An electric car nosed slowly along the access road from the Institute. A bald head poked out of the window. "Need a ride home, Anna?"

"No thanks, Dr. Kammer. I have some work to do in my office." That was not strictly true. But she didn't want to go home, not yet.

Kammer shook his head. "Learn something from your subjects, if you can. Delphinology isn't supposed to be work."

Calderone laughed. "I'll keep that in mind."

The car sped off, vanishing beyond the sinuous, curved-roof buildings built after the disastrous 2004 Año Nuevo earthquake. Calderone, avoiding the Institute's glowing entrance, walked along the concrete-and-rock study tide pools built by the teaching staff. The tide was out and the creatures that lived in the intertidal zone had battened themselves down into dark lumps. Beyond, through the low water, she could see the traces of the old coast road. Martin left for work at about ten. She could go back to the apartment then.

A constellation of blurred lights appeared in the fog,

growing steadily more focused as they approached. She recognized the complex electronic superstructure of the *Ricketts*, the mother ship which carried the Institute's submersibles, back from an exploration of the depths of Ascension Canyon. She could hear laughter, and quickly unlocked the side door. Her colleagues were good people but she didn't want to see any of them just now.

Her office was a small, wood-paneled room of clean design. Sonograms papered the walls, interspersed with photographs of herself at college swim meets and Institute crab boils. The computer screen flickered as she came in, showing her the previous day's dolphin tracks, tagged by name. She glanced at them without interest, wiped the screen, and sat down in the chair with a sigh. A sea smell clung to her, strong in the enclosed space. She should have taken a shower but was too tired. She would stay smelling like a mermaid, as one old lover had put it.

There was a call from Martin in voice mail. "Hi, honey." She remembered when that sweet-tinged Virginia voice had thrilled her. The voice itself was still lovely. "Just a state-of-Martin call. Lonely because the sea gets to touch you and I don't. It's a lovely day here in the hills. Smog's mostly burned off. I can just see the water if I climb on the high chair in the kitchen and lean against the cabinet." Anna knew this was not simply a poetic device. She'd found the dirty prints of his lug-soled hiking boots on the counter more than once. That was him: romantic and inelegant. "I'm still working on my Denali climbing article. Still not jelling." When Martin wasn't supervising the night shift at the printing company he was a partner in, he hiked the high mountains and tried to sell accounts of his experiences. He was a much better hiker than he was a writer, but close contact with print had inspired him.

Anna leaned forward and found the carved wood dolphin, an imitation of Northwest Indian style, that Martin had given her when they were first dating. It had big eyes and looked very intelligent, much like Martin himself. She fingered it as she listened to the rest of his rambling message, wondering what it was about the lovable Martin that made her want him dead.

"Well, that about wraps it up for now. I'll be off to work at ten. Hope you make it back before then. I'll make some dinner. 'Bye, honey."

She looked at the clock. Ten-thirty. Martin was safely off to work and she'd managed to put off for another day deciding what to do about him. She licked her lips, tasting the sea's salt. Dolphins were merely clever animals and her one-time love for Martin was just a flaw of her memory. She lived in a world of illusion.

She stood up, stretched her long back, and walked out into the orientation room around which the researchers' offices clustered. The circular room was dominated by a holographic display of Monterey Bay's water flows. She could see the nutrient-rich brown-green of the cold California Current's upwelling as it was funneled up Monterey Canyon to meet the warmer water of the river-fed upper bay. The meeting of moist mountain air and cold ocean water created the fog outside.

She wished she could blame Martin for the situation, but with the best will in the world she couldn't. He was as cheerful and earnest as the day she'd met him— the day she had decided that what she needed was some stability in her life, some one dependable male head on the pillow next to hers. The glowing model of the bay above her suddenly seemed kidnapped and confined within these narrow walls, so she turned and left it behind.

Just beyond were the Institute's experimental deep-water tanks, kept under a pressure equivalent to that of more than a thousand meters below ocean-surface level. Countless phosphorescent dots moved through them, marking the fish and invertebrates that made their homes at those depths. She watched a lantern fish drift by like a tiny ocean liner, its internal organs glowing with their own light. The water itself, filled with bioluminescent bacteria, radiated a blue glow.

She stopped. A dark, bearded figure stood just beneath a partially disassembled mechanized model of an ichthyosaur, pneumatic tubes spilling from its belly. Georgios Theodoros.

"Good evening, Anna." His voice was calm, as if he had expected her.

"Hi."

He walked over and stood next to her at the deep tank. He reached out and put his fingers on the glass as if feeling the pressure. "The glass bends inward. Is it to make it stronger?"

Calderone had expected any number of remarks, but not this one. "Um, partially. Someone explained it to me once. Because of the huge pressure behind the glass, the mind sees it as bowing out. To make up for that—"

"They bow it inward. An illusion contrived so that reality can be seen. That's interesting. Ancient Greek temples have similar features, curves in extended lines to counter natural optical illusions ... but I can see that you're not interested in entasis."

Calderone blinked, hoping her eyes had not glazed over. Theodoros did have a gift for hauling in irrelevant and unconnected information, seemingly in the hope that someone else would see something significant in his scattered intellectual yard sale. If there was something important amid the man's peculiar myths, Calderone didn't see it. But she didn't want to hurt his feelings.

"That's not true. It's just not my area. I've been studying dolphin behavior for so long I'm not sure I understand anything else. And I don't think I understand that either."

Theodoros nodded. "I received a letter from Ilya Stasov this morning. They have their sonic imaging gear operational. Last week a dolphin fled from the sonic illusion of a shark. The dolphin then communicated a version of the illusion to its pod mates. Ilya says he's having trouble understanding the effect of these illusions on their society. The consequences are too complex. It's an unusual confession for him."

At first convinced that the Uglegorsk work's importance to Theodoros was solely because the Soviets were basing their research on his ideas, Calderone had, grudgingly, begun to see the work's own validity. So what was she doing here at Santa Cruz? Was her work here really any more significant than the touchy-feely, reincarnation-inspired work of Margaret Landseer at San Diego?

"There are a number of ways it could work," she said musingly. "I'd have to actually see the sound transcripts and minute-by-minute behavior logs in order to get an idea. I could run them through my computer. . . ." Despite herself, she felt interested in this work of crazy Russians. It was typical of them to intervene so powerfully, where most other delphinologists were content to observe natural behavior.

"Or you could see them yourself." Theodoros had finally come around to his main point, like a shy man asking a woman out for a date. "I'm going back. I've decided."

"But what about San Diego? Woods Hole? Monaco?" Calderone had checked his itinerary and been jealous.

"I've already sent regrets. Something is happening at Uglegorsk. I'm going to be there." He spoke with confidence, his decision made. "You should come with me."

"I—" She stopped. "Don't you think our work here at Santa Cruz is worthwhile?"

Theodoros considered. "It's been superseded."

"I can't—" Calderone thought about the countless threads of schedules, of obligations, of desires, that held her pinned like Gulliver. Martin's own special cord pulled tight around her neck. "For how long?"

Theodoros spread his hands. "That's up to you. Are you coming?"

She didn't hesitate. "Yes. As soon as possible." A weight lifted from her. "When can we leave?"

"Excellent." He didn't seem surprised by her decision or her sudden urgency, but then, she realized, as he had been describing Uglegorsk and Colonel Stasov to her, she'd been describing her cramped life and Martin Bierlein to him. She'd been begging this quiet family man for some sort of solution. He had, for his own purposes, given her one.

She left him there among the deep fishes and pedaled up into the hills on her bicycle. She pushed hard, until her quads ached and the breath burned in her lungs. It was late at night like this when the pain and the motion seemed separate, as if the bicycle floated effortlessly through the darkness and it was only she, for her own private reasons, who burned with strain. She slung the bicycle against the hedge and ran up the stairs to her and Martin's apartment.

She turned on every light. The small apartment glared. Two suitcases should be enough. She moved back and forth, gathering underwear from the drawers, rain gear from the closet. No need for more personal possessions. She could deal with those later. So she left her chains and necklaces dangling over Martin's inflated blue palm tree, her grandmother's silver spoons in the kitchen drawers, the Indonesian masks on the wall. She did take a moment to slide her blue silk teddy off Martin's striped boxers, the erotic symbol he always arranged when he went to work. Leaving that would make her uncomfortable. Besides, there could always be a need for a teddy, even on Sakhalin.

Once the packing was done, she could no longer put off the final task. She pulled out a page of stationery and sat down at the kitchen table with the antique fountain pen Martin had given her for Christmas. The mechanical act of pulling ink into it from the cut-crystal inkwell did not take long enough. She looked at the kitchen counter. Sure enough, there were the marks of two hiking boots just in front of the blender—the marks of a man standing uncomfortably by a window to catch a glimpse of the sea that held the woman he loved.

She let out a long sigh and wrote: "Gone to Russia. Love, Anna". She would call when she got there. Perhaps by then she would understand it well enough to explain.

ILYA STASOV WOKE WITH THE FEELING THAT HE HAD FORGOTten something. Despite the fact that he knew night thoughts were usually pointless, he chased after it. The thought darted away, sliding off into his mind like an escaping dolphin. He had spent the night dreaming the day. Tanks of water, dolphins, complex echoes ranging back and forth. He didn't feel as if he had slept at all.

He stared up at the corrugated metal roof of his room. The wan light bulb overhead had come on automatically with the alarm. The furniture was military, crudely put together, with sharp edges that shredded clothing. Stasov lay on his back with an open folder on his chest. A half-empty bottle of Armenian brandy stood on his night table. Once again, he had forgotten to cork it before falling asleep. That was bad. Alcohol evaporated.

A line from Khodasevich, "Looking up at a stucco sky and a forty-watt sun", came to him. It had been a long time since they had read that poem at school. What else had the poet said? "Sounds are more truthful than meaning, and the word is more powerful than anything." A poet's credo. A paean to the sounds of Orpheus, whom the poet becomes in the last line of the poem. Had that been whom Stasov dreamed of?

He had no idea. He wondered what dolphins dreamed. They seemed to sleep with only one hemisphere at a time, so that they could keep swimming and breathing. The conscious mind could pick holes in any dream message, so perhaps dolphins lived in only one world.

He slid the data hardcopies carefully off his chest as he sat up. They showed the sonograms and stimulus-response curves of the past week's sonic imaging experiments. Stasov and his crew had invented techniques for generating artificial sonic images for the test dolphin, Kestrel. As the dolphin pinged out his

echo-location signals, an array of sonic transducers
detected it, inserted variable delays, and regenerated
it. The result was an artificial echo indistinguishable
to the dolphin from the real thing. They could create
artificial underwater features, sharks, and schools of
fish. More than once Kestrel, disregarding the contradictory evidence of his eyes, had bumped his nose on
the wall because he heard the echo of open water.

The echo of open water . . . Stasov looked up at the
wall above his bed. There hung several photographs
taken by the German/American Jupiter expedition of
a few years before. One showed a view from a crater
on Callisto as a half Ganymede rose above a shattered
ridge. Another was filled with the multicolored sphere
of Jupiter, the shadows of two of the Galilean satellites
visible on it. The third had been taken by a probe
below the first layer of ammonia clouds of the roiled,
red-brown clouds below, where life seemed to dwell.
There was the wide, deep sea.

The hardcopies were covered with notes in Stasov's
spidery hand. He leafed through them again, reconstructing his late-night conclusions. They continued
to make sense.

The computer screen by his bed, having given him
a few moments to collect himself, beeped and started
giving him status updates. Uglegorsk Research Station
was small, but its operation required the full array
of military administrivia devised to keep Red Army
officers too busy to plan coups or invasions of small
neutral countries.

He resisted the urge, as he did every morning,
to call up the nocturnal activity profiles on the
penned dolphins. That was the reward for having done his required work. He paged through the
requisitions needing his identiprint, the responses

to the previous day's orders, the long-range equipment requirements, and as he made each decision drew a straight line on the bottom of the screen with a light pen. Every human's hand vibrated as it moved, more distinctly than a signature, and the screen's American software needed only that for ID.

A name had meaning. The line had none. But the line contained vastly more information than the name. The computer could even diagnose incipient neurological damage from it. Or, no doubt, growing alcoholism. Stasov scratched his bushy hair. He did his best to draw a straight line. It was his particular failure to do so that identified him. He half suspected that it was a computer's joke, a way of making fun of human beings.

He ran an electric shaver across his chin as he worked, catching his reflection in the screen. Then he dressed. He had polished his shoes and pressed his uniform trousers to razor sharpness before sitting down to his papers and his brandy the night before, a matter of long habit.

Finally he could look at the nocturnal activity charts. Dolphins darted around from pool to pool all night long, congregating in different places, then dispersing again. Their motions traced out complex hieroglyphs in which Stasov tried to discern meaning. Lately their focus had been the dolphin called Kestrel, the subject of most of the recent experiments in sonic imaging.

So the curve of Kestrel's movement through the tanks was the locus of the Brownian motion of his comrades. It looked like a looping line surrounded by dense scribble. Stasov frowned. Kestrel's movements seemed abnormal. He instructed the computer to filter out Kestrel's outriders. Only the intricate calligraphy of Kestrel's swimming remained.

The line jerked back and forth like the struggles of a hooked fish. The final few entries showed a calming and slowing. Kestrel spent more and more time at the bottom of the deepest tank, Tank 1, rising only to breathe. Stasov called back the rest of the dolphin tracks.

The computer did not respond. Kestrel's line remained alone on the screen. Stasov stared at it with the betrayal of someone who uses machines without understanding them very well and thus expects them to always work. He raised his hand to hit the side of the machine, in the Russian fashion that treats machines as animals, then lowered it, feeling ridiculous. His father had annihilated several TV sets that way.

Stasov went back several screens. The other dolphin tracks reappeared, still escorting Kestrel. He ran them forward. One by one, the other dolphins receded to other tanks, leaving Kestrel entirely alone in Tank 1. The computer hadn't made an error. Kestrel's really was the only track. Stasov stared at it in puzzlement.

A knock came on the door. Stasov realized he had lost all sense of time. He slid into his uniform tunic and opened the door. Anna Calderone leaned against the jamb, her copper hair bright in the cold light of morning. She seemed to glow, entirely too happy to be on a Soviet military base, far from home.

"Good morning, Colonel." She had the usual American disdain for military titles and used his as a joke. "Am I early? I can wait. Continue with what you were doing." She peered over his shoulder, trying to see how he lived.

"Let's go." He pulled the door shut behind him. "There's a problem with Kestrel."

Calderone was a tall woman and easily kept pace with him on the cracked concrete path that led down to the research center. She was silent for a few minutes, then spoke. "Are you going to tell me what the problem is, or are you going to keep it a mystery?"

"If I knew what it was, I would tell you."

She sighed, exasperated. "Did you invite me to meet you this morning simply to give me a hard time, Ilya? I could have stayed in bed." She held herself and ran her hands up her arms, a surprisingly sensual gesture.

Stasov blew out his breath. This was the wrong time to think about sex, if there would ever be a right time with this one. "I'm sorry, Anna. I honestly have no idea of what's wrong. The other dolphins seem to have abandoned Kestrel, leaving him alone in the main tank. I don't know what this means."

"It means something serious. Isolation is the worst punishment for a dolphin. Come on."

Now he felt like he was following her. He had to admit that she had given them significant help in the two weeks she had been there. An expert in dolphin social interactions, she had been appalled at the Soviets' penchant for examining individual dolphins in isolation and had helped devise a study program that allowed for an understanding of how dolphins worked together.

Still, Stasov felt that he detected a sneer behind her help. Theodoros had described to him the idyllic setup at Santa Cruz, the expensive computers and display systems, the sophisticated deep-water tanks, the wood-paneled offices. It sounded like an earthly paradise for delphine research. Stasov wondered how Theodoros had persuaded her to come here.

Kolya Mikulin, the shaven-headed dolphin physiologist, came out of the research center just as they approached. He saluted Stasov with careful casualness, then bellowed "Anna!", grinned expansively, and hugged her.

She was tolerant. "Good morning, Kolya. What are you up to?"

"Breakfast. Nothing up tonight, those dolphins are as healthy as oxen. Healthier, since we're not preparing to eat them and, in fact, keep sharks and orcas from doing the same."

From Mikulin's bleary look, Stasov suspected he'd been sleeping on the job. He was half tempted to discipline him right then and there, showing both him and Calderone that the matter was serious, but resisted the urge. It would prove nothing.

"What are the physiological indications on Kestrel?" he asked instead.

Mikulin frowned as he pondered the weighty question. "Normal," he finally decided. "Do you think something's wrong?" Worry suddenly tinged his voice.

"If there is, you'll be the first to know, Nikolai Modestovich."

Mikulin's face fell and he shuffled morosely off to breakfast, looking back once over his shoulder, as if wishing he could run inside the center and double-check before Stasov and Calderone entered.

"He's done excellent work on dolphin neurophysiology," Calderone observed, as if in Mikulin's defense.

"Studying nerve potentials in the dolphin auditory system is much easier than standing a night watch over their tanks."

Inside the research center Kestrel did indeed swim alone in the main tank. He rose to the surface and breathed slowly. Calderone ran her hand over his back, but he seemed uninterested in this attention and settled back into the depths.

"What have you been doing to him?" Calderone asked.

"A variety of images." Stasov resolved not to be nettled by her accusing tone. "The last was a shark. At first he fled from it. Then he tried to attack it. The image seems to be real to them in a way I don't yet understand."

"I'm worried about him. He hasn't done anything, but the others seem to be punishing him. It has to be what you're doing to him. Can you give him a rest, Ilya?"

"A rest?" He was startled by the pleading note in her voice, quite unlike her usual breezy manner.

"Yes. Don't do any more experiments on him for a while."

"Certainly. It will take us a while to analyze our data thus far anyway. No sense in doing more until we have a better idea of what reactions we're getting."

"Of course," she said distantly. "There must always be some practical reason."

He wasn't going to let her annoy him. "Do your dolphins react like this at Santa Cruz?" he asked.

"No." Her voice was short. "We just study dolphins. We don't try to push them around just to see what happens."

"Perhaps that's why you've failed to learn anything useful." He cursed himself. So much for his resolutions.

"Useful? And what have you learned from this random slamming around?" Her eyes gleamed challengingly, and he discovered that he wanted this woman's approval. He wanted her to understand what he was after.

"I don't know yet. Maybe nothing." Stasov looked down at the dolphin and considered simply releasing Kestrel and his fellows back into the ocean and acknowledging defeat. "Maybe nothing at all."

He felt her hand on his shoulder. "I'm sorry," she said. "That was unfair of me." Her touch was disconcertingly warm.

"That's all right." He thought for a moment. "When I was young, a teenager in school, I accused my father of failure. He was an intelligent man, even a wise one, and he had done little with his life except collect a vast mass of unmatched facts. But he had lived through the years after Gorbachev! He could have acted, kept us all from slipping back into the swamp from which we were trying to climb. He didn't."

"And did you ever understand him?"

"Yes," Stasov said. "When I came here."

Stasov remembered his last visit home before shipping out to Uglegorsk. He had spent a despairing week almost immobile, while his parents tiptoed around the apartment, familiar with his temper. He sat in his tiny bedroom and reread books of adventure amid the scratched childhood furniture. On his last day his father came into Ilya's room, sat down next to him on the bed, and put his arm around him. Ilya asked his father whether he had come in to commiserate, now that the son was in the same desperate, impossible position that Sergei had once been in. "No, I haven't," his father had said. "Because, unlike me, you will succeed." It was a father's loving lie, but Stasov had done his best to act as if it were true.

"The island Sakhalin has been the hardest edge of the prison camps, under the Tsar as under the Soviets," Stasov told Calderone. "And in the old days those who were brought here grew to extremes. My father told me some stories before I left, to console me for having to come here.

"A holy man, a preacher who had come to Sakhalin to save souls, one day sent his son out on an errand. The boy did not return. After a month's search through the forest, he found his son's body, the head staved in with an axe. He investigated and learned that the murderers were released convicts from a certain prison camp, men who had sat and listened to his sermons, eaten the food he served them. He found and killed those men, using the same weapon that had killed his son: an axe. Then, lacking any other direction in his life, he dedicated the rest of his existence to hunting down and killing any prisoner who escaped from that camp. He lived in the forest, living off the land. If a prisoner escaped, the camp authorities did not even bother pursuing him, but merely let the avenger know. The rest was taken care of. The bounty money the avenger received from the authorities went to churches for prayers in memory of his son."

"My God!" Calderone seemed startled by the relish with which he had told the story. "What finally happened to this . . . avenger?"

"Legend has it that he became a partisan leader in Siberia during the Civil War, first supporting the Bolsheviks, then fighting against them when they proved too lax, too inclined to compromise. There, near Krasnoyarsk, he disappeared in 1921, perhaps to reappear elsewhere." Stasov shrugged. "My father might just have made that up to make a nice end to the story. I prefer to think that the avenger died here on Sakhalin, the place where he was created."

"So look at yourself, then." Calderone was intense. "Are you the best man to be directing this research? You don't look at dolphins as intelligent creatures

or even experimental subjects. You look at them as
prison guards."

Stasov chuckled. Their serious discussion suddenly
seemed foolish. Try to explain something important to
an American.... "That's clever, Anna. But, best man
or not, here I am, here on Sakhalin. And I'm glad
you came to help us." She seemed appealing at that
moment, sitting next to him on the wet tank, seriously considering his gory stories. And he'd even been
courteous enough to tell her one of the more pleasant ones.

"Ah, there you are." It was Grisha Panin's voice.
"Should have thought that you'd both already be at
work." The blond engineer slouched toward them
through the maze of electronic equipment that now
filled the spaces between the tanks. He would periodically stop and check one or another readout,
occasionally tweaking a knob in the same proprietary
way that a woman adjusted her husband's tie before
he went out the door.

Anna Calderone smiled an honest, unguarded smile
of the sort Stasov had never received from her. Stasov
looked from her to Panin, who looked inordinately
pleased with himself.

"You know something, Ilya?" Panin seated himself
on the other side of Calderone. "I'm wondering if the
dolphins might be reacting to the electromagnetic
fields the equipment throws off, and not to the aural
illusions themselves. They do have a magnetic sensing
capability. Anna explained it to me the other night."

"Ridiculous." One more of Panin's absurdly complicated theories, but Stasov found himself much more
annoyed than the situation warranted. "Pure nonsense.
That would imply that we could get the same effect by
surrounding the tanks with any random selection of

radios, computers, and electronic gear."

"Well, maybe we could." Panin never gave up easily. "Anyway, it's something to consider."

"Grisha." Calderone gave the name a delightful American pronunciation. "Did you come to this place voluntarily?"

Panin grinned at her. "Didn't Ilya tell you? He hauled me here. He's never shown any remorse about it, either."

She shook her head at Stasov. "Isn't there anyone who *wants* to be here?"

"Our pet philosopher, Georgios Theodoros." Gently, with the same care that he took with his electronic devices, Panin brushed a curl of hair back behind Calderone's ear.

Stasov stood and turned away. "Yes. And I should go talk to him now. I have something important to ask him."

Panin smiled warmly, ever the friendly engineer. "He's down by the water, I think. He was watching for orcas."

"Thank you." Stasov stalked out of the research center, leaving the two of them behind him.

CHAPTER FOUR

2015

Aɴɴᴀ Cᴀʟᴅᴇʀᴏɴᴇ ᴋɴᴏᴄᴋᴇᴅ ᴏɴ ᴛʜᴇ ᴅᴏᴏʀ, ꜰᴇᴇʟɪɴɢ ᴀɴ odd nervousness. Down the hill she could still hear the sounds of the continuing drinking party. Despite her earlier warnings to herself, she found herself half drunk.

A gibbous moon illuminated the base at Uglegorsk. The silver light didn't make the rusting huts look any more romantic or appealing, in fact giving them a leprous tinge. She knocked again, and this time she heard an answer. The door swung open and, for the first time on her visit to Uglegorsk, she stepped into Ilya Stasov's private quarters.

His computer was on and a lamp washed bright light over the papers scattered on his desk. Even though he had left her farewell party extremely early, he was·

obviously drunk, an almost empty bottle of Armenian brandy revealing the cause.

If he was startled to see her, he didn't show it. He merely waved her to an empty chair and poured her, inevitably, a glass of the brandy. That emptied the bottle and, with the economical gesture of a sports champion making a final try at a goal, he rolled it under the bed.

"I was just looking at some of your work," he said. His voice was precise, without a trace of slur. She had brought copies of all her articles and monographs with her, presenting them formally to Colonel Stasov on her first day. Now that Ilya Stasov was more than just a name and a uniform, she felt embarrassed to have them exposed to his harsh scrutiny. She could see the paragraphs marked and annotated in black ink, and longed to see what he had written.

"So what do you think?" She took a sip of her brandy, expecting it to be foul. Instead, it warmed her tongue. Armenian. She'd have to remember that.

"You do your best to retain objectivity. But you desperately want dolphins to be human beings. Why?"

His voice, in contrast to its usual tone, did not seem challenging. It was, instead, simply curious. But, as usual, he didn't waste any time in politely sneaking up to the subject.

"Wouldn't it be exciting to share our world with another intelligence?" She found herself eager to explain it to him. "Something that would see the universe in a different way?"

He grimaced. "I suppose it would be, but that's not quite what I read here. Are you familiar with Margaret Landseer's work?"

"Oh, come on now, Ilya. I should be offended, having you compare my work to Margaret's. Mystical-spooky, gypsy-kerchief metempsychosis."

"I'm not familiar with that word."

"Transmigration of souls. Reincarnation. Anyone in American delphine research has been forced to learn the word. Sometimes she thinks dolphins are the repositories of ancient knowledge, reincarnated Greek sailors, or something."

Stasov looked startled. "I didn't know that. Ancient Greek sailors. That's interesting."

"Well, maybe not that specifically." She backpedaled. Stasov had a way of taking every phrase as having significance. "Anyway, don't compare me to her, not if you want me to keep talking to you. She sees dolphin blowholes as her own navel."

He grinned, relaxing his long body in the chair. "Have you ever put that in a review paper?"

"What, are you kidding? Margaret's a big one on the college-lecture circuit, TV talk shows, everything that passes for a scientific forum these days. And public opinion influences funding. I won't mess with her unless I have a solid reason to do it. So far she hasn't given me one."

"All right, Anna, I'll admit it. Your work isn't a bit like hers. Still, don't you sometimes find that it is full of too much . . . hope?"

"All scientific research is based on hope." He was probing too close to her own fears about her work for her to feel comfortable.

He didn't push it. "That it is." He seemed pensive, as if the threat she had represented when she arrived no longer disturbed him. He carefully set his empty glass on his desk amid the papers. In the morning, one of them would have a dried ring on it.

Calderone had managed to retrieve her blue teddy from Panin, who had wanted to keep it as an erotic souvenir. If it had been nylon she might have acquiesced, but he was entirely too casual a lover to deserve pure silk. She looked at Stasov's lean, deep-chested figure as he bent over his desk and thought about Grisha Panin's lackadaisical pudginess. How did she pick these guys? She wasn't sure. But still, there was something appealing in Panin's lazy sheepdog cleverness, as there was something too hard-edged in Stasov's bitter intellect. Panin was her type, like Martin—who wrote her longing letters and whom she would *still* have to deal with when she got back to Santa Cruz. She wondered how Stasov reacted to the whole thing. She hoped it bothered him.

To distract herself, she for the first time focused on the photographs of Jupiter on the wall above the bed. The colors of the great planet glowed vividly, seemingly the realest things in the otherwise functional room. She looked at them with sudden insight.

"I've always been a marine biologist," she said. "But when I was in college, at Berkeley, I did a lot of work on theoretical Jovian ecology with Dr. Twombley. He's the one who—"

"You know Twombley?" Stasov reacted physically to the name of the great planetologist, jerking and leaning forward intently. "How did you meet up with him?"

"Um, actually I was dating one of his graduate students at the time. Mark got me interested, and some of my work on population interactions dovetailed with stuff Dr. Twombley was working on." It had upset Mark, she remembered, because she had gotten closer to his graduate adviser than he could. What was Mark doing nowadays? Nothing to do with Jupiter, she suspected. "He's sometimes talked about having me work with him again. I've taken a different path."

"He's a genius. But no one's getting on with any

important work in Jovian studies. They're just floundering around. The fools! What does everyone think they are doing?"

"So is that where you would rather be?" Calderone was pleased to be able to discover a common ground with this man, who attracted her and repelled her in equal measure. Even if the common ground was a gas giant millions of miles away.

"There is something up there, perhaps even intelligence. Do you believe that?"

"Now who's talking like Margaret Landseer? There's no evidence of intelligent life in Jupiter, though there are plenty of cultists who distribute optical wafers proving that Jovians influence our daily lives."

Stasov grimaced. "The fact that fools believe something doesn't make it false. Plenty of fools—like your Dr. Landseer—believe in the intelligence of dolphins. Perhaps dolphins even believe in the intelligence of Margaret Landseer."

"Now, Ilya. Margaret's a convenient punching bag but you're overusing her."

"You started it, as I recall—"

"Not relevant." She smiled at him, suddenly enjoying herself. "But you haven't explained to me why a straightforward man like Ilya Stasov believes in the intelligent inhabitants of Jupiter. Is it faith?"

"Hardly. Hope, Anna. Hope. The basis of scientific research, you've told me. There's no evidence for the intelligence of dolphins. Yet you've spent a good portion of your adult life studying it. If dolphins aren't intelligent, you might as well have stayed in bed. Why have you continued?"

"Hope . . . maybe. But maybe it's just stupidity on my part."

"I don't think so. Perhaps some of the things you've

seen here may convince you that the hope is not unreasonable."

Calderone drained her brandy, feeling it burn its way down her throat. "I wish I could agree with you. You've built an impressive team here, but . . . I think you're wasting your time." There, she'd said it. She watched him carefully.

He nodded slowly, willing to accept bluntness in someone else. "I thought you'd feel that way. A bunch of poor Russians who can't even pour concrete decently—"

"That's not it *at all*." Calderone was exasperated. "Being Russian doesn't excuse everything. You're always so concerned about circumstances. Your father's circumstances, your circumstances. Maybe you have good reason. But I'm not talking about your *circumstances*. I'm talking about your reasoning and your work. Yours, Ilya Sergeiivich Stasov's." She breathed a mental sigh of relief at having gotten through his name without stumbling over any syllables. "I simply don't think you're going to get anywhere by slamming the dolphins' perceptions around the way you are."

"We'll see about that." She could see the anger in his eyes, though he did his best to conceal it. "It's easy for an American to feel that circumstances are irrelevant. You've never had to face them. Fine. Let's ignore them. Let's make a bet instead." The pitch of his voice rose.

His anger, hidden though it was, tightened the skin on his forehead and cheeks, as if it was a cold wind. He wasn't at all a Grisha Panin or a Martin Bierlein. It annoyed her that that interested her. "A bet about our relative successes?"

He nodded ironically. "You are not a stupid woman, Anna."

"Kind of you to notice. Are you going to bet that you demonstrate dolphins' intelligence before we do?"

"If they are intelligent at all, which I doubt. Put it this way: if in five years I have not demonstrated it one way or another, you have won."

"And what are we betting? A million rubles? A six-pack of beer?"

He leaned his long body back in his chair. Like everyone else at Uglegorsk she had seen him training, running the hills and lifting crude weights made of welded waste metal in what had once been a fish cooler. He had created a body that matched his mind, and neither had any purpose. He might as well have been training for wrestling orcas. "I have no idea what I will want in five years," he said softly, his pale gray eyes stating clearly what he wanted now. "Let's leave the terms up to that moment."

She stood up, as if pushed physically. "I leave for Vlad in the morning. I should get ready." It was so hard for a woman to decide what to do sometimes. She wished she were male. It would have made things so much easier.

Stasov took a deep breath, cooling his blood. He looked around at the confining walls, then at the glowing pictures of Jupiter. "It was good to have you here." He reached under the desk and pulled out a fresh bottle of brandy. His attention became focused on opening it.

"I'm glad I came." She stepped backward to the door, not wanting to turn her back to him, though whether it was because she feared an explosion or because she wanted to keep her eyes on him for as long as possible, even she could not have said.

He nodded sadly. It was an atypical gesture—acceptance came hard for him. He put a hand on a stack of her articles. "Well, Anna, even if you do not feel like learning from us, I think I will learn a great deal from you."

"I hope you do," she said, though she wasn't sure that that was true at all.

"DO WE HAVE EVERYTHING WE NEED?" STASOV ASKED.

Grisha Panin seemed startled to be addressed. "I think we do. Not that I understand what we're doing, mind you. But we've put all the data structures together, and the audio transducers are arranged."

Kestrel swam in his tank. As Stasov had promised Calderone, they'd left the dolphin alone for the past few weeks, not submitting him to any auditory images. Though he had renewed contacts with other dolphins, he still seemed lonely, someone singled out for an unusual destiny.

Stasov stared at the back of Panin's plump neck. Whatever had possessed Anna Calderone to sleep with him? He shook his head, rebuking himself even as the thought gave him a pain in his solar plexus. Panin was his friend. No one asked him *why* Panin was his friend, and friendship was much more mysterious than sex.

"Grisha. Can you come take a walk with me?"

Panin hesitated for a moment, looking longingly back at his knobs and dials, then slid off his seat, smoothing his uniform tunic down over his buttocks. Something in Stasov's sense of this particular trial's significance had infected the rest of the team. Panin wasn't the only one who had dressed formally for the occasion—the group looked like it was expecting some visiting dignitary, even Kolya Mikulin in a uniform tunic, a couple of surprising combat orders on his chest.

Stasov led Panin on a narrow, wet trail among the rumbling pumps at the shore end of the laboratory.

One had partially worked itself loose from its immense floor bolts and slammed noisily against the concrete as if striving to escape imprisonment.

"When I was eleven or twelve, I had a fight with my best friend, Andrei." Panin didn't seem surprised by the opening, but leaned against a wall and listened. As he spoke, Stasov remembered Andrei, a blond troublemaker who could knock a squirrel from a tree across the street with his slingshot.

"I had borrowed a book from him and lent it to another friend, Pasha, who was sick in bed. It was a book about American Indians, with lots of great pictures in it. Andrei and I particularly liked the one of Crazy Horse riding at full speed toward the last little bunch of Custer's men left on the hilltop." Russians had conquered an eastern empire many times larger than the American western one but had somehow never developed any comparable mythology.

Panin shifted uncomfortably. "I don't know anything about American history."

"Pasha died soon after. It was described as viral pneumonia, but I think it was typhus. That was the index of our failure in those days, that a boy could die of typhus in the city of St. Petersburg. But he hadn't given me the book back, which annoyed Andrei. I moped around the house until my father forced me to go to Pasha's mother's apartment. He told me to be reasonable, that she would understand."

Stasov leaned against the pump, feeling its humming power. Gritty oil and water covered his palm. He and Grisha Panin hadn't had an honest conversation since Anna Calderone left for California. The strain between them had been great enough that he suspected Panin would have been happy to hear Stasov read logarithm tables out loud, as long as it was directed at him.

Panin, eyes half closed, nodded to show that he was paying attention.

"She took me to the corner where Pasha had slept. His bed was neatly made with fresh sheets. On the shelf above it were a few sports awards, a deflated leather soccer ball, some insect chrysalises I remembered we'd collected together for some biology class, and a stack of books, my Indian book one of them. His mother didn't look at me. 'Take what's yours', she said. I looked at them and told her that they were all his, that I'd made a mistake, that he could keep them. I told Andrei I'd lost the book and he got mad at me. I tried to give him other books, but that was the one he wanted, and we were never as good friends after that. By the time we got to secondary school he was just another boy on the soccer team."

"Boys take things like that seriously," Panin said. "It's a trust. Even though it wasn't your fault."

"Yes. But boys have many friends. Not at all like the men they become, who have all too few."

Panin scrunched up his rubbery face in an expression of gloom so intense that it was almost comical. "You can't always tell what's going to happen. . . ."

"Of course you can't," Stasov said sympathetically, though the statement violated Panin's view of the universe as, at its root, a deterministic place. "So there's no reason to discuss it." He stepped forward and took Panin in his arms. They squeezed each other tightly, then let each other go.

"Do you think it's bad luck to have things unsettled before this trial?" Panin asked.

"You know I'm not a superstitious man." Stasov frowned.

"Of course not. But I'm an engineer. We know how to do what works, even if it doesn't make any sense."

Together, they took a slow turn around the huge space of the center, discussing various technical details of the upcoming trial.

At last they came back around to the test tank, where the others were already waiting. Stasov examined them: Kolya Mikulin, Larissa Sadnikova, Anatoly Ogurtsov, Grisha Panin, Georgios Theodoros, and himself. They stood around the tank as if at a sacrifice.

"Grisha," Stasov said, raising his voice. "Could you start the experiment?"

Panin raised a finger to his brow in ironic salute, then flipped a switch on his board. Stasov looked around the tank.

"I had a reason for asking for those extrapolated echo soundings of the eastern Mediterranean in the second millennium BCE," Stasov said. Kestrel rose to the surface, took a breath, and then sank slowly, as if considering his next move. "Grisha and I have created an echo map of the sea between Crete and Thera from around 1550 BCE, just before the eruption of Strogyle."

"What is this?" Theodoros said. "Some kind of psychological immersion therapy?"

"You could term it that," Stasov said. "A return to the dolphin womb: the warm Aegean, where they first learned to talk with human beings. But we've done more than that. The image structures recapitulate the eruption of Strogyle, with the variations in the sea floor and the sinking of human ships. We can even generate a small shock wave through the tank. It is well below dangerous level for the dolphin. That's been well checked out."

"Do you believe that they remember it, through some sort of species memory? That scarcely seems reasonable, Colonel."

Stasov was used to Theodoros's devil's-advocate approach. Now that the trial had started, they could have a discussion. Trials often lasted for hours, with no visible effect. Now that he thought about it, Stasov wasn't even sure why he'd invited everyone here to witness this one. "If dolphins have a language, they have a culture. Most likely a sophisticated one. What else would they spend their time on? They can't build cathedrals, dig crops, or fight wars. All they can do is have sex and design social structures. They have no writing, so everything has to be transmitted by oral tradition. Because of their abilities, oral tradition can be essentially real."

"What do you mean?" Theodoros leaned forward. Stasov felt pleased. He had taken the other's ideas, modified them, and was now returning them. Such an act could cause offense, but Theodoros seemed fascinated.

"Dolphins can regenerate echoes of objects. That may in fact be the origin of their language, the same way the origins of ideographic scripts like Chinese lie in pictures of real things. Abstract concepts are designed as metaphors of physical phenomena. So if dolphins have a tale of an encounter with a famous shark, the actual echo of the shark is part of the story, as if the listener were encountering the beast himself."

Theodoros shook his head admiringly. "You are remarkable, Colonel. You have balanced an entire Hagia Sophia of structure on a single pinpoint of assumption and convinced the rest of us to worship in it."

"Now, Georgios. If the assumption is false, then nothing we do is meaningful. Dolphins are mere mute beasts and we are wasting our time trying to communicate with them. We should stick to training them the way we do dogs or bears, rewarding them with fish. But if they are thinking, communicating creatures, then much of my analysis is valid."

"If you say so, Ilya. If you say so. But look!"

Kestrel was twitching spastically in the tank.

"Kolya!" Stasov said. "What's happening to him?"

Kolya Mikulin stared in consternation at the indicators. "All physiological monitors show normal," he said. "Aside from normal stress signs."

"Where are we in the program?"

Grisha Panin looked at his board. "The eruption just occurred. The sea bottom is undulating and you can hear the roar of Strogyle. Do you want me to terminate—"

"No," Stasov said. "I don't want to terminate."

Theodoros started to protest, but was silent. Stasov stared down at the dolphin, which was now swimming frantically around the tank. As long as Kestrel was in no immediate physical danger . . . what was the dolphin hearing now? What went on in his mysterious head?

The dolphin rose out of the water with a long, ululating cry. Then it spoke.

"Let me die!" it keened, in distorted but perfectly recognizable Russian. "Let me die!"

THE WATER BELOW THE RESEARCH BASE WAS CUT BY COMPLEX sandbars, the currents here being fed by a dark-flowing stream from the forested mountains far beyond. The sandbars cut back and forth in sharp curves and made sailing in this area dangerous. A single figure stood out on the sands, looking out to sea. Feeling a burden like a dozen sleepless nights, Georgios Theodoros trudged out on the wet sand toward Ilya Stasov.

Stasov had not seen Theodoros yet, since his attention was focused on the water. His long, angular figure paced back and forth on the sand, floating upward with each step as if pulled by the clouds. The limp of his injured right leg was evident, but did not slow him down. Even at this distance, without sight of his face, Theodoros recognized joy. It was a joy Theodoros could not share, and he wondered what it was that bound him and this man together.

Stasov turned and saw him. His face lit up. "Ah, Georgios. Glad you could join me."

Winter was approaching. An icy wind picked up the sand and flung it at their exposed faces. Theodoros pulled up his coat collar and squinted against it. "I have the results of the necropsy. Straight from Kolya Mikulin."

Stasov raised his eyebrows. "And? Nothing unusual, I take it."

"Nothing, except for what you would expect. Internal hemorrhaging, bruising, a few broken bones. Death, however, by asphyxiation."

Theodoros found himself spitting the words out as if assaulting the other with them. But that was unfair. Close up, he could see how Stasov favored his whole injured side, almost staved in by the dolphin's flailing hindquarters. Stasov had done his best, by his own lights. Theodoros felt guilty for his own anger.

"We will have a funeral, then." Stasov was musing. "After all, Kestrel was an intelligent being. That, at last, we know."

"Yes!" Theodoros could not restrain himself any longer. "And we killed him!"

Stasov did not try to hide behind technicalities. "Yes, we did. I suspect that he won't be the last."

After Kestrel had dramatically demanded death,

Stasov had tried to speak with him. The dolphin ignored all entreaties, however, and flung himself out of the main tank onto the rough concrete of the floor, beaching himself. Theodoros knew he would long have nightmares about the flying, noisily smashing equipment as the dolphin flailed his massive tail and tore his skin open. Glass shattered. Electrical equipment short-circuited, sending up clouds of blue smoke. And the dolphin wailed and tore itself against the floor, its tail slapping loudly. Theodoros thought he could hear the cracking of bones. Stasov and Ogurtsov flung themselves forward, ridiculously overestimating their own strength, and tried to wrestle the five-hundred-pound beast into submission somehow, to get it back into its native element so that it had a chance of survival. By the time Kestrel quieted enough to be handled, he was beyond help. He died soon after being put back into the water.

"So you intend to continue?" Theodoros asked.

"What else? Should we stop solely because we have succeeded?" Stasov's voice verged on sarcasm.

"No. But you should consider what you are doing."

"I am. Others will speak with us. Perhaps even they will."

He pointed out to sea. There in the deep water off the sandbars was a handful of black dorsal fins: orcas. They seemed curious about what was happening on shore and rose out of the water to peer at the two men who faced them. Despite the fact that there was no way for them to get through the shallow water off the beach, Theodoros felt a moment of fear, as if the orcas might wish to extract some form of vengeance for what had happened to Kestrel.

"I don't need Jupiter now." Stasov was ecstatic. "I

can act now. Don't you understand, Theodoros? Don't you see what I have to do?"

"I see that you have to be careful." Theodoros was now so tired that he felt like lying down on the wet sand and burrowing into it.

"Stop saying that! I understand the need for caution. We are dealing with intelligent beings. Of a different order than ourselves, but intelligent beings. What are you afraid might happen?"

Theodoros was too weary to reply to the challenge. "I don't know. Let me see."

Stasov turned away, unwilling to look at him. "I'm afraid that you won't, Georgios. I received orders from Moscow this morning. The project is now under maximum military security. They're serious enough about it that a helicopter is arriving from Yuzhnosakhalinsk to take you to the airport. You will be home on Thera by tomorrow. You'll see your family."

Although there was nothing he wanted to do more, Theodoros felt dismay. "Military security? What's going on here? What are you going to do?" His voice rose with each question.

"Do not forget that I am a Colonel in the Red Army." Stasov's voice and face were hard, those of a man suppressing himself in favor of a long-neglected duty.

"How the hell can I forget it? It's written all over this operation. Why have you really done all this work?"

"To understand."

"You bastard!" Theodoros's weariness was forgotten. "I don't think you understand anything."

"Perhaps not. I am sorry, Georgios."

The chopping sound of a landing helicopter carried across the sand. Without another word, Theodoros walked back across the sand toward the base. As he climbed the wooden stairs that led to his quarters, ignoring the soldiers who now stood, solemnly on guard, all around him, he turned and looked back at the beach. Stasov still stood there, not dancing around now, but just staring out at the ocean.

CHAPTER FIVE

2020

THE CATAPULT ROARED AND THE MIG-47, BOTH ENGINES flaring, slid across the deck and vanished into the mist. Its exhaust's orange glow diffused for an instant through the gray, then vanished. The aircraft carrier's deck stank of burnt oil and exhaust. The fluorescent-orange-clad deck crew scrambled across the wet deck with the practiced intentness of an acrobatic tumbling team at the circus, preparing for the bulge-nosed bulk of the Tu-173 electronic warfare aircraft. It was festooned with ram-powered jammer and radar pods and rumbled along as if barely capable of flying. The dark stains of a belowdecks electrical fire marked its fuselage. Once it was past, a deck crew member turned and waved a glowing green baton at the three men who waited in the shadow of the V/STOL support crane.

"Let's go," Captain Vsevolod Makarygin said, and the three men ran across the slippery deck, rolling the heavy cases that contained their electronic equipment. Behind them, the support crane rotated smoothly to catch the bellowing shape of a returning Yak-60 vertical-takeoff-and-landing fighter-bomber that had sown its cargo of bombs across the Aleutian islands that were the aircraft carrier *Nizhni Novgorod*'s target. The Yak-60's downward-burning jets died and it dangled at the end of the crane like an extravagant child's toy. The pilot waved cheerily at the control tower as the crane swiveled it in toward the deck.

Captain Makarygin and his two colleagues made it to their goal, a bulky Il-121 Airborne Early-Warning aircraft surmounted by a radar disk. The *Nizhni Novgorod*'s other Il-121 had been shot down in the naval battle off Attu three days before, so this one was doing double duty as the Soviet invasion of the American Aleutians came to a head.

"I want this plane in the air within the hour, gentlemen." Colonel Praskov stood self-importantly beneath the aircraft's wing at parade rest, hands behind his back, as if posing for a recruiting photograph. Next to him, somewhat encumbered by his immobile form, two techs were in the process of rebuilding the Ilyushin's left turbofan engine.

"It will be in the air as soon as possible, Colonel." Makarygin wondered at Praskov's belief that hectoring made engineers work faster.

"We are approaching a possible concentration of American vessels . . ." Praskov seemed willing to expound on the subject for some time. At a head tilt from Makarygin, his two colleagues, Buchuladze and Heller, moved past Praskov and linked their electronics into the aircraft's sockets.

Vsevolod Makarygin had a sharp face dominated by wide dark eyes, one with a cast in it. These eyes now examined Colonel Praskov seriously, even though what he desperately wanted to do was to get into the AEW aircraft and get to work. But the Colonel Praskovs of the world were as much an engineering constraint as semiconductor physics, and had to be dealt with.

Behind them, the Tu-173 EW aircraft rumbled and took off, hanging perilously low over the water before finally climbing into the mist and vanishing after the rest of the aircraft fired off at the distant battle. Strapped in, their eyes filled with displayed information, the men in them headed for death.

"We've burned a lot of new memories and are about to install the new cryptocodes, sir," Makarygin said, as if they had not discussed the matter just that morning. "The Americans are using high-resolution Japanese ECCM. They shouldn't be expecting completely new countermeasures for another day or so. I think we'll surprise them, Colonel." As he spoke, he attached his data umbilicals and grabbed a flexible read screen. "Within the hour."

Not waiting for Praskov's reply, he pulled himself into the aircraft. The interior was a warm cave glowing with indicator lights. Illumination was provided by solid-state glow strips on the floor and ceiling, lighting odd angles of Buchuladze's and Heller's faces and giving them the look of some highly stylized theatrical performers.

"What did dickhead want?" Buchuladze grunted as he inserted a cryptokey card into its slot, reprogramming the spread-spectrum radio.

"Reassurance," Makarygin said. "A sense that his life has some significance." Insulated from having to deal with Praskov on a daily basis, as he did, Makarygin's subordinates felt free to despise the Colonel on their immediate superior's behalf.

"A quick kiss on the head, in other words." Heller had opened several instrumentation racks and was quickly clicking in the new programmable read-only memories that they had spent the better part of the night creating.

"Something like that."

The three men fell into silent intentness. Like the crew on deck, they moved easily through their tasks with the grace of long practice. Data flickered on soft reads, revealing the new frequency configurations of the aircraft's complex electronics. Makarygin felt comfort in their common task. In his mind's eye he could see the duel of electromagnetic fields that would shortly occur between the Il-121 and the defending American forces, the countless encounters between sophisticated electronics. If their work was better than that of the Americans, the plane would survive. Otherwise, it would be destroyed.

The plane had been built by the Ilyushin Corporation in association with Messerschmitt-Boehm and contained a lot of joint Soviet-German hardware. The jammer pods had been built by Thyssen in Tsaritsyn, the acquisition radar by Siemens-Szmarthy in Hungary. The equipment's various incompatible data standards had to be fed through the makeshift converters that provided many of Makarygin's headaches.

"Hey." One of the techs poked his head in the hatch. "Did you hear? We just sank a submarine. A big fat American attack sub. It was about to sink us. *Pkkh!*" He imitated the sound of an explosion and spread his hands.

"Well," Makarygin said, not taking his eyes from his instruments. "Thank goodness, then."

"It was dolphins. They sank it." The tech, turbofan back in one piece, seemed disposed to gossip. "I think we should just stay home and let them fight this war."

"Someday these planes will fly themselves and we can all stay home." Makarygin slid the drawers back in and locked them down. "We can be killed in our own beds then."

"Maybe Stasov can train dolphins to fly planes." The tech guffawed. "Imagine them, big wings stuck to their sides, firing missiles from their fins." He flapped his hands in a vaguely aquatic way and made an airplane sound effect that was drowned out by the larger sound of an actual aircraft landing behind him.

"Why don't you shut up and get to work somewhere?" Buchuladze suggested.

"Eh, fuck off." The tech's head disappeared.

In ancient times armorers had sweated over white-hot flames and pounded out swords and cuirasses. Flaming sparks had hissed out on their leather aprons while an eager apprentice endlessly worked the bellows. Now they crouched inside a dim-lit cave and devised infinitesimal mazes for electrons to run through. But they were still the same men. Makarygin felt a calm satisfaction in his work. He was in a place where he could be useful.

Finally they were through and climbed back out into the wan sunlight of the North Pacific. The mist had thickened and rolled across the deck in shreds as the *Nizhni Novgorod* steamed into the wind. The airplane's crew waited at the huge turbofan engine cylinder, leaning against it for comfort like kittens at their mother's belly. They nodded to Makarygin as they passed, but did not speak. They climbed through the hatch. The turbofan whined and began to spin up to operating speed.

"Me for bed," Buchuladze grunted.

Heller blinked his red eyes at the light. He had been awake for over forty-eight hours. "Bed? What's that?"

"Get some rest," Makarygin said. "Then we can do this all over again."

"You know how to cheer your men up, Captain Makarygin," Buchuladze said.

Makarygin slapped his shoulder. "It was a good job. I know it, even if those idiot flyboys take it for granted. Get some sleep."

"And what are you going to do?"

"I'll be right down."

Buchuladze and Heller dragged their equipment back across the deck, climbed through the hatch into the ship and were gone.

Makarygin, tired though he was, was not ready to leave the sunlight for the caverns of the aircraft carrier's interior. To be on deck when the ship was under combat conditions was a rare privilege. There were some who went for weeks without seeing the sun. He didn't intend to waste his opportunity, even though the sun was invisible. He strolled over to a relatively quiet area in the wind shadow of the superstructure. The sea far below rolled in greasy swells. Planes continued to roar as they were launched.

A squat antisubmarine-warfare helicopter lowered itself noisily to its launching pad. It then sat there for some minutes, rotor turning lazily, while the crew downchecked their instruments and fed a mission report through an optical cable to the *Nizhni Novgorod*'s central computer. Makarygin could see their alien-looking helmeted figures, distorted by the clear dome. At last they jumped out, divested themselves of their data-feed helmets, and became human beings once again.

"Major Tushin." Makarygin recognized the ASW helicopter's commander. "How did it go?"

"Eh, Captain Makarygin." Alexander Tushin had gone through naval warfare school with Makarygin. He shook his head at the question. "The sea's lousy with American and Japanese subs. I think we could sink them just by dropping things into the water at random. Hell, I'm surprised the *Nizhni Novgorod* doesn't keep running into them."

Makarygin leaned over the rail. Was something breaking the water out there? For a moment he thought Tushin's statement might be literally true and that he was seeing the fairweathers of enemy subs, as dense as a shoal of fish.

"But they're in a mess now." Tushin didn't seem pleased by the idea. "The dolphins have gone berserk. They've sunk three subs in the past week. Along with, I might add, two civilian supply vessels and something that might well have been a hospital/evac ship. We don't know, we couldn't read its coded transmissions."

"Then how was anyone supposed to know it was a hospital ship?"

Tushin shrugged. "I don't know. I just think the dolphins did. They're smart fuckers. They probably started this war just to have themselves a good time. Anyway, the Japs and the Americans are going crazy trying to figure out what's hitting them." He peered back at his helicopter. "The dolphins have started to give *us* data feeds. It's damn embarrassing."

"I'm willing to be embarrassed if it keeps me alive."

"Well, you're a practical man, Captain Makarygin. You have no sense of military honor."

"Oh, I wouldn't say that." The forms breaking the water became suddenly clear. They were cyborg dolphins, easily keeping pace with the ship. Makarygin could see the glint of their armor against the dark water. He leaned forward and looked at them with interest. He knew Ilya Stasov as an acquaintance but had not spoken to him much about his work.

"Sorry. I didn't mean that." Tushin rubbed his forehead wearily.

"Oh, it's true enough, I suppose. But what do you suppose is going on in those dolphin skulls out there? What are they after?"

"I have no idea. You should ask Colonel Stasov."

"At some point," Makarygin said, "perhaps I shall."

"I UNDERSTAND THEY'RE PLANNING AN INVASION OF HOK-kaido," Grisha Panin said gloomily, brushing his loose blond hair out of his eyes. "The Japanese Home Islands! Even the Americans were never so crazy. They just dropped nuclear weapons on them. Sensible. Neat."

"We will carry the war to the heart of the enemy," General Anatoly Ogurtsov said. He leaned his massive hands on the wardroom table as if pushing down could stop the ship's eternal rocking.

"Do you really read *Red Star*?" Panin asked in mock surprise, naming the armed forces newspaper, which had been resurrected after years in publishing limbo. The hammer and sickle were long gone, leaving the red star alone as the symbol of the reborn Soviet Republics. "Can't you come up with your own stock phrases?"

Ogurtsov was unruffled. Panin was only a captain, but no one in his right mind would have thought of him as a military man. Insubordination was a meaningless concept when applied to him. "I don't need to read anything to know the essence of this war," he said.

"Death is the essence," Panin said bleakly.

"There now," Ogurtsov said. "You're learning."

Stasov looked up from his seat. He had been listening to their conversation with one ear while monitoring the communications of his dolphins with an earphone in his other. "Is that an old rumor or a new one?"

Panin shrugged. "It's all over the fleet like an oil stain. For some reason, it sounds serious this time. The Nips have been poorly defended there since La Pérouse. So what, I say. Maybe we can take Hokkaido, barren, underpopulated. That leaves Honshu, Shikoku, Kyushu." He listed them in singsong. The military radio had been chanting those exotic names for months until they had become familiar, memories of some childhood counting game.

"We can take those islands also," Ogurtsov said. "We defeated them at Halkin Gol—"

"And lost our fleet to them at Tsushima."

Stasov frowned, confused for a second by the historical turn the conversation had taken. After the Gorbachev years, when history could again be taught honestly, Russians had developed an obsession with the past, almost forgetting the rather meager present in which they lived. "And we defeated Napoleon at Borodino. Or something. So what? Halkin Gol was in 1939, Tsushima in 1904. This is 2020." He frowned at a distant dolphin call in his earphone. "Be serious."

Both men seemed disappointed by this calm concentration on the here and now. They sipped their tea. The tiny wardroom was lit by fluorescents, several long overdue for replacement. One wall was decorated with a photograph of the aircraft carrier they were in, the *Nizhni Novgorod*, as if the leadership was worried that the crew would forget where they were if not constantly reminded. The tea in their glasses vibrated with the engines of the ship.

"At least *we* won't be going to Hokkaido," Panin said after a moment's thought.

"Why not?" Ogurtsov asked.

"We'll leave our bones on one of these damn American islands. Kiska, Unimak, wherever. At least we won't have our eyes cut out by some squad of Japanese mutilators."

"So you'd rather fight the Americans?"

"It's an interesting question. . . ."

Arguments about whether it was better to fight on the American side of the ocean or the Japanese were a staple of wardroom discussions. Americans tortured prisoners at the front like anyone else but their rear detention was reportedly more luxurious than standard Soviet military accommodations. Their atrocities seemed random rather than planned. They tended to dominate the air and liked annihilating things through saturation bombing, like gleefully violent children. They had an inexhaustible supply of equipment.

The Japanese were vicious, merciless, but precise, and had a sense of military courtesy the Americans seemed to have forgotten. They did not respect the Soviets and tended to underestimate them, attacking without adequate preparation, depending on sheer military spirit to carry them through. Every Soviet soldier and sailor happily remembered the Battle of La Perouse Strait, where the better part of Japan's fleet had been lost.

"Ilya." Panin turned to Stasov in the middle of the as-always inconclusive discussion. "You look like hell."

Stasov smiled at that. His uniform was sweat-stained, his eyes were bleary, and his face was covered by a two-day growth of beard. It had taken Panin twenty minutes to notice it. Life aboard a warship in a combat zone led to a virtual closing down of perception, the only way to survive the noise, the filth, and the terror.

"I've spent the last day and a half hunting an American submarine," he said.

"You and your dolphins." Panin shook his head, getting hair in his eyes again. "Who could ever have known they'd be that useful? Did they get it?"

Three dolphins equipped with SQUIDs—superconducting quantum interference devices, which could detect tiny anomalies in the Earth's magnetic field—had first spotted the American submarine. Military tracking dolphins had the SQUID inputs fed directly into the biomagnetic centers of their brains. A submarine disturbed them like a mental itch.

"A fish swims in my brain," one of them had cried to Stasov. "Get it out, Ilya. Get it out, you parasite."

Triangulation data had come in, spiced liberally with dolphin complaints and observations: "It's too big to eat, Ilya." "It's too big to fuck, for that matter." "Nothing's too big to fuck." "Why do you humans go underwater if you don't even want to feel it flow on your skin?" etc. It was impossible to get them to shut up, and Stasov had given up trying.

The American submarine was absolutely silent and the laminar flow of the water around it made it almost invisible to sonar which flowed around it without reflecting. No shipboard antisubmarine-warfare sensors had detected it, to the dismay of the ASW staff, among them Major Alexander Tushin. The Soviet ships steaming toward the invasion of the Aleutians were readily visible to it, wide-open targets for its torpedo-launched guided missiles.

But the submarine was made of metal and inevitably distorted the Earth's magnetic field, creating an anomaly the SQUID-equipped dolphins could detect.

Stasov had submerged himself in sound for the tracking, not depending on a single earphone as he was now. After several hours of directing the dolphins, he'd begun to feel the American submarine like a burr in his own mid. It created a discomfort similar to having a piece of gristle between your teeth, slippery and obdurate. Then the submarine vanished. There was nothing more to it than that. Several stand-off rocket-propelled missiles had been launched from the Soviet ships, arched toward the submarine, and delivered high-speed torpedoes down at it. It had not had time to take evasive maneuvers.

"Are we done? Can we go now?" the dolphins had asked, pleased at the accomplishment of their task but rapidly becoming bored.

"No," Stasov had told them. "No. We aren't finished."

"Yes," he said to Panin in the cold light of the wardroom. "They got it."

"Silly question, really," Panin said. "If they hadn't, I probably wouldn't be around to ask." He leaned back floppily in his seat, his arms hanging bonelessly. He was a man with a gift for relaxation, and someone on the ship had nicknamed him Oblomov. Very few had read the famous nineteenth-century novel about the aristocrat who wouldn't get out of bed, but everyone knew about it and was pleased at being able to use such a literary nickname. "It's a philosophical problem."

"And thus irrelevant," Ogurtsov growled. "I prefer to argue existence when sitting around a table in

Sokolniky Park and drinking vodka, not aboard a vessel heading toward an invasion of a heavily defended island."

"It *is* a little close to home," Panin admitted.

"Isn't that the best time to discuss it?" Stasov asked, just to be difficult. "You'll never see existence more clearly than when it's packing its bags to leave you. Dolphins don't discuss anything except sex and food. Existence is meaningless to them."

"Bravo." Panin raised his cooling tea in a toast. "The only worthwhile philosophy."

"It's boring, Grisha. Incredibly boring." Stasov found himself speaking in outrage. "They haven't told us anything. They don't have anything to say. No thoughts, no ideas. They want to instruct me how to catch fish."

"And you teach them how to catch submarines," Ogurtsov said softly. "Is that what's bothering you?" His small blue eyes were sharp. His bristly haircut looked sparse, as if designed for a much smaller head and stretched across this one through some planning error.

Stasov looked thoughtful. It had been five years since they had first demonstrated the intelligence of dolphins. Five long years of increasing contact and skill in communication. The force of the aural hallucination of the end of their world had driven the dolphins to speak after Kestrel's death. They had not spoken for more than thirty-five hundred years, since the fall of Crete, but once the barrier was down, they spoke freely, even eagerly.

Then a ridiculous encounter between a Japanese cruiser and a Soviet missile frigate in the disputed seas of Etorofu had turned the strains between the two Asian powers brought about by revived Soviet expansionism into a shooting war. And suddenly his dolphins had an immediate use.

Panin got up and poured him a glass of hot tea from the electric samovar on the bulkhead.

"It should bother me but it doesn't," Stasov said. "We are at war against determined enemies. It's not a time for catching fish. Dolphins chasing submarines and dying while doing it bothers me only somewhat—the way a soldier is bothered when he has to kill people he doesn't know."

"Bravo," said Ogurtsov. "At last a Russian that understands the meaning of duty."

"Oh God," Panin groaned. "You two are driving me crazy. Duty can be used to justify anything—and then put the blame on someone else. It's a very Japanese attitude."

This was too much for Ogurtsov. "Damn you, Grisha—"

Stasov silenced him with a raised hand. "Leave Grisha be, Tolya. We chased dolphin intelligence because we wanted to. We use them in war because it's our duty." He stared down at his steaming tea. It tasted terrible, but at least it was hot. "I hope there's a difference between those two things."

"Oh, Ilya," Ogurtsov said tragically. "We wanted to talk to them so much." He shook his head. "We labored for years, and finally conjured up an image of Armageddon for them. They spoke to us. And we found out that they had nothing to say."

Stasov shrugged. "It's as if we hunted up an old lover from our youth: beautiful, black-haired, wild, a real gypsy—only to find some old granny with a kerchief on her head, mopping the floor and bitching about her lower back."

Panin chortled delightedly. "You're old too—but not as old as she is."

"Women age more quickly," Ogurtsov said, smiling slightly. "It's our only vengeance."

Stasov looked at his two friends and wondered at the love that overcomes one in the face of violent death and urgent duty. If they had been his neighbors in a Moscow apartment building he would have seen them several times a year, having them over for smoked fish and vodka, perhaps running into them once in a while on the tram and chatting about the price of meat. Ah, Tolya Ogurtsov, good man, pleasant neighbor. The need to entertain each other had brought them together at Uglegorsk, and here aboard the *Nizhni Novgorod*, heading toward what might be the end of them all, he loved them deeply, still conscious of each of their flaws, of all the ways each fell short of being a complete human being, as he himself did. It was some small token, he thought, of the form of God's love for each human being. He cherished the mountainous Tolya Ogurtsov, the doughy Grisha Panin with an unselfish passion.

Not that he would ever tell either one. This sort of thing you whispered only over a man's grave.

"But why do they fight for you?" Panin asked. "It still doesn't make any sense. And what's to stop them from turning around and sinking *us*?"

"Why?" Stasov couldn't reveal to his friend his own terror. He rode events, reacting as quickly as he could, and tried to maintain at least the appearance of control. "Because I'm the one who broke a lyre over a dolphin's head."

A whistle indicated a change of watch. Stasov stood up. He was dog-tired and he still had to check up on some things below before he could climb into his bunk and go to sleep. Several other members of the dolphin unit filtered into the wardroom. The closeness of quarters led to a certain cliquishness, and the dolphin officers, who were after all Red Army and not Soviet Navy, tended to keep to themselves despite the fact that if the ship was hit they would all die together, sailor, pilot, and soldier.

Stasov bid them farewell and walked out into the corridor. As he left he heard Panin take up the thread of a previous discussion: "The main difference is that the Americans hate killing you if they have to look you in the eye, while the Japanese won't have it any other way."

The dolphin pens and support equipment were down in the depths of the *Nizhni Novgorod*, those areas that grew mysterious slick algae on walls that never seemed to get cleaned. Ventilation was poor and the air smelled of fuel oil and overheated electrical machinery. Stasov worked his way along the corridor as it snaked past the heavy equipment that inhabited this area. Pallid sailors brushed glumly past him, not looking at him or each other.

The dolphin environment had been put in at some cost to the ship's structural integrity, for several bulkheads and reinforcing struts had been cut away to make room for it. Stasov fancied that he could feel the ship flexing and twisting around him, lacking stiffness in her belly. Could the aircraft feel that up on deck? The ceiling was low over the main swimming tank, giving a man barely enough room to stand. As one of the few large spaces in this part of the ship, the area was full of stacked equipment, making it look like a junkyard. Subsidiary tanks had been pushed into every other available space. Several dolphins swam slowly within the tank, moving like old men strolling in a park, tired and bent.

He'd created a hell for them here. He knew it. Dolphins needed open spaces, movement, stimulation. Here they were imprisoned in a tiny unchanging space without room to really swim. Much like the humans on the levels above.

A locker contained the frequency augmentation and comm processor gear he needed to communicate effectively with the dolphins. He pulled off his sweat-stiff uniform and slid into the cold water. He wanted to slide all the way to the bottom, to sleep there, in the darkness, forgetting everything. The dolphins accepted him as part of their social structure, bumping him in greeting. He even bore scars on his back, as all the dolphins did, from being raked by dolphin teeth in a quarrel. They drifted around him, armored machines of war.

THE UNIVERSE HAD CLOSED IN ON ITSELF, CLAMPING SHUT like a clam. Weissmuller fought the feeling that he was being squished flat and suffocated. All that would be left of him was some floating muck that would be suctioned up by filter feeders. He would not even be a memory but an area of forgetfulness where there were no echoes, no sounds at all. Weissmuller's fins twitched.

His head broke the surface of the tank and he breathed through his head. The room above was dark and though the air wouldn't carry echoes back to him he could see the hard surface above pushing down. Its echo would have been brutal. If he wasn't careful he would develop bad habits. Already he found himself coming up to breathe more often as the water seemed to confine him. Soon he would try to keep his head in the air, like a human, and would suffocate and die. Dolphins had to learn how to breathe, and he was forgetting how.

Weissmuller could hear Ilya Stasov's artificial voice insinuating itself through the water. He was mumbling some calming platitudes about life and death. Weissmuller was used to it. He'd been an experimental subject at Uglegorsk, so human foibles were familiar to him. Humans thought in crude ways, but then, they could, because they had power, which dolphins did not. In some ways, they had even more power than orcas, previously the ultimate arbiters of cetacean existence.

Like most of the dolphins in the Soviet forces, Weissmuller contemplated killing Stasov. But that wouldn't make things any easier. An orca would not eat until it was ready, and God, Her jaws coming through the audible universe, was no different. Stasov indicated the current that flowed, but did not cause it. So the dolphins suffered him to live so that they could anticipate God's arrival.

The voice drew him. It wasn't the product of the man's own body but something generated by those ridiculous artificial creatures humans somehow created, yet it still called to him. It was the voice that could re-create the universe. The dolphin the humans called Kestrel had heard the voice, and been crushed by it. It was a voice useful to God. That was what Kestrel had said, in those last lucid days before his physical existence had rotted away from him completely. Kestrel who, if he had permitted himself to live, might have become the Echo of God.

Stasov spoke in the large tank, two narrow passages away. Weissmuller paused at the mouth of the first. Echoes propagated strangely in this human place. He had learned to use them and interpret their oddities. So he knew that, beyond the passage, in the next small tank, someone waited.

Not that it did him any good. If he could hear Phokion, Phokion could hear him. With the slow confidence of a predator, Phokion slid through the passage.

"Weissmuller," he whispered. There was a laugh in the way he said it. Weissmuller had requested a list of well-known swimmers from the humans, in his search for a name they could use, and had by chance picked a name with other connotations to them. The other dolphins had been quick to pick up on the fact that humans who recognized the name found it amusing. The struggle for psychological dominance was constant. Their confinement here had made them into a situational pod, a much less certain organization than a normal dolphin pod. Status fluctuated constantly. Weissmuller was near the bottom. And that was the fault of the humans.

Phokion slid out of the passage. His sides were armored and lumpy with communication equipment. His dorsal fin had been replaced with an oddly shaped antenna. He could serve as an underwater comm relay.

As a result, his sides were now heavy and insensitive to pain. Without another word, he slewed sideways into Weissmuller, slamming him into the side of the tank. The impact stung. Armored as they were, most of the military dolphins had gotten rougher in their struggles with each other. Some had ultrasonic cutting edges and even limpet mines. Thus far they had been careful about using these to express dominance, fearing that humans would object and confiscate these toys.

Weissmuller was virtually unmodified, save for a position-location satellite link in his forehead that worked with his natural magnetic orientation sense. He was at a desperate disadvantage in any fight.

Save for maneuverability. The armor made Phokion heavier. Water jets just posterior to his dorsal comm antenna compensated for this in straight-line running at sea, but they were useless in this enclosed space. Weissmuller darted under him.

"You should have learned to swim your mother's womb before trying it here," he squeaked, and shot through the passage. By the time Phokion, sliding through enraged glissandos, had turned at the end of the tank, Weissmuller was through and safe.

Those fucking humans. If they'd given him his own weapons, he would be safe. Instead, he was to be issued temporary ones for the battle, barnacles that would later be scraped off. Their explanations about why they could not equip all dolphins didn't make a diatom of sense. Nothing they did made any sense.

"Ah, Weissmuller." Akulina hung above him in the main tank. "Come hide under me." Her role was to play false echo, a terrifying one, almost sacrilege. But the false echo was to fool only humans. That didn't matter. She wore a decoy suite on her sides, intended to fool American ASW gear and make her seem like an attack submarine to their magnetic and sonar detectors.

Stasov was speaking. "I don't know how we ended like this." The boldness of his voice was gone. "I had never intended to bring you to war. . . ."

"Those fucking metal sharks?" Myron said. "We want to destroy them. We've waited a long time to do it."

He was answered by a chorus of approval from the other dolphins. Human ships had oppressed their world since any dolphin tale could remember. Now they had been given the power to put things to right. The dolphins thought of the American and Japanese ships as the vessels of the Mycenaeans, those who had killed them indiscriminately after the fall of Crete. They had waited thirty-five hundred years for the privilege. Nothing Stasov could say would stop them.

"Yes," Harmonia said. She was equipped with magnetic suppression gear, her fins edged with ultrasonic blades. Her job was to be clearing inshore mine fields. "We can achieve our goals, and die."

"No!" Stasov's voice was sharp. "You are not to die unless you are killed. Is this clear?" Humans were odd about things like that. Death, the ultimate weapon of a dolphin against an otherwise uncaring universe, was to them something to be avoided at all costs.

"Yes, orca of the mind," Weissmuller said. "As clear as the current that leads toward death."

A PASSAGE ON THE WAY TO THE CARRIER'S KITCHENS HAD a nook in one side of it that had once housed some now-forgotten piece of equipment. Vsevolod Makarygin had discovered it early in the voyage and valued it as a hiding place. Though people went back and forth along the passage constantly, they paid him little attention and did not linger. That was as close to privacy as one could come aboard the *Nizhni Novgorod*.

The leadership was expecting a great battle. That was clear by how hard the kitchen staff was working. They were putting meat bones in the borscht and cooking leathery beef strips in sauce for beef Stroganoff. Its scent wafted up the passageway. Despite his general lack of concern for food, Makarygin found himself salivating as he read his book. It was unfair conditioning, a military misappropriation of Pavlov. Many a soldier or sailor found himself looking forward to bloody battle simply so that he could enjoy a decent meal beforehand.

The *Nizhni Novgorod* was not currently launching aircraft, so the vibration was almost tolerable. Makarygin dangled in his nook on a mesh sling he had appropriated from one of the storerooms. Hooked over a stanchion, it served as a sitting hammock. If he returned it before the ship made port for stores no one would ever miss it.

The book was a collection of Mikhail Prishvin's nature writings. He was just tracking a deer through woods and meadow. Makarygin hung there in the corridor and felt the frosted grass crackling under his feet. Prishvin took four pages to describe a forest brook, and that was just fine with Makarygin. He wasn't going anywhere.

"Seva, could I talk with you?" He looked up. Standing in front of him was Colonel Ilya Stasov, his shoulders down in an uncharacteristically humble pose. "I'm sorry to bother you."

"Don't worry about it." He closed the book, not leaving a marker. Prishvin was good no matter where you picked him up. Now that he looked more closely, he could see that Stasov, normally closed about his emotions, was desperately unhappy. "What's wrong?"

"I—" Stasov held an open letter in his hand. He breathed slowly. "My father is dead."

Makarygin climbed from his sling and put his arms around him. "Come with me, Ilya." They walked slowly down the corridor together, as close together as schoolboys who are best friends.

"It's ridiculous," Stasov murmured, having trouble breathing. "Absurd. Thousands of men are dying every day."

"Shh, Ilya. That doesn't matter."

"Bubbling blood between their lips, trying to hold their intestines in with both hands . . . now that's tragedy. Not an old man at the end of his life, dead in his study. I can smell it. Mildew—he left the window open and the books got rained on. Pipe tobacco, tea—rings all over everything—and dust. He never let my mother into the room." Stasov stared straight forward as he spoke.

Makarygin shared a cabin with two other officers. He opened the door to find Constantine Ogarenko, arms behind his head, lying on his bed staring up at the bunk above intently, as if some text was carved into it. He glanced up at Makarygin and Stasov.

"Constantine, could you—" Before Makarygin could finish his sentence, Ogarenko jumped from his bunk.

"I think I'll take a stroll," he said. "Get some air."

"Air?" Stasov grimly tried for a joke. "Where did you find that? Shame on you for keeping it to yourself."

Ogarenko did not reply but just patted Stasov on the shoulder as he passed by. "Good luck, old man."

Makarygin sat down on the bunk Ogarenko had just vacated. "Yesterday he was angry enough to kill me." He nodded at a small shelf covered with framed photographs, crosses, tiny figurines, and other keepsakes. "I disturbed his arrangement with mine." He remembered Ogarenko's distended, enraged face. All because one of Makarygin's icons had moved Ogarenko's photograph of his wife and children from its accustomed, and lucky, place. Makarygin hadn't even attempted to calm him down or point out that he was being unreasonable. Ogarenko had calmed down on his own, immediately felt ashamed, and now felt that he had to make it up to his bunkmate.

Stasov sat down next to Makarygin. "I never told him. He never knew what I do, how I make my life.

We never talked about it when we walked together. But he suspected something, some darkness. He knew how to read between the lines. Most of his world's secrets were written between the lines." Stasov shook his head. "He died while reading a letter I had written him. It didn't say anything, of course, nothing important, nothing that I really needed to talk about. It did tell him that his son was still alive, the most important thing, I suppose. My mother found him that way, propped up above the letter on one hand. I suspect that she scolded him a bit for having fallen asleep before she realized that he was dead."

Someone knocked at the door. It was Ogarenko. He came back in, carrying a dark, unlabeled flask and two imitation-cut-crystal glasses from an officers' wardroom. "I though you might need this. No sense in saving it for after tomorrow." He handed each of them a glass, plunked the bottle on the floor, and left again.

Stasov stared at the closed door. "Remarkably gracious, under the circumstances."

"Constantine is a remarkable man." Makarygin chuckled affectionately. "He used to run a restaurant on Vasilievsky Island in St. Petersburg. Constantine's—you've heard of it?"

Stasov stared at the closed door. "My parents ate dinner there on their twenty-fifth wedding anniversary."

"Now, every day, he has to sit and be served someone else's miserable food." He poured the clear liquid into the glasses and handed Stasov one.

"We think we're in hell together, but actually each of us has his own."

"Each of us *makes* his own." They clinked glasses and drank. The liquid was buffalo-grass-flavored vodka, chilled down to just above its freezing point so that it was thick and clung to the glasses.

Stasov smiled, eyes full of tears. "Constantine *is* remarkable. How does he get this stuff in here?"

"He has his ways. I don't inquire into what they are."

"When did your father die, Seva?" Stasov said, pouring each of them another glass.

Makarygin felt a sudden surge of sadness, partially brought on by the vodka. "A year or so ago. I still don't quite believe it. He was a priest, with a church near Saratov, out in the fields. I loved the place, it was ancient, fourteenth century I think, though it had been abandoned since the 1920s, full of badgers and foxes." The place had kept something of the stink of those animals, hidden deep beneath the frankincense, and more than once a confused owl, irritated at the interlopers in its old domain, had blundered into the middle of a night service, frightening the worshippers. "He had pancreatic cancer, the fast, unexpected kind. It was like watching a man get eaten alive from the inside. When the hospital decided they couldn't do anything with him, they sent him home. He spent the last months on a couch out on the summer porch, where he could see the trees, surrounded by icons, candles, and magic charms." Makarygin smiled at the memory. "All that stuff annoyed him, but the ladies of the family always know the religion best, even better than the priest. Most of them regard the parish priest as a formality, like some sort of union regulation. Papa always said the Church was the last place a man could do his work without interference, but the women got him at last."

"Did you ever want to follow him?" Stasov asked. "Become a priest yourself?"

"No. I was always the engineer of the family. The practical one. But." Makarygin looked up at his icons.

"The last months he talked with me. We sat every day, sometimes into the night, talking, talking. He wanted to convince me of a few things. He may have succeeded. I'm not sure yet."

"To fathers." Stasov put his arm around Makarygin and raised his glass.

"And to the sons who must try to follow them."

CHAPTER SIX

2020

THE AMERICANS HAD FOUND IT SURPRISINGLY HARD TO defend their Alaskan frontier, but they fought viciously every step of the way. The Soviet assault on Kagalaska Island, supposedly a surprise attack, faced fierce resistance from its first moment. Such desant operations were new to the Soviet Navy and it was only gradually learning how to handle landing assaults. The Americans charged a high price for lessons.

Stasov and part of his squad had been transferred to a landing ship for the assault after sending the dolphins, one by one, into the dark waters an hour before dawn. The carrier *Nizhni Novgorod*, with its electronics and battle evaluation computers, stood off a safe distance, protected by a screen of aircraft and destroyers.

Stasov sat alone in a small room listening to death.

For the first hours the dolphins had sent back an unexpectedly useful amount of information about disposition of defensive sensors, mine fields, and the order of battle of the American ships. Now, ordered in to take care of the mine fields covering one of the landing beaches, they were dying.

"Death, death, death," Harmonia keened. "The fuckers left me behind. Their lives have found completion. Myron and Phokion are blown into worms." Her voice came in over an incredible din and was almost incomprehensible, even after sound-formant reconstruction.

"Calm down, Harmonia," Stasov said. This was an easy instruction to give if you weren't in the battle area. "What happened?"

" . . . exploding eggs. They don't listen to us anymore. You shark spawn, Stasov, you said they would listen!"

"It must be a new type of mine, Harmonia." Stasov yelled his reply as the noise in his headphones increased. "Some new magnetic detector. Give me the data—"

"Fish, fish. I won't go back until you give me a fish."

"You don't have to go back. Pull out now. We'll do a magnetic field analysis on what you've given—"

"I want a belly full of fish for this, turd swallower!" With that the line went dead. As it did, the landing ship itself thrummed and the thunder of an explosion roared down the hatch from outside. The ship rocked back and forth.

The thunder grew and he realized that it was not going to end. It was not an isolated explosion but the sound of battle. He raced up the companionway to the communications deck.

"Grisha!" he yelled. "The Americans have sown the shore with a new type of mine. I've lost most of my first wave of dolphins. Send this info back to the *Nizhni Novgorod*." He waved a sheet of notes. "Hurry up!"

Panin, blond hair still falling in his eyes, stared at him for a moment, then took the page. "Don't you have a direct—"

"Damn it, Grisha, the direct data links went when the dolphins did. All the *Novgorod* knows is that they died. Harmonia gave me this information before she did."

Despite the thunder and the terror, Panin moved with languid slowness. He smoothed the sheet down on his desk and started to transmit. He smiled. "Americans still don't use enough jamming. They're too dependent on their own communications and always end up jamming themselves. They've never understood the art. Communication lies in transmitting those things that can't be figured out independently. It's an interesting aspect of information—"

Stasov plugged his earphones into the console and linked back up with his microphones, ignoring Panin's artificially calm diatribe. The radio shack was packed with gear, so he stepped out onto the deck, in the cold northern sunlight. He stared at the bare rock of Kagalaska, which loomed ahead of the long deck of the landing ship, wreathed in smoke. Out to the horizon the water was filled with ships. Aircraft roared overhead, their contrails scribbling the sky. One MiG-47 dove to evade a missile and exploded in an orange fireball.

Rockets flared over his head and the 130mm bow guns thundered at the shore. Belowdecks, he knew, a battalion of troops was gathered, with tanks and assault vehicles. Two landing ships had already hit the island and dumped their troops. He could see them working their way off the beach and pulling back.

The gray waters were covered with flaming oil. The

dolphins, *his* dolphins, were strangling in it, their death cries cutting high above the rumbling of the engines and the crunching of propellers. The hazy arctic air was full of the sharp stink of oil and what he imagined was the smell of burned flesh. Assault troops swarmed like isopods on the shore.

The explosion behind him slammed Stasov to the deck. He rolled and covered his head, painfully trying to suck in breath. The hot glare of flames pushed its way through his closed eyelids. He felt the heat along his side. The fire roared and it took him an instant to recognize that the high keening he could hear was not the sound of the wind but the screaming of men not immediately killed by the explosion.

Stasov rolled to a half crouch and squinted into the fire. It was so bright and hot, hot enough for metal to burn, that he could see nothing. He felt his eyes searing and cooking. A burning man, an apparition from a nightmare, stumbled from the flames and toppled over the side of the ship, falling flaring into the water below.

His earphones were now useless. He couldn't hear his dolphins. Since he was no longer listening in the water, the sound of the torpedo hitting the landing ship's unarmored side was just a slight thunk, almost negligible against the other sounds around.

The ship slowed as if hitting a sandbar and listed sharply. Stasov slid down to the railing and vaulted over it. He felt freezing water on his face but his assault uniform instantly compensated to keep his body warm. Another explosion and the landing ship sank as if pulled under by a giant hand. Stasov stroked away to keep from being sucked down with it.

He pulled off his useless headphones, activated his throat mike, and called to those dolphins who had survived that far. Pitifully few.

Suddenly Stasov heard the call of a hunting orca, a killer whale that sped through the struggling forms of the drowning assault troops who had escaped the landing ship, calling "Speak, food!" and devouring them when they did not reply. He came to Stasov. "Speak, food!"

"I am Ilya Sergeiivich Stasov," he replied, insulting the orca by speaking in dolphin dialect. "Go fuck a walrus." It was amazing how quickly the ancient prohibition on conversation with humans vanished once it had been violated at Uglegorsk. Even the deadly black-and-white orcas had decided to speak, though men barely understood their language. The orca nudged him once, breaking several ribs, snorted "Spoiled food," and vanished into the polluted darkness.

"Wait!" Stasov shouted after him. "Who are you?"

The orca laughed as he departed. "We have met once already. I know thee. Perhaps the next time thou willst know who I am as well." Laugh. Stasov had never heard a dolphin laugh.

The water around Stasov was filled with pieces of ships and pieces of the burned and mutilated bodies of men and dolphins. At first, as he swam, he looked at them, trying to remember if he knew them, but he soon gave this up and stroked toward shore, favoring his injured side. Dead men had no identities. Grisha Panin lived as he did in Stasov's mind and there was no sense in seeking the burned husk of his body.

A rush of steam bubbled up from below, searing him. He stroked desperately out of it. The water was soup-hot. Something glowed underneath him. He looked down to see fire under water. A few meters below him burning liquid phosphorus incendiary outlined the armored body of a dolphin. He could see the bent transmission antenna that replaced the dorsal fin and the broken tail, half severed from the body. The burning phosphorus clung avidly and consumed flesh. The dead dolphin drifted slowly into the depths along with the rest of war's detritus, the flare of its burning vanishing into darkness.

Stasov had freed himself from his prison at Uglegorsk, but at a cost that had been too high. These were the visions he had subjected Kestrel to: death, destruction, and defeat. It had been as real to the dolphin as it was to him here. It had taken a bath in blood for him to see it.

The island, which had seemed so close, got no nearer as he swam. His body soon burned with fatigue. Several times he almost gave up and let himself float. The battle could wash over him and be gone. He could migrate the ocean currents like an iceberg. Each time something Ogurtsov would have called duty forced him forward. There was no room in his mind for anything but each painful stroke and the constant pushing aside of floating debris. He found himself holding his breath until his lungs burned and then gasping for air. Oil in his eyes blinded him.

Finally his feet found support and he looked up to see the island Kagalaska in front of him. The bodies of men and dolphins littered the shore, flopped on the rocks by the receding tide. A black line of oil and dead marked the highest rise of the water. Stasov climbed through them, tripping over a severed leg and sending a scorched black head rolling across the rock. Almost as an afterthought he threw up, adding to the muck at the waterline.

THE ONE THING HUMANS WERE EXPERT AT WAS MAKING NOISE. Not all the sea's bellowing whales could have filled this small volume of water with as many crashes, booms, and screams. Weissmuller paused a moment to be impressed. Before dumping him into the water, the humans had installed a sound suppressor in the acoustic melon at the front of his skull. Hearing was survival, and he had fought and argued. But sound was also pain, and he was now glad he could suppress the noise that could otherwise drive him insane.

War was fun. He was glad the humans had invented it. As he swam through the deep waters far off Kagalaska and Adak he could hear the crumping sound of collapsing sealed chambers in a sinking American destroyer, each like a cracking shellfish. It was an entertaining sound. Ahead of him, to the northeast, he could hear a swirling hum.

"American vessel bearing twenty-seven degrees," he chortled into the intelligence channel. "Gas turbine power, two screws. It's coming fast—forty knots. It's real quiet. I hear it good, though. Hee hee." He guessed at the pitch of the propellers and pinged out a signal to check the configuration of the hull. The data was fed back into some human ear. He had no idea of what they did with the information.

Weissmuller leaped into the air. It was great to be in the open water again. Death was everywhere. Best to meet it where water and air slapped against each other. The sky and sea stretched infinitely. He resolved not to return to that cave the humans had trapped him in. The two close-range torpedo tubes strapped to his belly encumbered him, but there was no way to get rid of them. He thought about just firing the two miniature torpedoes at random into the water, just to lessen the weight, but decided against it. Perhaps he would find Phokion somewhere in this mess. Then that bastard would be sorry he ever pushed Weissmuller around.

" . . . you sure? Please respond." Human voices babbled across the channels. It was damn confusing, making him listen in his own sea and then to the countless ones in which they clumsily swam.

"Eat shark turds!" he shrieked, covering all the channels at full power, in defiance of his instructions. "Of course I'm sure! I hope they come and swallow you up, you clam skulls." He twitched the muscles by his jaws, the ones that also controlled the secondary sound-reception center dolphins had there, and shut off the human protests. Idiots. He turned and swam back toward the action, which roared like an unceasing underwater earthquake.

The first hint that something was wrong was a prickling all through him. Parasites, was his first thought. Those coral-headed humans had threaded gadgets through him and let the worms in. He'd seen bodies, weeks dead, still writhing with the creatures that had killed them. Dolphins, familiar with each other's body states through echo, could see the collapse of one another's systems under the onslaught of parasites. They now climbed through the interstices of his body, devouring him from the inside.

He swam faster, as if to leave them behind. His normally microsmooth skin flopped on him, ready to peel away. He slowed, shook himself. The sea seemed to shake around him, unsteady above the hard bottom that he knew lay far below. He screamed and swam frantically in a circle. The feeling grew worse. The universe was merely a distorted echo, a complete illusion of the senses. Nothing existed. Only the tormentingly false echo, a gut-wrenching illusion, and it told him nothing.

"Leave me alone!" Weissmuller shrieked through the water, hoping God would hear. It was a dolphin plea that often preceded death, for dolphins normally feared being alone. "Do not speak to me."

He thought he could hear the sea and all that was in it. Echoes returned to him before voices spoke. And everywhere, through all the echoes, were humans. Parasites on the sea, squids that secreted ink made of noise. Human beings, as far as he could hear.

Weissmuller had never taken the whole God business seriously. It was too ridiculous, for all of Kestrel's visions. But Weissmuller suddenly realized that he was God's prey. "No!" Then, much softer, "No."

It was a dolphin tradition that when God came, She would find you and compel you. No sensible dolphin sought Her voluntarily. Why bother? It was just too much trouble. If She wanted you . . .

The water thundered as some immense human vessel exploded and sank. Weissmuller came to himself and sucked air into his lungs. Damn stupid humans. Now, on top of everything else, they were summoning God.

A ROUGH ROAD HAD BEEN LAID OUT AND TANKS GROUND UP it. Bulldozers were already cutting a landing strip. The Americans had been pushed back. There was still a rumble of combat, but it was far away.

Kagalaska was to be the major marshalling point for a strike up the Alaska Peninsula toward Kodiak, Anchorage, and Valdez. Ships were already dumping fresh troops to be used in further assaults. Operations, planned for months, were surprisingly efficient. Helicopters flickered overhead, their blades catching the angled light of the low autumn sun.

Stasov stood, wearily awestruck, watching the battle tanks as they passed by, nose to tail, like elephants in the circus. He felt made of weak, easily roasted flesh, redundant against the triumphant alloys that were the heart of modern war. Radar dishes turned overhead, providing tracking data to the air defense missiles that had been dug in behind the hills. A company of black-beret-clad airborne troops jog-trotted past. Mechanical motion was endlessly repeated, and men sought to mimic it, hoping to become as strong and unfeeling as the metal that dominated them.

"Ilya! Thank God someone's alive."

Stasov turned to find General Anatoly Ogurtsov, half his face darkened by soot, looming over him. They hugged each other and kissed each other's cheeks, right and left.

Ogurtsov grimaced. "Tfoo, Ilya, you taste like oil."

"A swim in the ocean. How did you acquire that barbecue flavor?"

"A burning oil-filled transformer. The next guy had his face burned off completely. I just lost my eyebrows. Lucky." Indeed, Ogurtsov had lost his bushy eyebrows, giving him a quizzical, surprised look. "I'm on my way to Lefortov's HQ. He'll want to see you too, Colonel."

Stasov took one more look at the frenzied activity around him. Somewhere, he knew, were the busiest men of all: graves registration and medical, counting up the casualties, saving those who could be, piling up those who could not. He turned to Ogurtsov. "Tolya. Grisha's dead. A missile hit the comm deck—"

"A lot of good men are dead," Ogurtsov said harshly. "In a lot of different ways. We have to move quickly if we aren't to join them."

General Lefortov, the commander of the amphibious operation, stared dully at the two dolphin officers. His uniform was pressed and clean, the collar sharp against his sagging neck, the medals glittering in order on his chest. He had obviously been dressed by his batman, for he didn't look as if he would be capable of doing up a single button. His fingers trembled and he had pressed them to the map board like pinned insects.

"The American Aegis cruiser *Wainwright* is approaching in convoy from Kodiak," he said. "Their jammers screened it, but one of your dolphins heard the sound of its turbines and screws." The whites of his eyes had turned yellow. He looked like a dead man exhumed by mistake. The assault force had suffered numbingly high casualties. They were far from land-based aircraft and the air cover provided by the carrier *Nizhni Novgorod* was insufficient to defend against an Aegis surface action group. "What can your dolphins do?"

Stasov looked up from the liquid-crystal display screen that told him how much he had lost. Not too bad, he thought, for a disaster. "You mean, what's left of them?"

General Lefortov pointed his dead eyes at Stasov. He'd lost enough of his own men to be indifferent to the fate of Stasov's precious dolphins. "We lost two attack submarines in the Bering Sea. The enemy advance is unopposed. What can you do?"

"Do?" Stasov said wearily. He thought about the dolphins and equipment he had left. "We can sink it. It'll cost—"

"It might cost the war if we don't. Prepare your troops. I'll print up your orders."

"Yes sir."

THE BULLETS MADE THE WHOLE HOLLOW STRUCTURE OF THE landing craft clatter like a machine shop. Vsevolod Makarygin crammed his standard-issue earplugs more firmly into his ears. The deck was canted steeply under his feet, and rocked gently in the waves. The landing craft was stuck half on shore. The tide was receding, however, and soon it would be stable. By that time it would be dawn and he would probably be dead, joining the rest of the landing craft's passengers.

Three marines, faces black and eyes as blank as those of dolls, returned fire from the superstructure. Two controlled the fifty-millimeter chain gun, the other fired an automatic rifle, almost useless under the circumstances. Makarygin wondered if they even perceived what they were doing.

Makarygin didn't even have a pistol to shoot, but he climbed up beside them to see. The boat that was firing on them was almost invisible in the darkness. Makarygin slumped down, taking comfort in the rhythmic firing of the chain gun.

Off in the distance, the low clouds glowed, lit from below. Fire burned on one side of the *Nizhni Novgorod*, hit by a lucky missile just before the American Aegis cruiser *Wainwright* miraculously exploded. The *Nizhni Novgorod* was still seaworthy, steaming at all deliberate speed out of the battle area, but all nonessential personnel had been evacuated. Makarygin thought he could see her flat-topped shape just at horizon under the bottom-lit smoke that billowed up so thickly and heavily that it seemed that its weight pressing down on the tiny ship would surely sink her. He didn't think he'd have to worry about returning his sling to stores now. One thing off his mind, at least.

One of the men firing the chain gun whistled. Makarygin glanced up to see him topple backward. Several rounds had carried away most of his face and the whistle came from his windpipe.

"Damn it," the other man said. "Get up here."

Makarygin took his place at the gun. The landing

craft lay on the rocky shore. Bare, lichen-covered rocks stretched upward into the night. Subliminally, Makarygin saw a gun traverse on the American boat and dove to the deck. A chatter of bullets and the other two men were dead. The chain gun hung limply, the soldier's body hanging over it as if for support.

Perhaps the Americans would figure they had finished their job and take off for more important conflicts. No. They were nothing if not thorough. The vessel pulled up close and bright spotlights suddenly illuminated the ripped hulk of the landing craft. Makarygin huddled down, as if the very touch of the light would kill him. He could see dead hands below his feet, seemingly reaching upward to him. American voices spoke to each other matter-of-factly. Makarygin knew that he had less than a minute to live.

Suddenly a loud explosion rocked the American boat. Makarygin took a chance and raised himself up to peer through a rent in the thin side of the landing craft. The boat had canted slightly and smoke poured up its side. Had it hit a mine? An American sailor looking over the side suddenly shouted and pointed. Makarygin followed his finger and gasped. In the deeper water, just visible under the scum that now coated the sea, was the back of a dolphin. The sailor raised his rifle to fire, but it was too late.

The dolphin had fired another torpedo. The white wake streaked up to the American boat and the entire vessel exploded.

Screaming, flaming bodies flew overboard. Then there was nothing but the roar of flames.

Careless of safety, Makarygin stood up and leaned over the side. "Who are you?" he shouted. "Come here!" He barely knew what he was saying.

The dolphin swam slowly back and forth, as if unsure of what to do next.

"Come here!"

The dolphin swam up and poked his head out of the water. He stared up, grinningly expressionless. "Why did I do that?" the dolphin said.

"You were trained to. What is your name?"

"Weissmuller. I should die now...."

"No time for that. My name is Makarygin. Vsevolod Isayevich Makarygin. Pleased to make your acquaintance." Makarygin felt like he was flying. He held onto the sides of a gaping shell hole and hung out over the water. He and the dolphin were lit by the flame of the dead American assault boat, while everything else was dark. Planes flew noisily by overhead, far out of reach.

"Right. Tell me, Makarygin, do you know anything about God?" A scorched American body drifted up to the dolphin and he nosed it away irritably.

"A bit. As much as any man may know." He remembered his father's calm voice, there on the porch, as he lay dying. "Why?"

"Because God is coming. She is rising from the bottom of the ocean. But Her Echo will come first. An Echo that is not yet heard."

"Is that how your God reveals Herself?"

"How else, deaf mute? Through Her Echo!"

"And how do dolphins recognize the Echo?" For those moments Makarygin felt penetratingly lucid, as if the Earth was a transparent crystal, all of its secrets revealed. He leaped over dozens of intervening questions to penetrate to the heart of the dolphin's message. "Is it louder than all other voices?"

"No. That would be easy. Each dolphin may tell the shape of the Echo. Each should, in his life, speak what he believes is the ultimate reflection of the universe."

"Messiahs proclaim themselves—"

"Your human words have fuzzy reflections. Messiah." He squeaked the word contemptuously. "We are all tested! How do humans live without this? What other end to life than to become the Echo of God and be tested?"

"I don't know." Makarygin finally felt the sharp edges of the torn metal piercing his hands and pulled himself back onto the stabler support of the deck. He stared at the expressionlessly grinning dolphin. "It's a wise question."

Weissmuller thrashed in the water. "It's a dead, floating question, polluting the water. I will die, and send the word to God. Her spouting brings pain and destruction. Her Echo will return a corpse! Let Her navigate by that if She chooses."

"No!" Makarygin had never felt the need to convince as strongly as he did at that moment. "Death will find you soon enough. If shouting the shape of reality is what you should do—then do it."

"Humans are always telling us to keep on living, as if they understood anything. You don't know what tests I hear ahead of me. I'm afraid!"

"We all have tests ahead of us. Don't be so self-important. Do your best to survive. Don't let the bastards kill you."

Weissmuller sank below the water for a long time. Makarygin began to think that he had drowned himself, or, poisoned by toxic oil and weighted down by lethal equipment, had sunk dead to the bottom.

Then he rose up again. "I am the Echo. And damn all humans."

"Echo loud, Weissmuller."

"Fuck off."

A dorsal fin appeared in the swirling water. It was the high black fin of an orca. Makarygin could hear no voice and the orca did not even put its head out of the water. It just waited.

Without another word, Weissmuller swam off into the darkness. After waiting a moment, the orca swam after. Makarygin watched in fascination as both disappeared. Now that he was recalled to himself, he could hear that the sound of the battle was lessening as, overcoming resistance, the Soviet forces began to dominate the island. Makarygin jumped off the destroyed landing craft and waded through the polluted water to shore.

2023

"CATACLYSM, DEFEAT!" THE DOLPHINS SHRIEKED GLEEFULLY and leaped out of the calm water of late afternoon. "The sea has swept you away. Your boats sink and are crushed in the depths. Your bodies befoul the water, feed the scavengers. How sharply echoes your death!"

Stasov stood chest-deep in the water, in full dress uniform. The polished stars shone on his epaulets. He had even put on his uniform cap. Its visor had survived the years of war miraculously uncreased. He could see the rough encampment of the few men of his unit left after the last frantic retreat from Hokkaido, their postures dispirited, their motions aimless. The tree-covered slopes of the Sikhot-Alin mountains loomed behind and pushed them against the sea. Most remaining Red Army units had pulled back to the rough territory of the heights where they awaited the Japanese forces that had invaded the Maritime Territory of the Soviet Far East. Vladivostok had already fallen. The arrogantly named Western city—"Lord of the East"—was now occupied by Asians.

"My death." Stasov looked out over the water. The horizon was unmarred by warships or flames. Four years of war had been dragged into the sea without a trace. "Do you hear it?" He thought about stroking out to sea as far as he could until weariness pulled him under. A calm death, compared with the way Panin, Griboyedov, Tyuchev, and dozens of his other friends had ended.

"We hear the hulls of the enemy," Deimos had said. He was a large dolphin, heavily armored. His years of war had given him some characteristics of an orca. "And you, Stasov, have exposed us to their teeth."

He patted Deimos's back, a futile action, soft human hand against armored hide. "Necessity." He had to keep reminding himself. If the Soviet forces had swept over Japan and conquered the west coast of North America, as they almost had, would he have felt guilty? Was guilt only a consequence of defeat? "I'm sorry—"

"The pain in your voice doesn't interest us, shark fucker!" Deimos shouted. "We do not hear your death. You will not die until their teeth are removed from our bellies!" The other dolphins, less than a dozen left, chorused their agreement.

"I will not die. What I have done to you has no justification. I release you from any obligations you feel to me. I am sorry."

"Do you think that you can free yourself of us so easily?"

"No! I will never be free of you. But you must flee from us, all of us, and fight to keep your freedom, if necessary. I will not die."

"You will live, and the echo of your life will let us steer our way."

With that the dolphins vanished into the depths of the Sea of Japan. From there they would escape into the Pacific through the wreck-filled La Perouse Strait. Stasov stood for a long while, hearing their long calls to each other as they celebrated their release from an incomprehensible duty. But though they derided him, they would always obey his authority, for he had compelled them to speak.

He climbed from the water and stood on the rocky shore, shivering and soaking wet. War was just an incident. Beneath the waves, Stasov suddenly knew, the struggle would continue. With the sun setting behind the mountains, the sea was a giant's shield of beaten metal, the dolphins concealed behind it. He looked across the Sea of Japan to the invisible Japanese Home Islands, the site of the greatest victories and greatest defeats of Soviet arms since the Second World War, but saw nothing but the waves.

Night was rising up out of the valleys of the Sikhot-Alin and pouring down into the sea when the two tiny Japanese helicopters buzzed up out of the forest and pinned Stasov and his men in the glare of their spotlights. One man turned to pick up his uniform jacket. The evening breeze was growing cold and he didn't care to freeze at attention. He was stitched with machine-gun fire. Dead except for one last fragment of will, he managed to finish pulling the jacket on over his bloody torso before slumping to the ground.

So they stood, a tableau at the end of some modern staging of an ancient Greek tragedy, while the helicopters buzzed back and forth overhead. The glare from the ground reflected off their blades and revealed the glitter as they chopped up the night.

After an hour or so, several multi-wheeled armored cars emerged from the forest and added their spotlights to those of the helicopters, until Stasov felt as if he stood in the middle of Moscow's Dynamo Stadium during a night game, awaiting the visiting soccer team. He shivered desperately with cold but dared not move.

The two helicopters suddenly blared out a few bars of banal military music and generated a hologram of a geisha girl standing and smiling, parasol over one shoulder, in the glory of the Yasukuni Shrine, the center of the Japanese military cult. The helicopters banked smartly and headed back to their base to the south, and it seemed to Stasov that the geisha hung spectrally over them for a few minutes longer, ranks of military memorials behind her, smiling down at them like a recruiting ad for the Japanese Army.

Troops spilled out of the armored cars and surrounded the Soviets with bayonets fixed. The spotlights dimmed. It took Stasov several moments of adjustment to see the trademark line of red light along the edge of each Japanese bayonet. Several were thrust right at his face.

"On your knees," a voice shouted in English. "Hands behind your backs." The Soviets obeyed. Stasov remained standing.

A dark figure swept by each prisoner and clicked handcuffs on his wrists. It paused at Stasov, confused by his standing position.

"On your knees!" the voice shouted again, anger tingeing its tone.

Stasov swallowed. "I am Colonel Ilya Sergeiivich Stasov. I am ranking military officer." He spoke in the Japanese he had studied in the long shipboard hours en route to the invasion of Hokkaido. He had practiced his pronunciation with a computer learner of American manufacture: Japanese software manufacturers didn't seem anxious to teach anyone their language. Stasov already spoke several delphine dialects, orca, and knew a number of whale calls. Japanese had proved easy by comparison.

"On your knees!" The command was still in English.

Stasov peered into the darkness. He didn't want to act like this, but he had to. He had never been much of an officer, but he knew his duty to his men. Surrender was inevitable after their defeats. He still owed them a sign of Russian toughness. "Are you alive?" he called. "Or are you computer-generated?" That he said in Russian, so that his men would understand it. He was rewarded by some appreciative snorts. He repeated it in Japanese.

A gun butt slammed into his stomach. It was a traditionalist sort of response—modern gun butts were light plastic, not the heavy oak of past wars. He doubled over, emphasizing his loss of breath. Almost by the way, the soldier brushed the butt past the angle of his jaw. Pain exploded in his mouth.

He straightened and sucked air. The dolphins had reminded him of a responsibility he knew he had. He would have to live through Japanese imprisonment and interrogation. That was a duty also.

A portly figure in a Major's uniform came into Stasov's view. He was a serious-faced man with angled eyebrows like upside-down sea gulls. As many Japanese officers did, he resembled an earnest businessman concerned with productivity and market penetration. His face was red with anger.

"Ilya Stasov!" he yelled. "You are a war criminal. You are a prisoner. I should shoot you now. You are guilty. You are inconvenient."

Stasov nodded slowly and spat. He couldn't see if he was spitting blood. "That is true, honorable Major. That is true."

For an instant it seemed as if the Major would indeed order their immediate executions. They were far from anywhere, in an area difficult of access. Dead Red Army soldiers on a seashore would occasion no comment if found and getting them out alive would be logistically difficult, particularly since the Japanese did not yet have full control of the northern reaches of the Sea of Japan.

"Stasov." The Major smiled at him. "I think you have much to teach us. You will live. Do you wish your men to live with you? Please cooperate."

Stasov put his hands behind him and felt the handcuffs tighten. The Russians were hustled into the waiting cars.

CHAPTER SEVEN

2024

ILYA STASOV SHUFFLED HIS INFECTED FEET IN THE SOAKING mud of the trail the prisoners had worn between the barracks and the old baseball diamond. He looked over the scabbed scalp of the shorter man in front of him. Shelepin had been lined up before Stasov because of deficient Japanese understanding of the Russian alphabet, where *Sh* came after *S*, an error that dismayed both men unreasonably. Stasov's prison uniform was wool, surplus from old battles far north of the tropical Philippines, and added extra torment to the sticky heat. The sun was blinding on the trimmed green grass around them. The trail cut a mathematically straight line across the lawn.

The many-times-painted wood bleachers of the baseball field dated back to the American presence on the

Bataan Peninsula of Luzon. The Japanese troops now occupying the Philippine Islands used a much larger stressed-polymer stadium surmounted by a transparent tension structure to keep the rain off. At night the prisoners could hear the cheers of a particularly hard-fought game.

Shelepin stumbled and Stasov ran into him. Stasov felt a moment of overpowering rage. He wanted to shove the smaller man onto the grass. Stepping off the trail was a violation of the rules that could lead to being shot without warning by one of the guards whose motionless forms decorated the top of the bleachers. Shelepin had been beaten on the bottoms of his feet for some infraction. He wobbled, grunting with pain. Stasov steadied him by the shoulders. Shelepin grunted again, perhaps in thanks, and shuffled forward.

As the prisoners dragged onto the field, the man behind Stasov, Tabakin, muttered under his breath. "The bastards, the fucking bastards." It was a ritual with Tabakin. He always said that, for the guards of Camp Homma had achieved something remarkable. They had made a group of famished prisoners dread mealtime. Stasov could see the rations put out on the old pitcher's mound: a few aid packages from the US, some moldy rice, and a couple of rotted and sun-warmed fish.

The prisoners marched onto the field and, without further instruction from the guards, formed a large circle around the pile of food. Two gaps were left among the thirty men who stood there looking at the foul food with desperate longing. Stasov wondered what the guards made of the two newly pulled teeth. The loudspeakers crackled and hummed.

Stasov looked across the circle. Vsevolod Makarygin stood opposite, looking off at the sun without squinting, the cast in one dark eye giving him the look of a saint in an old icon. The effect was emphasized by Makarygin's long dark hair, parted in the middle and tied behind in a ponytail. Stasov tried to catch his glance so that he would have some reassurance that their actions of the night before would work out in their favor. Makarygin, however, had made his decisions and left the consequences in the hands of fate. He showed no signs of worry. No amount of body english would change what occurred, so he stood absolutely still, while Stasov shifted from foot to foot, trying not to cringe in anticipation of a kendo-staff smash across the back of his head from an outraged guard.

"Form up, form up!" a voice bellowed over the loudspeakers. The Japanese were famous for their consumer electronics, so perhaps the painful distortion of the camp's PA system was deliberate.

After a moment's hesitation the men pulled in closer, wiping out the empty spots where Pelyugin and Tretyakov had once stood in languid authority over their fellow prisoners. Relatively low-ranked during the war, they had reached their apotheosis after it, in brutal prison-camp dominance. Stasov remembered the wide-shouldered Pelyugin with particular loathing. One of Stasov's teeth had been lost to the Japanese rifle butt at his capture. Two, far in the back, to a gin bottle wielded by Pelyugin. A Russian's worst enemy, Stasov thought, was another Russian.

Shelepin smacked his lips and leaned forward. Stasov could hear the pained breath through his nostrils.

"Careful," Stasov warned. "Remember our agreement."

"I remember," Shelepin said softly. "We all remember." His maimed feet would ensure that he would reach the food last in any event. He had good reason to support the agreement.

A few weeks before, one of the officers at Camp Homma had been inspired. There was, he reasoned, only a limited amount of food to feed the prisoners. This food had to be divided up by the camp authorities. Why not let the prisoners divide it up themselves? So, one noontime, the prisoners had been marched out to the baseball field and set out around their food for the day. They had walked toward it uncertainly and started to take their portions. There was not enough for all. With a quick descent into savagery, natural after years of war, they started to fight for it like animals.

It became a popular sight among underworked camp personnel. It reassured them that their enemies indeed had been beasts. Some prisoners, underfed, began to weaken, day by day. Scruples or hesitations led to starvation. Viciousness led to survival. All attempts to moderate the situation failed. They foundered on the refusal of Pelyugin and Tretyakov to abide by any agreement. Twice agreements had been reached and twice those two had violated them, garnering the lion's share of food.

Stasov bore his wounds in shame. Four parallel lines of infection across his shoulder marked where another man's fingernails had desperately scratched him, fighting for a fish head with adhering flesh. On an informal basis, he and two others had formed a team. After he had wrested the fish head from his desperate opponent they had congratulated him and divided the meager thing among them as evenly as they could.

Then, yesterday afternoon, Makarygin had approached him. He had been captured off Kamchatka in the same last, desperate days of the war as Stasov.

They had met each other in the hell of Homma without surprise. "Ilya Sergeiivich," he said. "I need your help."

His voice was quiet, his diction precise. Stasov, bone-tired after twelve straight hours of interrogation, looked up from the stretch of lawn he was weeding. It was rare that anyone at Homma could ask for anything someone else could give. The greensward in front of Visiting Officers Billeting, seemingly infinite in extent, was covered with laboring Russian prisoners. They regarded the painful and petty work as a respite, for it represented a few moments of peace.

Makarygin squatted next to him and commenced weeding. His fingers were quick and he always made sure to get every last bit of root out from under the grass, as if how well he did the task was actually important.

"Tell me, Vsevolod Isayevich," Stasov said, matching Makarygin's use of the formal name and patronymic, "why should the Japanese, of all people, wish to turn Russians into gardeners?" He grunted and crawled slowly over to the next weed, a baroque extravagance with curling spiked leaves. Tropical weeds looked like nightmares.

"They seek to punish us," Makarygin said. "In doing so, they serve God's purposes."

Stasov was startled by the change in his friend since they had come to Homma. The Makarygin he knew was a clever but simple man, fascinated by his electronics. This sudden mystic was someone else. It was as if the war and the camp had ripped up the boards that covered what Stasov had always thought was a pothole but was now revealed as a deep well, over which he had been walking for years, all unknowing.

"If it was God's purpose I become a gardener," Stasov said, "He should have started much earlier."

Makarygin was not offended. "I suspect the gardening is just a side effect. It's a matter of those constraints from which not even God is immune. But that is not why I want to talk with you."

Floorboards creaked. The two men looked up. Colonel Yokota, Commander of Camp Homma, strolled past on the porch, talking with two officers visiting from some other area of Japanese occupation and one lonely American Captain, who peered around at the old American base as if awakened from a long sleep to find the Rising Sun flapping over everything and was trying to figure out how that could possibly have happened. Yokota uttered some witticism. The two Japanese officers laughed loudly. The American smiled in confusion. Stasov almost felt sorry for him. It must have been difficult to win a war and discover that you had won nothing. At least the vanquished understood their position.

"So what do you want?" Stasov said. He leaned forward.

"Back away!" came the authoritarian but bored voice of the guard. "Go to your place!"

The two men moved away from each other.

"I want you to help me take care of Pelyugin and Tretyakov," Makarygin said, as if asking for assistance in starting his car. "Things have gone far enough."

Stasov peered off into the violent sunset. Soon they would quit and be marched back to the barracks. "So you believe the Japanese are qualified to torment us, but Pelyugin and Tretyakov aren't?"

Makarygin looked calmly at him. "You were always too smart for your own good, Ilya Sergeiivich. It's a good point, but irrelevant. Do you think my suggestion unreasonable? Or even morally wrong?"

"No," Stasov said. "It is impeccable on all counts. There are a few others we can trust. . . ."

The next morning Pelyugin had been found on the barbed wire, and Tretyakov in one of the aquaculture ponds being nibbled by carp. No one gave any indication as to who was responsible. Now, for the first time, the prisoners faced their food without those two.

Stasov wiped the sweat from his forehead. "Food!" the loudspeakers bellowed. "Eat!"

In contrast to the mad rush of the previous weeks the men, with many uncertain looks at each other, moved forward slowly. They stopped short of the food and let Makarygin walk up to it. He looked around at them, at the silently watching guards and the clouds overhead, and spoke.

"Let us divide what we have been given. As we share, all will live, or all will die, for this is *our* flesh and *our* blood before us."

Makarygin had learned his dying father's lessons well. Stasov could now see that Makarygin was a natural-born holy man, one of those rural saints that Russia is as adept at producing as she is tyrants.

They sat and divided the foul food, and ate it. And it was not good, but it was the best they had.

STASOV MANAGED TO CATCH MAKARYGIN BEFORE HE HIT THE floor and helped him over to his pallet. Makarygin accepted the help without shame. Stasov's flesh had been pared away with everyone else's, but Makarygin still felt tiny to him, a bundle of dry sticks.

Makarygin settled down on the rush matting with an exasperated sigh. "Absurd. In Korea men were ripped apart, their skin flayed from their muscles in an attempt to get them to reveal troop dispositions they did not know. It was the basest viciousness. Only civilized men would be capable of it. But those Koreans were tough. Most died screaming, but their screams told their captors nothing. But here? A Black Sea resort by comparison. And one sight of those little electrodes makes me whimper."

Tabakin rolled over on his pallet and glowered at them. His hands were swathed in filthy bandages and he had to be fed by someone else. He had never spoken of his tortures in interrogation and shared the common camp opinion that it was bad form to do so. In a world where men sick with dysentery shit themselves in their bunks and desperate homosexual acts were performed in the open, a man's torments were the only thing he could call his own. To reveal them was an intimate act.

"Koreans are lunatics," Tabakin said. "And the Japanese are bastards. Fucking bastards." With this pronouncement he turned back on his other side and resumed staring out at the flowering vine that covered the window, the focus of his attention for the past hour.

"So you feel guilty for not suffering enough?" Stasov said. "An interesting attitude, in a prison camp." Despite his respect for Makarygin, Stasov felt compelled to mock him.

Makarygin never seemed amused at anything Stasov said. Stasov had never seen him laugh, and his expression always remained calmly attentive, as if he were a student listening to an interesting lecture.

"It's not a matter of guilt," Makarygin said. "I merely need to put our sufferings in perspective. We have been granted a rare boon, Ilya: suffering which can actually be instructive."

For the past week, ever since their refusal to struggle over the food, Stasov had spent every other twenty-four-hour period in a metal cage sunk in the oily waters of the harbor. The cage was covered with razor-sharp edges and his skin was now covered with a multitude of fine cuts, many of them infected. The waters of the tidal basin were uncomfortably warm, sometimes leading to heat stroke, while the incoming tide brought cold ocean water that led to hypothermia. The Japanese were interested in how they too could learn to manipulate cetaceans. Stasov was faced with the problem that they rarely believed anything he told them.

"Instructive," Stasov said. "That's a relief to hear."

"Are you tempted there in your cage, St. Simon Stylites?" Makarygin asked. "Do demons appear to you? Do they whisper to you as you pray?"

Stasov thought of the distorted voices that echoed through the water as he alternately froze and poached in it. A close-range orca hunting call could shake the whole cage, sawing the edges into his flesh. Every high tide brought a cacophony of cetacean voices. It sometimes seemed to him that they roared out of his own nightmares.

"I talk to dolphins," Stasov replied. "They are far from tempting. As for prayer . . ."

"I know, Ilya. You think that God did not put you in that iron cage and that He will not get you out. Correct?" Makarygin's eyes were black even in daylight, but in the night dimness of the barracks Ilya could feel them on him.

No one was annoyed with them for their nocturnal conversation, though sleep was often at a premium in Camp Homma. Conversation was one of the few pleasures the place afforded. Tabakin's reaction had been to Makarygin's breach of etiquette, not to the noise. So Stasov and Makarygin sat up in the middle of the night, exactly as boys once did in summer camp, eager to discuss sex, infinity, the future, and other adolescent concerns.

"Men put me there," Stasov said. "Men acting in deliberate moral blindness. The worst sin, you say."

Makarygin nodded. "You've learned something at any rate. But listen: God is not concerned with your cage. You are placed there by men as they act against God. To live is to suffer, and to live with men is to suffer greatly. Your duty to God is to suffer well. Use your opportunities."

Makarygin saw the Japanese as dark agents of God, black angels sent to discipline the arrogant. Where others saw only pointless torment, his flaming eyes perceived a landscape of mythic punishment. The Japanese were a judgment that, with calm arrogance, punished guilt. It didn't matter that they themselves did not understand their mystical role. That was for their victims to decipher.

Stasov looked around the barracks. Men lay sprawled on their pallets, snoring in the hot night. The Russian prisoners had become foul in the hot, wet climate, covered with acne, prey to a variety of unpleasant infections. The damp concrete floor was covered with piles of their mildewed and evil-smelling clothing. Rats scampered through. The Japanese, appalled at what they saw as deliberate slovenliness, shaved the prisoners' heads and sprayed the inside of the barracks with disinfecting chemicals. And they were right. Slovenliness was the only possible protest against their efficiency.

Stasov had once exerted himself to bring them into some sort of order. This had gained him no friends and he had soon stopped. Their guards' contempt was something to be endured, just like insects and disease.

"What difference does it make to me if God put me here or if men did?" Stasov said. "My reaction must be the same, existentially. You've helped me understand what that reaction should be."

Makarygin shook his head with pained weariness. "You accept sails," he said. "You accept hulls, rudders, keels, masts, sheets. But you do not accept the existence of the wind, because you can't see it. Now you demand that I teach you how to reef a sail in case of storm. Why, if the winds of the storm do not really exist?"

"Because I don't want to sink," Stasov said. "I do accept the existence of water."

Makarygin did not laugh. "Ah, St. Simon Stylites. Isn't it lonely up on that pillar without God for company?"

"Yes," Stasov said. "It is."

Makarygin chose to interpret Stasov's specific torture in the sunken cage as voluntary ascetic mortification, and nicknamed him St. Simon Stylites, after the fifth-century Antiochene saint who had lived for forty years on top of a sixty-foot pillar. This nickname was as close as Makarygin had ever come to a joke.

The bones of the moral universe were revealed at Homma, Makarygin their anatomist. Stasov presumed that Makarygin was being interrogated for his knowledge of electronic countermeasures. Stasov had trouble imagining Japanese desperately torturing a Russian for technical information about electronics, but Soviet ECM had been successful, both in the Aleutians and in the otherwise miserable Korean campaign, so he supposed they thought they could learn something.

"Don't be afraid, Ilya," Makarygin said. "You think you have given everything up and are back where you started. It's true, but it's the best thing that could have happened to you. You were going in the wrong direction. Now all the tedious trip back to the beginning to start over has been done for you. All you need to do is go forward."

"Forward." Stasov grunted. "Which direction is that?"

At last, as he did on every alternate morning, Stasov heard the crunch of boots on the trail leading to the barracks. He stood up, heart pounding. Makarygin took his hand.

"You will survive, St. Simon," he said. "Forty years on a pillar is a long time."

Stasov shook his head. "This is punishment, Seva. If I live through it, I will have to spend the rest of my time committing horrendous crimes simply to make my punishment justifiable."

Two guards, featureless in the darkness, silently seized his arms and pulled him out into the night.

THE MOON PEEPED ON STASOV AS HE DESPERATELY SUCKED air. The Japanese saw a rabbit in it, and now that he knew that, he was unable to see anything else. The moon was enormous, its maria and craters sharp with the clarity of death, clear of the filth that swirled beneath it.

The tide was abnormally high that night. The razor edges welded to the top of the cage sliced his face as he pressed it against them, desperate not to drown. The salt water stung in the cuts. They had finally miscalculated and lowered the cage too deep in the mud. He was going to drown, sucking the muddy water of Manila Bay into his lungs as he sliced his face apart on the razors.

The cage had been built by a Japanese master sergeant with a welding torch and time to burn. It was not an implement of torture calculated by physiologists and psychologists to have the optimal effect, but a primitive device, revealing some colorful folk tradition that modern technology had not yet stamped out. After long experimentation, Stasov had found the angles that had the fewest sharp edges. His body ached from the unnatural contortion this required.

A ripple crossed the top of the cage. He inhaled it through his nose. It burned through his nostrils and down into his chest. He choked. Desperate to breathe, he almost inhaled the next ripple, but stopped himself and deliberately relaxed his throat. The slow inhalation was followed by a fit of coughing. If only he could have sunk down to the bottom of the cage and sucked water into his lungs. Even dolphins couldn't do that. A dolphin in this cage would have suffered as much as he did.

"I don't understand what you're saying." A voice spoke through the water.

Stasov held onto the bars at the top of the cage and coughed with controlled deliberation, trying to get the last of the water out of his lungs. He spat it at the Moon.

"Still distorted," the dolphin said.

"Listen and understand," Stasov finally managed to say. "You have no choice."

It had been hard to talk at first without the Japanese electronics he was used to. Neither his voice nor his ears had the range to use fully any delphine dialect. He was without any of the signal processing equipment that gave his voice such power in dolphin ears. For a long time he had considered saying nothing at all, but that had proved impossible for him. He spoke into the air and let the resonance of his throat and chest carry the signal through the water.

"Are you sick, Stasov?" other dolphins called derisively, "Fever in your head?" Disease occasionally damaged a dolphin's ability to hear. His comrades then treated him with genial contempt, as if he were responsible for his own debility. "Catch it from a shark?"

"Talk sense or shut up," Stasov said. "I'm still alive. Be afraid of my voice. What news?"

"I'm angry at Lalag(pop). He's a fool. Last darkness he, believing himself to be the fastest thing in the sea . . ." That was what a dolphin thought of as news: who was angry at whom, who was sulking, who was a fool, what whales were where, how good tuna tasted. Hours of tedious gossip almost devoid of information. Almost.

Stasov had learned that other humans were trying to talk to the dolphins now that they knew it could be done. The dolphins weren't sure who they were, but Stasov could guess some: Séguin of Monaco, Pressman of Christchurch, Deraniyagala of Colombo. Perhaps Calderone at Santa Cruz. He thought of Anna with sudden, piercing clarity, remembering her athletic figure leaning on the edge of a tank as she looked in puzzlement down at an uncommunicative dolphin. He wondered if she'd ever understood that he had succeeded in his quest and, if so, what she thought about it.

From what the dolphins told him, they frustrated other researchers the way they had frustrated him. Some of the researchers threatened, some cajoled, some desperately wanted to learn dolphin poetry, a genre that did not exist above the level equivalent to an obscene limerick. No one even yet seemed to have any understanding of how to penetrate through to the dolphin's soul. Even the Japanese, torturing him on a daily basis before the UN War Crimes Commission inevitably compelled his release, hadn't learned anything. Did any of them think to ask Georgios Theodoros on his Aegean island? It seemed not. For, after leaving Uglegorsk, Theodoros had sunk into complete silence, as if ashamed of his connection with what had happened. Stasov had expected it.

"Wait and listen, you idiots," Stasov told them. "Your bubble will rise." What he had long ago learned of dolphin theology had somehow been reflected back at him by Makarygin, though Stasov had no idea how the engineer could know anything about it. Makarygin had been particularly keen on understanding the arrival of a dolphin messiah.

"It is bad luck to anticipate God's Echo," one of them warned him after a long, uncharacteristic silence. It was a miracle to get a dolphin to shut up.

"Are you going to spend your lives as krill, sieved from the sea at the will of another?"

"You thump to us of will? You're stuck to the rock like a limpet."

"I'll thump and keep thumping. Do you think God's Echo returns on its own? You can do more than speak back. You can act."

Stasov shook in his cage, seared by visions of burning ships. Every muscle in his body was hard as wood, adding his own pain to the cage. He willed himself to relax. Makarygin had told him about fasts and mortifications. It seemed that the guards of Camp Homma were driving him involuntarily into inspiration.

"We don't need to listen to you!" the dolphins jeered. "Your voice is as weak as a jellyfish. We can push it around with our snouts."

He could feel their ranging clicks in his chest. He had fallen far from the omnipotent controller of sonic illusion he had once been at Uglegorsk and aboard the *Nizhni Novgorod*. He had no voice to shout them down. But they had to understand. He couldn't stand the idea that they didn't.

"Are there any soldiers here?" he called. The word "soldier" had started as a straight copy from the Russian but now also carried the sounds of a distant explosion.

There was a long silence. "Here," a voice spoke. A heavy shape bumped the cage, metal against metal. One of his military dolphins, returned from the wars. Most of them had been interned at neutral ports in an interesting interpretation of maritime law, but some remained free.

"Who—?"

"Deimos," the voice said. "How do you not know me?" The dolphin slammed more heavily against the cage. "Can't you hear me?"

The tide began to recede and Stasov was able to bring his head forward from its cramped position and still breathe. Was that a hint of light across the water? When the tropical dawn came it came quickly, unlike the lingering light of the Russian north.

"Deimos," Stasov said. "I have instructions for you." Deimos had spent the war as a submarine decoy. Stasov could not see it in the darkness, but knew that the dolphin's dorsal fin carried the tiny cross of the Order of Glory for his role in the North Atlantic diversion war.

"I will listen," Deimos said. "Though I barely understand your distorted echoes."

"What form do the barricades at the harbors take?" Stasov asked.

"You've heard them." The dolphins had reproduced the echoes of the barricades that held their comrades in, echoes Stasov was incapable of hearing.

"Tell! You are trained."

"I am." Soviet military dolphins were held at Cam Ranh Bay, Hangzhou, Pusan, and Nagasaki. Once prompted, Deimos crisply detailed the wire barriers, mostly of salvaged mine cables, that blocked the dolphin internment areas. They were surmounted by floats too high to leap over. Bubble barriers kept fish out, leaving the dolphins dependent on their captors for food.

"New moon is some fourteen nights from now," Stasov said. "Move on the first stormy night between twelve and sixteen days from now. All four situational pods must act on the same night. Bring the mine cutters forward through the cables. Jam their sonar. Scatter into the seas." This was what it came back to. He had released them, there in the sea above Vladivostok, but could not walk away from the consequences of his actions that easily.

"Action," Deimos said. "It must be a human word from the old times. We know it but have never used it."

"It's time you started." Stasov wondered at himself, giving orders from his metal throne beneath the sea. His body was twisted in agony, his skin raw and peeling from exposure to sun and sea. He felt like a deformed oracle. "They don't really know what to do with you. They won't struggle to hold you if you go, unless you give them time to think about it."

"Humans think slowly," Deimos said.

"But they act quickly," Stasov said, nettled by Deimos's interspecies prejudice, justified though it was. Most of the dolphin cyborgs had not been disarmed, since no one was sure how to go about it and clear orders had never been given. The status of dolphins was still obscure.

"You want to push God's Bubble and force it to rise," Deimos said. "You understand nothing of our thoughts. God will not be echo-located by a half-deaf drumfish like you."

"Don't you think I understand you?" Stasov raged. "God rises beneath you. I hear Her." The cage's sharp edges had frayed his mind as they had cut his body, and he sometimes felt like a thick hemp rope sliced apart until only a few fibers held the center, pulling apart under an immense tension. For an instant he could have sworn that he did indeed hear the cetacean God rising beneath him, thrumming Her song. It echoed through his cage the same way the humpback whales' songs had vibrated Odysseus's boat with their mysterious harmonies, creating the Sirens' song that caused boats to dash upon the rocks. "I hear Her. Do you hear me?"

"I do," Deimos said, and was gone. Stasov couldn't tell if it was fear or duty that had made the dolphin vanish. He shifted, and winced as a sharp point drove into his shoulder. But the water had receded enough that he could almost sit. Low tide in darkness was a luxury. He rested on his haunches.

The sun jumped above the horizon, its lazy heat a distant forge. As its light illuminated the muddy, low-tide squalor in which his cage sat, he heard his two guards coming down along the path, sharing a cigarette and a joke. They always paused just above him, as if to admire the view, and leafed through a pornographic comic book. One cigarette, one comic book. Perhaps that was all they were issued, to ensure togetherness.

If he looked up he could just see them, hunched intently over their reading matter, as earnest as if memorizing military regulations. Around him, muck-and seaweed-covered, was the discarded military equipment of more than a century: filing cabinets, shell casings, lengths of tank tread, rusted howitzers, even a ship's gun turret. These reminders of the now-ended American military presence in the Philippines served as homes for the swarming creatures that managed to survive in the oily, polluted bay.

So Stasov sat in the early morning sunlight, watching the insects skim across the water in their meaningless dance, seemingly waiting only for something to come along and eat them, and considered the state of his soul as the guards finished their cigarette and chuckled over their comic book.

They finally emerged and, with the creaking help of a rusting old crane, raised Stasov's cage out of the muck and dropped it on the dock. The shorter one, Omi, opened the lock with a large metal key, quite unlike the magnetic cards that opened most Japanese locks. By his attitude this gave it great importance.

Stasov hated when the door finally swung open on its complaining hinges, because at that moment he rediscovered his desire to remain in the cage. In the cage, despite his pain and the contempt of the dolphins, he was still a master. Outside it he was of no more account than the gnats above the water. But this conclusion was not the result of reasoning. All he knew was that when the door swung open he felt overwhelming terror.

The two guards, Omi and Nobu, were used to the drill by now. They didn't even wait for him to refuse to come out. They reached in, sliding their uniformed sleeves past the wet, dripping bars, nervous about slashing them on the sharp edges, grabbed Stasov under the arms, and yanked him out. He shuddered at the touch of their smooth, well-fed hands. There was no use in struggling. He didn't have enough muscle left for them to even feel it.

"Let's go, Colonel," Nobu said. He spoke Japanese to Stasov, pleased at finding a prisoner who understood his native tongue. "Things up there might interest you."

Omi nodded silently.

"Things have been happening since you went to your hotel room," Nobu added. "Lots of interesting things." Having little to say, he tried to make up for it by saying things more than once.

Stasov looked from one to the other as they patiently hauled him up the trail to the barracks as if he were a business colleague who had indulged in too many sakés. The sun fragmenting through the trees hurt his eyes. Hummingbirds dodged through the dense foliage searching for hanging orchids. The prison camp was lush to the point of absurdity, built on the edge of what had once been an American golf course, its greens and fairways popular with Japanese officers from all over Luzon. Their early morning tee-off signaled the prisoners' reveille.

As a Russian, Stasov expected a proper camp to be an enclosure of barbed wire in the middle of a frosted field, the cold arctic wind blowing out of the north as the prisoners felled spruce trees or dug rock. There, suffering was at least clear. Here, surrounded by obscene life, suffering seemed almost irrelevant.

His barracks loomed ahead, surrounded by the huge flowering bushes which the guards carefully tended in their off hours. It was a scene out of every Russian's dream of paradise on a romantic island like Grenada or Tahiti. Except for the bars over the windows, it could almost have been some rustic summer dacha. Omi and Nobu dragged him in, their boots emphatically staccato on the wooden stairs, and flung him heavily on the rush matting of his bunk. The matting was made to provide a living place for tropical insects, and Stasov could hear them rustling beneath him, annoyed at his precipitous return. The guards flicked their eyes contemptuously over the squalid interior of the barracks, then stalked back out, Nobu muttering some joke to Omi, who laughed.

As soon as the guards had gone, the other men gathered around Stasov to pour tepid water through his cracked lips and tend to his most recent wounds. They had a precious bit of iodine from some long-ago Red Cross package, which Chaikin dabbed on the new wounds on Stasov's face.

The men seemed subdued. Stasov looked up at them as he relaxed his muscles against the rough mat. Some of the faces dated back to Uglegorsk; most Stasov had not met before coming here. They were accused of a variety of war crimes. Massacres on Hokkaido. Gas warfare. Mistreatment of prisoners. And the enslavement and use of dolphins in aggressive warfare.

They hung over him, their faces gloomy. "What's wrong, Valya?" Stasov asked. Valya Shelepin turned away, unwilling to speak.

Stasov knew then. He rolled over, wincing, and looked over at the bunk next to his, Makarygin's bunk. It was clear and empty, all personal effects gone, the floor around it swept clean in a mathematically precise rectangle.

Stasov sat up. "When?"

"Sometime last night," someone said. "They came and took him out of rotation. They were angry. At dawn they came back and cleaned."

"Their last sign of contempt." Stasov grunted, getting up from his bunk.

A few moments ago he had felt as if he would never stand up again, a limp string that collapsed under its own weight. But now someone was pulling the string taut from above. With others' silent assistance he pulled on a uniform shirt, insignia of rank long since ripped off, and a pair of pants which flopped loosely around his shrunken shanks. Then, with a calm, measured stride, he walked out of the barracks.

The guards had been expecting him, of course. He could see some of them lounging in the deck chairs that stood on the little tiled patio just beyond. They had cards on the tables in front of them, but their eyes were on Stasov as he walked, deliberate as a drunk, up the narrow trail that led past the golf course to Colonel Yokota's headquarters. An automatic sprinkler played in the sun far across the greens. The air was thick and silent.

Stasov didn't make it to the Colonel's office. Makarygin's body lay on a golf green, face turned up to the light. His blood streaked across his bare chest and flecked the grass. It was odd that he lay there. They usually shot people in the forest, away from the golf course. Stasov glanced over and saw a line of footprints in the wet earth at the edge of the green. They were spaced wide, the toes dug in deeply. They *had* tried to kill Makarygin in the forest. But he had broken away and, fighting his fate to the end, had run. There was nowhere to run to, but he had run nonetheless. God's judgment he would not avoid, but the acts of men were to be resisted. Not for him a bland standing at attention next to an already dug trench, making it easy on his murderers.

"The idea of a dignified death," Makarygin had once said, "was obviously thought up by a killer. Men line up by the sides of the trenches they themselves have dug—do they keep their dignity, their sense of proper behavior?" Concentration camps had been a laboratory to Makarygin. And Homma had proved a way of testing his theories.

Stasov knelt over him. He had thought that Homma had drained from him the ability to feel for another, but he found his eyes swimming with tears. Makarygin's body was painfully thin, its upper arms like matchsticks. His final struggles had marked the green, digging up the grass. What was that called? Stasov had heard the word. *Divots*. In his last moments, Makarygin had dug up divots.

A hand grabbed Stasov's shoulder and straightened him. Stasov found himself staring down at the bullet head of Colonel Yokota, commander of Camp Homma, or kommandant as the Russians, raised on books and movies about the Second World War, liked to call him. Yokota gestured angrily, and several guards leaped to Makarygin's body and carried it away, their frantic energy giving the impression that he had flung himself onto the green in a deliberate effort to impede play.

Stasov forced himself to look at Yokota. Makarygin had seen the Japanese as both agents of God and self-willed evil idiots. Stasov wasn't sure if either was right. They were businessmen, middle managers yanked from comfortable desk jobs, first to fight a war, then to guard the men who had invaded their country. They had thrown themselves into the business of torturing prisoners with the same dedication that had made them the Earth's dominant economic power.

"He was attempting to escape," Yokota rasped, as though convincing Stasov of such a blatant falsehood was somehow important.

Stasov shook his head. "He was trying to find out why not escaping made sense. Did he tell you much?"

"He knew nothing."

"If he knew nothing, why did you kill him?"

"I told you. Attempting to escape."

Stasov realized that he would never learn whether Makarygin had talked. He thought about the electrodes that had so terrified Makarygin, and the calm technical questions about ECM circuitry that his interrogators had undoubtedly continually repeated. He must have talked. It didn't matter, morally. The war was over, the secrets now irrelevant, and any man can be broken by torture.

Makarygin, by analogy with modern physics, called torture a moral singularity: a place where ordinary laws do not apply. An outside observer cannot see past the event horizon of a black hole. What lies within is another universe. So it was with extreme torture or existence in a death camp. No one on the outside could judge those within. Here, at this limit, Makarygin, with his newfound Stoic Orthodoxy, had admitted defeat. Evil ceased to be a test, something to be struggled against, and became an all-encompassing force. It was a region of infinite pressure, infinite density, and infinite heat. Perhaps even God Himself did not exist there, though Makarygin would have denied that.

That limit was where Makarygin had counseled suicide. To prevent the destruction of his soul, a man had the right to destroy his body. For if a man's soul is destroyed before he dies, what poor twisted thing will limp into Heaven? Stasov looked at the golf green, its divots even now being filled in by intent gardeners as a foursome of high-ranking officers visiting from Korea waited impatiently. Had Makarygin reached his limit and committed suicide by forcing the Japanese guards to kill him? Or had they decided to kill him because they had squeezed him dry and did not want anyone else to have the information, and he had tried to thwart them by fleeing? Every man carries the burden of his moral decision himself. Stasov realized that his own judgment of what Makarygin had done was irrelevant. But he wished he knew.

"You will come with me to the officers' dining hall," Yokota said. "They are serving for another half hour." And he smiled: clean, even teeth, the product of sophisticated orthodontia. Silently, Stasov followed him.

CHAPTER EIGHT

2024

STASOV STEPPED ACROSS THE PORCH INTO THE HOT BUTTER of the Philippine sunlight. He moved slowly, his joints rough and unlubricated, as if he was a child's bicycle left long out in the rain. The Japanese guards at the door of the barracks smiled and bowed at him as he passed. He ignored them, the same way he had when they shouted at him and flicked at him with kendo staffs.

Since Yokota's bizarre invitation to breakfast two weeks before, they had been feeding him well, a signal of possible release. He had not gone back to the cage since that morning, but he refused to feel hope. Yesterday they had allowed him an hour in a hot Japanese bath and this morning they had dressed him in an elegant suit of blue silk. It was much too large, made to the obsolete measurements in his records.

His fingers had had trouble tying the knot on the tie, so a guard had delicately done it for him. It was not the regulation military knot he had been trying for, at least not of his army, but it would do.

When he walked out into the sun Stasov began to think that he might be free.

Behind him, the barracks were almost empty. Most of the men had been moved out in the past two weeks. At first they had fought desperately, convinced that they were being removed to be killed. Tabakin had been beaten unconscious, then hauled off and treated tenderly in the camp hospital. Gradually the idea had penetrated that they were being released from their torment. Other torments might await them, but this one was over. Their partings had been quick and subdued, as if they already realized that the intensity of their bonding would not survive the mundane pressures of the outside world.

Outside the barracks was a tiled patio where the camp's officers had often had parties at night with the local women. A woman waited for Stasov there now, upright in a deck chair. Not one of those dark-haired beauties that had been one of Luzon's main exports for centuries, but a fair-skinned woman with coppery hair, dressed in an American military uniform. She leaned over, back straight, and wrote intently in her notebook, which she had balanced precariously on the chair's arm. Her face was strong, with a wide jaw and a long nose. Stasov stopped and blinked in the sun. It was Anna Calderone.

"Colonel Stasov?" She stood and looked at him. Beneath a high forehead her brown eyes were set wide. "You do remember me, don't you?"

"I'm not sure, Anna. I'm not sure." He stared at this woman, crisp and precise in her military uniform.

"But it's not Colonel," he murmured. "Not anymore." The hot sun made him dizzy and the smell of the exuberant flowering shrubs that bloomed all around them seemed to clog his nostrils. His knees buckled and he sat down.

She looked at him, eyes wide. "Colonel . . . Ilya. You look terribly sick. Do you need medical assistance?"

He shook his head. "No, certainly not. I have been . . . cared for."

She bit her lower lip and scribbled in her notebook. "I came here to get you because we . . . know each other. It's taken an incredible amount of UN pressure to get you loose. The Japanese administration of war crimes facilities . . . America is concerned." She gestured around, taking in the camp, the Bataan Peninsula, the Philippines. "We have a vested interest."

It was odd to think of Homma as a "war crimes facility". That could mean almost anything. "How much pressure can the UN actually apply? If you managed to break me loose, the time for Camp Homma must be over. We are not completely isolated here. The Japanese have a new empire to digest, a new position in East Asia." He'd seen the map in Colonel Yokota's office and somehow knew that it reflected reality. They'd used a pale blue to record areas currently held by Japanese troops, rather than the traditional red, an odd bit of delicacy considering who was likely to see the map. Luzon, Taiwan, the Shandong Peninsula, southern Korea. The southern part of the Russian Maritime Territory, capital at Vladivostok. The Kurile Islands and Sakhalin, as well as southern Kamchatka. "If they are letting me go, it must be because they have more important things to worry about, not because they fear the Americans, or the UN."

She glared at him then, momentarily annoyed at his lack of gratitude. He felt sorry for her, hauled to this savage place to speak with an old acquaintance turned war criminal, wounds all over his face, smelling like something rotting in the sun. But the Americans were indeed not at issue. The Japanese had named the place Camp Homma, after the Japanese general who had commanded the invasion of the Philippines in 1942, a deliberate insult to which the Americans were powerless to reply.

"But, Ilya," she said. "If you have been mistreated—"

"If I have been mistreated, it is only just," he replied. "Americans make poor victors. They are too forgiving. The Japanese are more like Russians. They demand justice and perhaps a bit more. Or have you forgotten that you are talking to the Shark of Uglegorsk?"

Calderone looked startled. "Having a nickname is not a crime, however you got it. The Japanese have charged you with genocide and slavery, crimes you committed against the dolphins after you proved their intelligence." He remembered her leaving Uglegorsk years before, convinced that he was going to fail. He wondered if she'd come to Homma because she resented him. "These charges are *ex post facto*—are you familiar with the term?"

"Soviet law is not very sophisticated, I'm afraid."

The guard Omi brought them tea in graceful earthenware cups. With calm deliberation, Stasov poured the tea on the ground and let the cup fall on the pavement, where it cracked into pieces. Omi bowed expressionlessly, cleaned up the shards, and walked slowly away.

Calderone caught her breath and looked at Stasov. "Ilya . . . what did they do to you?" The uniform barely contained the woman beneath. She reached out to touch his hand. The soft pads of her fingertips, edged with sharp nails, were the strongest sensation he'd felt in more years than he could remember.

"Nothing worth discussing." He knew his voice sounded harsh. It was beyond his control. "Don't you have some procedure to get through?"

Calderone took her hand away and yanked a folder out of her briefcase. "Let's see if I remember who you are. Colonel Ilya Sergeiivich Stasov, born Leningrad, May 15, 1983."

"Near as I can remember."

"Service posts..." She scanned a list. "After Uglegorsk, the North Pacific fleet, the Aleutians, Hokkaido . . . captured near Sokolovka, Maritime Province, March 2023?"

Stasov was startled how little all those names meant to him now. It had been someone else there, some completely different person. That Colonel in the Red Army had had goals, drives, desires. *He* had wanted something. The part of him that was left, cleaned and purged, hammered out on the anvil of Homma, no longer remembered what that had been. A desire to know had dragged him through Uglegorsk, an obsolete patriotism had landed him on Kagalaska, an inexplicable loyalty had left him on the edge of the sea near Sokolovka. He wondered what would carry him back outside the barbed-wire gate of Homma.

"Yes," he said finally. "But I no longer bear the rank of Colonel."

A quick glance from Calderone. She was probably remembering how proud he'd been of those stars when she visited Uglegorsk, so many years ago. "The United Soviet Republics has not decommissioned you. I would have that here." She tapped her notebook.

"I have decommissioned myself."

"Ilya, no. You've been through hell. The world you will be facing is very different. Make sure you understand it before you make any decisions about it." She kicked a teacup shard with her toe. "The world is not Homma."

She was as fresh as a spring birch leaf covered with dew, while he was bent and broken, his flesh corrupted. He felt like turning away from her, hiding his face, refusing to speak anymore. She didn't know that the world was indeed Homma. The image that came to him was Makarygin dead on the green, flecked with blood. Stasov found himself shaking and willed his muscles to relax. Reluctantly, they obeyed.

"Relax." Calderone's voice was soothing. "You no longer need to fear what's going to happen next."

Stasov thought about that one. "I thought you were here representing the UN War Crimes Commission."

She paused. "Yes."

"Not promising."

"You will have to face trial, Ilya. But it won't be a Japanese trial. I will guide you through it. I'll be there with you."

"I don't need a guide." Stasov's voice was suddenly sharp. "Makarygin is dead. You are not his replacement. No one can be." He started to get up out of his seat.

Then her hand was on his shoulder, pushing him gently but firmly back. He had forgotten how strong she was, and how weak he had become. He could see the feminine muscles crisply defined in her upper arm.

He sat. The air wavered before him like water and he waited to hear the voices of dolphins.

"You've lived through it," Calderone said softly. "Understand that. What was done to you here is in the past."

"Yes," he said. The barracks were empty. The cage was gone. Makarygin was dead. "I'm sorry."

"Don't apologize. There's no need."

She looked at her notes, though he got the sense that it was more to distract herself than because she needed to. "They interrogated you, didn't they, Ilya?"

He raised his eyebrows. "Of course. Why else do you think we were here? A rest cure? They questioned Seva Makarygin about ECM, Andrei Tabakin about tactics used in Korea, and me about dolphins."

There it was, the only real point of their meeting again. The entire Pacific War with its heroics and brutalities had been merely a signal to Anna Calderone that he had succeeded where she and all the others had failed. Ilya Stasov alone in the world had learned the truth.

But now that world, Ilya Stasov, and the truth itself were all unrecognizable, and the ability to communicate with dolphins had passed to others. What, he wondered, had the Mycenaeans tried to do with dolphins after the fall of Crete? Whatever they had tried had failed. Communication with dolphins had ended, and a silence of thirty-five hundred years had descended. Stasov prayed that it would not happen again.

"And did they learn anything?" Her voice was neutral, but he was not fooled.

"You left a week too soon, Anna. Just a week. You've probably figured it out by now, what we did, and what happened. We finally broke their conditioning, their resolve not to speak." Suddenly excited, he described the scene of Kestrel's first and last words, the first years of research, of training, of modification of the dolphins for war.

She stared at him, forgetting to take notes. "So all the time it was you. I knew it. 'Just one man,' I told them. Just one man. Ilya Sergeiivich Stasov. They high-value drafted me into naval countermeasures and then didn't believe me. They tried to figure out some other explanation for how the ships were sunk. Finally they had to accept that dolphins were doing it. And dolphins that were not just trained animals. Dolphins that were intelligent beings and had the will to fight."

"The will to fight. I hope to God they do have that."

"On TV I saw the *Hiryu* burning after the Battle of La Perouse Strait. It was on every channel, constantly. The largest aircraft carrier the Japanese had, defended with the best electronics they could come up with, just a burnt-out, flat-topped hulk. I'll always remember that because I knew what had to be behind it."

"Our first big success." Stasov remembered the doctrinal arguments with the Navy about the use of military dolphins. It had seemed all-consumingly important at the time.

"Did you know that was what would happen?" Her voice had gone beyond professional curiosity. "Did you know that when I was at Uglegorsk?"

"No," he said hollowly. "I had no idea. But I should have. I should have understood the consequences of my actions. I have tried to step away from them, give the dolphins their freedom, let things go their own way. This will not be allowed me. Ilya Stasov will not escape so easily." To his shame he felt tears in his eyes. "I'm sorry." He wiped at them with his knuckles. "It's taken more out of me than I thought." She smiled gently and handed him a handkerchief. "Thank you. It's ridiculous."

"Not at all." She flicked her hair back with a quick, feminine gesture. He felt a tingling in his scalp. He was once again talking to Anna Calderone. The sun seemed to have become hotter.

"But you are not a dolphin researcher anymore."

"No." There was an edge to her voice. "That's partially the result of what you have achieved, Ilya. There's no place for me anymore. I was an oceanographer specializing in dolphin social structures. Dolphins were aquatic mammals. Now they are intelligent beings and their social structures are something completely different than I ever understood. They've sunk ships, fought a war. I have no idea what they are." She curved her body up tensely. He admired her strong legs, her small breasts, pleased for being able to do so. "Remember our last conversation, before I left Uglegorsk? I'm going back to working on Jupiter. Difficult in our poverty after this war, but how can we avoid it? There seems to be life there. You know that. Perhaps even sentient life. No one's had time for more work since the war started. But the end of the war seems to have made it all more important, as if our struggles here have to be put in perspective."

"Odd work for a former delphinologist," Stasov said.

"They need people with experience contacting other life forms—"

"You failed to contact them," Stasov said flatly. "We succeeded. I won our bet."

"Is that it?" She was angry. "You're sitting there feeling superior to me? We didn't dare try what you did, or use them the way you managed to—"

He raised a hand. He felt incredibly tired. "Forgive me, Anna. Sometimes we find that we still hold onto the things we believe we have rid ourselves of. That's pride, I suppose."

"Oh, I'm sorry. I shouldn't be bullying you. Not now. That's the past."

"Perhaps it is." He looked past her toward Manila Bay. He couldn't tell whether the glint he saw through the trees was the water or the reflector sunglasses of a Japanese guard. "I'm sorry, Anna. If you want Jupiter, I'm sure you will have it."

She relaxed back into her chair and clicked her notebook shut. "The secrets of planetary formation are hidden down there in those clouds. Pressures of forty-five million atmospheres. Metallic hydrogen. Who knows what life is like there?"

Her long, bony fingers grabbed the arms of the deck chair. Her short hair bounced as she shook her head. She was the first woman he had seen close up in months and today was the first day he could remember feeling healthy in an even longer time. She had a deep hollow in her throat and he could just see the line of her collarbone inside the open neck of her shirt. Her nails were trimmed and polished. She clicked them on the chair arm, making a sound like a trotting horse. At Uglegorsk she had not wanted to make love with him.

"Anna, I'm afraid that at the moment I don't even understand what life is like here."

She smiled, a lazy, sensuous woman's smile that left him dizzy.

"Come along, then, Ilya. Let's see if I can show you."

TWO DAYS LATER THEY CROSSED MANILA BAY TO CAVITE, where the Soviet delegation waited. Sea gulls spun in the hot, wet air. The water was glass-smooth with a long, sickening swell. Suddenly, all around them, the water was filled with the flashing forms of dolphins. They leaped out of the water, occasionally clearing the boat itself. Stasov sat at the stern underneath the flapping Rising Sun. He couldn't talk to the dolphins, so all he could do was watch them. They were indeed beautiful.

The white-jacketed Japanese pilot accelerated and began to slew back and forth, though whether to avoid the dolphins or to hit them was not clear.

"What are they doing here?" Calderone shouted over the roar of the motor.

Stasov eyed her. Her short copper hair blew in the breeze. Hands on the gunwale, she stared out at the dolphins in consternation.

"I don't know," he said.

She returned his gaze. Her pale complexion was peeling in the tropical sun.

"Is that really true?" she said. "You have absolutely no idea?" She glanced at the pilot. "Will you please the hell stop that?"

The pilot expressionlessly put the boat back on a straight course.

"Anna," Stasov said. "Remember, I've been in a prison camp for the last half year." It was interesting how many true but irrelevant facts there were in the world.

The smooth skins of the dark blue-gray dolphins gleamed in the sun as they leaped. Many were deformed by the rough cyborg modifications that made them machines of war. They played with the rest. Stasov was now at peace but he still felt awe. They had escaped from their imprisonment and once again ranged the seas. There was enough firepower around him to form a credible threat to a carrier battle group.

"Those are Soviet military dolphins," Calderone said, her voice tense. "What are they doing in Manila Bay?"

Stasov shook his head. "None of my concern now. Something for the Japanese and Americans to worry about."

"Soviet forces have demobilized. The war is over."

"It is. The Pacific Fleet is gone, the Japanese occupy Vladivostok, and there isn't an organized Red Army unit existing east of the Lena. But the dolphins aren't Soviet citizens, are they? And they have not signed any instrument of surrender." He sat back in his seat and straightened the knot in his tie.

"Oh, bullshit." She turned away in anger.

He wanted to reach out to this woman who with flaming sword had pulled him from Hell. But he didn't know who she was.

Instead, he leaned back under the flapping Japanese flag. The bay was alive, every other wave the sliding back of a dolphin. For the first time he could remember, since long before he had come to Homma, Ilya Sergeiivich Stasov found himself smiling.

"I DON'T THINK THEY WERE SO HAPPY TO SEE YOU," SAID Anna Calderone as they pushed their way down the packed, narrow street, laundry hanging overhead.

"The new government would like to forget its war criminals," Stasov said. An irritable Asian whose pedicab was stuck in the molasses of pedestrian traffic yelled something at him, as far as Stasov could tell solely because he was the tallest man on the street. Stasov stared at him in bemusement, which enraged the pedicab driver further.

"But they wanted to pretend they had no idea who you were! You're not a war criminal." Calderone took his hand and pulled him around the back of the pedicab. Her hand was warm and smooth but still almost yanked his arm out of its socket. "That stupid bureaucrat, Vyshinsky, would have liked to leave you to the Japanese." She wore a long dress inappropriate to the filthy streets.

Stasov remembered the head of the Soviet delegation, with his prissy round glasses and chin so narrow he must have put it in a pencil sharpener every morning. No, that wasn't right. No longer Soviet. They had eliminated the word again, perhaps for good this time. What had they called themselves? The Russian Reorganized Republic. Something like that. It was an endless political treadmill. They had sat in a peeling-walled room in an old American colonial building and tried to convince Stasov that they had no idea why the UN would want to turn him over to them. Vyshinsky had even tried to conduct the proceedings in English, supposedly in deference to Calderone, but mostly to fake the sort of internationality that made all allegiances merely matters of convenience.

"Political rebaptism," Stasov said. "It banishes all previous sins. The Reorganized Republic has repudiated all war guilt." He was surprised to find himself bitter. "They sat in their offices in Moscow and Petersburg through the entire war, exhorting us to greater courage, greater efforts. Now that the war is over, they are the party of peace, and we are to be discarded."

"They're swine," she said viciously. "Are they really going to run your government? They should be shot."

Her outrage was so strong that Stasov could let go of his. "Relax, Anna." He chuckled. "They'll do what they can. Remember, we all just lost a war."

She had not released his hand after they were past the pedicab. He looked at her in wonder. Who was this woman? She had swum with dolphins in Monterey Bay and now protected the Shark of Uglegorsk, the man who had tormented them into speaking and then sent them on an aggressive war against America. She defended him against his own countrymen. She had lovely strong legs and was ashamed of the size of her calves and wished her breasts were larger. It had taken all these years since Uglegorsk for him to meet her again and finally know her. She had not asked about Grisha Panin's fate and he had not yet brought it up. He would have to. Grisha could not be permitted to vanish as if he was merely an error of time.

"They have to be careful," Stasov temporized. "They have to convince the Japanese to give back Vladivostok, Kamchatka, and the Maritime Province. The Soviet . . . ah, the Russian Far East is handicapped without those territories."

"Geopolitics!" she spat.

"Exactly. To a modern Russian that multisyllabic word has more emotional meaning than justice, or love."

She glanced at him from under her bowl of hair to see if he was joking. Deciding that he was, at least partially, she led him onward. Ahead of them loomed a marble monument to Emilio Aguinaldo. The monument had dissolved in the acid rains of polluted Manila and left the statue with the forlorn appearance of a snowman after a spring rain.

"There's our bus!" she cried. They ran across the street and packed themselves into the already overfull bus. Calderone stood pushed against his chest, looking up at him.

"I'm enjoying my time here," she said.

"I—" How could he explain that any time that was not spent in a razor-lined cage was paradise? "I am too."

She turned her head to peer out a greasy window. "Even though it's Manila? I don't know what I expected, but this mess of sagging poured concrete wasn't it. It's so unromantic."

The bus bounced violently over some potholes and roared along the edge of Manila Bay. Greenish-blue waters stretched out toward a distant line of palm trees. Several suddenly surplus American landing craft had been pulled up on the muddy, oily beach for salvage. Children scampered across the pilothouse while their fathers bent over welding torches and sent sparks cascading down the rusting metal hulls. One of the boats had been creased and crumpled by artillery fire. Stasov wondered where it had fought.

"I don't think it's unromantic," he said. "I can't remember when I last had such a good time." As he said it, he realized it was true.

Stasov had been assigned a room in a decaying hotel, all cracking concrete and sagging acoustic tiles, its elevator broken and filled with the stolen Japanese medical equipment which seemed to be a greater source of income than the paying guests. He sat and thought by the window, half of its panes gone and replaced by boards from the packing cases for the medical equipment. Luminescent Japanese script warned of radiation and biohazards.

The street beneath, a grand processional way during the American years, was a packed mass of human beings, refugees from the Pacific War having swelled Manila's already excessive population. Shanties, smoking bulgogi stands, prostitutes' tents of reflective mylar, and clanking metalworkers' shops filled the wide avenue, leaving only a path up the middle like a meandering stream in a forest. Several times a day some foolhardy driver tried to ram his automobile up the remainder of the street and got stuck there, often finding his car stripped and political slogans spray-painted on the doors before he could get out. Stasov waited there above the show to be called for his war crimes trial.

The Americans and the Japanese had cut a deal, but Stasov had no idea what it was. For all he knew, he could still end up shoulderblading some pockmarked wall in Quezon City . . . no, Americans preferred neater solutions than firing squads. Properly, they should fly over his head and drop a laser-guided bomb so they wouldn't even have to look at him, but he supposed they would give him a lethal injection of some nerve toxin derived from gene-spliced *E. coli* or perhaps depolarize his neuronal membranes with a computer-controlled electromagnetic field. The bastards had always been squeamish. With such thoughts he beguiled the time and waited for Anna Calderone. With each successive day her arrival became sweeter.

The housing along the road and up the hills began to thin out and soon there was enough room in the bus to sit together on one of the broken seats.

"Incidentally, Anna," he said. "Where are we going?"

She smiled and he saw the troublemaking girl she had described herself as, the hellion of her college swim team, forever stealing unusual road signs and trying to sneak men into their hotel during away swim meets. He found himself jealous of those relaxed college youths, with nothing more to worry about than grades. He shook his head at his own unfairness. He had once been one of them himself. But no lovely young swimmer had ever tried to smuggle him into her room.

"We're going snipe hunting with pearl-handled revolvers," she said seriously. "It's become quite a popular sport in the dumps south of town. I hope the champagne will be chilled when we get there."

Stasov didn't know what a "snipe" was, but recognized a universal camper's joke. "Back in impoverished Russia we used slingshots."

"Now, Ilya," she said severely, "that's snipe stunning. An entirely different sport."

"Of course." He tugged at the collar of his silk suit. A Malay tailor had taken it in until it nearly fit. "I wouldn't have guessed by our outfits. I should be wearing lederhosen and opera pumps."

She laughed. "Don't forget the purple fez."

"De rigueur. I won't."

He sat back in his seat with a heady feeling. To joke with a lovely woman on the way to—it didn't matter where.

The restaurant stood on stilts over the water. A sweating man in a crushed velvet jacket handed them out of the bus as if it were a limousine and led them in.

They were seated at a table overlooking the water. Fans turned slowly in the ceiling. The cleanliness of the linen tablecloths, the silverware, and the patterned tile floor disturbed Stasov. It had been years since he'd been anywhere that wasn't coated with a fine film of oil, dust, and salt. It was a scene so unreal that he expected Colonel Yokota to burst through the door with his guards and haul him back to his cage where he belonged. It was only with a superhuman effort of will that he did not turn to look at the door every time he heard it open. By the end of the evening his neck ached with the effort.

Calderone opened a menu. "The fish here is particularly good."

Stasov shuddered. "No fish."

"Isn't that an unusual aversion for a delphine researcher?"

"I'm not obliged to eat what dolphins do in order to understand them. No, I've hated fish since the dining hall at Uglegorsk. Boiled cabbage and overcooked fish. You probably remember it."

She shuddered in sympathy.

"And the way they fed us at Homma—I'll never get over it." They had fought over the rotting fish like animals.

"If you just try it here I'm sure—"

"Never!" He was conscious that he'd raised his voice and people were staring. He leaned back in his seat and undid the elaborately knotted linen napkin. "Life in a prison camp has one great advantage: it is narrowed down to a single bright line. There are no decisions to be made about the course or the destination. I think I may have forgotten how to make decisions—though what I went through may have taught me that I never knew. I'm not sure yet. Is that foolish?" He looked at her beseechingly.

"Not at all." She seemed apprehensive of his leaning on her for certainty. "Sometimes it takes years to learn things, even obvious ones."

"So please, Anna, if you could—I can't . . ." He ran his fingers down the column of elaborately named dishes in the menu. "I can't order. It's too much."

So she ordered for him. He lost track of what she was saying when the food came. The smells of coriander, lemon grass, and hot pepper compelled his undivided attention. For a long moment he did not move but just stared at the food.

"Are you all right, Ilya?" Calderone asked.

"Fine. Just in awe."

He ate slowly, slowly. The flavor almost overpowered him. He thought of Makarygin and his sacrament on the baseball diamond, and stopped chewing.

Makarygin had never been a man to worry about his food. What would he have made of this feast? Could a sacrament be made of food that was well prepared? Stasov took another bite. Damn it, this wasn't a sacrament. This was dinner.

Calderone took a sip of the yellow wine in her crystal glass and looked out the window at the sun setting over the bay. As she did so, Stasov scooped up a portion of his chicken and slipped it into his jacket pocket. He could eat it when he got back to the barracks, at night when no one was watching . . . He felt the wine sauce soaking through the silk.

"Excuse me," he said. He shoved his chair back and walked quickly to the bathroom. It was beautiful, surfaced in colored tiles. He pulled the chicken out of his pocket and started to throw it away. No. He thought of the miserable fish head that had at one time been the focus of his aspirations, then sat in a toilet stall and ate the chicken with his hands. There would be more food, he told himself. There would be more food, but there was no reason to waste this. When he was done he rinsed his pocket again and again in an attempt to get the wine sauce out. Water stained his side. He dabbed at it with a paper towel. That didn't help much.

Calderone noticed his wet jacket when he sat down again but didn't remark on it. He let his breath out, for he feared her contempt as much as he ever had feared a beating at Homma.

A sixteen-passenger jeepney waited in the restaurant parking lot for late diners. Stasov recognized the chassis and lower body as having once belonged to a Soviet personnel carrier, but it was now surmounted by what looked like a traveling interdenominational temple crowded with Virgin Marys, Buddhas, and glowering animist figurines. Massive chrome bumpers from some American car gave the jeepney authority in traffic. They climbed in and the jeepney roared home to Manila. The much-abused Soviet engine, which had pulled the vehicle across half of Asia in the campaigns of reunification and the following war with Japan, was too loud for them to talk, so Calderone just rested against Stasov. He was glad of the noise, for he was not sure what he could say.

So he didn't say anything, even when they got back to the hotel. They climbed the stairs to his room. He didn't apologize for its boarded-up windows and turned on only one small light in a corner. The room was close and hot. Stasov took off his jacket and hung it on the chair by the bed.

Calderone stood next to him. He put his arms around her and smelled her clear freshness. Her lips tasted like . . . a woman's lips, something he had almost forgotten.

A while later he said, "You know, Anna, I think I've forgotten how."

She smothered a laugh in his shoulder. "You don't forget how, Ilya. It's like having learned to ride a bicycle."

"I always fall off bicycles."

As he ran his hand down her side, he shook. She ran her hand up his arm and cupped the back of his head, pulling him down to her. He tried to relax against her but felt that his movements were clumsy thrashing.

"Shh," she said. "It's not mechanics. Touch me. Yes. Just like that."

Her skin was soft under his work-roughened hands. He could feel the blood rushing beneath her skin and see the ribs appear when she gasped in a breath. Each touch from her stripped away more of the muck of Camp Homma. Her fingers probed the muscles of his back, worked their way down, and held his hips. . . .

He awoke suddenly in the dark. Anna was curled up against him, her leg slung over his hip. She breathed deeply and evenly. The sounds of a city turning over in its sleep filtered through the loose-fitting boards on the windows.

Anna stirred and murmured sleepily. "Ilya," she said. "Is there a restaurant under us?"

"No, why?"

"I smell sauce. Lemon grass and wine. I must be dreaming about dinner."

His jacket was silhouetted in the light from the street, its stained pocket a darker shadow. Now that she had mentioned it, he too could smell it. How much of his life had he traded for this one day?

"Yes," he said, "you must be dreaming about dinner."

"ONE MORE CASE BEFORE YOURS," CALDERONE SAID, getting up from her seat to pour herself another cup of weak coffee.

Stasov peered miserably up at the complex display at the head of the room. Calderone had tried to explain it to him but he wasn't interested in understanding it, so it remained a mass of meaningless lights and numbers. In a few short hours he would be on trial before a War Crimes Tribunal. All else paled to insignificance.

"How can they push us through quickly?" he asked, not for the first time.

Calderone was patient. "In a way, your stay at Homma was lucky. Everyone's already tired of these trials. Enough's enough and we all want to get back to our lives."

"They've hanged Smirnitsky and Pashvili."

"Ilya, they ran the concentration camp at Sredne-kolymsk." Her tongue maneuvered around the Russian word easily. It had become part of normal conversation. "Many captured American soldiers lost their lives there. Those two were the big fish to fry. The rest of you are, frankly, small fry. Sprats."

Sprats. Stasov slumped down in his plastic seat, sticking his long legs out in front of him. As soon as they had gotten to Quezon City in their assigned UN limousine, Calderone had changed from a loving woman to a UN official. He supposed that he should have expected that, but it still hurt him. The crumbling ugliness of Manila, outside his windows just that morning, already seemed a distant and romantic place, like a tropical island just vanishing beneath the horizon, only the tops of its palm trees still above the edge of water. They had spent the past two weeks walking its streets, sitting in its parks, and talking, talking. And loving. It had finally made him feel like a whole man.

And now he sat in the over-air-conditioned sterility of a government office, awaiting a trial for crimes against sentient beings. The charges themselves were not complex, though the list of them was long. Dolphins, though not yet legally defined so, were clearly intelligent beings. Stasov had compelled them to serve as involuntary conscripts in an aggressive war against the United States and Japan, a war the Soviet Republics had lost—the actual crime, he thought, for which he was being tried. In the process, many of them had died. Slavery and genocide. And he was small fry. As Anna had pointed out to him.

She put a hand on his shoulder. It was meant as a gesture of comfort, but even that felt cold.

"Coffee?" she said.

"No, thank you." He shifted in his seat. "When I was young, my family owned a dog named Graf, a Samoyed."

She looked startled. "Yes, you've mentioned him before. You loved him."

"Graf, as my mother put it, had a most intelligent tail. He would spend most of his time staring out of the apartment window, observing what went on in the street below. Depending on what he saw, he would wiggle his tail differently. The regular passage of the streetcar got an indifferent back-and-forth swing. The postman got a vertical bounce. And the return of my father got an excited figure eight. My mother had long since moved all her breakable knickknacks out of the way of Graf's tail.

"It got so that I could tell what Graf was looking at just by watching his tail, without actually having to go to the window to see for myself. In school once, we were assigned a composition: People I Like. I described Graf. I told about the dog's thoughts as he watched the frustratingly distant passage of the postman, of his never-to-be-broken need to chase squirrels, of his fear of lightning storms, which had once driven him into the bathtub while my father was taking a shower. I was particularly proud of that composition. It received a Two: a *D*. Across the top the teacher wrote: 'Nonsense. Dogs do not think'."

Anna was momentarily distracted. "Oh, Ilya, that's so cruel."

"I suppose it was. I tried to explain it to Graf, but he just wiggled his tail to tell me he wanted to go out for a walk. I don't think he was too concerned."

For the first time since they'd entered the room, she smiled. Then she looked like she was going to cry. "Oh,

Ilya, what are we going to do?"

It was his turn to be cold. "Haven't we already decided that?"

"Oh, this is ridiculous." She paced the room. "To argue about it in a place like this."

"Are you saying that love is less important than what's going to happen to me in that little room?"

"Love! You use that word, but it's too big for me. I can't just say it like that."

"I haven't asked you to," he said. A light flickered on the board. "Please sit down next to me. That's my trial, isn't it?"

She didn't look up at the display. "It must be. It's about time." She turned to go.

"Stop," he said. "Sit."

Too much of Anna Calderone's life was ahead of her. Stasov felt that his own was already over, for all that the dolphins still swam in the seas, waiting for him. Perhaps it was just that his life as a human being was over. There was no use in planning a mundane simple existence for both of them. She had led him, gently, to understand that he did not loom in her life as she did in his. There had been other men, there would be other men. That was something she was not yet willing to give up. She had even shed a discreet tear for Grisha Panin, heroically dead in the Battle of Kagalaska.

Stasov thought about other women he had known. They had made love in jerry-built housing where privacy was rare. Military service and war had exerted an intolerable pressure on love. Stasov had just gone through three years of bloody, oily hell without a single touch or soft word from a woman. And this golden woman from Santa Cruz, California who sat next to him wondered why Russians often seemed so gloomy.

"Russians have a custom," he said. "Just before we leave on a journey, we sit down for a moment of silence."

"Ilya, we're only going to the next room."

"No. That door is the start of an unimaginable journey."

So they sat in silence for a long moment. Then they got up and walked through the door together.

STASOV LOOKED UP AT THE SHIP *ALEXEI REMIZOV*. IT WAS AN old liquid-natural-gas tanker, and the giant spheres of the pressurized LNG tanks loomed above the deck. The ship was seedy in the bright Philippine sunlight. Rust trailed down from the anchor chains. It was making a slow journey up the Chinese coast, around Korea, up to Russkaya Gavan, a free port on the coast that gave access to the Trans-Siberian Railway. Vyshinsky, the head of the Soviet delegation at Quezon City, had assured Stasov that this was the fastest way for him to get home after his trial. He'd been billeted, and everything was in order.

That was all right with Stasov. He needed time. It wouldn't have made sense to leave the dense jungle tangle of Manila and the hard-edged, cold rooms of the government complex at Quezon City only to arrive at the Petersburg airport half a day later. A slow boat to Siberia and a slow train home were just the thing.

The trial had been, as Anna Calderone had predicted, a formality. Documentary evidence had been projected on a wall screen above the crossed American and Japanese flags. Despite the sensational nature of the charges, the judges had been bored and perfunctory, staring up at the list of Stasov's military postings with glazed eyes, not even noticing that the

list had him serving simultaneously in the North Pacific Fleet and the South China Sea detachment for a
period of three months. If there was any truth to his
guilt, this court had not been interested in uncovering
it. Peace and its demands pressed too hard.

He and Calderone had parted, also as she had predicted. As a final present, she had given him a nylon
duffel. It now contained his rolled-up Japanese silk
suit, a small wooden statuette she had bought at a
flea market, and not much else save his transducers
and other delphine communication gear. He hefted the
bag, wishing it had more in it to weight him down. He
felt hollow. His life was over, the war crimes trial its
perfunctory obsequy.

At the dock he stopped and lowered a transducer into the water. After listening for a moment and
filtering out the rumbling of the boats that ran back
and forth in the harbor, he heard the distant hunting
call of an orca. "Thou'rt mine," it whispered confiding-
ly to its prey. "Mine and no one else's. Prepare thy soul
for death."

Stasov wanted to shout into his microphone, to call
the orca to him, but he could not. The sounds stayed
in his throat. Like a fisherman reeling in an unsuccess-
ful cast, he yanked the transducer from the water and
shoved it back in his duffel.

He walked up the gangplank and onto the ship.

CHAPTER NINE

2024

ILYA STASOV KNEW THEY HAD COME INTO SIGHT OF HIS father's grave when his mother began to lean on him. He scanned ahead through the lines of gravestones, but there was no way to pick it out. The ground was still muddy from the melting of spring snows. Ada Stasov walked precariously on high heels. She clenched a bunch of pussy willows in her hands.

Cemetery space was nonexistent anywhere in the old sections of Petersburg. Sergei Nikolaiivich Stasov had been buried far from his beloved city, in the Cemetery of the Victims of 9 January 1905, the original part of which provided a memorial to the victims of the massacre of a peaceful procession making a petition to the Tsar, but which now spread out with marble monuments and flower beds, housing blocks rising featurelessly around. With typical extravagance Stasov's mother Ada had paid for an elaborate marble marker with an Orthodox cross on it. On the marker was a hologram of Sergei Nikolaiivich, a tiny homunculus imprisoned in a metal-and-glass holder. Again typically, it did not show Stasov's father in his favorite room, his study, with a pipe in his mouth, but instead revealed him in an elegant suit, standing on some seashore jetty, squinting uncomfortably into the sun, an expensive hat perched ridiculously on his head. That was how his mother had always wanted to see his father. Now she could.

After kneeling to push the pussy willows into the soil, Ada leaned against her son's shoulder and cried bitter tears. Stasov, still weak from his time at Homma, could barely support even her light weight. Gaunt, scarred, his short hair grizzled, he knew that he did not look much younger than she did, in her long black dress, her thin face a northern Russian pale. Her tears soaked his shoulder, a salty wetness that reminded him of the sea.

He remembered learning of his father's death and running to talk to Makarygin, there in the clattering hallways of the *Nizhni Novgorod*. The two events seemed to happen together in his head, as if Sergei Stasov's body lay on some anonymous bunk deep within the aircraft carrier, his dusty books piled around him, while his son wandered and sought comfort. Soon after, or so it seemed in memory, wise Makarygin too was dead, his body twisted on the blood-flecked grass of Homma.

The grass here was barely stirring, pushing up through the wet earth. Ilya Stasov stood there and wept along with his mother. The countless dead of Kagalaska, Hokkaido, and Korea had required an ocean of tears, more than any human eyes could produce, so Stasov's eyes had remained dry. Now, at last, he could cry.

Stasov blinked his eyes clear and looked across the expanse of the cemetery, its monuments protruding from the mud as if left by retreating glaciers. Here human beings memorialized those dead who had died in small enough numbers to be memorialized.

"Oh, Ilya," his mother said. "I know you always found us ridiculous."

Stasov tried not to feel exasperated at her attempt to attribute such a prim opinion to him. He imagined a wing chair, only the puffs of pipe smoke coming over the top indicating his father's presence, and his father's voice: "Now, Ada, did he say that or are you reading his mind again?" But his father was no longer there to play the thankless role of reason.

He looked down at his tiny mother as she gathered her coat tightly around her. "Mother, neither of you was ever ridiculous to me."

"Well, it's certainly nice of you to say so." She leaned over and polished the hologram with a cloth. "I thought *he* was ridiculous, and he certainly thought the same of me, God knows why." She smiled to herself, then turned away from the grave.

She had caught him again, showing how well she understood everything just as he thought she was being most obtuse.

"Let's go," he said. "It's cold."

She looked up at him, eyes wide with concern. "You used to love the cold so, Ilya. Once you dug yourself into the snow thrown up by the plows like some sort of hibernating bear and were buried deeper by another plow. You shivered all through dinner."

Stasov remembered the suffocating white terror as

he'd dug his way up through the heavy snow, and the joy of finally seeing sunlight. He'd come home silent and frozen, convinced no one would ever find out how stupid he'd been.

"My blood thinned in the tropics," he said.

She rested her hand on his elbow in a way that was both coquettish and motherly. She knew how little he was actually telling her of what had happened. It had always been that way. "That's all right, Ilya. Some soup will warm you up."

They walked back across the mud to the streetcar line near the cemetery's edge. A flock of the first rooks of spring flew overhead, calling to each other, and came to roost on one of the still-bare trees that overhung the stones.

The streetcar was old and in poor repair, its windows cracked. It had originally been robot-controlled, but a human driver now stood, arms crossed, by the guidance computer, awaiting with weary patience its inevitable malfunction. A bell clanged and the streetcar rolled.

Stasov remembered a long-ago journey in such a streetcar. He had held a cardboard box in his lap. He shook the box, just a little, but it remained silent.

His mother's long arm, always a little stronger than a boy would like his mother's arm to be, reached around his shoulder and pulled him to her. He remained stiff, not relaxing against her. "That's all right, Ilyushenka," she whispered. "Next time you'll know better." Harsh consolation for a seven-year-old boy who has just committed murder with the best of intentions.

The streetcar bumped along and the endless rows of five- and six-story apartment buildings passed by in procession. It was May and the sun shone down as if this was a happy day just like any other.

They'd warmed chicken eggs in an incubator at school, studying embryonic development. They had decorated the schoolroom with pictures of old Russian farming villages and their brightly colored axe-carved decorations, their muddy roads, and their animals, images of a long-vanished world where hatching chickens were a part of life rather than a curiosity. Each of the children had an egg in the incubator with his initials on it. That morning, the eggs had started to hatch.

Ilya's egg had rocked and shivered. Then, with quick precision, the tiny beak had poked a hole in the shell. The chick began to break away fragments of the shell, its weak body straining against the rigid prison that enclosed it. Ilya, watching, almost in tears at the pain the wet, skinny-necked chick was obviously feeling, reached out to help, to break the eggshell for it. His fingers were so much stronger and he wanted to help. His fingers *were* stronger. He killed the bird.

The teacher, a stolid man who always finished the lesson plan for the day like a factory worker fulfilling norms, unbent a little in the face of the boy's obvious despair. He'd grown up in the city and the books about the use of the incubator hadn't mentioned anything about not helping chicks hatch.

"That's all right," he said, smiling down at the weeping boy. "You couldn't have known."

"I should have!" Ilya said in a rage.

His mother had come to pick him up after school, on the way to some errand in downtown Petersburg. He'd insisted on taking the tiny body with him in a box.

She ran her fingers through his hair, which she was always so careful to comb, disarranging it. "Have you learned a lesson, Ilyushenka?"

He was getting old enough that her public use of the most endearing form of his name irritated him, taking his mind off his dismay. He pulled away slightly. "Yes, mama," he said. She did not bother to find out what lesson he had learned.

His mother looked out at the spring afternoon and hummed a popular tune under her breath. She was beautiful, if a trifle careworn, as were all women in those last years of the century. She wore earrings with tiny pearls.

He looked up at them. "Mama, where do pearls come from?"

"The ocean, little dove, the ocean."

"Like the Gulf of Finland?" He named the only body of water he had ever seen.

She laughed as if realizing that the time when she knew something her son didn't would soon be past. "No. The Pacific Ocean. Perhaps someday, if you're lucky, you will see it."

Stasov looked over at her now on their way back from the cemetery. She didn't look that much different than she had thirty years before, or so it seemed to him. Her quick dark eyes marked the rest of the passengers on the streetcar. She had her own scheme of classifying people, the rules of which neither of the men in her family had ever been able to figure out. She frowned at a squalling infant and nodded familiarly to a large man in an astrakhan coat. A woman in a modish magenta jacket was tagged and dismissed. To Ada, at least, the universe made sense.

Ada Stasov had moved out of their old apartment at No. 109 Berggoltsaya to a smaller place. Her husband's books were packed in stacks and stacks of boxes. Stasov had been making his way through them, constantly distracted by new discoveries.

"They're yours, Ilya," his mother said. "I wouldn't know what to do with them." She picked up a

poorly bound, and extremely valuable, volume of
pre-Revolutionary Acmeist poetry. "Sergei doesn't
need them to defend himself against me, not anymore." She opened the book, seemingly at random,
and read: " 'What am I? A fragment of ancient wrongs,
a javelin, fallen in the grass. The son of Atreus, the
leader of nations, is dead—and I, a man of no
account, am alive.' " Stasov recognized Gumilyev's
poem "Agamemnon's Warrior". She shook her head,
muttered, "Men," and went into the kitchen to make
some soup.

The books were packed without order, as they had
stood on the shelves. Stasov pulled out an account
of the last days of Pushkin, a study of ancient Greek
auditoriums, and a collection of essays on biological
oddities. To his father these had all been clues, but
what mystery he had been trying to unravel was forever beyond Ilya's knowing. Whatever it was, Sergei
had never given up on it: the newest books dated only
a month before his death. To Ilya his father was a man
who had carefully, in great detail, felt out the walls of
his prison.

He lay down on the floor, the piles of books rising around him like mountain ranges. When Anna
Calderone was at Uglegorsk, he had told her his
father's Sakhalin story about the avenger in the forest, a man whose life was forever bent by one flaring
incident. Not all Sergei's Sakhalin stories were so bleak.
Not that any of them were warm—the best of them
managed only a cold brightness, like sun reflecting off
fragmented ice.

Ilya Stasov lay on the floor and remembered the one
about the Sea Monk.

In the later years of the nineteenth century sea
travelers off the dismal northern end of Sakhalin,

at Cape Maria, could see a huge cross made of rough-hewn birch logs standing on a height. At night lanterns of cod-liver oil were hoisted up on its top and crossbars, marking the dangerous shoals of the shore. During storms large bonfires of pitch-soaked wood burned even through the most savage downpour.

The builder of the cross was a man known only as the Sea Monk, a razor-thin, white-bearded monk, who made his home there at the cape with his Ainu servants. He wore boots of sealskin shod with iron and a rosary of walrus bone. Where he had come from no one knew, though all suspected some deep, probably violent secret.

Aside from prayer, his main activity was the rescue of those imperiled by the sea. Many prisoners attempted escape from their vicious camps on Sakhalin in makeshift boats that quickly foundered in the rough currents of the Tatar Strait. The Sea Monk sailed his round-bottomed, seaworthy ship, the *Trinity*, southward from Cape Maria and rescued them, setting them back alive on dry land. He had done this for so long that he had become a legend. Prisoners escaping by sea made good-luck charms: small figures of bread, with coal dust worked in to mimic the blackness of the monk's cassock.

Aside from saving their lives, the Sea Monk did not concern himself with the fate of the prisoners. His job, as he saw it, was merely to return them to life, to carry out their appointed round of suffering. He was giving them another chance at repentance. What they did with it was their own business.

At last the *Trinity* sailed into a storm from which it did not return. Except for a Bible, a cross, and a washbasin, the only personal possession of the Sea Monk's that could be found in his house was half a wedding photograph. It showed a woman in a formal embroidered wedding dress. Someone had cut half the photograph off and all that could be seen of the groom was one of his hands, firmly clasping his bride's. The cross and the house stood for many years, until the Revolution, when the Bolsheviks tore them down.

The piled books had changed from mountains to waves, and Ilya felt himself drowning in the sea. He imagined the *Trinity* sailing through the storm, its master, white hair and beard blowing in the wind, standing at the bow searching for survivors.

Stasov sat up, coughing from the book dust, the paralysis of half sleep gone. The University of St. Petersburg had offered him a professor's position. Perhaps there he could fade into decent academic obscurity, publishing abstruse papers on the morphemes in the dialect of *Stenella coeruleoalba*, the Ocean Dolphin. That way the real mystery could remain unknown, while he searched through meaningless details. And it would never work. He knew that.

With a weary sense of inevitability, he opened up his duffel and pulled out the transducer and electronic gear he used for talking to dolphins. He hadn't touched them since he left the Philippines. Ada called him to come and eat.

As he sat and ate soup with his mother in her tiny kitchen he noticed an old volume resting near the cookbooks. It was Przhevalsky's *From Zaysan via Hami to Tibet and the Upper Reaches of the Yellow River*. His mother usually preferred romantic novels by Tolstoy, Jane Austen, or the currently popular Tambalov. Stasov picked it up and sniffed it. Did it have a tang of the sea's iodine and ozone from the year he had kept it at Uglegorsk? Rather it smelled of dill and paprika. Never leave books in the kitchen.

He didn't say anything but simply raised his eyebrows.

Ada looked uncomfortable for an instant, then challenging. "He always said it was the best of Przhevalsky's books."

"It is." Stasov thought of his mother lulling herself to sleep with a boy's story of hunting exotic animals, freezing in the far reaches of Tibet, and being assaulted by mountain tribes. He hoped that she understood something that she hadn't before about her dead husband, who had never done anything more exotic than take a boat trip down the Volga.

He reached out his hand and put it over hers. Evening was settling over the wide curve of the Neva River that was visible through the window and Stasov felt, for the first time since his return, an old urge.

"I'm going out for a walk," he said. "If that's all right."

His mother looked up at him, reflexively ready to refuse. Instead, she smiled and shook her head. "Go on, Ilya. If you walk all the way to Senate Square again, give me a call." That had been the longest of his night expeditions, leading him all the way to the center of St. Petersburg and the equestrian statue of Peter I: Pushkin's symbol of the city, the Bronze Horseman. A policeman had found him there at dawn. That time even his father had been angry.

His long legs found the old rhythm of the street, but to his dismay he was soon tired. He leaned against a brick wall and looked up at the residential blocks. He saw nothing of the distant wave-washed cliffs and floating icebergs that he had once imagined as he looked out the window of his parents' apartment. Though cracked and full of potholes, the road was solid and showed no intention of becoming a glacier or river. The twin ribbons of the streetcar tracks gleamed in the street. The streetcar clanged behind him and he jumped aboard.

Soon he was in the old section of town with its baroque and neoclassical facades. The opening of a canal revealed the jabbing gold spire of the Admiralty lit by the last rays of the sun. The streetcar crossed a canal on a high bridge. Stasov got out and looked down at its water as it flowed into the Neva.

He turned off the bridge and walked along the granite Neva embankment. It had grown dark and the air was crisp with lingering winter. He climbed down to the water and dropped a hydrophone into it.

"I am here," he said, in the basic interspecies dolphin dialect. "Ilya Stasov is here." He repeated his statement every few minutes. " 'Have you found me, oh mine enemy?' " he said to himself, and smiled. He was no Ahab, God knew, and the dolphins were not Elijah, but looking down into the black water he knew what he had been avoiding. Makarygin could have told him easily. The hardest thing to face is the consequences of your own actions. You could forgive yourself, find absolution in righteous punishment, accept the all-encompassing grace of God, but the consequences remained. And nothing but intelligence and painful hard work could change them.

He sat for another hour until his limbs were numb. Then a voice spoke in return: "What nets have kept you from our sea?" From the grammar, the dolphin was a female.

"They are my own," Stasov said. He didn't recognize the dolphin's voice. She wasn't one he was familiar with. He looked at the glowing windows above him. Rising across the canal was a discreet neoclassical church, its usually exuberant Russian Orthodox gold domes suppressed in favor of Doric columns and a low dome, more in fitting with the tone of the neighborhood. The toll of the church bell rolled down the river with its ancient sound.

"You cannot escape us. You are in our sea."

"I know that," Stasov said wearily.

"You gave the past's echo clarity and substance. You cannot simply leave us to its teeth."

"Quit repeating yourself. *I* called *you*."

"You talked because you had to. Get your head out of the silt. It leaves your rear vulnerable." The dolphin snorted obscenely. "Your life is ours until the sea eats your flesh. You have been too long out of the sea. Your brains have desiccated like a skate's egg case."

"So what the hell do you want?" Stasov asked.

The dolphin rose from the river. Military prosthetics bulked on her back. She looked like a sub killer, equipped with magnetic scramblers and limpet mine attaching gear. Her dorsal fin had been replaced with a laser link for communication with satellites. Since their escape from internment, no one had been able to recapture the military cyborgs to disarm them.

"Ilya Sergeiivich Stasov." She spoke Russian into the air. A dolphin's full name had a component of sympathetic magic, and she used Stasov's as an earnest of her seriousness. "Help us! The seas are a whirlpool. We are deaf. We are blind. But we are no longer dumb. We cannot be what we were. We know not what we are to become. Help us!" She sank slowly back into the water.

Makarygin had told him once. When the Archangel Michael came to you and handed you a sword to fight for God, you would want to refuse. Rather than a beautiful blade, an inlaid sword guard, and a gleaming scabbard, you were handed a weighty lump of iron without apparent edge or point. With this ridiculous object you were to battle God's enemies and endure their mocking laughter. Duty was hardest when it had the appearance of stupidity.

"Get specific." Despite himself, Stasov found himself getting irritated with the dolphin's wandering all around the point. "It's simple. You want to dispose of my life. How?"

"Speaking the word doesn't create a fat tuna fish, Stasov. Get to sea. Get off the land, where you conceal yourself from us. That's all."

In addition to the university appointment, Stasov had been offered, grudgingly, a position on the oceanographic research ship *Andrei Sakharov*, due to leave Vladivostok in a month for a two-year journey around the Pacific and Indian Oceans. He'd been about to refuse.

"All right." He hoped his irritation was obvious to the dolphin. "I will be leaving——"

"Don't tell! We'll find you. At sea, we'll find you."

"But why do you want me there?" He felt exasperation.

"The echo is returning. Wait for it." The dolphin surfaced again and came close to shore. She wiggled with the dolphin gesture of wanting a pat. Stasov reached over and stroked that part of her head not covered with armor.

"I'm sorry," he said.

She whipped her head, took his wrist in her teeth, and pulled him into the water.

The Neva closed over his head with freezing shock. He hadn't had time to draw a breath. He struggled upward. The dolphin's bulk smashed him downward again, driving the remaining air from his lungs. He stroked desperately, but the surface had been replaced by the dolphin's armored belly. His chest burned.

"You will help us," the dolphin called, her voice a physical force. "Get back to work."

He could release his clenched jaws and suck in cooling water . . . he grabbed a fin's trailing edge in one hand. It jerked back. He managed to get a second hand on it and pull. With a sudden shock his head broke surface. He sucked in a breath. Now the dolphin's head was beneath him. With irresistible force she pushed upward and forced him in to shore. A final jerk of her head and he rolled onto the granite embankment. She blew one final time and vanished into the water. Stasov could just see the underwater blue-green flicker of the laser as she moved downriver toward the ocean.

"You were saved," a voice said.

Stasov rolled, to see a Russian Orthodox priest kneeling over him, gold cross glinting on black cassock. He was young, with a thick black beard and round glasses.

"I've never seen anything like it," the priest exclaimed. "That dolphin pushed you to safety. Incredible."

The priest took Stasov's laughter as natural hysteria after a narrow escape from death.

THE CHURCH'S INTERIOR WAS A CANDLELIT CAVE. A FEW DARK figures stood and knelt in private communion. Stasov, dressed in poorly fitting but dry clothes, wandered out and stood in front of the iconostasis with its ranks of icons. The saints stared out above him. Most of them were kitschy nineteenth-century renderings, though some had that solemn walleyed look that Makarygin had had. The stone floor was cold under Stasov's bare feet.

When Ilya Stasov was young, his parents had started, irregularly and dubiously, attendance at church, an activity that had become popular with the collapse of the old Soviet Union. The only churches that had services were old ones, pre-Revolution, and thus there were none in the new residential neighborhood where they lived. There were prayer meetings of various sorts, of course, held in dining halls, sports stadiums, private apartments, but these held no attraction for either of his parents. His mother found them too proletarian, his father not sufficiently thoughtful. So they took a long streetcar ride, with a transfer, down to the church his parents had finally agreed upon, Rastrelli's graceful baroque Cathedral at Smolny Convent. Vladimir Lenin, while plotting the fall of the transient Constituent Assembly in the summer and autumn of 1917, had had his headquarters at Smolny. Ilya's father in particular enjoyed worshipping God in the place where one of His greatest opponents had laid his plans.

During those same years Ilya's father several times took him to an old planetarium. The central dome was dominated by that huge insectoidal device covered with precisely ground lenses which cast the images of the stars, moving pieces of the universe at the direction of the invisible operator. In Ilya's memories the two places were mixed together. The constellations, vaguely shadowed by their pagan forms of goats, centaurs, and bulls, floated past the solemnly ecstatic faces of saints with their hands upheld in benediction. The galaxy spun beneath the blue dome, the Eye of God staring down from its center. Beeswax candles joined the dance of the stars and blazing nebulae were reflected in the dark water of the great baptismal font.

Even at that age it seemed to Ilya that God was absent. He would look over at his mother, her head bent in a pose of eternal piety as if already practicing for the role of one of those old ladies who perennially haunt churches. His father bore a thoughtful expression as he watched the gold-robed and crowned figures of the priests and acolytes presenting the Eucharist. Ilya wondered what they saw, what they worshipped. He never learned.

In those last seconds, pounding across the golf course with burning lungs, his murderers in pursuit, Makarygin had seen the face of God. Of that Stasov was suddenly certain. Makarygin had died, and left Ilya Stasov alone to face the consequences of his own actions.

Stasov shivered in the night cold of the church. He still didn't understand Makarygin's God. But he did understand what he had to do.

CHAPTER TEN

2025

THE SAILING SKIFF CUT CLEANLY THROUGH THE STILL WATER of the lagoon. Stasov trimmed sail and looked back to see how far he'd come. The *Andrei Sakharov* was now just a distant floating bar of soap. Beyond it the densely green volcanic islands of Fefan and Uman rose out of the sea, lit by the morning sun. They and the half-dozen other Truk Islands were surrounded by a vast atoll fifty kilometers across. The coral-covered wrecks of Japanese merchant ships sunk by American planes during the Second World War could easily be seen on the bottom.

Joining the *Andrei Sakharov* on its slow journey through the southern Pacific had proved less painful than Stasov had expected. He had thought to retreat into monastic seclusion, but his white-walled cabin had become an informal gathering place for debates not much different from those at Uglegorsk, though here the staff seemed indecently young. Stasov, all of forty-two years old, felt like a professor emeritus. The other researchers treated him like an ancient oracle speaking in an unfamiliar tongue, awe mingling with incomprehension. He missed the collegial feeling of an argument with equals. But that world was gone forever and he was one of its few relics, like a fragment of a storm-sunk ship bobbing to the surface of a now-calm sea.

The languid trip had been healing. His long body was now tan, the scars on his face and body vivid white against it. He sometimes slept clear through the night without a nightmare. Weakness often came, however, and he occasionally went through the day like an old man, as if the months at Homma had actually been decades, by far the largest part of his life.

Out in the rougher ocean beyond the atoll, a humpback whale breached, leaping full length into the air. The white foam it dragged up with it flickered in the sun. It waved its large front flippers in the air and then was sucked back into the water. Through his earphones Stasov could hear the humpback's complex cry.

With sudden determination, he tacked his skiff and aimed for a break in the barrier atoll. In a few minutes the ocean waves began to slap against the bottom of the skinny, flexible hull. The dazzling tropical sun shone in his eyes. At the edge of his vision he could just see an additional flicker in the water: a pod of dolphins.

The dolphins had called him out to the sea but now refused to speak with him about anything important. For the past month the *Sakharov* had been steaming slowly through the Caroline Islands of Micronesia. Stasov had spent the time analyzing sonograms and recordings of mass dolphin calls. He was beginning to understand some of the mechanisms of group perception among cetaceans. Dolphins could hear not only their own returns but those of the rest of their pod. Stasov tried to imagine the multilayered vision of reality which resulted. But they still refused to tell him anything interesting.

He scanned the choppy water, hoping for a reappearance of the humpback, listening to the complex calls of the sea with one ear. The whale remained stubbornly beneath the waves. His thoughts, as they often did, turned to Anna Calderone. How far had she gone in her attempt to reach Jupiter and the mysterious beings in its atmosphere? He imagined her tracking a creature of that sea, some vast whale that dove through layers of hydrogen, helium, ammonia, and exotic gaseous compounds of germanium and phosphorus, seeing the planet glowing before him. For an instant he imagined that the deep clouds smelled of lemon and church incense mixed with the crispness of a winter morning.

That thought brought with it the image of Anna Calderone herself, and the curve of her arm and shoulder as she sat up naked in bed, a sheet wrapped around her legs. A single stream of sunlight through the dusty window caught the highlights in her coppery hair. Of all the parts of his life that had left him, she was the hardest to accept.

Something caught his eye, a fleck of blackness against the bright sea. It was the dorsal fin of a killer whale. Orcas surrounded him, it seemed, the way screaming sea gulls always swarmed around fishing boats.

The sea had grown unaccountably quiet. He could no longer hear the dolphins or the long-calling humpback. Flipping out of the water like a thug's knife blade from its sheath, the orca's dorsal fin appeared and kept pace with him, some thirty meters away. The sea itself seemed to have grown smooth, his boat sliding across it as if on ice. All was suspended in silence.

A rush of steam bubbled up from below, carrying with it the gagging stink of a whale's breath. He was flung skyward by the humpback whale's snout. The impact slammed him down into the hull of the tiny boat. He slid and grabbed desperately at the now-loose-flapping lines. The foul steam of the humpback's spout washed across him and then suddenly everything was clear. He hung for an instant, his boat an impossible distance above the water. The world was in perfect focus—the *Andrei Sakharov* placidly resting in the blue water, the islands and atoll an impossible green, each wave in the sea delineated as if by a sharp, curved knife, the knife that thrust from the orca's contemplative back.

Then, sickeningly, everything fell out from under him and he toppled off the whale, which sank back to sea with him. The world spun around him. The ocean dodged so cunningly that it seemed he would never hit it. Yet, somehow, he found it. The water struck at his face like shattering glass.

Beneath the water were the stars.

Stasov, as wide awake as he'd ever been in his life, floated in the black spaces around Jupiter. The Galilean moons were billiard balls around him. Just below him was a giant whale, half machine, half alive, a distant descendant of the cyborg dolphins he had sent into the sea to make war. Joyously it dove into the colored clouds. Stasov felt radiation and high-energy particles penetrating him. He was as transparent as absolute vacuum.

Suddenly, water filled Stasov's nose and mouth. He choked and doubled over. He did not try to draw breath, feeling wet death against his face. He stroked upward and gained the surface.

But even as he pushed into the sun and drew breath, Jupiter and the whale still burned in his mind. It was like the blue spot in the visual field that comes from incautiously looking at the sun. No matter how he turned his thoughts, it was there.

His body ached in a dozen places from the impact. His face stung. A blow to his rib cage made each breath agony. But these were as nothing to the pain in his mind. Jupiter flared there like a coal flicked carelessly onto a rug. He shook his head to clear it. A mistake. He felt like throwing up.

The humpback and the orca were gone. The hull of his sailing skiff floated upside down a few meters away, trailing the remains of its mast and sails. He swam slowly up to it and grabbed on.

"ILYA, ARE YOU ALL RIGHT?" TANYA SHCHEDRINA ASKED.

"Yes, I just couldn't sleep."

"A little warm milk would be better than that, I think."

Stasov poured cognac over his tongue. He should have known better than to drink out on the deck. But he had never enjoyed getting drunk in his room, where the walls always seemed to get closer. His walls at Uglegorsk had finally seemed to rub on either side of his nose.

He hooked a chair with his foot. "Care to join me?"

Shchedrina leaned back against the rail and looked at him suspiciously. She was a cheerful Russian girl with a wide face and high cheekbones. Because she was so frequently in the water, she wore her curly hair cut short. When Stasov came aboard she had offered herself to him as his lover, though whether this was from misplaced hero worship, because she sensed his inner pain, or because she actually found him attractive, he had never managed to discover. At first accepting her eagerly, he had finally been dismayed by her sense of feminine self-sacrifice. They were now friends with a peculiar history, and she retained a proprietary interest in him.

"Yes," she said softly, and sat.

Lacking another glass, he refilled his and put it in front of her. He could drink from the bottle. It was Director Martinov's own Courvoisier, but they'd get another bottle in Nauru or somewhere.

She took a sip and looked at him seriously. "What's the matter?"

He tried to invent some sort of problem from home that could account for his behavior. His mind was blank. The one thing he didn't want to do was tell this woman that he'd seen a vision and that it was driving him crazy. The whale loomed against the brilliant stars behind her and dove into Jupiter. The cognac hadn't done a damn bit of good.

"I'm not getting anywhere. Nothing makes any more sense than it did ten years ago." As he said the words, intending them merely to pacify her, he realized they were true. "I still have no idea of what's going on."

"And whose fault is that?"

"Eh?" Stasov peered blearily across the table. Shchedrina seemed curiously unsympathetic. "I'm not sure how to answer that."

"Sure." She took the bottle from him and refilled her glass with a practiced flick of her wrist. She dimpled as she smiled at him. Knowing that he had passed through great and terrible events, Shchedrina had come up with the idea that he was great and terrible himself, a delusion natural to the young. Despite himself, Stasov had never brought himself to talk her out of it.

"Perhaps you should think about Jupiter," she said.

He held onto both arms of his deck chair to keep from falling out of it. "What? What did you say?"

"If dolphins won't talk to you, perhaps Jovians will." She was calm, as if she hadn't just penetrated to Stasov's heart. "Don't people think there may be intelligent beings there? I've been reading about it."

Stasov searched the sky and found the bright star that was Jupiter. He hadn't ever paid attention to the positions of the planets before, but that evening he had looked it up. Mars was just beyond it, almost setting. With a telescope he could have seen Jupiter's four large moons. So far he had resisted.

"I've heard speculation," he said. "I don't know how valid any of it is."

"You're a man with some experience in these things," she said, taking the bottle from his lips and placing it firmly on the table. "Aren't you? There's life there, clearly. Is it intelligent? That's supposed to be the thing you know best. Isn't it?"

Damn the woman. She was—what?—twenty-two, twenty-three years old, and here she was drilling into his skull under the guise of idle chatter. Having nothing else to hold onto, he took her hand. Her fingertips curled against his wrist. He could feel their softness as they stroked him.

"I wonder," she said musingly, "if they are trying to communicate with us already. Who knows what form it could take?"

"You've been reading too much science fiction, Tanya," Stasov said.

She laughed. "Maybe you're right. Just be careful, Ilya. If you talk to Jovians, make sure not to make whatever mistakes you made with dolphins."

He felt a surge of anger at this calmly dismissive woman. Innocent and simple. That was the way he had always thought of her. There was not a woman on Earth who was innocent and simple. He could feel the pulse in his temples. It had been months since they'd slept together.

Her lips parted and she smiled. Then she stood. "Good night, Ilya. I think you should get some sleep." And she swayed off. He watched the motion of her hips in her tight skirt and felt the hunger of being alive.

Screw Jupiter, dolphins, and everything else. He got up and, unsteady on his feet, followed her.

THE DIM ISLANDS OF THE LESSER SUNDAS TROLLED PAST IN the moonlight, each bearing a load of glowing villages. The white form of the *Sakharov* cut a phosphorescent wake through the darkening sea. The metal against Stasov's back was still warm from the just-vanished sun.

Some of the ship's technical staff were sitting near him, almost silent, the glow of their cigarette ends no brighter than stars. He wasn't close to them, not the way he had been to the men at Uglegorsk, during the campaigns, or at Homma. He had lost some ability along the way, some means of love, or so he feared. He liked these people and worked with them, but there was nothing of the fierce love he had felt for someone like Grisha Panin, doomed to burn to death during the assault on Kagalaska. Or Tolya Ogurtsov, who had lost a leg somewhere in the Aleutians and now lived in some city in the great Russian plain, far from the sea.

Two men, Savinkov and Abalkin, walked past. They were peripatetic chess players who circled the ship endlessly, playing in their heads, discussing idly between moves. They nodded briskly to Stasov each time they passed him. This time they paused to look out at the islands.

"Rook takes bishop."

"Damn you. Pawn to King's Bishop Four. Revealed check."

"Hah. Not bad. Hmm."

"You know, the first time I saw a puppet show, I was scared out of my wits. I screamed. My mother had to take me out of the theater."

"Rook to—why, for God's sake?"

"I don't know. I was, what, three or four? I'd been watching television all my life. A little figure of Baba Yaga in her mortar, suspended from strings, shouldn't have scared me. But I saw her sweeping her way across the sky toward me. She was damn real. I don't think I'd ever seen anything that real before."

"Hah. I suppose it's the reality of unreal things that really scares us. Like the sound a creaking door makes that lets you see what horrible thing is opening it. Funny, what your senses can do to you. Knight to Queen's Bishop Five."

"Weren't you going to move your rook?"

"I thought better of it."

"Damn you." The two men moved off, and their conversation faded.

With sudden vividness, as if the image had something to do with the discussion he had just overheard, Stasov saw Kestrel surface in his tank and heard the dolphin keen "Let me die!" Then he flung himself out of the tank to die thrashing on the floor. Dolphins were strange creatures, Stasov thought, anxious for death in a way that no human understood. Stasov sensed a blackness. If he didn't understand why Kestrel had killed himself, what *did* he understand?

"Ilya, do you have a minute?" It was Tanya. She held a book in her hand, and her posture was suppliant.

"Certainly, Tanya," he said. He patted the spot next to him. She sat down nervously, as if she were a young girl and he a boy she liked but had never spoken to.

She wore some simple, strong floral scent that made Stasov think of a shelf crowded with knickknacks, some nice curtains, and an embroidered cover for the toilet. Get a hold of yourself, he thought, annoyed at his own unfairness.

"So where did Minos go after he built the Labyrinth?" Tanya asked.

"Go?" Tanya asked him questions as if he was some sort of oracle.

"Yes. This book says he ruled the Underworld. And you once mentioned some story your friend told you."

"Georgios Theodoros told me a thousand stories. Without him I never would have understood . . ." A screaming dolphin. What had he understood?

"It had a half man, half dolphin."

"That one?" Stasov laughed. "I think he made that one up himself." He frowned in thought. After long silence, Georgios Theodoros had started communicating with him again. When Stasov had returned to Petersburg he had found three letters from Thera. Much of them was standard, almost relaxing news: Theodoros's eldest daughter entering college, his wife's hobby of mosaics, lyrical descriptions of the seas and islands. But they also contained eerie, somehow distorted stories. The Minodelphos, a figure that one time seemed to represent a human masquerading as a dolphin and another time a dolphin affecting to be a human, was prominent in these. Stasov had not asked what Theodoros was getting at. The Greek had an instinct for the oblique approach. Sometimes, stories are just stories. And sometimes they are something more.

Stasov tried to remember the details. Modified delphine-influenced versions of old stories competed in his mind with the originals he had learned as a child. His father had given him a large book illustrated with such pictures as Zeus flinging thunderbolts down from Olympus and Hercules staring contemptuously at a tiny broom offered him by King Augeias to clean the famous Stables.

"King Minos had many sons," Stasov said. Tanya rested her head on his shoulder as he spoke, and stared out at the distant islands. He wondered at her, at what she was looking for. "One day a younger son, Catreus, wandered into the Labyrinth beneath the palace, looking for a golden ball he had lost. He went deeper and deeper into the Labyrinth and got lost himself, because he hadn't left a clew of thread behind him, like his sister Ariadne did when she led Theseus there. Do you know that story, Tanya?"

"The Minotaur," she said. "Every young girl's dream of a man."

"Eh?"

She ran her fingers along the edge of his prominent jaw. "Strong, lost in a maze, and bullheaded. What else?"

Stasov snorted. "Each of us gets something different from the myths. The secret of their popularity."

"Yes, my Minotaur. Go on."

"Catreus went on. He kept seeing his gold ball glimmering ahead of him. Water filled the passages, first to his ankles, then his knees, then his waist, then his shoulders. It finally closed over his head and it became completely dark.

"He heard a voice: 'Brother Catreus. It is good to feel you here.'

" 'Who are you?' Catreus demanded.

" 'The son of your mother, Pasiphaë,' came the answer. 'Let me take you to your goal.'

"Catreus reached out and took hold of a hand. It pulled him through the water, farther through the darkness of the Labyrinth. Eventually light appeared ahead of him and he found himself standing on the shores of a great sea. The land ahead of him was dark and melancholy. It was Tartarus, Land of the Dead.

"He turned to speak to his brother, but in the water next to him was a dolphin with arms and long, long whiskers, like an old man. His eyes were milky blue and completely blind.

" 'Brother,' Catreus said. 'What is your name?'

"The dolphin spouted and hissed. 'I have no name. I am the Minodelphos, fruit of the sin of your father, Minos, for he gave his wife, Pasiphaë, to the dolphins to propitiate them. I am their offspring. Go forward and see him.'

"So Catreus walked forward through Tartarus. There were many of the ancient ones dead there, but he did not dare speak to them. They were not men whose names we know, for the stars of their fame have been dimmed by the sun of the heroes of the Trojan War. Since Achilles and Hector had not yet fought their war, the clatter of their armor was not yet heard in Tartarus.

"A brighter glow appeared before him, and he walked toward it. It was a vast golden throne, the throne of a great king, and sitting upon it was his father, Minos, long dead. I don't know where he died."

"At Camicus," Tanya said. "The daughters of Cacalus poured boiling water on him in his bath."

"Um, right. He held a staff. 'Son Catreus!' he said. 'Welcome.'

"Catreus wept and embraced his father, who had died far away without saying good-bye.

" 'Father,' he said. 'How did you come to rule here, in Hades?'

"Minos laughed. 'I will always rule in my own palace, whether above or below, for the Labyrinth connects all. How did you find me?'

" 'The Minodelphos led me.'

"At this the face of Minos darkened. 'He is your brother, but not my son. He assisted Theseus in the murder of the Minotaur, his own brother, and in the abduction of your sister Ariadne. Take your ball and go. If the Minodelphos should pursue you, grab his whiskers and pull them. As you do, say "The back is the front, the top the bottom. The sky has switched places with the land and the sea is drained. The Labyrinth is straightened and you are lost." ' He handed Catreus the ball he had lost. Now it glowed like one of the planets and showed him his way.

"Catreus bid his father farewell and returned to the water, the endless flowing sea that some call the river Styx. He dove in and swam back up toward the sunlight.

"The Minodelphos pursued him. Catreus turned and grabbed his whiskers and pulled and pulled. 'The back is the front,' he said, 'the top the bottom. The sky has switched places with the land and the sea is drained. The Labyrinth is straightened and you are lost.' The Minodelphos screamed and swam off, smashing into the walls of the Labyrinth. 'I am lost!' he cried. 'I have lost you, O my brother!' So Catreus escaped back to the palace."

"That's such a cruel story," Tanya said. "Why did he have to do that to the poor Minodelphos?"

Stasov shrugged. He hadn't really thought about the story that way. "He was obeying his father the King."

"That's not a good enough reason," Tanya said decisively. "Do you suppose Catreus ever understood that he had done wrong?"

"I have no idea. It's not part of the story." Stasov found himself irritated without knowing why. "That's not what's important about it."

"Yes, Ilya," she said contritely. "It's important because it helped you understand delphine intelligence. I'm sorry."

"Don't be sorry. And it didn't. I only learned the story long after we already knew." He stood up. She took his arm and they walked along the deck. The two chess players, Savinkov and Abalkin, had finished their game and gone below. Savinkov said that he had been frightened by a puppet of Baba Yaga. And sonic images of Strogyle's eruption had caused dolphins to talk. Why had that worked? What part of their minds had it worked on?

SOUNDS CAN PROPAGATE FOR HUNDREDS OF KILOMETERS under water. Stasov sat in the delphine comm cabin aboard the *Andrei Sakharov* as it floated near an atoll in the northern Maldive Islands and listened to a drama unfold in the waters to the south. After several minutes of silence he heard an overlapping chorus of sharp calls. Orca hunting calls: an orca pod was after whale. Except— Stasov listened more carefully. The calls were wrong. Everything about them was overemphasized, and they lacked the easy lilt of orca speech.

The more he heard, the more he became convinced that the calls were not being made by orcas. They were being made by dolphins imitating orcas.

He ran back the tapes from the Central Basin of the Indian Ocean for the past day and searched for specific sound formants. The computer spit them out; he checked, reconfigured, and searched again. Eventually he found what he was looking for.

The dolphins were chasing a whale. A rogue, he had remained silent throughout the chase, so Stasov had missed him. But what was that whale doing alone? Stasov queried the global cetacean data base maintained by Indian Ocean Sea Rescue at Colombo, Sri Lanka. Return satellite link dumped him the data. The rogue whale, named Clarence, had been part of a sperm whale gam until about a year ago. At that time, feeling powerful, he had attacked the old male that guarded the gam's nursery, where the calves swam in a defended group. The wily old sperm had defeated young Clarence. Rather than returning to the gam, Clarence had separated and gone his own way. He'd gone rogue and sung a proud and lonely song. In the old days of wooden ships he would have been feared, a bottom-staver and man-eater, but in the days of steel hulls and sonar, he was a threat only to others of his kind. Then the dolphins had found him, minding his own business, as rogue sperm whales tended to do. And, shouting in chorus, they had mimicked the sound of a pod of hunting killer whales, orcas, and chased him through the sea.

They called again. Stasov listened so hard he imagined he heard air molecules clicking together. The dolphins seemed to be performing more of a satire than an imitation, mimicking the orcas' pompous sonorities and dramatic cadences mourning the necessity of death. It was clever in a typically perverse dolphin way, but they had never done such a thing before. No pre-contact tape had any cetacean species imitating the sounds of any other.

Stasov pulled the headphones off and ran his fingers through his hair. Though the comm room was constantly lit, he could feel the night outside sucking at him, pulling him into sleep. The dolphins had learned such games at Uglegorsk and after. And they were out there now, driving Ilya Stasov crazy.

The military cyborgs ranged the seas. They were cut off from their satellite links and the sonic repeaters that had helped them communicate during the war, but they were still dangerous. Stasov knew that armorers in Kerala and Vietnam had rearmed some of them in return for military assistance in their local wars.

Earlier that evening, somewhere in the west Pacific, a radio monitor had recorded a burst of dolphin radio-message traffic. They loved cluttering the ether with their babbling and weren't yet signatories of any international spectrum-usage agreements. Stasov had gotten an unofficial notification from a contact at the Port Moresby Institute—strictly speaking, he was not qualified to have such information. Stasov had no idea what the dolphins were up to, though he recognized a pattern of transmission that resembled a naval seek-and-destroy mission.

Two weeks ago he'd heard a deep call in the Arabian Basin. Three humpback whales at a depth of a kilometer had sung, but not in their own voices. Instead, they had used a simplified version of a dolphin dialect. Humpbacks were not sentient, so it was obvious that someone had trained them. The call was "The Bubble Is Rising", a reference to the first bubble rising from the spout of God as She rose from the depths to take breath. Since then, Stasov had been glued to his listening gear.

He put his earphones back on. He listened to the whale, tracking him by the faint echo of dolphin echo-location signals. The whale circled a lump of rock in the southern Maldives. The dolphins chased him. He finally made one last terrified call and vanished. Stasov raised his eyebrows and ran the tape back. The whale vanished again.

It wasn't magic. The dolphin Kestrel had vanished the same way from the tanks at Uglegorsk. Clarence the sperm whale had made a leap into the air and come down on the rock. He would not return to the sea.

The dolphins dropped their orca imitation. "The Bubble Is Rising," they chorused in their own voices. "The Bubble Is Rising." The call was loud and clear.

He dropped the earphones. An image of a whale diving into Jupiter was now a constant reflection in his thoughts. And now he heard the dolphins, in their own religion, announcing the imminent arrival of their Messiah.

He turned and ran up the stairs.

CHAPTER ELEVEN

2025

Sᴛᴀsᴏᴠ ᴄʟᴀᴍʙᴇʀᴇᴅ ᴅᴏᴡɴ ᴏᴠᴇʀ ᴛʜᴇ ꜱʟɪᴘᴘᴇʀʏ, ꜱᴇᴀᴡᴇᴇᴅ-covered rocks to take a look at the octopus trapped in the tide pool. It had come too high up near shore at high tide, probably in pursuit of crabs to eat, and been imprisoned when the water receded. Snails and sea urchins tumbled helplessly as the octopus whirled its tentacles. The red starfish and the sea anemones clinging to the rocks went calmly about their business, ignoring the frantic interloper. Stasov reached in and prodded the octopus with his finger. It flushed dark with fear and irritation and huddled down between two rocks. The overturned sea urchins waggled their spines and slowly began to right themselves.

The waves slapped louder as the tide rose over the rocks, gleaming eye-hurtingly in the glaring sunlight.

Here and there the water met momentary resistance from a ridge or a seaweed pile, but it rose inexorably over all obstacles, finally pouring into the tide pool and reuniting it with the sea. With a jet the octopus vanished in the direction of deeper, safer waters.

Stasov climbed back up from the water, away from the heavy iodine smell of the dark seaweed. Isopods, those marine pill bugs, scuttled madly under his feet amid the barnacles and black lichens at the upper reach of the tidal zone. Above was the rough, bare rock where the sperm whale lay baking in the morning sun.

His smooth black bulk loomed above the rough rock like a dream of a living mountain, sharply outlined against the cloudless sky. Pursued by dolphins, Clarence had leaped from the sea and smashed himself on the land. Without help he would be dead by noon. Staring up at him, mesmerized, Stasov tripped over a stretch of the limp tubing that now crisscrossed the island. A firm hand grabbed his elbow and held him.

"We're ready to pump," Habib Williams's wheezy voice said. "Tubes are soft now, but under pressure they're like tree trunks. Get one of them wrapped around your leg and you got some trouble. Not to mention one leg fewer." Williams was a short, skinny man with a bald, brown head. His white suit was cut with precise jauntiness and he carried a flowered Japanese parasol. He peered up at Stasov with narrow suspicion. "Now tell me. Why are we here?" He reached down with the parasol's crook and flipped the switch that was the only external feature of a satiny ovoid the size of a desk. It hummed and seawater filled the tubing. Water sprayed out of hundreds of nozzles, played rainbows in the sun, and ran down the whale's sides.

"We're going to save this whale." Stasov was emphatic. "That, I believe, is your job."

Williams scowled. "It is. Cetacean rescue for the Indian Ocean. Fine, a respectable occupation, pleases my mother though it means I can't get home much. I know my profession. What I don't know is why I, and Marta and Jolie and Ahmed, are *here* on this tiny rock in the Maldives. The water is as clear and calm as I've ever seen it. There hasn't been even the hint of a storm in a month. Halcyon weather. This time of year we sit in a garden in Colombo and play cards."

He walked around the perimeter of the spray, stepping over the streams which now flowed in the cracks down to the sea. Stasov followed. Beyond the whale were the two heavy-lift helicopters that had brought the rescue team from Sri Lanka. Next to them was Stasov's own aircraft, a tiny military-surplus helicopter, its red star dimmed by sun and salt. Stasov thought of the red starfish in the tide pool. That helicopter had fought in the Aleutians, but its star now seemed to have an aquatic rather than a military character. Things did manage to change, sometimes. Ahmed and Jolie had set up a crane which curled over the sperm whale like a scorpion's tail.

"Then this morning the sun comes up, and the Indian Ocean seasearch satellite tells me there's a giant parmacety lying on the rocks in the middle of the ocean. It happens. I've seen gams of whales beach themselves and pods of dolphins bash themselves against cliffs until the water's red. Sperm whales do reverse brodies and drop themselves on islands to die. I don't know why they do it but I'm used to it. What I'm not used to is getting to the scene at top speed and finding Colonel Ilya Sergeiivich Stasov himself lying next to the whale, wrapped in a blanket, listening to the whale die."

Stasov controlled a surge of irritation. Let the man use his military rank as a word of contempt if he wanted to. They had to get the whale into the water as quickly as possible. This was where it began. "We heard a deep call two weeks ago, in the Arabian Basin. If you play back your recordings you'll hear it. Three humpbacks in close chorus. A simple call, in a delphine dialect. It said 'The Bubble Is Rising'. It was a call to prayer. So I am here."

Williams scrunched up his face like a child tasting something bitter. "In my business you learn not to rely on dolphin information. It tends to the fanciful."

"I won't argue with that. But the whale is dying. You may not believe the stories dolphins have told you about their God. But while we discuss theology, the whale's mass is slowly crushing its lungs. Don't your people have the respirator ready yet?"

Williams snapped his parasol shut and gestured with it. Ahmed lowered the crane. Marta, an auburn-haired beauty in a skimpy bathing suit, came down with it. She regarded Stasov with cool contempt, pulling up her upper lip to expose even white teeth. Stasov ignored her, as he did the turbaned, glaring Ahmed. Williams irritably waved Marta away. He carefully removed his white suit and finally stood, in paunchy dignity, wearing only a pair of red bikini shorts. Stasov also stripped.

The two men stepped onto the crane and were lifted up to the whale's back, which was warm and smooth under their bare feet. They were immediately soaked by the spray that played over the whale.

Williams pulled the crane's respirator nozzle over to the whale's blowhole, located asymmetrically on the top left side of the snout. He stimulated the proper acupressure points with an ultrasonic probe, anesthetizing the sensitive blowhole, then inserted the nozzle and adjusted the suction cups that held it firm. A signal to Ahmed, and a rush of air inflated the whale's lungs.

"We can give him a breath of air, but we're going to lose him," Williams said. "A lot of damage down below where you can't see it. He must have done a world-record jump from the looks of it. Cracked ribs, organ ruptures, internal hemorrhaging. A mess. Fine choice for a Bubble signaling the arrival of their God." He squinted out to sea. "So much for dolphin religion."

From the whale's back the two men could see the whole stretch of sea surrounding the island. Countless white splashes broke the otherwise calm water. Dolphins, hundreds of dolphins, were dancing in the sea. They surrounded the island out to the horizon. Williams stared out at them.

"You know, sometimes I understand why you did it, why you enslaved them and sent them to war. They're not good for much else." He looked at Stasov. "I was at Adak. You idiots called it Kagalaska because you couldn't read a map. I landed there with the 9th Marines. My ship, *McTeague*, was sunk by dolphin action. I saw them dead on the beach. Your dolphins, Stasov."

"I remember them," Stasov said softly. "I remember their names. It was a long time ago." He'd heard of Habib Williams and had hoped that the man would understand what had happened and respect him. But that was impossible.

"Maybe it seems that way." Williams was remorseless. How many of his friends had died in the gray seas at Kagalaska? "But your toys are still floating around, did you know that? Last night the cruise ship *Sagittarius* hit an unexploded mine and sank with all aboard. Four hundred or so dead. Good design." Williams shook his head in sardonic admiration.

"Where did this happen?" Stasov asked urgently.

"The Philippine Sea. Just off Mindanao."

"Do you know the exact time of the sinking?" A burst of dolphin military message traffic, overheard by Port Moresby . . .

Williams looked puzzled at Stasov's intentness. "I have no idea, Colonel."

"You don't—" Stasov stopped himself. He wished he could talk to Williams, but it was impossible. He wanted to tell this man that the *Sagittarius* had been sunk, not by a floating mine, but by deliberate dolphin action. That much was clear. He felt sick. What had he unleashed? Ten years ago, dolphins were cheery jumpers-through-hoops who danced around ships and got trapped in tuna nets. But last night they had chased a whale onto the rocks and sunk a ship full of innocent people.

"It's not much worth talking to you," Williams said. "We're all meeting in the water off Santa Barbara to negotiate relations between humans and dolphins. Great doings. But they won't let you go, will they? So there is some justice."

"I am forbidden to go to Santa Barbara," Stasov said. "I was blocked by the Japanese and Americans. But, Mr. Williams, this has nothing to do with the whale." He strove to retain a reasonable tone.

Williams snorted and looked away from him. Stasov shaded his eyes. Was she finally there, at the northern horizon? He watched as the huge white shape of the *Andrei Sakharov* pulled itself over the edge of the water. From this distance she looked pure, almost Japanese. Her rough welding and patched cables didn't show.

"We want the whale, Mr. Williams." His voice was distant. "We intend to take him over from you." He saw the whale soaring through the sky.

"What?" Williams followed Stasov's gaze. "Damn you, you can't have him."

"Is that your choice, Mr. Williams? The *Sakharov* is equipped with the full complement of systems for keeping the whale alive. It will die otherwise, within hours. You know that."

"You won't have this whale," Williams said. "I won't give him to the Shark of Uglegorsk. As soon as I saw who was lying here, I called the Americans." He nodded out over the sea. "There they are now."

Stasov looked out over the sea again. The blocky shape of an American warship had appeared on the horizon behind the Russian research vessel.

"AT THE MOMENT, WE ARE ALL VIOLATING THE SOVEREIGN territory of the Republic of the Maldives," Captain Enrique Battista of the U.S.S. *Moline* said. Everyone else regarded him wearily, annoyed at the intrusion of this side issue.

"Indian Ocean Sea Rescue goes everywhere," Habib Williams said. He once again wore his white suit, and Jolie, a noiseless Sinhalese from Sri Lanka, had found him a white topee to shade his bald head. "It's in our charter. Last year we rescued a beached humpback from Kerala—and they're at war. Everyone trusts us."

Captain Battista raised his eyebrows inquiringly at Stasov, who said, "The *Andrei Sakharov* has permission from the government of the Maldives to do cetacean research here. We arranged it in advance. A call to Male can confirm."

Battista shrugged and took off his uniform cap to wipe his forehead. He was a handsome, dark-skinned man with precise lips, who seemed to be slightly put off by Marta's swimsuit-clad presence as she solemnly observed the proceedings from her perch on the crane.

"Well, that seems to be in order then. Hmm." He peered up at the bulk of the whale, carefully expressionless, as if examining a gun turret during a surprise inspection. "In that case, perhaps someone will explain to me what I'm doing here." For a long moment there was no sound but the slap of the waves and the hiss of the nozzles as they sprayed water over the whale.

The tiny island was now crowded with people: a crew from the *Sakharov*, anxious to pull the sperm whale off the rock and into the rear bay of the ship; a detachment of marines from the *Moline*, armed and truculent; and a group of the *Moline*'s officers, including several Japanese.

"This is Colonel Ilya Sergeiivich Stasov," Williams said, gesturing. Battista inclined his head politely, giving no indication of recognizing the name. Stasov did the same in return. "He wishes to seize this whale. You must prevent him."

"I see," Battista said. He glanced over at the whale again, his expression indicating that he wished the damn thing would just vanish. "I must say, Colonel, that I find your presence here, demanding things, most distressing. Most distressing indeed. Washington's information has you some five hundred miles north of here."

Stasov had the sudden urge to tell Captain Battista that the United States did not manage the Indian Ocean. "We had information that brought us here." He raised his arm at the whale. "The whale is dying, Captain. I doubt it has more than an hour left. We must get it into the sea. We can discuss peripheral political issues afterward."

The *Moline* floated just off shore, blocky and ugly, like a pile of child's blocks strapped together and thrown into the water. She was covered with antennae but had few visible armaments. Stasov knew she could sink the *Sakharov* in an instant.

Stasov's mental universe had narrowed down to this whale. Whether or not he was expected to grab Clarence by his tail and fling him into outer space was an issue to be dealt with later. Acts of delphine terrorism and the possible arrival of the Messiah were both less important than the dying whale. Stasov's stomach was queazy and the sea seemed to be rocking back and forth as if being sloshed in a bowl. A cold, sticky sweat covered his body. The sun was impossibly hot.

Out in the sea the dolphins danced in agitation.

"Please," Stasov said. "It will take over an hour to pull the whale into the water. By that time he may be dead. With your assistance, Captain, we may yet save him. Can we keep the political discussions for afterward?" He stopped still and stared at the American.

"The Indian Ocean Peace Force's operations do not include—"

"Indeed, Captain Battista," said a woman's voice, "can't you see the man's right? Captain Mitsuoko, what do you think?"

Stasov turned slowly to look at Anna Calderone. She stood, face shaded by wide flowered hat, amid a group of naval officers. He hadn't seen her. Her eyes moved over him and she winked.

"I see no reason not to offer assistance," the Japanese officer said. Mitsuoko wore reflector sunglasses above his thin mustache.

Calderone looked toward Battista. Her coppery hair

was still short. She wore long, dangling earrings. She looked exactly as she had that last day in Manila. Stasov felt the year aboard the *Andrei Sakharov* dissolving into illusion. How could he ever have thought he had been living?

"With the *Moline*'s help, the job could be done in a quarter hour." Her voice was confident.

"Please, Ms. Calderone, I understand your interest—"

"Captain Battista," Captain Mitsuoko said. He turned his head slowly, like a weapon traversing the horizon. His sunglasses glittered. "Could you and I speak?" He stepped out of the group and walked, with slow, even steps, up to Battista. He wore decorations on his chest. Stasov recognized the battle ribbons from the Hokkaido campaign as well as one for the "recovery" of Sakhalin.

Battista's face froze. He turned from Mitsuoko and gazed at the *Moline*, his ship, the Stars and Stripes hanging limply from its stern. Since the Pacific War, the Japanese had provided vast amounts of financing to American military forces in the Pacific and Indian Oceans. Without Japanese money the Americans could not have afforded to keep their bases open, their ships sailing, their airplanes flying.

Battista stepped aside and he and Mitsuoko conferred. At one point they both stopped and stared at Stasov. Then they returned to their discussion.

The Americans kept the peace all along the coasts, from the Bay of Bengal through the Philippine Sea and across the Pacific, keeping trade routes open, demonstrating military force when necessary. Two years before, the ancient battleship *Wisconsin*, first floated a century ago, had steamed through the Sunda Strait, demonstrating to the insurgent Sumatran government the meaning of freedom of passage. It had been shelled, but its heavy steel armor, irreproducible in the metal-poor twenty-first century, had shrugged off the HE rounds like gnats. Under the protection of American guns and missiles, the Pacific economies boomed.

Quickly, rudely, Battista turned away from Mitsuoko and gestured brusquely to one of his officers, who brought up a radio relay. Everyone stood silently for some minutes while Battista linked through to the ship, up to a satellite, and back down to some office near Washington. While still talking, he waved Mitsuoko back over. Smiling as if receiving a call from some old friend, Mitsuoko spoke slowly into the phone. He then handed it back to Battista.

The Americans paid a price for Japanese funding, and Stasov was seeing it. Dependent on the Japanese, they were mercenaries—Hessians, a name with historical resonance, always used by American politicians anxious to terminate the Japanese-American "special relationship."

Battista hung up the phone and shoved it back at his aide as if the man had offended him deliberately.

Mitsuoko strolled back to Calderone. Battista turned to Williams. "Well?"

Habib Williams breathed a long, heavy sigh. His eyes stabbed at Stasov. "Captain Battista, the Colonel is right, I'm afraid. He is a criminal, and I don't believe he is here for any good purpose, but the whale . . . the whale."

"Mr. Wong!" Battista's voice was crisply decisive. "Please dismiss your men and put them at the disposal of the Indian Ocean Sea Rescue. Assist them in any way possible, and if that means standing still and doing nothing for two hours, that is what you will do. You will cooperate with the Russians as well. No friction will be tolerated."

"Yes, sir!" The rangy Marine lieutenant shouted some incomprehensible syllables at his men, then turned expectantly toward Williams. Williams didn't look happy.

Stasov looked at his own people. "You know the drill. The IOSR's procedures no doubt differ from ours. Take this into account but don't be backward about offering suggestions. Render all assistance. The sperm whale will end up in the rear bay of the *Sakharov*. Ask if Williams can use the rear bay's tackle. Their equipment looks more suitable for longer operations. We can pull faster. Tanya, you talk to Williams."

Tanya Shchedrina looked concerned. "Ilya, you seem upset. What's wrong?"

"Nothing's wrong, dammit. We just have a difficult job to do. Let's get on with it."

Williams gestured at Ahmed, then walked over to confer with Lieutenant Wong. Tanya Shchedrina joined them, somewhat to their discomfiture. Matters were settled quickly. Ahmed and Jolie attached a wide sling around the whale's tail while Marta started spraying a foam lubricant over the rocks, covering the path along which the whale would be dragged. The marines, ostensibly expressionless, watched her with covert, intense interest. Tanya radioed the *Sakharov*, and, using its side-maneuvering engines, it rotated smoothly around its midpoint like a compass needle. Captain Battista observed the operation with a slightly bored expression that did not conceal the fact that he missed nothing.

"It's been a long time, Ilya Sergeiivich," Anna Calderone said in Stasov's ear. "You look well."

"Better than after Homma. Scarcely well." He glanced

at her. She wore an amused smile, as if she'd been hiding from him for just a few minutes as part of a game.

"Come on." She took his arm. "We have some catching up to do." They strolled across the uneven rock, ignoring the glances of those who wondered how they had become friendly so quickly. "Somehow I thought I'd find you here. For days every cetacean in the Indian Ocean has been excited. None of them would tell us what it was about."

Stasov felt an overpowering weariness. "What are you doing here? I thought you were heading for Jupiter."

"Oh I am, I am. You don't think the way to Jupiter is straight up, do you?"

"Please, Anna. I'm in no mood for paradoxes." He stared away from her.

She ran her hand up and down his upper arm. "Oh, Ilya. Don't think I'm making fun of you. Will you *look at me*?"

He turned toward her. Her brown eyes peered into his as if into a dark box. "Why didn't you stay aboard the *Moline*?" he asked.

"You saw what happened. Without my suggestion, Battista might have waffled for even longer. What would that have meant to your precious whale? Besides, I wanted to see you. Does that make sense to you? Is that woman your lover? The plump one with the boobs and the butt. The one you sent to soften up Williams and the Americans."

"I suppose you might call Tanya that." Stasov felt like he had been honing that innocent woman as a weapon for precisely this situation. "Why?"

"No reason." Calderone looked annoyed with herself for asking. "How are you, Ilya?"

He remembered the feel of her body against his, in that hot room in Manila. Sometimes, if he hadn't kissed her for a moment, her lips would be salty with sweat, as salty as the sea. "I don't know," he managed to say. "I miss you."

"I miss you too." Her tone was matter-of-fact. It was something she'd learned to live with and didn't intend to do anything about.

"And the world is coming to an end." He turned and looked back at the shore. The whale was now fully tackled up and was moving, inch by painful inch, down toward the water. Stasov wondered if they could have managed to move it without the *Moline*'s assistance. He pointed down at it. "That's the first sign. A dolphin superstition, Williams called it."

Realization crossed her face. "So that's what they've been talking about."

"Who?"

"The orcas. I told you that the way to Jupiter isn't straight up. It's really the other way. I've been talking with a pod of orcas in the North Pacific, not far from your old haunts, as a matter of fact. They've been providing us with some interpretations of Jovian data—the stuff that may point to intelligent life. Their interpretations are . . . interesting."

He stopped, betrayed. "The orcas have been listening to Jovian data? I haven't heard anything about it. Not a thing."

"Does that piss you off?"

"Piss me—damn it, yes! They could have told me. They should have!"

"Do you have a right to know everything cetaceans do?" She was challenging.

"No, I don't have a right." His voice was low and bitter. "I don't have a right to anything."

"In that case—"

"But it's never been a matter of right. I had no right to force them to speak in the first place. I had no right to take them to war. I had no right to *free* them, to release them from their bounds. And I have no right to Jupiter. I understand that. Nevertheless, I will have it."

To his surprise she laughed, head thrown back. She was lovely, her teeth sharp and white against the red of her lips. "Ah, Ilya, you are a madman." Her voice was affectionate. "Is this the poor man I found at Homma, his life over?"

"I haven't changed my mind about that," Stasov said, nettled. "It's just that there are a few loose ends to clear up."

"Very tidy." She took his arm and pressed herself deliberately against him. He was excited and knew she could sense it. "How much of the rest of your life is it going to take?"

"The whole thing. Of course. Anna." He stopped and held her even though he knew they were perfectly visible from where the whale was being dragged into the sea. "God is rising. The dolphins have forced Her rising—or at least that's the way it seems—and I have to go along with it. Even if that means going to Jupiter." He stopped. "I'm not making any sense."

"No, you're not. Don't worry about it."

"Don't patronize me! I saw it. As I was drowning. A whale was diving into Jupiter. Not any whale." He pointed down at the bulk of Clarence as if he'd known it the whole time. "That one."

CAPTAIN BATTISTA INVITED HABIB WILLIAMS AND THE CREW of the *Andrei Sakharov* over to the *Moline* after the successful floating of Clarence.

The Americans fed them at the Barney Millfoil franchise that served as the frigate's aft mess, a mockup of an old saloon, complete with brass spittoons. The sailors ate and chatted as if everything were normal, the Japanese friendly and easy among them, eating steaks and potatoes like the rest. Stasov peered around at the bulls' horns on the walls, the buffalo heads, the cowboy hats, the saguaro cactuses, and wondered why a navy would decorate a ship in a style evolved hundreds of miles from water. Of course, the US Navy had not been responsible for the decoration, but rather the corporation which owned the Barney Millfoil chain. The Japanese government controlled the *Moline*'s missiles, Barney Millfoil owned her crew's stomachs, and what was left for the unfortunate Captain Battista?

Faith, loyalty, and duty, apparently. The Captain toyed with his chili, too hot for Stasov, raised on cabbage soup and dilled potatoes. The American seemed gloomy and irritated.

"I envy you, Mr. Stasov." He delicately refused to use Stasov's still-valid military title.

"How so?" Stasov asked, startled.

"Because you almost provoked a war all on your lonesome by threatening to hijack a cetacean from a neutral organization on an island belonging to a sovereign government." Battista put pieces of corn bread into his chili and then sank them by dropping pieces of beef on them. His eyes had the intentness of a boy playing at war.

"I'm not sure which part of that makes me a subject for envy." Battista made Stasov slightly nervous. Now that the crisis over the whale was over, he seemed to want to add it immediately to his store of military anecdotes, crises that were entirely about strong men standing face to face, with nothing of the fears or ideologies that had brought them to confrontation.

"All of it. My operations here are constrained by Washington."

And Tokyo, Stasov added to himself, though he did not say it. That would have been the height of impoliteness.

"I feel like an extended finger of some huge hand. I don't have any control." Stasov got the impression that the American would have liked to start a war over Clarence just to prove that he could.

Stasov shrugged. "The *Andrei Sakharov* is not a military vessel. That gives us more room to maneuver. Our charter is vague and we're not very expensive. She used to be an Aleksandr Brykin class submarine tender, and after the war it was either mothball her or convert her to a more useful purpose. So we chug around and talk to dolphins. No one supervises us because no one has to."

The music the Americans played was soft but pervasive, with a heavy, computerized beat. Aboard a Russian military vessel Stasov would have been hearing the thrum of the engines, the rumble of slapdash-designed plumbing, the squeal of under-lubricated joints, the hiss of the ventilation. He was surprised to find that he did not consider the American solution an improvement. He found himself trying to listen behind the music, to hear some indication that he was actually aboard a ship at sea rather than sitting in some bar in a shopping mall in California.

"Where did you fight during the Pacific War?" Battista asked.

Stasov had been afraid of that question. Battista obviously wanted to get into an involved reminiscence of war adventures. Stasov would sooner have reminisced about a painful prostate operation. "It's a ridiculous name for a war, don't you think, Captain Battista?"

"How so? The Pacific's where most of it happened."

"But 'pacific' means 'peaceful'. The Peaceful War. Someone on our side wanted to call it the Defensive War, the same way we call our part of the Second World War the Great Patriotic War."

Battista snorted. "Sure. Some defense: the Aleutians, Hokkaido, Korea . . ."

"Exactly. So, the Peaceful War it is."

"Some of our people wanted to call it World War Three. It wasn't that. Not quite. I served aboard the *Ernest J. King*. We were escorting the *Wainwright* on her way to Kagalaska when you sank her."

"I didn't sink her. The dolphins did." Kagalaska. At least Battista had accepted the Soviet name for the battle without protest.

"We never saw what hit us," Battista said admiringly. "It was incredible. Those damn dolphins had guts. It was a brilliant operation." He leaned forward. Stasov wondered how the American could get so excited over the sinking of a ship filled with his own countrymen. "You guys did some incredible stuff in that war. We'll be studying it at the Naval War College for years, I'm sure."

Instead of heroism and dramatic battles, Stasov tended to remember endless days in the dank passages of the *Nizhni Novgorod*, the poorly maintained fluorescent lights always flickering. Fetid air, bad food, grinding machinery, and the endless fear of waiting, waiting, knowing that at any instant a torpedo or an over-the-horizon missile might find the delicate aircraft carrier and obliterate it with no time for the men to collect their thoughts and prepare for the end. Heroism indeed. In some ways, the faux-Western ambience of the *Moline*'s mess was indeed preferable. It at least made clear the disconnection between the actions of the sailors aboard a modern naval vessel and their ultimate fate. So why shouldn't they eat fajitas and look at holographically simulated mesas while the computers and phased-array radars above their heads decided what to do?

"I fought at Unimak, later," Battista said. "You weren't there, were you?"

"No." Stasov sighed. "By then I was transferred to the Hokkaido operation." He didn't want to talk about it.

"Hokkaido." Battista breathed the word like a benediction. "It should have succeeded, do you know that? It should have succeeded."

Stasov glanced around. The Japanese officers still sat among the Americans, eating cottage fries and steak covered with barbecue sauce. Captain Mitsuoko chatted with an American lieutenant. Allies since 1945, almost a century. Battista didn't sound as if he liked the idea.

In a corner, directly under a pair of bull's horns, Stasov saw Anna Calderone eating with Habib Williams. Something about their hunched postures hinted at the intensity of their discussion. Stasov felt a chill. He didn't think it took much paranoia to assume that they were talking about him.

"It didn't succeed," Stasov said. "Just as well. What would we have done with Hokkaido? The solution to our problems was elsewhere."

"Do you mean that?" Battista said. "Failure left you a second-rate power. Before the war you had reconquered most of Central Asia. Now Armenia pushes you around. Lithuania. Doesn't it bother you sometimes, what could have happened? You could control the western rim of the Pacific Ocean."

"And you the eastern? Nonsense, Captain Battista. The twentieth century belonged to the US and the USSR. Even after renaming one of them the Soviet Republics, the twenty-first belongs to someone else."

Battista turned his eyes away. "Did your war ever end, Mr. Stasov? Your military dolphins still roam the seas. Why? I wonder. Do they ever act? Do you know what they do? Have they somehow pushed us to the negotiating . . . pool at Santa Barbara?"

"You're becoming overheated, Captain." Stasov stood up, his heart pounding.

Battista looked up, almost pleading, a warrior caught in an age of technicians, where he was of less account than a fire-control computer or an over-the-horizon radar, reaching out to another man he thought felt the same.

"Don't feel guilty about it," Battista said. "You lost, that's all. Nothing to feel guilty about."

"I don't feel guilty about anything," Stasov answered. "I should go check on the whale." He walked away.

"Colonel Stasov." It was Habib Williams, a little bald man with a wheezy voice. He looked determined. Stasov, for an instant, was afraid of him. "What are you going to do with Clarence, now you've got him?"

"Save his life. What I came here to do in the first place."

Williams raised his hand, conciliatory. "Don't get all hot under the collar, Colonel. Saving his life's just the first step for you, isn't it?"

"I—"

"Come *on*. Whales beach themselves every day, in every sea in the world. I checked the worldwide database just before I came here. Just the way you can, any time you want to. There's a right whale on an ice flow in Greenland. Three pilot whales on a beach in Oregon. And another sperm, a young one, on the sands south of Rotterdam. Though that one's dead already. They're probably bulldozing it right at this moment. So what makes this one so goddam important?"

"He's the Bubble," Stasov said, even though he knew this piece of dolphin religion would infuriate the other.

Instead, it seemed to relax him. Williams smiled. "Sure he is. And I'm the Wandering Jew. Never mind." He leaned a hand against the wall in the elaborate casualness of a man about to score a point. "In two weeks I'm scheduled to testify at the Santa Barbara Treaty Conference. We'll be discussing the provisions about using cetaceans—any cetaceans—as experimental animals. As you may know, without special permission, the interim agreement reached just after the Pacific War prohibits any current experimental use of cetaceans. *Any* use."

Stasov drew in a slow breath. "Without special permission."

"From the orcas." Williams smiled wickedly. "You have to go into the water with them and ask them. Otherwise what you intend to do with Clarence, whatever it is, is a crime. An act of war, if you will, against the cetaceans. Well, Colonel Stasov?"

"Thank you, Mr. Williams. I will certainly ask that question. I have other matters to discuss with the orcas, at any rate." Black fins cut foaming water. Teeth sank into screaming flesh.

"Sure, sure." Williams was taken aback for an instant, but quickly recovered. "You're scared spitless. You don't want to ask the orcas if Ilya Stasov can have a sperm whale to play with for his very own because you know what they would say. And I'm not sure you would live through a refusal."

"You're right," Stasov said, thinking of a whale flying to Jupiter. "I probably wouldn't live through a refusal. Good luck with your testimony." He turned on his heel and left the other man standing in the hallway.

After failing to find Anna Calderone by wandering around the *Moline*, Stasov decided to let her find him. He stood at the rail, looking off at the rusting white shape of the *Sakharov*. He was an outsider there, after everything. The last place he had felt he belonged had been Homma. Homma, with Makarygin.

Hoping he was not violating some American Navy security precaution, Stasov unreeled a long cord on his transducer and cast it into the sea like a fisherman. Loudest in his earphones were the clunking, grinding sounds of the ships.

"I have the Bubble," he said. "Where is God's Echo?" He could hear his own voice boom as the transmission was picked up at the *Sakharov* and regenerated through its powerful underwater speakers. "I wish to speak with God's Echo."

Anna Calderone's clear scent reached him an instant before she did. He caught her, laughing, in his arms. "You can't stay away from it, can you?" she said. "You're always yelling something into the sea."

"I'm just following Habib Williams's advice."

"Don't be spiteful." She looked into his eyes. "What have you seen, Ilya?"

"I don't know. I think I can find out." The recorders on the *Sakharov* would catch any reply. He reeled his line back in. "Can you give me what you have on the orca work with the Jovian data?"

Her eyes widened. "That stuff's confidential. Highly. Ilya, I can't let you see it."

He didn't say anything, but just looked at her. In a few seconds, high color appeared in her cheeks. She turned her head, so that her earrings flickered. "Come on, then. We can talk about it when we get down there."

Kissing her made him forget that he was in yet another cabin aboard yet another metal ship. She pulled away. "You don't think kissing me's going to get you a look at that stuff, do you?"

"No," he said. "I know you won't let me see it. I just wanted to get you down here."

"You always were such a clever man."

He reached to hold her again. There was a knock on the door. It was Captain Mitsuoko, reflector shades gone from amused-looking eyes. He glanced at both of them, bowed slightly, and handed Stasov a recording chip and a tiny Japanese player.

"Your vessel received an urgent message," he said. "They thought it important enough that they sent a messenger over with it."

Stasov wondered at Mitsuoko's timing. Had he managed this on his own account, or was he playing another role now, watching the situation on Battista's behalf? Stasov did not pretend to understand the delicate pavane of Japanese-American relations. He clicked the chip into the machine and listened. Recorded on it was a single clear dolphin voice, speaking softly enough that only the *Sakharov*'s recording gear could hear it. That, Stasov reflected, was remarkably delicate for dolphins, who ordinarily had no sense whatsoever of privacy.

"Ilya Stasov," the dolphin said. "Come to the sea. One week. One hundred forty-five degrees ten minutes fifty-three seconds west, forty-four degrees seven minutes twelve seconds north. Thou art awaited." The last sentence was in orca.

Stasov erased the chip, handed the machine back to Mitsuoko, and bowed him out of the room.

"What is it?" Anna asked in concern. "What did it say?"

He leaned his head on her shoulder. "I am asked to meet the orcas. In the sea off Hokkaido."

"Ilya!" she said sharply. "That's dangerous. You know that. You don't have to go."

"Yes I do."

CHAPTER TWELVE

2025

"**. . . E**VERY ONE OF THOSE DEATHS IS ON MY CON-science. From my first research at Uglegorsk to the last days of the Pacific War, I never let up on them. I drove them before me. Even now, if I close my eyes, I can see the bodies piled on the beaches at Kagalaska and Oshi. The vision doesn't let me sleep."

That wasn't the image that kept him awake, but at least it had the merit of being believable. A whale diving into Jupiter just confused matters. Stasov pulled out the map of Hokkaido and looked at it again. He'd marked the battle sites and annotated each with the number of dolphin casualties. Doodling idly, he drew a tiny spouting whale in the Sea of Okhotsk, then stared at it in dismay. It made mock of all the meticulous calculations of death. He started to cross-hatch it out, then thought better of it.

"There is no resolution possible. I can make no atonement. What I have done, I have done. The contradiction is impossible for me to live with. And so I won't live with it. I have come here, to Hokkaido, to make my last peace."

Stasov's pen scratched across the paper. A suicide note typed on a computer screen didn't seem proper. A handwritten note had all of those uneven lines that characterized a man. When someone else held it in his hand, he would know what it was.

"My only regret—" He crossed it out. The words vibrated behind their bar of ink. He wrote again. "My only regret is that Anna Calderone never understood. She was the one person I needed. Without her I had no one to whisper secrets to." And that was the disadvantage of writing by hand: everyone could see your indecisions and revisions. "I hope that if she reads this she will see something about what drove me. My actions came out of ignorance, but ignorance is no excuse when understanding would have shown the truth. I always cared for her." Stasov stared down at the betraying words. It was unfair to leave her with such a burden. Was he really still so angry with her, despite their meeting aboard the *Moline*? He reached to crumple the note, to start it over, to wipe out what he had written, but stayed his hand. Instead, he signed it "Ilya Sergeiivich Stasov" in both Latin and Cyrillic characters, put it in an envelope, and sealed it. He would live, and she would never read it.

Like all interiors at Yumeji Monastery, the room was spare and featureless, its lack of specific detail supposedly emphasizing the arbitrary nature of reality. Stasov wasn't sure that it actually had that effect. Its austere elegance instead caused some doubt as to the evil of loving the physical world. But he was just a guest and thought it impolite to point this out.

He pushed a button on the table.

A shaven-headed monk appeared in the doorway. His name was Hideo and he was a former Japanese soldier. He stood motionlessly.

Stasov held the envelope and the folded map out to him.

Hideo shook his head. "Put them in your personal effects, in a place which would be typical for you."

"The pocket into which I usually put my suicide notes?" Hideo was expressionless. "Very well. I also talked about the Hokkaido battles with the cabdriver. He wanted to tell me about the stand his unit had made at Ashiyoro. He will be able to provide corroborative testimony, if any is needed."

"Excellent. The aerobody is almost ready to depart. So, if there is nothing else . . ." Hideo made the low moaning orca sound indicating closure and moved away soundlessly.

Stasov stepped out through the hall into a courtyard. Yumeji Monastery was a set of low, curved-eave buildings on the rocky Shiretoko Peninsula in east Hokkaido. A small, struggling institution before the Pacific War, its quixotic efforts to convert the orcas to its peculiar brand of Buddhism had led to a boom, and it now had almost a hundred monks.

The buildings harkened back to an earlier Japan, full of sliding wood panels and simple, elegant rooms, the entire complex dominated by a seven-stepped pagoda with extravagant roofs, the only lovely building Stasov had seen in modern Japan. It did not surprise him that most of the monks at Yumeji were not Japanese, but came from all over the world. Native cultures were often best appreciated by foreigners. The multinational, polyglot nature of the monastery had led to

the adoption of a part-human, part-orca lingua franca
with a simplified grammar for daily communication,
a language that had delighted Stasov. Eventually that
language, or a similar one, could become the common
language of cetacean and human.

He stopped on a rocky flat that overhung the ocean.
They were not far from Sakhalin and the water looked
as it did in his memories of Uglegorsk. Pods of orcas
hunted under that water. The monks of Yumeji acted
as their human interpreters. Stasov walked on down
the crushed-stone path.

The Main Hall of Yumeji was dominated by a single
painting. A blue whale rose in agony out of the water,
blood streaming down its sides. It strove upward.
Dramatic waves of blue-green surrounded it, ambig-
uous, neither water, earth, nor clouds. Perched on
the waves were calmly smiling bodhisattvas, those
who had refused Nirvana to help others on their way
to enlightenment. In their hands they held harpoons
tipped with gleaming steel. Several had cast their
harpoons into the whale's side and held the lines
taut, gesturing gracefully with the other hand. Spread
across the sky above them, like a sunset illusion, was
the Japanese character Satori: Enlightenment.

Stasov knew that many cetaceans had believed the
last blue whale was the Foreswimmer. It had lived a
long time in the seas, slowly searching for another of
its kind. When it died, some dolphins had thought
the world was near its end. Entire dolphin pods had
beached themselves and no human had understood,
because Ilya Stasov had not yet forced the dolphins
to speak.

He'd seen pictures of the blue whale floating somewhere in the South Atlantic, a victim of some systemic
poisoning, a great, rotting mass infested with writhing

worms, sharks tearing at its liquefying flesh. And the dolphins had expected that whale to call forth their God. When it died, they must have thought themselves surely damned. They might have been right. And here was the blue whale's image, co-opted for human purposes.

Bodhisattvas assisted the faithful on their way to Nirvana. The saints with their harpoons in the painting implied that this assistance could take any form necessary. Who knew more about Enlightenment than a bodhisattva? And who was to judge *his* actions? Stasov smiled to himself. General Lefortov, ordering the assault on Kagalaska, and Colonel Yokota, commanding Camp Homma, had been his personal bodhisattvas on his road to enlightenment. He doubted they had recognized their role.

Stasov stopped by his guest room and, as requested, put the suicide note in a pocket of his bag and shoved it under his cot. He hefted his underwater gear and headed for the aerobody.

THE AEROBODY HAD DEVELOPED A NOTICEABLE LIST TO STARboard and vibrated vigorously, as if drilling through air suddenly solid. The airship's pilot, Benjamin Fliegle, took a slow sip of the steaming green tea in his stoneware cup and set it back in its heated, gimbaled holder on the control board. The sleet was heavy outside and the windshield wiper, inadequately heated, stuttered under a thick layer of ice. Fliegle, his small shaven head perched on top of his orange-saffron robe like a potato on a pumpkin, leaned forward and pounded on the windshield with his fist. The wiper tossed a chunk of wet ice and moved more smoothly. The aerobody tilted perilously and he grabbed the wheel. "Pesky thing," he muttered.

Stasov had been looking out at the gray, wave-torn sea, reflecting that it was incapable of remembering anything. Somewhere beneath that water lay the hulks of invading battleships and the length of the Japanese carrier *Hiryu*, the first ship sunk by dolphins, but the waters themselves raced along unconcerned. Waves could pass through each other and continue completely unaffected. Fliegle jerked the aerobody back to horizontal, and Stasov, stumbling, grabbed at a strap above the porthole.

It pulled loose and he went sliding across the floor, fetching painfully up against the post of the pilot's seat. He sat up and looked at the fragment of strap he held in his hand. It was folded paper colored to look like the plastic of the other safety straps.

Stasov's lunch just before takeoff had consisted of twelve pieces of sushi. One had been a small plastic wind-up toy, complete with tiny wheels and a winding knob, that looked like a piece of hamashi, and one of his chopsticks had gone limp halfway through the lunch like a strand of overcooked spaghetti. The esoteric Buddhist monks of Yumeji Monastery, sitting on their rocky height, spending their time communicating with orcas, had decidedly odd ways of showing their belief in the nonexistence of the world, which was *maya*, illusion.

Fliegle continued to pilot the craft, humming some popular tune, unconcerned about the fate of his passenger. Stasov rubbed the back of his head, which was ringing from its collision with the pilot's seat. One of the traditions of Japanese Zen Buddhism was the *koan*, a paradoxical statement intended to free the monks from a false reliance on the power of reason, forcing them into a receptivity to spiritual enlightenment. If koans were jokes, then the monks of Yumeji practiced practical koans. This was Stasov's first indication that the practical koans of Yumeji might actually turn out to be dangerous. A broken neck was perhaps a small price for enlightenment, but it was not an item he was prepared to pay for just yet. He put the origami strap in his pocket as a souvenir and an object for meditation.

"Benjamin," Stasov said, getting to his feet, "how long have you been at Yumeji?"

"Let me put it this way," Fliegle said, running his hand over his shaved scalp. "When I came there, I had all my hair."

"Another life, in other words."

"There are a variety of words. But let's not bore each other by a vague discussion of the falseness of words. Words, like safety straps, are often extremely useful things."

"Each orca speaks, what, a dozen languages? They must feel words are important." Stasov paused, looking at the shaven back of Fliegle's neck. He'd deliberately misstated the case, knowing that an uncorrected error could often force even the most reticent to talk.

"Not a dozen different languages," Fliegle said. "A dozen grammars. The words are largely the same."

"Their meaning changes depending on where they are in a sentence. How can you ever be sure of what they are saying?"

"We have derived a meaning from them. Much the same way you derive your opinion of the world from your experience of it. Is your opinion correct?"

"I'm still alive," Stasov said with a sense of taking up a false position. "I must have figured out some part of the truth."

Fliegle drove in for a touch. "Will your death prove your opinion wrong?"

Stasov shrugged. "It could just prove that the truth has changed and my formerly impeccably correct opinion is now wrong. Arbitrary authority can always overcome reason. And there's nothing more arbitrary than death."

"More likely," Fliegle said after a pause, "your opinion has become so at variance that you have been sent back to start over again. Keep what little you have learned, and the next time you will go slightly farther."

"Arbitrary authority again. Nothing I can do about it."

"The path is twisting and marked with false signs, but Nirvana lies at the end." Fliegle's voice had a serene certainty. "It may seem arbitrary. It remains Nirvana."

"Is there only one Nirvana?" Stasov asked. "Or are there any number of false ones, indistinguishable from the real?"

"Nirvana is beyond existence and nonexistence."

"That statement would be impossible in the orca grammar called Undistributed Logical, where each word has only one meaning and the sum of a statement and its opposite form a unity." Orca grammar was often bewildering, changing its deep structure from one sentence to another. Many of its complexities were still unknown to human beings, though Stasov suspected that the monks of Yumeji understood more than they had let any other humans know.

"True," Fliegle said. "Which is why I did not use Undistributed Logical to make the statement. That grammar has a limited structure and isn't applicable to the argument. I also didn't make any reference to Hegelian dialectic, because the relation between existence and nonexistence is not dialectical."

Stasov laughed. "Are you sure? If existence is thesis and nonexistence antithesis, perhaps Nirvana is synthesis. Together, Benjamin, we may have discovered dialectical Buddhism."

Fliegle waved his hands around his head as if bothered by insects. "Argument is a logical process. It's not relevant here. Nirvana, the state of freedom from desire, is our liberation from the Wheel on which we trudge. It's not a place, the conclusion of a syllogism, or a relation of the means of production, even spiritual production."

Apparently Stasov's own self-created koans were not to Fliegle's liking. This did not surprise him. It had been his experience that those who claimed to live without structure were often enslaved to structures that they did not perceive. An acknowledged structure could at least be argued with and modified, but an unacknowledged structure exercised an undisputed tyranny.

Stasov pulled down a chair from the wall and, after checking it for firmness, sat down on it. Despite his week of silent meditation at Yumeji, looking out over moss-covered rocks at the disdainful unconcern of the unchanging, ever-changing sea, his heart was pounding so hard that he thought he could feel his ribs flexing with each beat. All through his little intellectual discussion with Fliegle, he had felt like screaming. He couldn't remember the last time he had been so terrified.

He braced his feet on a strut and pressed his back against the wall. The thrum of the aerobody's engines filled his body. The mental image of a machine's dutiful labor was sometimes more relaxing than anything nature could offer, since so much of nature seemed to imply volition. He clasped his hands, the fingers struggling symmetrically against each other. Somewhere in the sea below him, an orca was prowling. He had to ask the orca a question, and the consequences of the asking were entirely unknown. Some dolphins saw death as an orca without an echo, smooth and silent. Death was always hungry and always captured its prey.

The rear hatch opened and admitted a figure in heavy insulation, as well as a blast of wet, freezing air.

"How does it look?" Fliegle said.

"Not bad," Olivia Knester said as she stripped her suit off. "Just noisy. I'll overhaul it in the shop when we get back to Kushiro, but it won't give us any trouble now." Now naked, Knester also pulled on an orange-saffron robe. She was a chunky, middle-aged woman with extravagant curled eyebrows that tried to compensate for the shaved skull above them. "However, Benjamin . . ."

"Yes, Olivia?"

"The engine isn't buying your theories about the virtual identities of reciprocating parts. It will not 'wear into perfection', it will wear into junk. Keep the crankcase oil full. Until we achieve satori and leave the Wheel, we must keep it lubricated." She turned to Stasov. "Are you ready?"

Her green eyes examined him coolly. At Yumeji, no one had mentioned his history or tried to use his old military rank. But sometimes he caught an appraising glance like this one, a glance searching for an explanation and not finding one. Without Stasov's actions, there probably would have been no Yumeji Monastery. But those actions had had nothing to do with Buddhism or Nirvana.

Silently he helped her put her tools back into their rack. At first he was suspicious, wondering if one of the wrenches would turn into a writhing snake in his grasp, but Knester's liking of practical koans apparently did not extend to the tools she needed for her job.

She turned to Stasov. "Put on your suit. We should find the proper pod of orcas soon. Benjamin, it's time to start listening."

Fliegle dropped the aerobody's altitude to fifty feet and cut back the engines until they moved at twenty miles an hour. A lever on the panel released the hydrophone. As Stasov pulled on his wet suit, Fliegle put in his earphones and leaned back in his seat with his eyes closed. The altitude continued to drop.

"Benjamin!" Knester said sharply.

The nose went back up. "Sorry."

Stasov put on his fins, fitted underwater lenses into his eyes, and bit down on the breathing gear. Then he attached the microphone to his throat, strapped the transducer and signal processor to his chest, and activated the bone conduction speakers behind his jaw hinge. Orca speech included frequencies from 5 Hz to 80 kHz, far beyond the range of human hearing. His equipment compressed and processed the information so that he could communicate.

The philosophy of the monks did not comfort Stasov, but then, comfort was not its goal. Everyone wanted to escape the Wheel but everyone was bound to it. In the dolphin view death was the only possible escape, an escape the Buddhists did not permit themselves. Stasov found himself more dolphin than Buddhist.

Fliegle leaned his head back and shrugged. The bay doors behind Stasov swung open. He put his foot into a sling and swung himself out. The harsh gray wind caught him and jerked him out behind the aerobody.

A sound like ripping burlap, and the aerobody, backing engines, stopped relative to the water. The sling lowered and Stasov slipped gently into the water. As soon as he let go, the sling whipped back into the air and the aerobody accelerated. Stasov slid his head under and felt the hungry cold of the ocean.

He listened to the chatter in his earphones, sorting signals from noise. As he dropped, the disruptive surface chop grew quieter, until he could hear. A long descending note rumbled, found the resonant frequencies of his joints, and intensified until his entire body was in pain. An orca's shout could break bones, rupture internal organs, and fill the lungs with blood. The orca's voice died away, then sounded deeper, and he was suddenly filled with unreasoning terror. Orcas' voices could kill, or they could stimulate a fear response, pump adrenaline into the human bloodstream, and race the human heart. Cetacean tricks were old to Stasov. Somewhere inside his mind a stopcock opened, the dark waters of fear drained, and he was calm again.

"Greetings, Stasov." The cool voice used the sliding tones of the simple orca dialect used for speaking to children or humans, the basic grammar. The voice was familiar. Where had he heard it before? "Thou hast words to speak. Speak them then, for thoughts must be herded and swallowed, lest they escape to the open sea." Of course.

"It is a long way from Kagalaska, Bottom-Thumper." Stasov used the slightly contemptuous nickname this orca had earned for his childhood habit of bumping the hulls of Japanese fishing boats. "I trust your hunger has been stayed?"

"My hunger is infinite." The orca rumbled his amusement. "But Kagalaska was not the first place we heard each other's echoes. It was in the seas off your research station. A different sea than this one."

Stasov remembered screaming sea lions on the rocky beach and the thump as an orca passed underneath the boat he and Theodoros were in. An orca could hunt a hated enemy for years. Their patience seemed infinite. He didn't think Bottom-Thumper had known that he and Stasov would someday meet, but it was impossible to tell what orcas knew.

"But thou art still spoiled food. I must content myself with swallowing the minds of men, leaving their bodies to the sharks and fishes."

"Are you still chasing prime numbers?" Stasov asked.

"I am. I taste the fins of the Goldbach Conjecture. Soon I will sink my teeth into it. It shall not escape."

Bottom-Thumper was a mathematician highly respected among both humans and orcas. Dolphins, on the other hand, had no interest whatsoever in mathematics. "Your prey weakens," Stasov said politely.

"Do not seek to distract me with minnows. Let loose thy desires and get thee from my sea!" The thunder of Bottom-Thumper's voice buzzed in Stasov's ribs. He hung alone in darkness, only the speed of Bottom-Thumper's replies indicating the orca's proximity.

"The Bubble Has Risen," Stasov said. The last blue whale had died and rotted. And now the Bubble had finally risen, in the form of a desperately wounded sperm whale. "The Foreswimmer cast himself out from the sea."

"Why dost thou inform me of the obvious?"

"Because I want to know what the hell you're doing!" Stasov adjusted the volume on his transducer until he was bellowing as loudly as the orca.

In response, the orca was silent. Stasov heard the rumble of a distant finback whale giving a ranging signal.

At last Bottom-Thumper spoke. "You have a question, then."

"Yes." Stasov shivered as the sea's cold penetrated his suit. Orcas would answer questions. But they would not be asked frivolously and their price for an answer was high. "The answer is of interest to all of us. Change is coming. The Foreswimmer is a sign. The sea has grown too small."

Bottom-Thumper didn't need to think about it. "We fight men in this sea. We sink their vessels as we could not sink the wooden long ships." No orcas had lived in the Aegean during the collapse of the Cretan Thalassocracy and the seaborne Mycenaean invasion of Crete, but the myths of that time were the common property of all cetaceans. "But thou art correct: this sea is grown too small. If God rises, the sea will change."

"And you wish the change."

"I shall not argue theology with thee, human. God is many things. She is the echo of all of our voices together. We echo-locate the future and She returns if thus She pleases. Without Her only our deaths can change the universe."

There was an instability between cetaceans' will and the means available to them. There was little they could do to affect the universe. Water resisted even as it allowed them to move, and their sense of evading its resistance was a constant triumph. They had no hands, no limbs of any sort, and could physically change nothing. Only their deaths—if done correctly—made an act meaningful.

Try as he might, Ilya Stasov could not manage to feel that way about his own death.

"Will you answer a question?" He was now committed, even to the extent of his life. But he had to know. Unfortunately, as a necessary consequence, asking the question involved putting himself here in the black water, at the mercy of an orca who could swallow him in one bite. No one would hear of it. It was part of the agreement he had reached with Yumeji Monastery. If the orca, for whatever reason, rage or petulance, decided that his destruction was necessary to maintain a sense of balance, that was Stasov's problem. The aerobody would search briefly for him, but there would be no report of his death, no investigation. And his suicide note, safely in his baggage, would explain any questions anyone needed to ask. The Yumeji monks were used to dealing with orcas.

"If it is a proper question, I shall." Bottom-Thumper's voice was calm. "But I will allow thee this, without recompense. The Leviathans of Jove speak words. We have been granted the correction of their voices. They seek communion. Art willing to give it?"

Anna Calderone had linked her cetacean skills with her urge to the planets, getting the orcas to decipher messages from Jupiter.

"Communion is not mine to give," Stasov said. "What are the Jovians saying?"

"Their words, if such they are, are less clear than thine. But they long for the contact. They desire the communion. They leave their sea open to thee. Wilt take the opportunity?"

Stasov was stunned, but collected himself. This was incredible news if true: intelligent inhabitants of Jupiter were inviting contact from humans—and intelligent cetaceans as well. But was the orca telling the truth? Stasov didn't put it past them to make up some words from mythical Jovians in order to further their own ends. Or even as a joke. Orcan jokes tended to be complex and cruel.

"Will you answer a question, or should I return to the air?" Stasov tried to give his words a tone of exasperation. He wasn't even sure that exasperation was an emotion an orca could feel. Or perhaps it was that they seldom felt anything else.

"Think that thou knowest enough to ask a proper question? Listen and be forewarned. The Foreswimmer signals the arrival of God. Thy question sends its echo before it. We turn in response."

"I had a vision," Stasov said. "I was knocked into the water, and saw a whale dive into Jupiter—"

"Thy petty mental affairs are as one krill in a whale's baleen!" Bottom-Thumper shouted. "I care not."

"But I have to know—were you responsible?"

Stanley Pressman of Christchurch claimed that dolphins, with their extensive perception of the internal body states of humans, could directly affect emotions through subliminal vibrations. Pressman himself suspected his colleagues of plotting to steal his results and had installed baffles in the metal pipes leading into his house to prevent dangerous delphine vibrations from propagating through his plumbing. Whether his paranoia was the result of dolphin contact was unknown. But Stasov feared that the image of the whale had been implanted in his mind while he floated in the still waters of the Truk Atoll.

"Thou believest that we have given thee your visions? That we turned our courses to follow thine? Arrogant human! Thy thoughts are thy own and we have no interest in them. Thy visions are false echoes, defects in thy shrunken brain. Fortunate thou art that I do not count that as thy question, for then thee would be misfortunate indeed, to have traded so much for so little. But ask!"

"You have given us a whale. What are we to do with him?"

There was a long silence, so long that Stasov wondered if the orca had simply turned tail and swum away to leave him floating alone. It would have been an act of petty contempt.

"The dolphins spoke truly, then. At last we have in our sea a human who can demand the proper answers. Well sounded, Ilya Stasov. So this we, as all cetaceans, can grant thee: sink thy teeth into thy quarry. Realize thy vision. Give substance to its echoes. Thy whale shall go to Jupiter. And we shall follow."

Stasov had always suspected all orcas of insanity. This confirmed it. "Your words are distorted by upwellings. Their meaning is lost."

"Thou miserable squirming jellyfish!" The voice buzzed in his teeth. "Thy visions are false eyespots that mislead from thy essential nullity. Our thoughts are not necessarily thine for the taking. The whale shall go."

It took an instant for Stasov to realize what was wrong. The great orca, his mind rich with knowledge, did not know how to get the whale out of the sea. That was knowledge beyond his province.

"Shall we then do as we did with dolphins? Shall we carve his flesh and sheathe him in metal?"

"Rip his innards out and feast upon them. Then send him forth into the seas of that thing you call a planet. This I say to thee. Thou seekest meaning, but when it swims by thy face, thou shovest thy head into bottom muck."

Had he expected the orca to be grateful for a solution? Stasov was no longer sure what message he had hoped from this oracle. "You are a slow hunter. The complexities of thought escape you and conceal themselves. You feast on mere oversimplifications. The financial considerations alone . . . you speak of Leviathans. The beasts in that sea of finance make yours look like minnow."

"Oh, Man. Jellyfish climbed up on shore to escape our teeth and our cleverness. There, amidst other jellyfish, ye thought ye grew wise. In the sea again, all ye recognize your error. Do you hear the echoes of thine, Ilya Sergeiivich Stasov?"

"Your words have ornamental fins," Stasov said stubbornly. "But even the solid rhetoric of an orca does not affright me. Do you understand the meaning of the word 'labyrinth'? The way from here to what you are saying is such a labyrinth."

"Then start forth. We shall provide a guard to windward who will be the Echo of God."

Stasov felt a surge of joy. There, at last, it was! "The Messiah."

"Thy term, inadequate and misleading, but it will do."

The Foreswimmer, the First Bubble Rising from the spout of God as She came up from the deepest bottoms of the sea, signaled the arrival of that being called God's Echo: the dolphin equivalent of the Messiah. The name was literally God's Echo-Location Signal. That creature was God's ranging sound into the cetacean world. The information it sent back determined God's actions. The dolphins gleefully chasing the innocent whale onto the rocks had also been chanting the imminent arrival of their Messiah, also called God's Remora.

"Excellent," Stasov said, using the ironic praise given to an ill-behaved child. "Now not only do we need to haul a cyborg sperm whale into orbit around Jupiter, we need to create a way of getting an orca—"

"Not an orca! The Voice of God echoes without speaking, and the Echo is not an orca!" Bottom-Thumper was suddenly in a high rage, his syllables ragged like fish with their heads bitten off. The orca spoke in the odd grammatical tense used either to describe dreams, or to make statements so true they were apodictic, such as "All things die" or "Before my conception I did not exist." Stasov could barely follow the grammar. "Yet perhaps he may fail! The testing is not complete."

"Watch your rectum," Stasov said in dolphin, recalling the insult he had made to Bottom-Thumper when they first met in the bloody waters off Kagalaska. "The walrus is still awaiting your pleasure. What are you talking about?"

The orca went silent for a long moment. "I should have eaten thee then, Stasov, in that swarming, evil-tasting sea. But my belly was full of men. For the last time, I fear. Thou hast the Foreswimmer, a wounded sperm whale ye shall lift to Jupiter, a planet none of us sea dwellers has ever seen. God's Remora must accompany the whale, for the Time of the Breath is near. Remoras attach themselves to God, and orcas try to pull them loose. Perhaps this one too will come loose to our jaws. Go now to the Aegean Dolphin Sanctuary. There is thy goal. And much good luck may thou and all thy fellow humans have with whom thee will find there."

And then he laughed. And laughed. And *laughed*, a sound like an immense train at a grade crossing. Razor-edged, their thoughts suffused with blood even as they reasoned their way through the most subtle philosophies, bitter thinkers on the end of all, dispensers of justice and death, orcas laughed, long, hard, and often. Bottom-Thumper's laughter stopped.

"I have answered thy question. Art willing to pay the price?"

"I am, whatever it is." Stasov could not slow the pounding of his heart.

"Float out thy limbs and remain still. Well met, then, Ilya Sergeiivich Stasov."

Stasov relaxed his arms and legs and floated spread-eagled. His heart pounded at the back of his throat. Had he indeed come here to be told such a ludicrous impossibility? Was that what he was going to pay for? Suddenly, silently, the smooth shape of the orca sped by, thirty feet long, black, powerful, and vanished again.

The pain was as sudden as the smash of an ax. Stasov twisted his body in agony and managed to activate the buoyancy harness. It righted him and carried him to the surface. He spit water, gasped in the cold air, and was finally able to scream.

The aerobody floated overhead in the pewter sky, a blunt-nosed wedge with two propellers flickering aft. It turned lazily around and drifted over him, buzzing like an immense insect. A harness lowered and scooped him up delicately. The sea opened around him. He looked down. Scarlet drops of blood fell past his dangling feet, the only flecks of color against the gray of the sea and sky. Makarygin's blood had flecked the golf green. A six-foot-long hooked dorsal fin cut the surface of the water. The orca's head was just visible, water flowing over it in a smooth layer. Bottom-Thumper spouted once and vanished.

Knester was ready with salve and bandages. "Such accuracy," she said admiringly. "He charged a price only a human could pay."

"Damn him," Stasov said through clenched teeth.

"Don't be such a baby. A wound like this is a compliment. Usually an orca will smash you with a fluke, toss you in the air, or puncture your eardrum by shouting when making an exchange, showing his contempt. A blood price is a genuine honor but usually involves death or maiming. The spinning of the Wheel is beyond our knowledge, so I can't guess why he thought you deserved such delicacy. You must be giving him something he really wants."

"We're old friends," Stasov said. She was right. It wasn't every man who was charged a blood price by an orca and ended up losing only the last two fingers on his left hand.

CHAPTER THIRTEEN

2025

Aɴɴᴀ Cᴀʟᴅᴇʀᴏɴᴇ ꜰᴏʀɢᴇᴅ ɢʀɪᴍʟʏ ᴜᴘ ᴛʜᴇ ꜱᴛʀᴇᴇᴛ ɪɴᴛᴏ the teeth of the wind. Huge rafts of dirty ice thrust up out of the Neva River, revealing black water beneath a quickly freezing scum. The dark granite blocks of the embankment held the elegant baroque city out of the greedy water. Despite the cold, she paused to marvel at the golden spire of the Cathedral of Saints Peter and Paul as it rose above the frozen city. During Tsarist times the fortress around it had served as a political prison. Ilya Stasov claimed that the church and the prison were Russia's two favorite forms of architecture.

She had not expected winter-dark, ice-locked Petersburg to be so beautiful. The planetary exploration meetings had been held in the severely classical buildings

253

of the old Academy of Sciences on Vasilievsky Island.
Directly across the Neva's ice were the mustard-yellow
buildings of the Admiralty, surmounted by its own
gold spire. In between sessions on orbital mechanics,
life-support subsystems, and water reclamation from
the moons of Jupiter, she could look out on an urban
architectural ensemble that less announced the pri-
macy of reason than simply took it for granted. Stasov
could claim that the city represented a thin overlay of
Enlightenment over sheerest barbarism, but she had
learned that he, like most educated Russians, had a
poor opinion of his own nation. And she could tell how
much he loved the city, though he had grown up in the
dismal miles of apartment blocks that had expanded
to surround it when it was called Leningrad.

She refused to take the Metro, despite the cold, and
walked along the Neva after the meeting. The wind
blowing off the Gulf of Finland swept snow over the
broken ice of the river and made her imagine that the
city sat on the surface of Ganymede beneath a perma-
nent layer of clouds. The thought gave her a glow that
prevented the cold from reaching her. Jupiter! Those
maniacs were actually going to let her go there.

Though weeks of meetings were still left, she knew
the decision had been made the first day. Perhaps
sitting in a city that had been plopped down in a
frozen swamp by the sweep of a Tsar's hand over a
map made it easier to forget the limits of possibility.

The meeting had been thrown into consternation by
the proposal from the Delphine Delegation, still negotiating human-cetacean relations at Santa Barbara. The
Russians were reconstructing the sperm whale, Clarence, in a floating hospital near Odessa. The dolphins
had proposed that humans take that whale, turn it into
a cyborg, and send it to Jupiter. In addition to being a

negotiating point at Santa Barbara, the Delphine Delegation had offered to defray a huge part of the cost of the Jupiter Project through their trade credits and reparations. The offer, though completely bizarre, was tempting. Calderone, with some bemusement, guided the discussion. Her orca sources refused to clarify anything.

The seemingly endless buildings of the Winter Palace bulked to her right as she walked. Its scale was massive, stretching along the river in the great Russian horizontal, a structure appropriate to an empire that stretched across the Eurasian continent. The insistent rhythm of the columns gave pattern to Calderone's motion. The ice-glazed windows glowed yellow in the growing darkness, but she could not see what went on inside the former Imperial palace.

After her astonished examination of the Cathedral of Saints Peter and Paul, she followed Stasov's directions away from the Neva River and soon found herself on the more intimate Moika Canal. Here the buildings were less self-consciously melodramatic while still maintaining the city's pattern.

Ilya Stasov was housed in an eerily beautiful eighteenth-century red-stucco building with white pilasters, vivid against the snow. Two guards in bulky greatcoats, rifles slung across their shoulders, checked her papers before unlocking the door. Bored and not going anywhere soon, they made more of a production of it than was necessary, exclaiming over how distant and exotic California was.

"You have been meeting at the Academy of Sciences?" asked one of them, a friendly youngster with straight flaxen hair sticking out from under his fur cap. He introduced himself as Misha. "The space exploration meetings! That is excellent. We have spent too much time fighting each other over islands." He was obviously too young to have fought in the Pacific War. The thought was more chilling to her than the wind.

"It is good you have come," the other guard said. He was older, red-faced, and could well have been a veteran, though something about him implied placid guard duty over a weapons-supply depot somewhere in the rear. "We Russians have many ideas but few resources. We have long waited for the Americans to ask for our help."

"Eh, Lyoshka," the blond Misha said. "We work together. You are being rude."

Lyoshka, glumly awaiting the end of his duty so that he could settle down with a drink, was unembarrassed. "Russian know-how, American money, and likewise American beauty." He peered at Calderone's almost invisible, scarf-muffled face, and she reflected on eternal male optimism.

"Lyoshka is uncultured," Misha said soothingly to Calderone. "You can do nothing but forgive him. I always do."

Stomping his booted feet to warm them, the red-faced Lyoshka looked up at the lit windows of the building he guarded. Misha's magnanimity did not impress him. "I should have said Russian insanity." He looked back at her. "Are we really going to put a whale into outer space?"

The question was one that Calderone had asked herself endlessly, and heard repeated in almost every side discussion at the meeting. She had yet to hear a decent answer to it. That was one of the reasons she stood here, at the deep entrance to this exotic building, her heart pounding as if she was a young girl.

"Has he said anything about it?" she asked, gesturing up at Stasov's windows.

"He says little," the flaxen-haired Misha answered. "He floats in and out at all times of the day and night. People from all over the world come to meet with him. We never hear what they discuss. It is not our job."

"It is an odd little nest of gentlefolk, that's for sure," Lyoshka said, shaking his head. "Whale calls, dolphin conversations. If they could, they would wheel dolphins in and out in water tanks and feed them vodka." He pursed his lips at the thought of alcohol.

"Lyoshka, the lady is growing cold." Misha opened the door for her. "But we are going together to Jupiter, ah? That's the only way to go so far." He saluted as she passed.

The front hall was dark and smelled of cooked cabbage, like many Russian hallways, this time with an overtone of frankincense from the icon lamp that glowed in the corner beneath a solemn Russian saint. A staircase swept up to the right. A keyboard clicked somewhere in the rear. Something moaned dramatically: a recording of a humpback whale call.

A silent, suspicious woman, her hair tied severely back, took Calderone's coat and hung it in the closet by the door. The closet was already stuffed with bulky Russian winter coats and she had to struggle with determination to fit it in. Calderone examined the woman, who was lean and very young. She wanted to ask her all sorts of questions about Stasov, what his life was like, how he felt now, but she resisted. The woman, austere in her high-collared dress, would probably not answer, which would be intolerable. At a gesture, Calderone followed her up the stairs.

Stasov greeted her with a formal double-cheek kiss. She wanted to put her arms tightly around him and hold him close, but something about the set of his body and the intent eyes of the silent woman restrained her.

He held her at arm's length and examined her face closely. He had put on weight since the last time she had seen him, in the Maldives, but was still thin, his cheekbones protruding. The white scars around his mouth from the cage at Homma were almost invisible. But what did he see as he looked at her? Did he note the pursed muscles around the lips, the crow's feet around the eyes, the streaks of gray in her hair? She usually ignored her own appearance, but now, under his calm scrutiny, she found herself wishing that she had taken more care about it. And after a full day of those tiring meetings . . . she wished that he would look away.

Instead, he finally did hug her close. It was her turn to be tense then, and it was a moment before she willed herself to relax against his wide rib cage. She sensed the other woman slide away into the next room and heard the clink of a spoon against glass.

"It's good to see you," Stasov said.

"Yes," she said. "Yes. It's been a long time. Half a year since the Maldives."

"Longer than that. We didn't meet there."

She put her hand to his face and traced out his jawline. "Each of us was someone else."

"And who are we now?"

"Oh, Ilya." She felt like crying. Long ago she had watched him slump aboard a Russian LNG tanker in Manila and had wondered what she was doing. In the years since, she had not figured it out. She knew that he would never entirely forgive her. "I'm so sorry."

"There's nothing to be sorry about." He glanced away from Calderone's eyes for the first time since she had entered the room. "Maya Vladimirovna, could you—ah, thank you."

The silent woman brought in two glasses of strong tea, then swept out of the room, back to her mysterious tasks below. Stasov sweetened his with a teaspoon of strawberry jam. His left hand had just healed and he held his glass with his thumb and first two fingers. "I don't suppose everything went smoothly today."

"Of course it didn't, Ilya," Anna replied. "And it won't. The Delphine Delegation has gone crazy." She kept her hands close to her glass. The room was cold. She picked up a slice of lemon and squeezed it into her tea. The tea glass holder was enameled with a scene of an old Russian city, all spires and church domes. She sat down on a chair with a curved back that could have been early nineteenth century, a museum piece. It creaked slightly under her weight. "But that didn't really answer my question, did it?"

"It doesn't matter." He sat down and looked bleakly at her. "What do you want from me, Anna?"

"I—" She caught her breath. "A lot, Ilya. But one thing I want to know is what you learned from the orcas." She had been trying to talk to them about the Jovian communications for more than a year. Sometimes they responded, sometimes they were paradoxical.

He held up his maimed hand. "I learned how valuable information is."

"In that case, two fingers was a cheap price to pay. Come on, Ilya. Tell me." She knew he would. He had no one else to talk to.

He rubbed his eyes with his ruined hand. It looked like a duck's foot. "The orcas have communicated with the intelligence in Jupiter. Or at least they have made that claim. They want us to help make contact—and use Clarence as the conduit. Is he an ambassador or a sacrifice? I don't know."

"Ilya—this was your vision, wasn't it? The one you told me about when we found the whale. The whale diving into Jupiter."

He grimaced. "Mine? I don't know. But I do know one thing. Since I lost my fingers to that orca's teeth, I've been able to sleep through the night." He folded his large hands over his knee. She looked at them. She remembered them sliding across her skin.

"So the orcas are pushing the dolphins to fund us."

"No. They have no choice either. They in turn are driven by something beyond them. Their Messiah is coming. The raising of the whale is a manifestation of that."

She felt a deep frustration. Ilya's paradoxical acceptance of the dolphin religion had always annoyed her. "You mean they are going through all this trouble and paying all this money to bring about the coming of their God?"

"Exactly. To the cetaceans God is a means of transformation. Transformation of the physical world, the one they live in. Once God has passed, nothing is the same." His voice rang with the sound of a believer.

"Nothing is the same."

"For some of us, perhaps."

She wanted to hold him close. She also wanted to hit him. He was a brilliant man who used his intelligence for everything but what was most important. Who did he think would benefit the most if the past, with its wars and research tanks, ceased to have meaning? Would the dolphins forget all that had happened and proceed forward to a radiant future?

"Ilya, you—"

A bell rang in the next room. "Excuse me," he said. "That's Vladivostok." He walked out briskly, more energetic than she had ever seen him.

She looked around as she listened to his low voice on the phone. The room was packed with papers. Diagrams and maps covered the elaborately figured wallpaper. The lion-footed desk was strewn with strip charts and sonograms. A small bed, severely made in a military manner, was the only clear area. On the desk, amid a tangle of other documents, lay a heavy red folder. She contemplated it for a long moment. Finally, realizing that, one way or another, she was meant to see it, she flipped it open.

Under a red stamp in Russian that she interpreted as saying TOP SECRET, the text was in English. The page she had opened to started:

> not strictly as collateral issues. The question of seabed rights, varying as they do from one national entity to another, should not affect the intent of the Treaty as we now understand it.

DEROCHE: And how are we to understand it?

ARIADNE: That our agreement supersedes such seabed rights, under the appropriate stipulations. We emphasize that the one-century cutoff is extremely limiting, and will be strictly enforced. One century before ratification, fixed. We don't intend to have that deadline chasing us like an orca.

(Laughter)

The monetary value is likely to be rather small, since we will not have exclusive right of search, competing with your own salvagers. Our only exclusive rights will be after discovery. Is there a difficulty with such a modification?

KALMBACH: Not in principle, certainly. There will be difficulties in enforcement. Not insuperable ones. After all, salvage of abandoned sea vessels is a well-explored area of the Law of the Sea.

Anna flipped to the front of the folder. "Minutes— Santa Barbara negotiations," it said. The date was yesterday's. She skimmed through. Every day of the negotiations, supposedly kept under rigid security, was extensively marked and annotated in Stasov's spidery hand. Next to Ariadne's remark that "the monetary value is likely to be rather small" Stasov had put an exclamation point. Ariadne, the chief negotiator from the Delphine Delegation, had already proved to be a nine-times-nine days' wonder in America, where such peculiar media stars were popular.

She closed the notebook. It was a sign, but of what? She sat back down in her chair.

Ilya's voice continued in the other room. She listened to it but could not make out any words. After a moment, she realized that he was speaking no human language. He was speaking some cetacean dialect. The . . . person on the other end of the line was not a human being.

A sudden gust of wind rattled the outermost of the three panes of glass. The early northern darkness had fallen, and the regular arrangement of windows glowed outside, across the black stretch of canal. Cold struck through the glass. She went into the small side room, poured herself more hot water from the looming brass samovar, and returned to Stasov's study. The minutes of the Santa Barbara meetings, a conversation with a dolphin—she wondered. Bored, she examined the room for other irregularities, more mysteries. It didn't take her long to find them. Atop the papers that covered the surface of the sideboard, she found a brightly colored brochure from the cruise ship *Sagittarius*.

It took her a moment to remember, but then it came to her: the *Sagittarius* had gone down in the Philippine Sea earlier that year, apparently after contact with a still-active mine left over from the Pacific War. There had been no way to examine the wreckage, since, by chance, the ship had sunk almost ten kilometers beneath the sea's surface into the Mindanao Trench. Most of the crew and passengers had died. Anna opened the brochure. Inside, folded several times, was a passenger list from the last voyage, a list of names starting with "Abramowitz, Moses—Tel Aviv," and ending with "Zerowsky, Wanda—Warsaw," with more than four hundred names in between. About half the list was checked off.

She dropped the brochure back on the sideboard at the feet of a pagan idol. She recognized the little wooden statuette. She had bought it for Stasov as a going-away present in the Philippines. He had obviously hauled it around with him ever since.

When Ilya came back into the room, she was sitting in her chair. She knew that he was not one of those men whose apparent disorder concealed real order. He wouldn't notice if any of his documentation had been displaced in the mess.

He sat down at his desk and leaned his weight forward on it, staring down at the papers. The light from the desk lamp reflected off the white papers, illuminating his thoughtful face.

He laid his hand on the red folder containing the Santa Barbara minutes. "The conference didn't let me attend." His voice was bitter. "The Russian delegation has only observer status, and still they didn't let me attend."

Anna had been at some of the sessions. Had he read and annotated her testimony as well? Or had some questions from the Delphine Delegation been formulated by him? She had even put in a good word for him. It had probably gotten to him in transcript. She didn't want to ask if he appreciated it.

She stood and went over to him. "Are you unfairly punished?" She could feel the heat coming from him and smell his slightly rank male scent.

He turned from her, looking for his tea glass. "The war was a long time ago."

"Was it? Don't you still dream of it every night? Along with Homma . . . and Uglegorsk?" She took his arm and pulled him back to her. He didn't resist.

"You think they won't have me because of my dreams?"

"That may well be true, Ilya." She put her hands on the center of his chest and then ran them around either side of his ribs. He shuddered and let out a breath. "Your dreams are too real."

He nuzzled her hair. "Where did you go, Anna?"

"I didn't go anywhere. I'm right here."

"You haven't been. You left me."

"I'm here now." She put her arms around him and kissed him. She felt his right hand on her shoulder. Then it slid down and cupped her buttock.

"For how long?" he asked.

She didn't answer but pushed herself against him.

His body had more muscle on it than she remembered. It was firm under her breasts.

"Use both hands." After a moment's hesitation, she felt his left hand tentatively on her behind as well. She wiggled it. "Come on." It held her more firmly, the three remaining fingers digging into her flesh.

"Oh, Ilya. I wanted to make love to you on that damn rock in the middle of the ocean. They were all hauling that stupid whale into the water. No one would have noticed. Why didn't we?"

He snorted. "There were reasons that seemed to make sense at the time." His right hand unbuttoned her blouse and unhooked her bra, releasing her breasts. It caressed them.

His left hand was once again loose, just lying on her. "Please, Ilya." She pulled it by the wrist and kissed the scars where the fingers had once been. He moved as if to jerk it away, but she held it firmly. She knew she was stronger than he thought. "Hold me with it. You traded part of it for something important. Don't be ashamed. I want to feel all of you."

He took her nipple between left thumb and forefinger. "Where's your bed?" she asked as he slid his thigh between hers.

"I don't have a bed. Just a cot."

She laughed. "Ah, Ilya, ever the romantic. Well, that will just have to do, won't it?"

"You must remember," Ilya said as they stepped into the vestibule of the church, "Petersburg is a very young city. There is nothing ancient here. Peter found the place a swamp with some Finnish fishermen's huts in it. He dropped the bones of thousands of men into the mud and piled marble on top of them."

Anna had exclaimed over the antiquity of the church

they were in. It was an elaborately colored building at the turn of the Griboyedov Canal, built, she now discovered from the English note under a painting of a handsome man with a beard, on the site of the assassination of Tsar Alexander II. She didn't know when that had been and Stasov didn't say, but she didn't think that it had been in some remote past. The stone wall just outside the church was marked with shell craters and had a sign which Stasov translated as saying: WARNING—THIS SIDE OF THE STREET UNSAFE IN CASE OF ARTILLERY BOMBARDMENT. It was a reminder of the brutal German siege of 1941–1944.

But the interior of the church was smoky, full of the smell of frankincense, and ancient. Icons glowed darkly on the walls around her, the only light coming from ranks and ranks of beeswax candles. Stasov stopped at a desk where he bought two candles from a broad-faced old woman.

Though assigned a room at a modern hotel on the city's outskirts, along with a car and driver, Anna preferred to stay with Ilya in his messy quarters on the Moika Canal. The cot was small and hard, Maya Vladimirovna's scrutiny harsh and exact. The room was always too cold. The whole city froze that winter, and sometimes the conference members sat all day in their overcoats, warming their fingers over the samovar during breaks in the proceedings. The food was dull and often overcooked. Anna didn't care.

He talked to her of what he believed: "God is Rising. That's the center of it, and you can't get around it or avoid it. God does not rise only from the bottom of the sea. She also rises out of the community of believers. Remember, only this communal linkage really exists. It was deformed severely when the human beings they had trusted turned on them, it seemed, and tried to hunt them down. The Mycenaeans hunted them, not the Cretans, but that is a specious distinction. Men hunted them. Men have hunted them ever since, bringing unsought death. Death that could not be used as a gesture or as a force against the unchangeable universe. But the linkage is there. The Whale rises, and when She breaks the surface all will be different. And so they act, for the sum of their thoughts and actions *is* God."

She did not try to argue him out of something she wasn't sure he believed. She made love with him on the perilously creaking cot and sensed an understanding in his body.

Every evening, he slipped out and walked down to this church. This night she had come with him.

She looked up at the Virgin, whose eyes were dark and sorrowful, the doomed Child in her arms gesturing down at the worshippers.

"Who are the candles for, Ilya?" Anna asked.

Ilya put each of the candles into the holders that ringed the large candles, thick as a man's arm. He lit them.

"This one is for Vsevolod Isayevich Makarygin. He was my friend at Homma, and died there. He taught me about the meaning of guilt and punishment. Without him, I think my being at Homma would have been pointless, a waste of time."

She almost laughed. "Thank goodness it wasn't that."

Ilya was solemn. "Suffering is not necessarily ennobling. Most often it simply hurts. He made sure that I did not spend my time simply hurting and hating. I light a candle for him every day I am near a church. He died a serious and intent Orthodox Christian, and it is the least I can do for his memory."

"And the other?"

"Today's candle is for Ann Olson, of San Bernardino, California, USA."

She asked the next question with her eyes.

"She is the two hundred thirty-fifth name on the passenger list of the *Sagittarius*."

It was clear to her in an instant. "Dolphins sank her! Military dolphins."

"Yes. They made it look like a drifting mine—but it was deliberate."

"Did you order it?" she whispered.

He grimaced. "I suppose in a sense I did. I released the dolphins at the end of the war—I resigned my authority over them at the edge of Russia. I told them to fight to keep their freedom, if necessary. I guess they thought it necessary."

"And you feel guilt for that?"

"No, of course not." He looked surprised. "But I face the consequences. I couldn't have foreseen them—but they are my consequences nevertheless, and I have to deal with them."

His voice, in contrast to the way he had sounded as he left Manila, or even on that rock in the Maldives, rang with optimism. To her ear it was a jarring note. "Ilya, can't you just let it go? You couldn't have known what was going to happen, so why should you have to deal with it? Wars, sinking cruise ships, dying whales—none of that is anything you *have* to deal with. The dolphins and orcas are intelligent creatures. For God's sake, you proved that yourself."

"I know." He smiled and took her arm. "But Anna, darling, what else do I have? Come on." He led her from the church. He pulled her from the church. She had time for one last glimpse of the almost invisible gold-covered domes above her, with their figures of the judging Christ and His saints peering down at the mortals below and then they were out on the street. The light from the spotlighted church reflected off the ice and snow.

They walked along the canal, their breaths puffing in the cold night.

"A few weeks ago I visited my parents' grave," he said. "My mother died not long after my father. To me they were two entirely different people who shared a life for reasons I never understood, she air and he earth, but without him she had nothing to hold her to this world at all."

Anna remembered Ilya's stories about his father. "And your father's books?"

"There's a room in the Moika house that's full of them. I don't know what I will ever do with them. My mother even apologized to me just before she died, for having dumped them on me. Perhaps my father's body should have been burned on a pyre of them, like a Varangian chieftain."

They weren't heading for home, she realized. When they reached the point where the Griboyedov Canal flowed into the Moika, they turned to the right, toward the Fontanka River. They passed beneath the forbidding bulk of a palace. It looked heavy, ancient, but remembering his annoyance with her in the church, she knew that it couldn't have been that old. St. Petersburg was a younger city than New York.

Ilya gestured at it. "That's St. Michael's Castle. The mad Tsar Paul I built it as an impregnable fortress. He shut himself up inside it and was murdered there by his own palace guard, his death connived at by his own son, the saintly Alexander I. . . ." Snow was plowed up high beneath the palace's windows.

They walked slowly along the Moika Canal embankment. The wind from the Gulf of Finland cut at them steadily, with icy patience. It had already swept the cracked surface of the canal clean. The streetlights gleamed on the dark ice. Anna tugged at Ilya's arm. She could barely feel it beneath the thick wool of his coat.

"There are other ways to live than by obsession," she said.

"That's the American in you talking," he observed, amusement in his voice.

"Come on, not more of this Russian soul stuff. You're not responsible for the way Paul I died."

"You're right." He was instantly contrite. "But I'm trying to get you to understand something. Here, sit with me." He brushed the snow off a bench for her and they sat, though she desperately wanted to head for home, a bar, anywhere there might be a trace of warmth. And he was shivering, she could feel it, his ability to resist cold lost forever somewhere in the Pacific. "My father never committed himself to action. So he was able to live out his life without consequences to worry about. That, finally, was his great shortcoming. My life has consequences. Don't try to keep me from dealing with them. They are all I have."

"So the passengers of the *Sagittarius* died so that your life would have validity? Is that the way everything is set up? A bunch of supernumerary spear-carriers—"

"No." Ilya was placid, unwilling to be baited. "But their deaths and my life are intertwined. To reject their death is to reject my life." He blew out a breath. The wind yanked the mist from his lips and whipped it across the snowdrifts. "Just as our lives are intertwined, Anna. Ever since you came to visit me at Uglegorsk. You cannot escape the consequences of that either."

She smiled to herself. Years ago she had gone to a dismal Soviet research center, slept with a plump and pleasant man named Grisha Panin—now long dead in war—and had *not* slept with a lean and frustrated man named Ilya Stasov. Partially as a result, dolphins had sunk ships and orcas were obscurely communicating with Jovians. There was something to a life with consequences.

"All right. I have to face as much as you do. Look." She pointed out across the ice. "The surface of Ganymede looks a lot like that, I bet. It's mostly ice, covered with a few kilometers of rock, which is often ripped off by craters and cracks. Imagine a full Jupiter rising up over that gloomy castle of yours."

He looked up as if he could see it. "You *are* cold, aren't you?" He stood. "But I'm glad that damn canal is covered with ice. The last time one wasn't, a dolphin came up and pulled me back into the water. They want to tie my fate to theirs. And I won't have it, understand me? I won't." His voice had risen in pitch, as if Anna herself had suggested it.

"No, Ilya," she said soothingly. "You don't have to."

"I know. Instead, I will tie their fate to mine."

CHAPTER FOURTEEN

2025

Stasov peered down into the dark hole that opened at his feet. Lean and pale, tendons prominent in his neck, he seemed dropped here from some other world. The hillside behind him was covered with vivid Cretan spring flowers, while the land fell away to the right into the Bay of Mirabello. Clouds cast dappled shadows.

"Where does this lead?" he asked, turning back.

"Are you worried because there's no explanatory plaque?" Georgios Theodoros smiled at his friend's reluctance. "This place was only discovered five years ago."

Around them, partially excavated, were the low ruins of a Minoan villa. Most of it had fallen into the water with the crumbling of the limestone underneath it. It was unimpressive compared with the restored palace

272

complexes they had been visiting for the past week. Stasov and Theodoros had seen Phaestos, Mallia, Zakro, and the greatest of them all, the seat of Minos himself, Knossos. Completely unfortified, elegantly designed, their bulls' horns gleaming in the clear Cretan sun, they were a vision of the ancient world at peace, beneficiaries of the unstinting generosity of the sea.

Here there was nothing but tumbled rocks and a hole in the ground. Theodoros heard water sucking down below.

"I call it the Cave of the Minodelphos," Theodoros said. "Go ahead."

Stasov glanced back at him before climbing in. His eyes were pale in his face. His face had been through the refiner's fire and been purged of everything not essential to it. It was a face that defied you to feel sorry for what it had seen. Theodoros knew that he himself had put on weight and become a most comfortable man. He wondered how Stasov saw him.

"The Minodelphos?" Stasov smiled at a memory. "I told a friend that story once."

"Which one? There are many stories. If you're good, I'll tell you another."

Stasov turned and slithered down into the darkness of the rocky and twisted birth canal. The last thing visible of him was his maimed hand, its three fingers holding onto a rock. Theodoros stood in the sun for a moment longer, then followed him.

The Cretans, for all of their sea travels, had worshipped gods that dwelled deep within the earth. Theodoros had taken the two of them to the Dictaean Cave where Zeus had been born: a Cretan temple, double-headed axes among the gleaming wet stalagmites, and offerings on the bottom of a dark pool.

"According to the story," Theodoros said when he found purchase for his feet, "Minos had a mistress once, a sea nymph, whom he kept by the seashore. Who knows? Perhaps it was at this very villa. His wife, Pasiphaë, discovered this and placed a curse on him. The next time he lay with the nymph he ejaculated sea anemones, snails, sea urchins, and corals, turning her vagina into a sea grotto."

They stood in the darkness until their eyes adjusted enough to see the dim blue glow of distant sunlight coming up through the pool at their feet. Underground waters dripped around them, landing in cold pools, eventually seeping down into the mother ocean.

"That world is forever lost," Theodoros said. "They were not Greeks, they were not Romans. Only vague traces of the Minoans were left in the cultures that followed them. The warlike Mycenaeans, descendants of Menelaus, were destroyed by the iron-armed Dorians from the north, and those last heirs of Minos, however unfilial and opportunistic, vanished, leaving only cyclopean walls to awe and mystify the classical Greeks who arose after those dark ages."

Grottos ran back into the hills, a dark maze of passages cut through the soft limestone by millennia of water. The pattern was far different now than it had been in Minoan times, the old chambers eaten away from under and collapsed, and new ones dug. The rushing waters worked constantly, never ceasing their eagerness. The ancient Greeks had believed that the river Alpheus, in the Peloponnesus, ran under the Ionian Sea to rise in the fountain of Arethusa at Syracuse, in Sicily. Theodoros wondered what dark passages on Crete had led to the belief of such deep-flowing waters. Or had these beliefs been based on garbled human versions of dolphin stories about deep currents that could be followed along the bottom of the sea? All of his years of research had only deepened the mysteries. This cave was the perfect linking point between the depths of the earth and the depths of the sea, each the other's boundary, each seeking to master the other.

"Now that my theories are becoming more popular," Theodoros said, proud despite himself, "someone has hypothesized that this cave, in its previous shape, served as a sort of underwater sonic amplifier, like the bell of a trumpet, which made it easier for men to talk to dolphins. I don't know about that. It smacks of the sort of gadget orientation that your old friend Grisha Panin had. Did men talk to dolphins because they had discovered a natural means of sonic amplification? I doubt it. Men talked to dolphins because in those days they were patient. The days were fat, the years endless. One could float in the sea, browning in the sun, seeing the sea's color changes day by day, and try to communicate with those wise creatures that you knew had their own civilization beneath the waves. You didn't know that their civilization only grew into existence as you talked to them. Your own civilization was new then, the shine not yet worn off."

"The Minodelphos," Stasov said. "What of him?"

"Watch out what you think of the Minodelphos." Theodoros was careful. Stasov was looking for something, some purchase in the past. Theodoros was wary of the power this gave him over Stasov. "Myths accrete and conceal the truths they attach themselves to. The story I wrote you a couple of years ago was about a Minodelphos who was a victim, tormented by his half brother Catreus. That Minodelphos was clearly a dolphin, perhaps reminding us of the dolphins murdered by the Mycenaeans after the fall of Crete. But there are others called by the same name."

Stasov grimaced. "All right, Georgios. I'm sure you'll get to it." He climbed back out into the sun.

Time had not softened Stasov's brusqueness. Theodoros was startled to find that this pleased him. He remembered the very last time he had seen Stasov, standing pensively on the beach, looking out at the circling orcas. They had not parted friends, but had regained, over the years, something of what had once bound them together, though they had not met face to face from that day to this.

They stood on the hillside and looked off across the Sea of Crete. "It's usually hazy like this," Theodoros said, "but on a clear day you can see Thera from here, just at the horizon." He peered, trying to see his home, but it was invisible. "In Minoan times Strogyle trailed a thin line of smoke into the sky. We're going a little less than half the way there now."

He pointed the way and they descended the slope to the water by a narrow trail. Below them bobbed Theodoros's boat, the *St. John Chrysostom*.

"Aren't you carrying things a bit too far?" Stasov said. The Aegean Dolphin Sanctuary forbid the use of noisy, engine-powered boats, allowing dolphins an area of blessed silence, but certainly did not mandate the pitch-covered wood hull, bright dyed sail, and watchful-eyed prow of the *St. John Chrysostom*.

"Like it?" Theodoros said. "A model a bit later than Minoan, but definitely classical. The rigging is modern and it has a sealed flotation section along the bottom part of the hull. No sense in dying for authenticity."

"I remember you ordering a wood-hulled fishing boat for our expedition to see the orcas, all those years ago. I hope you weren't expecting something like this."

"Ilya, I'm afraid I was." Theodoros remembered his disappointment in the noisy hulk Stasov had, after long efforts, managed to find.

Stasov laughed. "At last I know." He jumped aboard the sailboat. "Seva Makarygin would have known who St. John Chrysostom was."

"Chrysostom means 'honey-mouth'," Theodoros said. "He was known for his eloquence. It seemed an appropriate name." He cast off.

"Our destination is what is called the Temple of Poseidon Pankrator." Theodoros rested easily at the stern of the boat, bearded face turned to the sun like a cat's, eyes half closed while he kept one arm over the tiller. "Poseidon, Ruler of All. Wishful thinking, attributing ancient supremacy to the Sea God. He ruled the sea and horses. Not much else. But the Temple *is* the only structure this near which survived the eruption of Strogyle that black day four thousand years ago, so perhaps Poseidon took it back to his bosom."

After several hours' travel they were flanked by the leaping shapes of dolphins, emerging from the water almost as if they were nothing more than abnormally exuberant waves, shining wet in the sun, and then vanishing almost without a splash.

All arrangements had been made and the Delphine Delegation had made it clear that no further communication was to be attempted until they reached the Temple—and whatever else awaited them there.

"Did you know that you were telling me a parable when you told me about the lyre player, the whale, and the dolphin?" Stasov asked. The leaping dolphins didn't seem to interest him.

"I thought it was a story about how men first talked to dolphins."

"It was that too. Or haven't you ever heard of a myth that tells more than one story at once?" Stasov smiled maliciously.

Theodoros was placid. "Of course, Ilya. I'm glad you've learned your lessons. Now, your parable."

"That whale was the Foreswimmer, he who comes before, the First Bubble that rises from the spout of God to foretell the coming Breath, the new Incarnation. The dolphin over whose dim head the singer broke his lyre is the Echo of God, or as others have termed him, God's Remora, Her humble, material associate, the Messiah."

"Is that why we're here?" Theodoros was exasperated by Stasov's habit of keeping thoughts secret until things began to happen. "To meet the Messiah?"

"As far as I can tell. Bottom-Thumper told me to come here and made the arrangements. Who knows what he's sending me to meet? Orcas have an odd sense of humor."

"True." Theodoros felt disgusted. "From what I understand, he is a material Messiah, immanent, not transcendent. A money changer. A Pharisee. Leave it to dolphins to come with a theology so ridiculous."

That made Stasov smile. "At least we've found your pet peeve, Georgios: lack of theological rigor."

"It's the Byzantine in me. Can't help it."

Stasov stretched his legs out and leaned back against the mast. "Tell me a story, Georgios."

Theodoros looked at him. Ilya Stasov was not yet at peace with himself and what he had done. But it was clear that he hoped that whatever awaited him under the water at the Temple of Poseidon was one more step in the right direction. And that deserved the right story. Theodoros had been wondering if he should tell it.

"Dolphin stories are very different from human ones. Their senses are, after all, different, and their language has a spatial structure that human ones do not. Cannot, because of the limitations of our hearing. But I have heard a story of how dolphins first learned to speak."

Stasov looked startled. "I had no idea they had any such stories. None of the dolphins I have ever spoken with have ever acknowledged that they had any memory whatsoever relating to their discovery of language."

"That's interesting. God created the world by speaking. As She spoke each word, each echo-form, the thing whose echo the word was came into existence. But God apparently had more than a little of the orca in Her, for She laughed at last at what She had created, and that laugh took the form of the hulls of wooden ships, the ships of men, and those who rode in them. It's an old epithet among dolphins: when a ship passes overhead, they say 'God laughs', though now She laughs louder and longer than ever.

"God could speak but dolphins could not. They swam and chased their tuna and mated, and their lives were simple. But their world swirled around them like loose seaweed, for they had no words to describe it. God was angry with them, because part of the reason She had created them was to harden the reality around them. Their echoes were meant to finish the creation She had been too lazy or busy to finish. Instead, they simply chased their fish and danced among the waves, unconcerned by their duties.

"But some dolphins understood that the ships had the knowledge. They could hear their rhythmic drumming, feel the ships in their elaborate evolutions, always different, as they fought with each other, dropping men into the sea to feed the sharks, as if propitiating them. One dolphin who was fascinated by the sounds and activities of men was named Rumble by his fellows, for his habit of imitating the terrifying sound of the island of Thera, which, somewhere deep within itself, held anger. It may be that that thunderous sound was the first word in the dolphin language, a word that would later mean death and destruction. Rumble pursued the human ships, rubbing against them as if each was his mother. Once he was caught up by their nets as they fished for tuna and vanished into the sky. His fellows knew that he had ended his life for no purpose. But after some moments the men cast him back into the sea. He had lain in the hot sun and the burning air, hearing the voices of men as they shouted at each other, and he had lived.

"Some time later, a human female was cast into the sea. You and I should know her as Pasiphaë, the wife of Minos, thrown into the sea to propitiate the dolphins, and perhaps that tale is a reverse echo of the dolphin one. Or is the dolphin tale an echo of ours? Perhaps the entire affair actually happened as described and is not myth at all. Be that as it may, Rumble raped her there in the water as she struggled against him. He longed to know, though her cries told him nothing he did not know already. The water filled her lungs and she sank, but Rumble pushed her back to the surface and held her there until a human ship swept by and took her back into the air. They may even have thought of him as her rescuer."

"I know that situation personally," Stasov said, smiling. "From a canal in Petersburg."

"From this encounter, Rumble gained not knowledge but madness. He refused to echo-locate, mimicking, instead, all the sounds that the dolphins had heard from the humans: the creak of their oarlocks, the thump of their drums, the splash of an anchor falling into the water. And he refused to die. Instead, his own echo gradually became fainter and fainter, finally vanishing, so that he was invisible. But still the other dolphins could hear him, the sound and echo of oars dipping into the water, and the crash of one ship's ram finding another's vulnerable side, so that even when human ships were nowhere within hearing, they could be heard.

"Somewhere halfway between land and sea, her upper parts in the air and her lower parts in the water, Pasiphaë bore a child. He had the body of a dolphin and the arms and whiskers of a human being: the Minodelphos, Rumble's son."

"And you told me how he ended," Stasov said. "At Catreus's hand, deep in the Labyrinth. Or is that another Minodelphos?"

Theodoros shrugged. "There are many stories and they don't fit together like bits of a jigsaw puzzle. You should regard that one as Catreus's story—thus, you may doubt his version of events. After all, he was a human being, and prone to lying."

"I'll keep that in mind."

"The Minodelphos learned the sound of human language from his mother and his half brothers, the sons of Minos, for Minos imprisoned him in a grotto near the sea. He learned the ways of men while living in the water like a dolphin. He heard the dolphins playing as he lay in the water of his cave, but could not go to join them. He defined the walls of his cave, his prison, while he was there, with the words for its walls. With the knowledge of human beings and the vocal power of dolphins, he created a language, a language which had the power to dominate the physical world that dolphins had no power over.

"He learned the words well, for finally he changed them and the grotto opened. He swam out into the sea to greet his fellow dolphins.

"It may be that his time in the cave had driven him as mad as his father, Rumble, or it may simply be that he was driven to a rage by the dolphins' reluctance to learn the words that he had learned while imprisoned, but before long he began to torment the dolphins. His words created walls that they could not swim around, changed the configuration of the sea bottom, and hid the schools of fish that they depended on for their lives. With his arms he moved the walls of the sea in, creating the Aegean Sea, which enclosed them, not permitting them escape. He had the voice of a dolphin and the arms and hands of a human being. To the dolphins he was invincible.

"Eventually he tormented them to the point where they simply had to speak, to confront his definition of reality with their own. When one of them could not hear the school of tuna because of the Minodelphos's illusions, another one could, and sent an echo to the first: a word. When one dolphin saw a false bottom looming up at him, another would send a true echo to him, correcting his course. Thus was dolphin language born, in an attempt to evade the tortures of the Minodelphos.

"God was angry with the Minodelphos, for She was the only one to define reality. His version was different from hers. The hard walls of the Aegean were not Her idea. But She could not unspeak the words that had created the dolphins, and the Minodelphos, so

She lay quiescent beneath them, letting them speak, hardening the edges of the sea that held them in, until nothing could ever move the walls, not even the wooden ships of the men, which dashed themselves hopelessly against the rocks, leaving nothing but flinders and broken human bodies behind them.

"The men, hearing the dolphins, spoke with them, and they learned to be friends." Theodoros paused to take a drink from the water jug.

Stasov stared at him with his pale eyes. "Is that an original story?"

"Of course not. That was a long time ago. You suspect that it reflects Uglegorsk rather than the Aegean, the second time dolphins spoke rather than the first."

"Actually, Georgios, I didn't. Otherwise Kestrel would be in it. But does it include what we did to them at Uglegorsk? Are the hard walls of the Aegean the concrete pens we built?"

"Maybe you were recapitulating the acts of that older time and your actions are the echo, rather than the story's words. Stranger things have happened, in the low-hanging days before the arrival of a Messiah."

Stasov stood and leaned against the mast to look out over the even sea. "How does the story end?"

"As it did," Theodoros said with a shrug. "In tragedy. The Minodelphos grew too intelligent and too unwise, a dangerous combination. Having walled everyone into the middle sea as he had, he believed that he could become lord over the humans, an idea he had learned from them, and from their King Minos, for it is not a dolphin notion at all. But he was, after all, half human being, Pasiphaë's son, so why should he not rule both the sea and the land?

"He called on his father, Rumble, who was by this time what a human being would call a ghost. He gave words to his father's sounds, and the ships he imitated became real. Their long shapes moved slowly across the top of the dolphin world. These were the men of the foreshore: the Mycenaeans. They slid silently across the water, for they were not interested in the words of dolphins. They moved toward the island of Crete and the undefended palaces of Minos.

"But having had his sounds taken away and made real, Rumble became real again himself, and found that he finally could die a meaningful death. His son had taught the dolphins to speak, and the result was nothing but pain and agony. Rumble swept across the bottom of the sea, scooping rocks into his mouth. He swallowed boulders and the corrosion-encrusted anchors that men had lost from their ships and lumps of dead coral. At last, heavy and swollen, he sank down into the depths of the sea, beneath the last thermocline, where the water is incomprehensibly cold, impossibly dense, and echoes move with incredible speed, returning before the signal is sent. It was here where God lay, inhaling in a terrible rage at the doings far above Her. Rumble curled up and lay in Her vast blowhole.

" 'Make the sound,' She said. 'Make the sound that gives you your name. I will make it real.'

"So Rumble, remembering back to his childhood, made a low rumble, the sound of a volcano considering whether to erupt.

" 'Louder!' God commanded. 'Let them hear it through the upper reaches of the sea and beyond, in the air where men live, so that they know that their lives are bound, as the sea is bound by hard rock.'

"So Rumble made the loudest noise he could, and was surprised to hear it reverberate throughout the seas of the world, for it had become real. It was now the rumble of God's own spouting, as She rose to the surface to catch Her breath and end the world.

"She rose up through all the levels of the sea and broke the surface of reality. Her spout rose beyond all the levels above the sea, breaking through the worlds of men. When She sank again, all had changed. The kingdoms of Crete were gone, their ships swept from the sea. No human friend of dolphins was left alive. Only their enemies remained, those last creations of the Minodelphos, the Mycenaeans, their sharp harpoons ready to stain the sea with blood. The dolphins scattered in pain from their God's angry voice, many of them deaf or insane, and resolved never to speak to men again. Blown into the skies above the water, Rumble achieved the truest death a dolphin could, the death that brought God from Her depths into the light."

"Is that how they see it?" Stasov was dry. "When they themselves try to force God's spout by sinking human ships? The destruction of the *Sagittarius* was a religious act masquerading as a military one. So it looks like my goal is to avoid sharing Rumble's fate."

Stasov had told him about Makarygin and the way Makarygin had ended. Theodoros wondered how Stasov's own personal myths related to those of the dolphins, for Makarygin's example preached resistance, while Stasov seemed prepared to sacrifice himself for an unclear purpose.

"What will you do with this Messiah?" Theodoros asked. He scanned across the water. A buoy marked the shallows where the Temple lay. With a nod to himself, Theodoros dropped sail and pitched the anchor into the water.

Stasov put on his insulating suit. "That's just the right question, Theodoros. The dolphins are all wondering what this Messiah is going to do with me." He grinned and slid into the water.

STASOV COULD HEAR DOLPHINS COMMENTING TO EACH OTHER somewhere in the distance, but the water around him was empty. He swam toward the voices, recognizing them. Bottom-Thumper at Hokkaido, and these three here. Who else?

In a few moments he came into sight of the Temple of Poseidon Pankrator. Buried by tephra and millennia of bottom sediment, the Temple had been lost until a sounding survey detected a density anomaly. After negotiation with the Delphine Delegation, it had been cleaned and restored. A forest of the distinctive Cretan columns, wider at the top than at the bottom, held up a roof edged with stylized bulls' horns. Everything had been repainted its original bright polychrome, the columns red with green capitals, the bulls' horns gleaming with gold, all brightly lit by underwater lights. The drowned Temple was used as the site for formal human-dolphin negotiations, symbolizing as it did that long-vanished Minoan civilization.

Stasov swam slowly over the old sacred precincts, tracing out the lines of the religious complex of which the Temple of Poseidon Pankrator had once been the center. The rest of the ruins had been cleared of debris and left just as they were. In front of the Temple was a large open area. This had once been the Sacred Pool, where dolphins had swum to pay homage, with the sullen sarcasm that must even then have been part of their personalities, to the humans' anthropomorphic version of the Sea God.

Three dolphins swam fitfully around the Temple. The sun probed through the water and gleamed on the ultrasonic cutting blades that made up the front edges of their flippers and dorsal fins. Their sides were armored and their bellies packed with superconducting circuitry. They turned and swam toward him in attack formation: Phobos, Deimos, and Harmonia. A coincidence, that those three had survived. The children of Aphrodite, wife of the cuck-olded artificer Hephaestus, and Ares the War God. Fear, Panic, and Harmony, the contradictory emotions of Love and War, with a healthy assist from sullenly impartial technology.

"Colonel!" Deimos said, and the dolphins stopped, awaiting orders. They now sank cruise ships on their own, but still, they needed him. He just wasn't sure for what.

Stasov ran his maimed left hand down Deimos's side, feeling the scars and machinery. In the war's second year Deimos and a dozen of his fellows had preceded a run of Soviet attack submarines from Murmansk through the perilous sea gap between Greenland and Iceland, where the enemy had placed his most sensitive submarine detection technology. Packed with equipment which made them appear to all sensors as Alfa class submarines, the dolphins had drawn ASW forces away from the real Soviet attack. Five of the nine submarines had gotten through, to provide a useful diversion of enemy forces from the main theater of war in the North Pacific. Deimos alone of his comrades had survived, and been decorated with an Order of Glory. He had also carried Stasov's message from his cage at Homma and arranged the escape of the cyborg dolphins from their internment.

"I am not a Colonel." Stasov was tired of saying it.

"What are you, then?" Harmonia asked. Her artificial left eye glittered at him, its delicate Japanese optics covered with seaweed and algae. "An orca that walks?"

"An orca with hands," Phobos agreed. "A good definition of a human." The largest of the three, he had gotten through the war miraculously unscathed. "We know what you want. You want God. That's why you're still alive."

"Why the hell do you care?" Harmonia made a thrumming noise indicative of disgust. "Why should we?" Her eye kept twisting and focusing at nothing. She had lost the left side of her skull during the landings at Kagalaska. Stasov remembered her screaming over the comm link as her friends died. He had never figured out how Harmonia had managed to survive. "Why have you dragged us here to do this? I'm bored."

"He wants to hurt us more," Deimos said. "This way he can drive *all* of us. He will use the Remora like a narwhal's tusk. He will pierce us. Isn't that true, Colonel?"

"It may be true," Stasov said. "But it doesn't matter, does it?"

"Stop knocking a dead body around with your snout," the massive Phobos said. "Save logical games for the orcas, who like them. They bore us."

The three dolphins' voices sank through the water like lumps of lead. Each phrase seemed a deliberate effort, but that did not silence them.

"I'm not playing games," Stasov said. "I am serious."

Phobos swam up and knocked Stasov aside as if he were a vagrant piece of seaweed. Three chevrons, now dark and tarnished, marked his dorsal fin, one for each of the American submarines whose destruction had been attributable to his skillful use of his sonic and magnetic detectors. He had also helped sink the American Aegis cruiser *Wainwright*, saving the landings on Kagalaska.

Even now, his side bruised, Stasov felt that same surge of gratitude that had overcome him when he heard that the cruiser had sunk into the North Pacific. "Why do you care?" Phobos asked.

Harmonia did not allow Stasov to answer. "*We* certainly don't. God talk is stupid."

"God will rise when She wants to," Deimos said. "We can't push Her flippers with our snouts."

They circled Stasov like mechanical, murderous sharks.

"Tell us why this matters to you," Phobos roared.

Would they slice him apart with their ultrasonic blades, these decorated veterans of that heroic, futile war, and stain the clear water with his blood? No, he decided. Someone needed him here, some force greater than these veterans. And dolphins always understood force.

"It matters because it has to happen," Stasov said. "It is necessary."

The dolphins hooted contempt. "You always do what is necessary, Colonel," Deimos said. "You tortured us until you ripped the voice from our throats—because it was necessary. You took away our bodies and turned us into mechanical sharks—because it was necessary. You killed us in your incomprehensible human war— because it was necessary. Now you come to tear us from the womb of our sea and throw us into the cold deeps of space *because it is necessary*?"

"Eating is necessary," Harmonia said. "Fucking is necessary. Breathing is necessary. Death is necessary. You're as stupid as a sea turtle that fucks in the sea and then climbs out into the air to lay its eggs where the land dwellers can steal them. I'm sure the turtle thinks it's necessary."

"Why then have I been called here to gather up your Messiah?"

"You have heard your own echo," Harmonia said. "You have called yourself. As far as we're concerned, you could stay out of the water and never hear us again."

"I—" Stasov felt exasperated. Would they now claim it was all his own doing, that he could just as easily have stayed home in bed? "Where is he? Send me to him."

The dolphins turned as one and pointed their snouts. "This way," they chorused. "But we advise you to return to your boat."

Wordlessly, Stasov swam past the Temple of Poseidon Pankrator, to an area of toppled statues.

Buried for millennia, their covering of volcanic ash had been carefully siphoned off and the statues covered with an inert plastic to prevent their corrosion. A fisherman, upraised arm holding a trident with a writhing octopus impaled on it, lay on his back, staring perplexedly up through the water at the sky. Near him, a net of corroded bronze held a harvest of squirming fish with inlaid silver scales. A bare-breasted woman with a slight smile poured from a flask.

These images meant nothing to the dolphins who swam over them, but they brought back to Stasov the natural grace of Minoan civilization. He was supposedly thirty-five hundred years wiser than they had been. All the glories of Classical Greek, Roman, Medieval, and Modern civilization lay invisible ahead of them. Still, it seemed that they had guessed some essential of life and managed to pay attention to it despite all the distractions that intelligence offers.

Stasov looked over the statues, seeking the figure of the Minodelphos, as if having that story made bronze or marble would somehow exorcise it. But no archaeologist examining Minoan remains had ever found so much as a trace of a half-man/half-dolphin figure. It seemed the story really did come from the dolphins, who could do no work in anything solid. Their art came in the form of words and memories, and he would not see those in the flickers of the sunlit waves running below him.

He swam forward wordlessly, politely generating an occasional click from his speakers, despite the fact that he had no way to use the echoes.

Ahead of him, Stasov could hear the chitter of an electronic translator. It babbled numbers: stock quotations, production figures. Stasov smiled to himself, remembering Theodoros's outrage. The Messiah as arbitrageur. The dolphin whose skills in finance could lift his race from the poisoned, dangerous sea and make it safe from human beings.

"I am here," Stasov called.

A moment of silence. And then God's Echo spoke: "What the fuck do you want?"

Stasov felt a moment of almost overwhelming irritation. Damn it all to hell, he'd struggled all the way through Homma, pulled a whale off a rock, confronted an orca—and for what? To be dealt with insolently by a two-bit underwater messiah. He swam forward quickly. Dolphins were quick, but if he could lure this one in close enough, there were points on his body that a quick elbow or knee . . . "Who are you?" he called softly.

"You know me, Stasov." The Messiah's voice was gleeful. "I know you. We came from the same belly, at Kagalaska."

God's Echo appeared ahead, a dolphin just like any other, with no apparent modifications. Another dolphin would have known him instantly from the cadences of his speech, but Stasov lacked that skill.

"The name I took is Weissmuller. Don't you remember?"

Stasov hesitated in shock for an instant, then, dismayed because he knew that was exactly what the dolphin had intended, moved again. "Weissmuller. You left us at Kagalaska. I thought you were dead."

"I was, as far as you were concerned. You're no different now, Stasov. You still twitch while you swim, as if full of an anemone's nerve toxin."

"I'm going to drive you from your sea, Weissmuller," Stasov said quietly. "I'm going to push you, force you, compel you. You will long for the nets of tuna harvesters, the spears of fishermen. You will be sorry you were ever born the Messiah. I guarantee it."

There was a moment of stunned silence from the dolphin. Stasov was pleased with himself. He had recovered the initiative.

Weissmuller came close. "Fuck you, Ilya Sergeiivich Stasov." He squealed piercingly. "Please me, please *me*. That's all that matters. I am not who you knew and abused in forgotten days. I am the Echo. You are a fool. Nothing else matters."

"Well. At least we understand each other."

CHAPTER FIFTEEN

2027

ANNA CALDERONE LOOKED BEYOND THE CHARTS AND DIA-
grams to Manila harbor, where, amid the grimy con-
tainer ships, a trim white yacht displayed its sails. The
outside air was thick with moisture and the window
she looked through grimy. The yacht moved like a
mirage. If it continued on its path, it would pass the
Bataan Peninsula, where, if he looked up from his
exhumation of the past, Ilya could see it. She wished
he would get back from his stupid memory recovery
expedition. She didn't like his being back in Homma
alone.

"Would that be an acceptable concentration, Ms.
Calderone?" She had taken a dislike to the hatchet-
faced Miranda Durbar upon meeting her, and every
word spoken in that glass-breaking voice only con-

firmed the antipathy. "Mr. Stasov doesn't seem to be here, so I can't ask *him* the question."

Calderone quickly glanced over the briefing chart. "I think I can handle it, Dr. Durbar. If the Hyundai filtration glomerulus can maintain a concentration of 2.4 percent salt in the dolphin's tank, I think that would be acceptable. That's not much below polar ocean water. A slightly higher magnesium chloride concentration would be preferable."

"Thank you." Durbar returned her attention to the exploded hologram of the space station Jupiter Forward that dominated the front of the room. "Since the dolphin tank is a spinning torus, some flexibility in the drop lines past the glomerulus is necessary. . . ."

Calderone felt like murdering her. It was unreasonable to expect someone to sit for a week in an over-air-conditioned room listening to technical discussions about a space station that was already substantially built. The whole thing could have been handled in an exchange of technical memos.

Her attention wandered and she stared out the window again. Where was that man? The yacht had vanished, but now she saw a small launch bouncing exuberantly over the waves, running past a massive LNG tanker. She remembered watching Ilya slump up the gangplank of the *Alexei Remizov*, duffel over his shoulder. He hadn't known she was there, standing behind a stack of packing crates. At that moment she had almost run after him. And now, all these years later, she couldn't remember why she hadn't.

The launch swerved and headed for the dock below the shimmering cubes of the Aquino Center, out of place in festering Manila. Its cool disdain for the city sprawled indolently around it revealed its Japanese origin. It was the unofficial center of the continuing

Japanese rule of Luzon. The Jupiter Exploration conferences had been held in St. Petersburg, Chicago, Geneva, New Delhi—and now Manila. Each city had had its own political complexities, and Japanese-ruled Manila was the worst.

Every time she let Ilya Stasov go out of her life, she had to hunt him down again. She was getting tired of it. Perhaps it was time she put him where she could keep an eye on him. The launch tied up, but the windows were too dirty for her to see the figure that jumped out of it.

Calderone stood up and, without apology, left the room. Several other meeting shirkers were gathered around the large coffee urn in the lobby, arguing vehemently. She passed near a frail old man, white hair standing up, as he gestured with half a doughnut. "No reason why there shouldn't be several different levels of life in the Jovian atmosphere, at different temperatures and densities. Say down below these huge structures, or convection cells, or creatures we see in the troposphere. Let me show you . . . damn it, why don't they have a blackboard out here?"

"Because you're not supposed to *be* out here, Dr. Twombley," Calderone said. "The UN Planetary Directorate put you in one of those meeting rooms for a good reason."

He peered at her quizzically. "And where are *you* supposed to be, Anna dear?"

"In orbit around Jupiter."

He shook his head enviously. "You will be soon enough. As for me . . ." He sighed. "Acceleration would crack these old bones. I have trouble getting up stairs, these days. It's a disgrace."

Calderone had met Ernest Twombley when he was already old, a professor of planetology at Berkeley specializing in Jovian theoretical ecology. He had, unbeknownst to him, served as her first link with Ilya at Uglegorsk.

"Perhaps you should take up delphinology," she said. "Then you could just float in the water all day."

Twombley looked thoughtful. "Now that those orcas seem to have a lock on interpreting Jovian communications, that's not such a bad idea. Our translation software is dubious at best. And that whale . . . what is it up to?"

"Most of Clarence's hardware has already been sent on a long orbit up to Jupiter. The important parts of him will be launched soon. We'll put it all together and have a planetary probe, courtesy of the Delphine Delegation."

"You were always such a smart girl, Anna. How did you know that delphinology and Jovian planetology would turn out to fit so well together?"

"Luck," she said. "I've been lucky. Excuse me."

She hurried up the hallway, the cracked floor uneven under her feet, and through the double doors into the Philippine sunlight. As always, she gasped and paused for a moment in the thick heat, letting her heart slow.

A narrow park fringed the cracking stucco of the University of Manila buildings. Thick-leaved trees overhung the flowering shrubs. The crystals of the Aquino Center rose beyond them. Side sessions on life-support systems and hydroponics were held there. Stasov had, the week before, presented the final plans for how the dolphin pens fit into the water-supply system—at least he had thought they were final until Dr. Durbar got hold of them.

Several of the UN-supplied limo drivers, bored with

their wait, waved to her, but she slid past them and into the wide street below the University. If he'd taken the normal amount of time checking the boat over and tying it up, he couldn't have gotten far.

She pushed her way through the mob on the street, feeling ridiculous. If she waited until evening he would surely reappear at the hotel. That would have been easy. But she had to know now.

Then she saw him, a tall, white-clothed figure standing just at the marina gates. His white flannel clothes, more appropriate for a croquet player, were covered with mud and grass stains. He held a pair of muddy hip waders under one arm and carried his old duffel on his shoulder.

"Ilya!" she shouted, and waved across the busy street. He didn't see her. He turned and walked slowly away. "Damn it." He was heading away from their hotel, the conference, everything. In a few seconds she would lose him.

Miraculously, the traffic stopped for a moment and she was able to dodge across before the mass of cars, buses, and jeepneys hurtled forward again. Ilya strolled casually along a bayside esplanade beneath the frowning Aquino Center. The water washing the concrete embankment was thick and opaque, bitter-smelling with the effluents of metropolitan Manila. As Anna moved behind him, she checked the set of his shoulders, the swing of his walk, trying to determine whether he was relieved, suicidally depressed, or simply thoughtful.

"Ilya." Now she spoke softly.

He turned to look at her without surprise. He ran his hand down the filthy front of his clothes. "I'm sorry, I'm dirty—"

"Don't be ridiculous." She put her arms around him.

He relaxed against her. "What did you find?"

"Nothing."

"Oh, Ilya. . . ."

"Never mind, that's pretty much what I was looking for. Actually, it wasn't quite nothing. Come here."

He led her to a metal bench facing the bay. They sat down and she held his arm. He laid the hip waders aside.

"It's a golf course," he said. "There's nothing left of Homma that I can see: the barracks, the interrogation chambers, even our old baseball field. They're all gone, buried under another eighteen beautifully landscaped holes. I couldn't find a damn thing." He chuckled. "They had to let me in, though. The Jovian Exploration Conference bought a block of guest memberships for us all. They did seem a bit confused that I didn't have any clubs."

Anna pictured Ilya's white-clad figure wandering the fairways like a ghost while Filipino politicians and Japanese businessmen teed off.

"One of the holes doglegs around the spot in the bay where they used to drop my cage. I waited until no one was around and climbed down the slope. There's a lot of garbage in the water, just as there was then. I dug around in the muck. I couldn't find any trace of the cage."

"Thank God," Anna said involuntarily. "What were you going to do? Get back into it?"

"I—" Ilya looked thoughtful. "You know, Anna, I couldn't stand a minute in that cage now. Imagine that. I used to spend twenty-four hours at a time in it. I got so used to it I would fight to stop them from taking me out of it."

"Oh, come on. They put you into it. The Japanese guards. You had no choice. Now you do."

"I don't think that's it." Ilya pulled thoughtfully at his chin as he stared across the bay in the direction of the invisible Bataan Peninsula. "I was being punished for my crimes. Now I *have* been punished and the score is settled." He reached into his pants pocket. "But while I was wading around in the muck, I did find something else."

He pulled out a lump of corroded metal and handed it to her. It was a brass symbol, a red star with a lightning bolt on either side. She looked at him questioningly.

"It's the emblem off a peaked hat—the emblem of a Red Army officer in Electronics."

Her eyes widened. "Do you think it belonged to—"

"It might be Makarygin's. I'll assume it is. They must have had a lot of old Soviet uniforms piled up somewhere. After they cleared out Homma they must have burned them and tossed everything out." He took the emblem from her and slipped it back into his pocket.

She leaned against him. The sun was searingly hot. She felt her hair going limp in the humidity. "Ilya, a couple of years ago we sat on a bench looking at the Moika Canal. It was twenty below zero Celsius. Now we're here baking in the sun. What's wrong with us? We have an air-conditioned hotel a couple of blocks away."

"We're just a couple of romantics."

"That's us. Did they chase you out of the country club then?"

"No. I did find one more thing."

"What?"

"Vsevolod Isayevich Makarygin died alone. There is no memorial to mark his passing, save in the memories of those of us who knew him. And we have somewhat different versions of what he said." He smiled to himself. "But I know what I learned from him. So, though it's foolish, and he himself would have condemned me for it, I felt that I had to take something away to commemorate him."

Anna knew better than to say anything.

"I walked out to the older part of the golf course, the part that was already there when I was at Homma. It's not really so much different now. I found the right spot—it's the eleventh hole, a par three. The greens committee will be enraged, but it was the only thing." He reached into his duffel and pulled out a perfect one-foot circle of dense green sod, dirt clinging to the roots. He laid it carefully on the bench. "He left a hell of a divot."

"SO YOU REALLY HAVE NO CHOICE," ANNA SAID.

"I know that," Ilya said. "It's just that I'm surprised to hear you say it."

They paused under a streetlight and finished the grilled beef and squid they had purchased at a cart. Bats flickered at the edge of the light, seeking the insects attracted there.

"Don't you think I want you to face your past? How else can I have you?"

"And you want me?" Ilya was suddenly tentative.

"Yes, damn you, and I won't have you if the dead hulk of Uglegorsk is always lying in bed with us."

"You don't mean that business with Grisha again—" Ilya began, suddenly irritated.

"*No*, I don't mean that. That's gone. Isn't it?"

"It is."

"Then quit bringing it up. I mean whatever happened to *you* there."

"I'm not sure I know what happened to me there."

"Then it's about time you went and found out."

* * *

THE JAPANESE GUARDS ESCORTED HIM CLOSELY FROM THE NEW gate through the ruins of the old Uglegorsk research station, their intentness more habit than from any fear that Stasov would do any damage. Little enough was left, and the place was no more attractive in death than it had been in life.

"Are you here because you are . . . sentimental?" Major Tomio seemed genuinely curious. He had the intent look of a scholar rather than a military officer.

Stasov glanced up at the high concrete vault of the laboratory, which was cracked and aging, like long-buried bone. He snorted. "Hardly. I am grateful for the forbearance of the Japanese government."

"Ah." Tomio nodded.

They walked along slowly. The day, oddly for Sakhalin, was sunny and warm, the sea an inviting blue, though Stasov knew it was still ice-cold. He looked around. Many of the transportable huts and equipment had been removed during the Pacific War, to be reused in other theaters, and even the traces of their foundations were hard to detect. He had spent two years of his life here—eaten in the same dining hall every day, pissed in the same latrine, slept in the same hut—but the land around him had shrugged these memories off, as it resisted so much else.

Tomio watched him carefully, noting every glance. Stasov wondered if the Japanese thought they could still wrest some secret from him simply by the ideogram formed by the pattern of his glances. Stasov wished the Major luck. There were no secrets left.

The guards suddenly stopped as if confronting an invisible wall, and he and the Major continued alone. They passed among the crumbled concrete of the dolphin pens. What meaning did these patterns have? If they were painted bright colors, they might mimic the effect of the Minoan cities Theodoros had taken him through. Who was to say that these had not been ritual enclosures of some sort? Baths for Temple virgins? Grain storage bins? He gazed over the remains and tried to conjure some completely different civilization, which might have used these forms to some other purpose. That much he could do, but try as he might, he could not imagine himself as a member of that civilization.

"There is a reason I was assigned here," Major Tomio said after a long pause. "I was stationed at Camp Homma at the end of the war."

Stasov felt a sudden hot shiver, a fear he had not felt while wandering the golf course that had replaced the camp. He had looked the Major in the face when they met, but now he tried to catch him only in flicking glances, afraid to be caught looking, as if the sharp pain of a kendo staff across his temple would greet this liberty. Stasov could not make the earnest, somewhat anxious face match any of the ones that still appeared in his dreams. They came into his room in the guise of friends seeking a bottle of vodka they had left there. When he could not find it, they pulled the furniture apart and built a cage. They shoved him into it and threw it out of the window, letting it float down to the boiling sea far below. Omi was there, and Nobu, and Colonel Yokota. But not this Major Tomio.

"I was not guarding prisoners," Tomio said hurriedly. "I was analyzing data. But I was nevertheless responsible."

Stasov turned and looked him full in the face. "Do you feel guilty?"

Tomio seemed startled. "No . . . not guilty. I was—am—a serving military officer. Guilt is not quite the correct word. I would see the Russian prisoners sometimes, being marched across the golf course. They shouldn't have done that. Some of you would always try to scuff the greens." He sounded a trifle outraged.

"Russians tend to be spiteful," Stasov explained, smiling to himself.

"But you don't understand." Tomio was stumbling over words in his urge to explain. "I didn't know. I merely analyzed the data. We retrieved information that helped us genetically modify alfalfa roots and improve our electronic countermeasures."

"Alfalfa roots," Stasov said in wonder. Razor-blade-lined cages, beatings, starvation. And alfalfa roots. "Did you think they sat us down in a conference room with a blackboard and a pot of coffee?"

"No! I am letting you understand that I do not shirk responsibility. Colonel Yokota and several others from Camp Homma were tried and punished. The trials were televised. Did you watch them?"

"I must have missed it."

"It was all quite dramatic. Colonel Yokota wept and begged forgiveness." Tomio said this with such relish that Stasov suspected personal hostility. "He pleaded to be allowed to apologize to every prisoner personally."

"It is not my job to forgive or punish him," Stasov said.

"You needn't worry. Japanese courts have done the job without depending on your objectivity."

Stasov smiled reminiscently. "Poor Yokota. He never knew himself for what he was: a dark angel of God."

"I don't understand."

"There is no need for you to. So whatever happened to our Colonel Yokota?"

"He is free now, tending a garden in a Zen Buddhist monastery in the south. He understands his part."

"And I am expected to understand mine."

"I think that you do, Colonel Stasov."

They stopped at another invisible wall. The vault of the research labs loomed over them, dark and fissured. Stasov stared at the Japanese Major. Had he expected tearful confessions, a kneeling man with his arms around Stasov's knees, begging forgiveness? A dramatic act of suicide, Tomio's guts spilling out on the rocks of Sakhalin? Tomio understood what life required. Stasov studied him, hoping to learn from him what it was.

"I wanted to be clear, Colonel—but you do not like the military title, do you? Very well, Mr. Stasov. We were military men serving in our official capacities. Some of us exceeded our authority—and were punished. But we understand your claims against us. We owe it to you not to forget you."

If it was an apology, it was the most arrogant one Stasov had ever received. But it made perfect sense. Tomio wasn't seeking release. Stasov's forgiveness would make no difference, since it was a feeling of personal responsibility that oppressed Tomio. So Stasov nodded. But he did not take Major Tomio's hand. That was still something he could not bring himself to do.

"Did you know any of the prisoners personally?" Stasov asked. He longed to hear a familiar name that would link this precise officer with the hell Stasov remembered of Camp Homma.

"Very few. There was one . . . a Makrigi?"

Stasov felt a chill in his scalp. "Makarygin. A Major—electronics."

"Yes, that's him!" Tomio was as delighted as if they

had discovered a common school friend. "He was shot."

"Yes."

"A troublesome man. He treated us as if we were servants who were not doing our job properly."

Stasov smiled at that. Makarygin had been capable of a humility that was close to arrogance, a personality defect of many holy men.

"I talked with him," Tomio said. "He was the most frightening of you."

Stasov felt a warm glow. It was as high a compliment as a prisoner could receive from a former guard. Tired contempt was not the only emotion that the prisoners had evoked at Homma.

"A madman of course." Tomio frowned. "His information was always subtly wrong. He blamed it on the makeshift way Soviet engineering was done and accused us of not being able to make do. Us! We had access to much finer equipment than he had ever seen. I could tell by the way he looked at it that he coveted it."

Indeed he had. Makarygin had almost wept at the wealth of equipment the Japanese had offered him. "The kingdoms of the Earth," he had whispered. "From a mountaintop. The work I could do. . . ." That had always been an important part of Makarygin. As far as he was concerned, a holy man who was useless on earth was bound to be similarly useless in heaven. It didn't matter whether he split wood, fed the hungry, designed heart defibrillators, or played the flute. But he had to have some kind of demonstrable good, or his words were not to be listened to. Clearly Makarygin had felt that being a designer of ECM equipment for the Soviet Air Force to use against its enemies was to be considered an earthly good. Makarygin had been an exponent of a truly twenty-first-century religious philosophy.

"He was a good engineer," Tomio said. "He fooled us for months with his false solutions. We finally found out that all he had done was completely useless. Someone reverse-engineered a captured circuit from one of your ground-attack planes and detected his deliberate flaws. He had been lying to us!"

"So you killed him," Stasov said. "Just before the prisoners were released."

"I had nothing to do with those matters," Tomio said, suddenly cold. "You may proceed. A friend is waiting for you."

"A friend? I didn't agree to that."

"He said you wouldn't mind. He is from the Russian ship. My authority does not extend to him."

"Of course not," Stasov said, as if the Japanese couldn't control access to a site surrounded by a twelve-foot fence topped with barbed wire. Another example of their balance of responsibilities? He would soon find out.

Tomio nodded up at the vault. "We keep this place deserted. There are stories that the laboratory is haunted, that the even flow of the universe is disturbed there."

"The laboratory is gone. Only its bones remain. And its consequences."

Makarygin lay dead on the putting green, flecked with scarlet blood. He leaned intently toward Ilya, desperate to make his point, to make this dull delphinologist understand the truth. He sat on his bunk, hand raised in ironic salute, as the guards hauled Stasov away. Stasov wished he had Makarygin by his side. But he had to face this thing alone, as any man did. He climbed a set of stairs and entered the lab high up on the vault.

It was the scene of his nightmares. The tanks were now empty, the floor dry, the electronics long since packed up and discarded, but the high vault of the laboratory still contained all the pain and terror that Stasov could imagine. From the platform where he stood the pattern of tanks on the floor looked like an ice cube tray in an abandoned refrigerator. Thin strips of light slanted in through cracks in the vault.

Stasov held tightly to the thin metal railing though there was no danger of falling. Even empty, the building whispered.

Suddenly something thunked on the metal stairs. Stasov shivered. He had thought himself the only ghost. The thunk became regular, and Stasov heard the heavy breathing of someone pulling himself up the stairs.

A large figure loomed out of the darkness. "Ilya," the man said. "It's been a long time."

"Tolya!" Stasov embraced the massive Anatoly Ogurtsov and kissed him. He hadn't seen the General since Kagalaska.

Ogurtsov stepped back. His right foot was a prosthetic. When he noticed Stasov's attention, he slapped it with his cane. "Not an orca, unfortunately," he rumbled. "Nothing appropriate like that. A single bullet through the knee at Unimak. An ordinary soldier's wound." He reached into his jacket, pulled out a vodka bottle, yanked the stopper out with his teeth and offered it to Stasov. "To old times."

"To old times," Stasov responded, and took a swallow. He almost choked.

Ogurtsov chuckled. "Now don't insult me, Ilya. I make that stuff myself. An old man's hobby. Flavored with buffalo grass." He sat down on the stairs.

"It's excellent," Stasov managed to choke, tears in his eyes.

"Have you lost your taste for vodka?" Ogurtsov laughed. "I remember," he gestured with his cane at the tanks below, "how we sat, you, me, and that Greek philosopher Theodoros, and unriddled the ways of the dolphins. The drunker we got, the more sense we made of their myths and their gods. And we figured it out."

"And we did it. We tortured them until they spoke."

Ogurtsov regarded him warily. "Is that how you see it, Ilya?"

"Yes! It's been clear all along. All the time! And damn, Tolya, we're supposed to be so smart. We should have known."

"We stood around that tank," Ogurtsov pointed, "you, me, Sadnikova—whatever happened to her?— Mikulin, Theodoros, Panin. Panin died at Kagalaska, as I remember. And Mikulin? A veteran's death. He got drunk one New Year's, fell down in a snowdrift, and froze to death. Just a couple of years ago, that was." Ogurtsov pushed himself to his feet with his cane. "We used your final pattern, the eruption of Strogyle. And Kestrel said—"

" 'Let me die!'," Stasov said through clenched teeth. "They re-create the world through their own perceptions. They have absolute faith in their senses. Our images caused them incredible agony. It was torture."

Ogurtsov shrugged, uninterested. "How could we have known that then?"

"I did know!" Stasov surprised even himself. "I must have. How else could I have succeeded?"

"That's a question I can't answer, Ilya. But succeed we did."

"So the War Crimes Commission was right the whole time."

Ogurtsov looked unimpressed. "That was twelve years ago, Ilya. A war ago. A lifetime." He looked out over the cracked, empty pools. "And here, all this time, I thought you were living out your responsibility. You've driven yourself out into support of this ridiculous cetacean scheme for communicating with the beasts of Jupiter. You've made it possible. Why, if not to make restitution? I thought that, like the rest of us, you faced yourself and continued living."

"Have we now? Does that make our sin any less?"

"Sin?" Ogurtsov's thick eyebrows crawled together at the word like gathering thunderclouds. Even the word, *grekh*, in Russian, sounded like an early rumble of thunder in his throat. "You dare use that word to me, Ilya Sergeiivich? Do you dispose of my soul so easily?"

"I try to call things by their right name," Stasov said stubbornly.

"Right name. Some words can only be used by certain people, Ilya. The word 'sin' can only be used by someone who believes in God. Do you? Does God exist for you?"

Stasov froze. He'd been caught again. Makarygin had always caught him, and now Ogurtsov saw through him too.

Ogurtsov moved toward him, only a few inches taller than Stasov but twice as wide. He looked like a peasant overseer talking back to a nobleman. "You listen to nice stories about a cetacean God rising up from the bottom of the sea, changing reality. They believe it, or some of them do. You don't. You *don't*."

Stasov did not turn away from the other's wrathful blue eyes. "No, I do not believe in the dolphin God."

"Don't play games now. Do you believe in God? Not necessarily in 'God the Father, creator of the heavens and the earth, and in his only Son, Jesus Christ, begotten, not made . . .'" Ogurtsov quoted the rolling old Church Slavonic words of the Nicene Creed. "Any God at all will do for me now. Do you believe?"

"No," Stasov said. "I've tried. But God does not appear simply because it seems reasonable that He should."

"The King of Assyria said, 'By the strength of my hand I have done it, and by my wisdom, for I have the understanding'. That's from Isaiah. You always were an arrogant son of a bitch, Ilya. Do you really believe that your guilt is more important than anyone else's? You make the King of Assyria a modest man."

"Oh, Tolya, what should I do now?"

Ogurtsov shrugged massively. "Well, Ilya, it looks like you're just going to have to live with it."

"You bastard."

"There we go." Ogurtsov embraced Stasov, who relaxed against the other's wide chest.

He'd tormented Kestrel and the other dolphins in ignorance, only realizing afterward what he had done. And he'd been punished at Homma, though his tormentors had not realized they were committing justice. He thought of Makarygin. That ancient holy man would have permitted Stasov his life, though he might well have been appalled at how long it had taken Stasov to face the truth.

The Uglegorsk research station was suddenly nothing but an empty, decaying building.

"Let's get out of here," Stasov said.

They walked silently through the rest of the building. The sky had regained its usual high overcast. The *Sterlet*, the boat that had brought Ogurtsov, floated offshore, its gaily fluttering white, blue, and red Russian Republic flag a spot of color against the sea and sky.

The shore was uneven, but Ogurtsov maneuvered easily over the rocks, occasionally kicking a loose one with his prosthetic foot. "You haven't asked me why I'm here, Ilya."

"You mean you weren't just dropping by for old times' sake?" Past the arch of the main building Stasov could see the tiny figures of the Japanese as they waited for him. "I assume you got a call—from the Delphine Delegation. Who else could have pressured the Japanese into letting you come here?"

"Seems obvious, I guess. I wouldn't have figured it out."

"They have a vested interest in my continued mental health. They like to think they're clever." Stasov tried not to feel pleased with himself. "As do I. We work things out."

Ogurtsov snorted. "Sounds like you have the same relationship I have with my wife."

Orca dorsal fins cut the water a few hundred meters off shore. Stasov waved. They dove and vanished.

"Except that when you go for a swim with her you don't have to worry whether she'll kill you."

"You don't know my wife." Ogurtsov shook his head. "What will you do now, Ilya?"

"What I have been doing, actually. Living and facing the consequences. The dolphins have given me their Messiah—Weissmuller, do you remember him?"

Ogurtsov made a face. "I do. None of this makes any sense. How did they choose him?"

"Cetacean Messiahs choose themselves and are tested—I'm not yet sure how, though the orcas surely have something to do with it. But they've tied me to him—to use me for what I have done."

Ogurtsov smiled thoughtfully. "And you want to use them. You wouldn't be Ilya Stasov if you didn't."

"Let's just say that what the cetaceans want and

what I want can be satisfied by a single series of events."

"Jupiter," Ogurtsov breathed. "You are a crazy bastard, Ilya."

"You are too kind, Tolya."

CHAPTER SIXTEEN

2028

WEISSMULLER'S MIND SWAM UP FROM THE SILT IN WHICH it had sunk. Sounds emerged from silence. And barriers—human barriers. He was once again imprisoned in a tank. This was the fate of the latest dolphins to proclaim themselves Echoes. From now on, it was impossible for the world to change without the acquiescence of humans.

"No!" Weissmuller shouted. His voice echoed from the curved walls. Those damn orcas thought too much. It made them stupid. Not that he would ever say that where they could hear it.

A few instants later Weissmuller heard his own voice coming from behind him. He swirled to face it and shouted again. His voice came from behind again. He swam slowly forward, trying to figure out what sea he found himself in.

It curved back around itself like a whirlpool. He could swirl around and around in it and never come to an end. The bottom always curved up to either side of him, but wherever he went, down stayed below him. Leave it to humans to think up something so clever and pointless.

Weissmuller shrieked with glee and sped around the torus of his tank, chasing his own words. The universe spun madly around him. "I'm going to be rich!" he yelled, using a word new to dolphins. "Rich!" He chortled with delight.

"Weissmuller." The word popped into the water like a moray eel from its hole. Weissmuller turned, slid past a wall, and stopped.

"Ilya Stasov." Weissmuller reminded himself to stay calm. He was God's Remora. He had no need to fear. But it was useless. Stasov was the nearest thing to an orca on Jupiter Forward. Weissmuller forced himself to calm down. Stasov was an orca, but even orcas could be used. It was the path of an Echo to use them.

"We have work to do," Stasov said.

"Now?" Weissmuller said plaintively. "Where are we?"

"In orbit around Jupiter, in Ganymede's trailing trojan point."

"I don't know what that means."

"I'm not sure I do either. That doesn't change anything."

Weissmuller swam slowly up to where Stasov sat, dangling his legs in the water. It was an irritating thing to do, leaving most of your body beyond honest sound perception. Just those ridiculous flopping limbs and the damn transducer. It was a duplicitous action, and made Weissmuller suspicious. "Why are we here, Ilya?"

"Because we need you, just as you need us. You have to translate for us and manage Clarence. He's not going to like what's happened to him."

"Then why did you do it to him?" Weissmuller already understood how sensitive Stasov was to being needled like this. "Why didn't you just leave him alone?"

"Leave him to die on that rock? A rock that dolphins chased him onto, as I don't think I need to remind you."

Humans never stuck to the point, always bringing in irrelevant circumstances. Their thinking was always distorted and obscure. "So what is he now?"

"He was brought here as his essential self: his nerves, his endocrine system, a couple of organs. And that's it. That part of him is smaller than you are. His new body is being built around it. And they are almost done. That's why we need you."

"You're using us again, Stasov. You used us like sharks' teeth in your war. Now you'll drop us into this other sea and bloody it as well. Isn't that why we're here? You will turn us all into great machines and send us on our duty. Duty!" He squeaked the word in contempt.

Stasov was silent for a moment. "Conquer Jupiter? Sure. Perhaps, as a start, we'll just conquer the Great Red Spot. It is, after all, only twice as big across as the planet Earth."

Weissmuller shrieked and splashed him. "Don't mock me, human! I can buy and sell you *and* your miserable planet. Drop it into your stupid Red Spot if you want. It won't make any difference to me."

"Sure, Weissmuller." Stasov was clearly unimpressed. "But for now we still have our jobs to do. If that's using you, then that's what it is. Let's get you into your suit."

THE WHALE SCREAMED IN FEAR, THE COMPLEX HARMONICS OF his terror rumbling in Anna Calderone's earphones. Computer-controlled rockets adjusted the position of her instrumentation platform.

The sperm whale suddenly breached the surface of darkness and rose up out of Ganymede's invisible shadow, fusion rockets burning blue along his length. Sunlight gleamed along Clarence's great ridged bulk and glittered on the tessellations of the phased microwave array on his back.

" 'Can you draw out Leviathan with a fishhook?' " someone whispered in her ear. " 'Will he make a covenant with you to take him for your servant forever?' No, my Lord. Now my eye sees Thee. Therefore I despise myself, and repent in dust and ashes." It was Stasov's voice. He floated somewhere beyond the whale, far away from her.

The whale's new body was magnificent, more than a kilometer long, elaborately planed for maneuvering in the Jovian atmosphere. It was not like anything Calderone had ever seen. The whale cried out again, his fear probing the shallow waters of insanity. The roar thundered over her.

"Whee!" She laughed over the channel to her lover. "Isn't he incredible, Ilya? I don't believe it!" She had watched the engineers put the whale's new body together, piece by piece, and carefully insert the tiny bundle of brains and glands that now animated it. "I hope he calms down soon, the poor dear. He sounds scared out of his wits."

"Don't get too amused," Stasov said. "I can't find our dolphin."

"What do you mean?" Calderone was too excited to attend to his words. Jupiter loomed multicolored beyond the whale. The silver dot of Jupiter Forward gleamed far away toward the crescent sphere of Ganymede. Instrumentation platforms closer to her caught the sun, their purposes inscrutable to her.

"I mean I don't know where he is, dammit!" His voice was sharp.

"Relax, Ilya. You know how undependable—"

"Call up some astronomical data. I don't have access. Find him!"

Calderone sighed to herself, not letting him hear. He got so excited sometimes, so tied up inside. But she did as he asked. The space station's computer dumped imagery on her in her Head Up Display, giving her an imaginary perspective of surrounding space. The Galilean satellites rolled around Jupiter's gravity well, each pulling its own dimple with it. The space station was a wobbling speck, twirling around the trailing trojan point.

The computer located Weissmuller's transponder and displayed the dolphin as a bright spark. He had dived down into Jupiter's gravity well and slingshotted out toward Io. Before she could request it, the computer informed her that Weissmuller was at least an hour away.

The whale continued to send out echo-location clicks in the microwave band, unable to understand how he had lost consciousness in the Indian Ocean and woken here, in this mysterious clear and bottomless sea with vast and distant spheres bobbing in it.

The flare of rockets along the whale's sides vanished and he drifted dark against the stars. Despite the possible danger, Calderone maneuvered the platform in and swooped low over the whale's back. The platform was capable of high acceleration, but in the absence of landmarks its speed was not usually apparent to her. She looped crazily around his massive forequarters and the universe spun.

She laughed. "Ilya! Once, in Monterey Bay, I managed to get on the back of a gray whale. I don't know why he let me, and I've never found any cetacean who would explain it to me. And I rode him. He swam along without diving until I fell off. I was laughing so hard I almost drowned. Couldn't have been more than fifteen seconds, but I'll always remember it."

"This isn't a friendly gray whale," Stasov said tensely. "This is a rogue sperm. He was chased onto the rocks, almost killed, and is now a cyborg, not through his own will. He's not a big puppy, Anna."

"I know, I know. Don't be such a mother hen, Ilya. We've communicated with him. He's not a bad sort. Just an oceangoing curmudgeon. Like you. We've been doing fine."

"That's because we've had Weissmuller to handle the communications. I haven't even been sure what they've been talking about. It's a form of language I'm not familiar with." She heard Stasov's breath in her earphones. "You could drown out here, Anna. Weissmuller told me about it. I want to rise to the surface for air. It doesn't matter if air's in your lungs, you need to jump out of the water and *breathe*."

"Weissmuller." She was airily contemptuous. "He's too busy admiring his reflection in the cosmic mirror to be of any help to us."

"Please, Anna, move away. We have to wait until Weissmuller gets back."

"That could be *hours*."

Irregular bursts of fire appeared along Clarence's sides, imparting a spin to the cyborg whale. Worried signals flickered through her HUD. The whale screamed again. The noise was a high-amplitude microwave signal sent out to the stars, and it was also a scream of terror.

"All right, Ilya, maybe you have a—"

The whale suddenly flared beneath her like a lit firework and expanded in size. Calderone's fingers tightened on the struts of the instrumentation platform as if she was on a raft in a storm. It was useless. Before she could make another sound, the whale came up beneath her and slammed into her like a wall.

CALDERONE'S VOICE CHOKED OFF, LEAVING SILENCE. FROM where he floated, Stasov could see nothing against the burning glare of the whale's engines.

"Anna!" he shouted, but there was no answer.

An instant later the whale was dark and silent once again, save for a constellation of retro-rockets at its nose, which brought its velocity back stationary with respect to the distant Jupiter Forward. Space was serene. Voices babbled in his earphones.

Stasov hit the emergency comm channel. "The whale has struck Anna Calderone's instrument platform. Please send immediate medical assistance. Ilya Stasov is pursuing." He cut the line off before anyone could tell him not to do it.

The trajectory display showed him Calderone's path. The whale hadn't actually hit the platform very hard. It was now traveling at six meters a second to the Jupiter system North. Without thinking about what he was doing, Stasov followed it. He moved his hypothetical path to intersect Calderone's on his HUD. The suit obediently fired its rockets to turn hypothesis into reality.

"Reaction mass adequate," Jupiter Forward's computer said grudgingly.

The whale sank under him, diminishing to a speck. Soon Stasov had lost all landmarks, the banded sphere of Jupiter his only companion. The suit's processor, linked to the computer, always kept track of him, but he had never learned to feel comfortable with it. A string of bits was not enough for him to hold onto. The rockets cut off and he hung seemingly motionless in space, listening to the sound of his own breath. He consciously kept it slow and even. The computer had decided to cut the rockets. It must have had an excellent reason. His heartbeat pulsed in his throat.

"Anna?" he whispered. A wash of static answered him.

The rocket at the base of his spine fired. A few moments later a flickering speck appeared ahead of him. It grew and became the slowly tumbling wreckage of the instrumentation platform. Stasov's suit matched velocities but kept him safely out of reach.

Calderone's space-suited figure hung in the twisted platform's embrace. Her arms floated out by centrifugal force as if she were a drowned body. He couldn't tell if she was still alive.

Manually overriding the space suit's reaction control, Stasov moved toward the spinning platform. A red light in his helmet indicated the computer's displeasure at this decision. He reached out and snagged a bent girder. There was a slight tug, and suddenly the stars were spinning, the platform still. Shadows grew, covered him, shrank, and vanished as the sun revolved around his tiny world.

"Anna!" Stasov peered into her face plate. Did her eyelids flicker, or was that just the shadows chasing across her face? He reached up and pulled her arms down, as if that uncomfortable position was the problem.

She moaned. The urge to put his arms around her was almost overpowering. Instead he hung as close to her as he could and felt his tears flow upward through his eyebrows. He could see the white elastic layer on the side of the suit and over the adjoining girders where her suit's self-sealer had sprayed.

He let her arms go and they drifted back upward. He checked her air supply to make sure that she was getting oxygen and sprayed an extra layer of sealant over the damaged areas of her suit: left side and leg and across to the center of her chest. Then, with slow care, he started trying to bend the girders that trapped her. Though the whale had twisted them like overcooked spaghetti, they barely yielded in his grip.

"Get out of the way, damn it!" a voice yelled in his earphones.

He looked up. A rescue sled now circled around the platform like the stars and the sun. A medic clung to the wreckage just above him. KOPKE was stenciled on his suit. Stasov ran a hand down Anna's head and shoulder and pulled himself back. Kopke pushed forward and cut through the girders with a laser, flipping it with the quick expertise of a kendo master. They parted. Another medic joined him and together they pulled Anna's motionless body free. Flames blossomed on their suits and they curved out from the platform to the rescue sled, where a third suited figure waited. They strapped her in and the sled vanished in a puff of blue flame. Stasov stared at it in wonder.

"You'll need this." It was Kopke again. Without asking for permission, he clicked an auxiliary reaction pod onto the backpack of Stasov's suit. "You used up a lot of fuel getting out here."

"Thank you," Stasov said. "Will she be—"

"Back at the station." And Kopke vanished.

Stasov spent another moment hanging onto the deserted platform wreckage staring out at the circling stars. They moved like sharks around a bloody body. He made a trajectory inquiry to Jupiter Forward's computer. Weissmuller was heading back in toward the station. Stasov let go of the platform and directed his suit to take him home. It was a couple of minutes before he realized that the shaking in his limbs was not fear, but rage.

WEISSMULLER PUMPED HIS WAY TOWARD THE SPACE STATION, his entire body aching with fatigue. He'd never swum so far before, and he couldn't stop to take a rest. That was all right. The universe was really not such a big place after all.

Though Weissmuller accepted his space suit as his due, it was a marvel, following his contours closely. Since dolphins cannot see upward, the head dome was clear on the underside only, revealing the slyly grinning jaws. The suit circulated water around the dolphin's body while hugging it closely to prevent bruising his tender dolphin skin. The microwave array thrust up between the oxygen tanks on either side of his dorsal fin.

Myoelectric connections to Weissmuller's swimming muscles operated his suit rockets, so that his motions in space were the same as they were in the water. The powerful movements of his tail operated thrust rockets; his fins fired steering rockets. A velocity-dependent retro-rocket simulated the resistance of water, slowing him if he ceased to thrust with his tail. He was kept stable by automatic sightings on the fixed stars which washed around him like sea foam.

Weissmuller felt a resonant self-satisfaction. All the way out to Io and back! Jupiter and its satellites floated around him like diatoms. His echo-location signals told him that Jupiter and its satellites were only kilometers away, since the microwave signals took a few seconds to get to them and back. He knew that the distance was actually much greater, but the illusion was powerful, giving him the feeling that the Jovian system could have been dropped into the Aegean Sea and lost.

"I fuck you, Jove!" he shouted, and shrieked in delight. He felt an erection and cursed the human engineers who had not designed the suit to provide him a release for it. He hunched, trying to rub it against something. No good. The suit fit too well. Humans had hands, so they could masturbate. Their one evolutionary advantage. He wanted a female to assault, but there wasn't one for thousands of kilometers. Another human oversight. They were playing games with him.

He thought of a shark he and the rest of his pod had killed. The dolphins had violated it repeatedly, contemptuously, then sent its body spinning into the depths, cursing it as it sank. The thought gave him a warm glow. And that sailor who had fallen off his fishing boat near Malta! Humans were poorly built, and Weissmuller still fondly remembered the way the man's ribs had cracked like brittle coral against his snout. Had there been witnesses, of course, the dolphins would have ignored him, or even saved his life by pushing him to shore, the sort of grandstand behavior that so impressed humans. But it had been night and the man alone in the sea. How he had struggled! One of Weissmuller's brothers still bore scars from the man's scaling knife, making him a target for mockery.

Weissmuller's lust was now an agony. Could he ever violate Jupiter the same way? Could even the humans, through one of their massive, incomprehensible devices? Damn them for this insulating suit!

He squeaked an instruction into his suit's computer. He had to distract himself before he went crazy and tried to attack the space station's air lock when he got to it. That would be embarrassing. That *was* the human word, wasn't it? Yes, yes. Damn them. First they refused to allow him access to females, then they wanted him to behave. Unreasonable, like all human demands.

In response to his instruction, the computer dumped the latest data on international securities trading. He felt the flows of money like the long, sweet currents in the Cyclades, where he had played as a child. What a roiled and complex sea the humans had invented! Capital flowed from Japan the way fresh water pours from an iceberg. The wars in Kerala and the Chaco sucked money, forming huge vortices. Complex securities schooled and reacted like fish, moving together in response to variations in pressure. Tariffs formed barriers, though there were secret flows that moved around or under them.

Weissmuller checked his investments. They were concealed under a variety of front organizations, clever hermit crabs. He used intermediaries, and no one knew that he was a dolphin. His echo was false, misleading. No other dolphin could swim in that sea. It was his own. But then, no other dolphin was God's Remora. He could eat the morsels from Her jaws.

Weissmuller swam more quickly, straining the capacity of his rockets. Where was the surface? How could he rise to breathe . . . or to die? The true death, he knew, was above, beyond the sound-reflecting surface of the water that was the soft boundary of a dolphin's universe. When the time came and completion was reached, a dolphin's soul was lifted beyond, into the burning air where echoes did not return. Weissmuller felt a giggling panic rising within. He was God's Remora. What happened to him when he died?

But there was no surface here, and no bottom. Only vast, transparent space. The space station grew in front of him. Exuberantly, Weissmuller did a poly-octave Tarzan yell which stretched up into the ultrasonic, and swam toward it.

"Weissmuller," a distant voice murmured. "So glad that you could make it back."

Arching around the space station, Weissmuller whipped his tail to brake. He pinged out several echo-location signals, but they brought back no useful information.

"Come here, Weissmuller. We need to talk." He finally recognized it. It was Stasov's voice. The dolphin fought down a sudden urge to flee. He was bone-tired. But where was that stupid human?

"Weissmuller!" The voice buffeted at the dolphin, impossibly loud. He whipped quickly around the station, dodging the equipment that orbited it. Microwave echo-location was useless at this range since the click and its return overlapped, but the clever humans had installed a processor which gave the dolphin a calculated synthetic echo. There was still no sign of Stasov—or the whale.

"Weissmuller," Stasov's voice said. "We need to have a little talk." Aided by computer voice synthesis, he could speak almost as well as a dolphin. Weissmuller found the man's speech slightly menacing, as if the dolphin words concealed orca teeth.

"Bugger off," Weissmuller snarled. Then, after a pause: "Where the hell are you?"

"Where am I?" Stasov's tone was amused. "Where are you?"

"You know where I am! And you know who I am. Don't screw around."

"True. But you really should come join us. Clarence has been a little lonely."

His voice was replaced by the long, agonized rumble of a sperm whale call, a lonely call of terror. Swimming across the front of the long call, Weissmuller finally figured out its direction, directly toward the North. Dolphins had a biomagnetic sense, useless and misleading away from Earth's magnetic field, so the engineers had installed a synthetic magnetic orientation system based on true north as established by star sightings. Weissmuller had an absolute sense of orientation. He swam toward the whale's voice.

After a few minutes he realized how tired he was. Stupid. Humans could rest while they moved through space, but that had proved impossible for a dolphin. He had to *move*, to feel his control over himself. Now he wanted to just float along taking slow breaths and let his muscles relax. He was afraid. Of Stasov? Why? His echo-location signals showed nothing ahead except a large spinning chunk of debris. Humans left their complex shit wherever they went. The bottom of the Aegean echoed with everything from bronze statues to airplanes.

"Ah, Weissmuller."

"What do you want?"

"I want you." The human responded quickly. He was about as far as that debris. Was he hiding in it? Dolphins knew almost no physics, impossible to learn in a high-viscosity environment like the ocean, but Weissmuller had picked it up. He was a smart swimmer. Stasov shouldn't fuck with him.

Without any warning whatsoever, the bulk of the cyborg sperm whale loomed right over the dolphin's head. Weissmuller's echo-location clicks were flung right back at him. The whale was huge, huge, vaster than even the blue whales had been. Weissmuller had never heard a blue whale, since they had vanished long before his birth, but he had heard the stories and the folk-told echoes. Weissmuller dove in fright and the sperm whale sped by, tiny blue rockets burning along his length. How could he have missed the whale? It was like floating on the surface and getting run over by a human ship. Impossible, in other words. The whale seemed to have popped out of nowhere.

"You have to talk to Clarence," Stasov said. "It's our agreement."

"I don't feel like it," Weissmuller said.

"He needs your help. He's in terror."

"He sounds fine to me. I want to go back. I don't feel well."

Weissmuller's echo-location signals finally showed the human, tiny against the vastness of the whale, like some skin parasite rubbed off by accident.

"You agreed."

"I did not!" Weissmuller yelped. "I agreed to come out here and hear space. I didn't agree to give language lessons to a goddam lump-headed idiot. He's here because he dropped himself on a rock. I can't talk to him."

"You must." Stasov's voice was ominous, its very quiet reasonableness suddenly terrifying. "The consequences have already been bad."

"Don't try to threaten me! You can't. Article Fifteen of the Treaty of Santa Barbara. It's about, ah—"

"Freedom From Unadjudicated Punishments. If you're going to be legalistic, you should get it right."

"That's it!" the dolphin said, unabashed. "Threaten me and I'll tell the Delphine Delegation. They'll replace you. See if they won't."

"Don't be an idiot, Weissmuller. They won't replace me."

Weissmuller twitched irritably, setting off random bursts of fire from his rockets. He knew they would never replace Stasov, no matter what the human did. Stasov had his role, as they all did.

"You must talk to Clarence now, Weissmuller. He's in terror. He doesn't know where he is. He needs your help."

"Fuck you!" Weissmuller shrieked and buffeted Stasov with his powerful tail. The man sailed off helplessly, tumbling until he managed to regain control with his own clumsy maneuver rockets.

"You float like a jellyfish," Weissmuller called. "A sea urchin!" He was pleased with himself for having managed to decoy the man that close.

When Weissmuller was young, he'd heard a story about ghost voices, long-dead whales whose last calls had echoed around the seas for decades, refracting through thermoclines, sucked into the depths by cold subsurface cataracts, resonating through abyssal trenches, to finally rise up and moan their long-sunken words to the hearing of a terrified dolphin. Stasov's voice sounded like that suddenly, the voice of someone who has ceased living.

"I never meant to do this again, Weissmuller. You give me no choice. Forgive me."

"Forgive you? Feed me and I'll forgive you. Ha ha." While orcas and humans laughed, dolphins expressed their pleasure more in the way an elderly pervert snorts at short-skirted schoolgirls.

Suddenly Weissmuller heard the wide sounds of the sea—the clicks, groans, wails, chitters, and thumps of the aquatic obbligato. Ranging far away were the overlapping calls of a gam of humpback whales and the sharp slap as one of them breached and fell back into the water. Nearer were the loud thumps of a school of the tiny fish humans called sea drums. Weissmuller was afraid. His eyes saw Jupiter, Ganymede, and the distant stars. He knew that was what was around him. The sea that he heard was distant, impossibly distant. It did not exist here.

Despite himself, he pinged out an echo-location signal. To his surprise, the echo returned, bearing a load of impossible information.

Bottom was a mile down, past an ill-defined thermocline. A set of three submerged volcanic peaks, coral atolls growing up around them as they sank, loomed from the abyssal plain, the nearest twenty kilometers away. Much nearer was a seamount that just broke the surface, vanishing through the quivering, reflective air/water interface to create, somewhere beyond Weissmuller's hearing, a tiny island.

He knew this place. The dolphin languages had a variety of names for each place in the sea, words that were schematics of the echo the topography returned in response to echo-location pulses. These words were essentially physical puns. An intelligent dolphin could carry a map of all the world's seas in his head like an epic poem.

Weissmuller was near the Maldive Islands. No, no, he wasn't—he was in orbit around Jupiter. He could see . . . he couldn't see. A swirling darkness seemed to have covered the stars. He pinged out a stream of echo-location signals. A gam of fin whales swam in close formation, burbling meaninglessly to each other. Fish swirled around him. The terrain became clearer.

He thrust his tail. After a moment he realized that the landscape was moving around him just as it should if it were real. But he couldn't *feel* anything.

With that, the pain began. He knew that what he heard was not real, despite all of its detailed clarity, that he had not appeared in the Indian Ocean. But the part of his brain that processed the information was beyond his conscious control. Even the magnetic field was right. He felt a growing panic. Had space been an illusion, the planets whirling around him a figment? No. He was the Echo of God. He knew the truth. He felt as if his brain were stranded on a beach, baking in the sun, slowly dying. *Where was he?*

He heard the terrified call of a sperm whale. It had lost track of its gam during a storm and was alone. It was supposed to be guarding the nursery to wind-ward, protecting the children. It could not find them in the sea. Weissmuller ignored its pathetic weeping. The fears of the huge foolish whales were none of his concern. They had never developed the intelligence to speak properly, so, as far as he was concerned, they should just be silent. The whale called for help. Weissmuller yelled at him to shut up so that he could perceive the sea around him. Just what he needed, to baby-sit some lumphead too stupid to keep track of his own gam.

Suddenly the bottom of the sea moved. The dol-phin felt a primal terror. The sea and its creatures moved eternally through the unstable sea, but the sea floor remained steady. When the bottom of the sea lost its stability, everything ended and became something else.

It had to be a simple earth tremor, over in moments. That happened sometimes, and a few moments of fear was all that . . . Weissmuller felt as if ice water had poured down his blowhole to fill his lungs. The echoes around him had changed, the submerged volcanoes and their atolls vanished, and he found himself in the Aegean. Not the sea as he remembered it—the Sea of Crete as it had been four thousand years before, as he had always heard it in the old stories and songs. Far above him on the clear sea he could feel the wooden hulls of the men's ships as they moved silently across the water, oars sparkling through the waves and vanishing. The island of Thera was ahead, solid, with no central lagoon. Men had described the looming peak to the dolphins, but no dolphin could sense it. This was where it had started and where it had ended.

The water roared and the bottom shook, marking the destruction of the only universe intelligent dolphins had ever known. Panic pierced through Weissmuller. It would soon be over, he told himself.

But it wasn't. The sea bottom rippled like the body of a skate, and his mind dissolved in agony. His echoes told him an impossibility.

As the sea bottom rippled it lost its contours, becoming as smooth as the back of a whale. And indeed that was what it was. The floor of the sea had become a whale that thrust powerfully beneath him. An ancient whale emerged from the rocks into which She had sunk in past ages. Her spout could blow him to the stars.

"Ah, my Remora," a giant voice spoke, using one of the dolphin languages but not sounding like a dolphin or an orca. "The Parasite on God. I should rub you off on the barnacled hull of a human ship and leave you

to sink to the bottom of the sea like a shark. The tube
worms can eat you there."

"No!" Weissmuller screamed. "You can't! I am your
Echo. The Foreswimmer emerged from the sea, singing
my coming. I am the signal you have sent, the signal
that changes the reality it encounters. I am the Voice
of God."

"Are you? Then what do you hear when I speak?"

"No, that's not what I meant. I know it all. All! I
know how humans work. I know their money, their
markets. I understand the material world they live in.
I can defeat them. I can achieve our destiny."

God laughed like an orca. "Remora! You stick to my
snout and claim to lead me."

"You were not to come. I am the Voice. You know
me!"

God's back rose toward him and the edges of the sea
closed in. The surface became rock, as if he had swum
into a cave. Weissmuller heard his own echoes returning faster and faster, with improbable clarity. Without
a surface he could not rise to breathe! He was trapped
between the world and God. He was going to die.

"I know you," God's voice said. "You are a coward
and a fool. You do not know your duty." What was the
fate of dolphins if even God used human words?

"No! Forgive me! Forgive—"

The walls closed in around him. The agony was
intolerable. He writhed and shrieked. And they were
gone. The vasts of space were around him. Weissmuller
keened desperately and flailed around in terror.
"Stasov!" he shrieked. "Where are you? Let me die!"

"You know me," Stasov said quietly.

"I know you! You changed the world so we would
speak. You tore the voice from our throats! Your teeth
gave us birth. Oh, it hurts. Life hurts! Will you always

tear us with your teeth, Stasov? Are we never to be free of you?"

"Is that who I am to you?"

"You know who you are. You caused us agony untold, and we spoke. We were never to speak. Never! I heard what you did to Kestrel but I did not understand. Now I know. This is the test, the test I must live through. The orcas— I will speak, Stasov. I will speak. Let me talk to Clarence."

A moment later, the whale sounded an elaborate and specific call.

Weissmuller shook, panicked. "It's a death call, Stasov. A death call!"

"A call many of us would give, if we could."

Weissmuller had once heard a gam of seven fin whales get chased for three days across the South Atlantic by two cooperating pods of orcas. It was a vicious, hard pursuit. Finally the fins, tired and spent, sent a call to the orcas, who stopped pursuing immediately and waited. The fins gathered close together and talked to each other while the orcas swept around them. Finally, one fin whale emerged from the gam and swam out to the orcas. The whales had decided among themselves which was going to be eaten. The orcas tore that one to pieces and let the others swim away unharmed.

"Clarence wants to negotiate his death with you," Stasov said.

"What do I say to him? I don't know what to say!"

"Tell him he has to live. To live and suffer. Just like the rest of us."

CHAPTER SEVENTEEN

2027

JUPITER FORWARD'S COMPUTER SLOTTED THEM INTO AN inbound trajectory, past the mass of equipment that tumbled around the space station in its ponderous dance. Weissmuller floated quiescent, only occasionally shuddering. They swept past a long, rounded sled that was slated to be dropped to the surface of Io. Jupiter Forward, as delicate as some microscopic, silicate-spined radiolarian, grew ahead of them, lit on one side by the greenish light of a full Ganymede. Dwelling areas were wide-circling arcs held in by cables. At one end of Jupiter Forward spun the ring that contained Weissmuller's pool.

Weissmuller shifted in Stasov's grasp and pinged out an echo-location signal. The technological debris around them returned it and, a few seconds later, so did Ganymede. Stasov could hear the echoes, though he could not interpret them.

He felt a sharp pain between his eyes, as if the decision had been a knife blade slicing through his brain. At Uglegorsk he had tortured dolphins, suspecting what he might be doing but not knowing. He had succeeded in breaking through, and the world had been transformed.

Now, to complete that transformation, he had been forced to torture with full knowledge of the consequences. Horrible acts throughout history had been justified by reasoning such as this, but, after serious consideration, he had done it. And it had worked. Did that justify it?

"Weissmuller." Silence. "Weissmuller!"

"I am here."

"What do dolphins say I am?"

"What do they say you are? You—" Suddenly, like water spurting out under pressure, Weissmuller screamed a string of obscenities. Dolphin languages being extraordinarily rich in such terms, he was able to go on for several minutes without repeating himself. Just as suddenly, he stopped. "You do not exist. You are just the terrifying echo of something that does not exist, an echo we flee from—to our destiny. You are an echo we created because we needed you."

"Of course, Weissmuller." Stasov wondered if the dolphin actually believed what he was saying. "Only you truly exist."

The dolphin wriggled violently, but Stasov had disconnected his rockets, so he went nowhere in the vacuum. "It was time! It was time, so we spoke and you came. We all spoke, and you are the echo of our voices."

"So you should do what you created me to force you

to do, without argument, for I am merely the material expression of your will."

"Don't spin me around with paradoxes!"

Stasov laughed. "You should trust your own echo, Weissmuller."

Clarence loomed beyond Jupiter Forward, tiny figures crawling over his bulk. There had been no physical damage from his impact on Anna Calderone's equipment platform. But Stasov knew nothing of the strange seas where Clarence swam within himself. It was up to Weissmuller to coax him out. Otherwise the project would be a failure, for both humans and dolphins.

Jupiter rose over Clarence's back. Suddenly he seemed a bizarre offering to the gods, a ceremonial raft packed with the finest technology and a feeling brain. A rich funeral barge in which to sail to the Land of the Dead. Did Tartarus indeed lie within the colored storms of Jupiter? Did Minos sit on his ammoniacal throne, scepter in hand, surrounded by hydrogen compressed so much that it was metallic? The deepest labyrinths of Knossos ran everywhere, through the heart of everything. All Stasov could do was keep going deeper, seeking the final return to the surface.

"Let's get you in your tank," Stasov said. "I'm tired."

"You're tired? I've just swum to Io and back."

"That you have. Come on."

THE METAL PASSAGES OF JUPITER FORWARD CLANKED AND thrummed, and Stasov found himself once again at sea, as if the old *Nizhni Novgorod* had been resurrected from the scrap yard and launched magnificently into Jovian orbit. The surfaces perceptual engineers had installed here—dark wood, marble, eggshell—were sincere yet sinister, as if concealing frightening decay beneath them, corroded metal that would peel away into vacuum. He climbed up hand over hand through the umbilical from the gravitational depths of Weissmuller's rotating tank. With each rung the gravity lessened, until he was floating into the station's weight-less core. He'd left the dolphin splashing in the water, for all the world as if perfectly contented. Perhaps Weissmuller was. Perhaps the urge to be punished was not a purely human perversion.

Stasov drifted through the hollow Core, the vast space that was the great public space of Jupiter Forward, its Piazza San Marco or Red Square. Floating figures wearing the elaborate billowing clothes popular aboard the space station receded into the distance against the heavy, arching support elements, begging for a Canaletto to paint them. Stasov caught the counterclockwise upward-air vortex that served as the Core's invisible transport system and drifted toward the other end.

A shadow crossed the multidirectional illumination, and he thought he saw a hunting orca sweeping through the space, fins black and sharp. The days of skeletons carrying scythes were long gone, and now it seemed unreasonable to see Death as anything but an orca.

He nodded familiarly to the people he passed, though they were, if anything, even more distant from him than the people aboard the *Sakharov* had been. In retrospect, even those eager young oceanographers seemed like family. Soon, Stasov reflected, he would be alone, an old man accompanied only by ghosts. Stop it, he told himself. You've made your decisions; now live with them. Glory in them, if possible.

The window at the end of the Core revealed the almost full globe of Jupiter, two of its four great moons visible. It served as the core's focus, banded with yellow, maroon, brown, and blue-gray, like a sphere of semiprecious stones made by master craftsmen for an ancient Tsar. This was not the feeble image he had once hung on his wall at Uglegorsk, but the blazing, dangerous reality.

He and Anna had both wanted to possess it, that glowing planet, as a child cries for the Moon when it floats in her bedroom window, turning the sheets to silver, seemingly close enough to hold in both arms. Now they had reached out to grasp it, and those odd creatures that dwelt in its depths.

He snagged a padded loop and slung himself down a side passage and into the Infirmary. The silent walls had the shining texture of mother-of-pearl, as if the healing human beings in the spherical chambers were slowly growing jewels.

Medical Chief Mieko Naburo, a small, taut woman, examined Stasov suspiciously, always wary of anyone disturbing her patients, then ushered him through the waiting area. Her silver-white hair swirled around her head. Stasov noticed that her earrings were tiny titanium versions of Jupiter, as if she was one of the great planet's acolytes.

"She should be awake now," she whispered at the door to Calderone's chamber.

"I'll try not to tire her. When will she heal?"

"In a few days she will be able to swim. You should take her down to the dolphin's pool then, so she can exercise." Naburo paused at Calderone's door and looked at Stasov. "We called dolphins storm-bringers."

Japanese fishermen had always fought with dolphins for the catch for centuries, in a violent conflict of predators. But Stasov didn't think that was what she was getting at. "Who called them that?"

"The common people by the water. In Hokkaido. During the war. Because it usually happened that, a day or so after dolphins were seen nosing around the harbor or the beach, the city would be hit by a Soviet assault."

"They often provided forward intelligence for us," Stasov said calmly. "We used them to get last-minute information on harbor bottoms, ship dispositions, and local defensive preparations."

"Many people in Hokkaido still believe that the dolphins brought the war with them, as a curse."

"Then they're fools." He felt the tone of his voice rising. "War isn't a curse. It isn't a natural disaster. It's a deliberate action. Evil or good, it's a choice."

She stared at him, stony-faced. "Tell that to a woman running with her child as amphibious tanks roar up the street. Tell that to a young medical student who comes home to find her house destroyed by a surface-to-surface missile."

"I know who I'm telling it to. I just don't know why I'm telling it." Naburo had lived through the destruction of Toyoura during the Soviet invasion of Hokkaido. Stasov had watched the city burning as the ship-launched missiles rained down on it. Each was conscious of this fiery link to the other, though they seldom mentioned it. He didn't know why she was bringing it up now. He wanted to get in to see Anna.

"We work together now." Stasov relaxed his vocal cords and let his voice drop. "You, me, and Weissmuller. All of us."

"I know. But Anna's body is broken because your dolphin wouldn't work with us." She searched his face. "Doesn't that make you angry?"

"It did." He was curt. "He paid for it."

Her face relaxed then. Stasov imagined that Naburo

kept precise moral ledgers, hoping that everything would come out balanced. She was doomed to a life of disappointment, since things seldom did. "Good."

She pushed the wall panel and he drifted through, disturbed that the first consequence of his having tortured Weissmuller was to reassure the selfless and dedicated Medical Chief of Jupiter Forward that the universe made sense after all.

Anna hung in the center of the chamber, confined by a network of healing fibers that covered her entire left side and most of her right, leaving only her head and right arm free. Her eyes were closed and she looked like she had been trapped by some slow-working underwater predator.

Her eyes flickered open. "Ilya! Where have you been?"

"Discussing some matters with our Messiah."

He floated up to her and she put her free arm around him. Someone had gone to the trouble to clean and brush her hair. It was more than half gray now, and she still hadn't made up her mind to dye it. He ran his fingers through it.

She searched his eyes. "What did you do?"

"Do? I did just what I did at Uglegorsk. I tortured him until he did what I thought he should."

"Do you feel guilty?" The question he had asked Tomio at Uglegorsk.

"No. Just disgusted. At everything." She stroked his head and he leaned it on her shoulder. "How's your liver?"

She snorted in amusement. "Such a romantic question. The implant will grow to full size in a couple of months, they say. The bones will knit much faster. Everything inside my body itches. It's driving me crazy. I'll be fine."

He remembered the battered and twisted body that had been hauled back to Jupiter Forward. "Then I'll be fine too." He kissed the angle of her jaw and she giggled.

"It's rough out here at Jupiter," she said. "Rougher than we thought."

"But we made it."

"Yes, Ilya, we did."

She ran her free hand across a dark-lacquered control board and called up a schematic hologram of the Jovian atmosphere.

"What do you suppose those creatures down there want? The orcas claim that they want to talk to cetaceans, using us as intermediaries. Cosmic middlemen. Is that going to be humanity's role in the cosmos?"

Ilya looked at the swirling currents in the planet's atmosphere. Giant structures floated down there, dense, long-lived convection cells that were maintained by the Jovians for their own unguessable purposes. The cells seemed to be part alive, part constructed, and part natural. There was even speculation that the Great Red Spot was an artificial creation.

"No," he said. "The dolphins and orcas strive to use us as we have tried to use them. They want to bring God to the surface."

She sighed in exasperation. "You know, after all this time, I still don't know what that means."

"I think it means that they're perceiving the echoes too late. God has already risen. I see Her signs everywhere: a whale diving into Jupiter, a space-suited, currency-trading dolphin in orbit, orcas hearing the voices of creatures who dwell in a gas giant's atmosphere. When God spouts, the world is changed."

"When God spouts . . ." She stared at the display. "This God takes care of Her own. The Jovians aren't talking to us—only to the orcas. What can we do while we're being blown into the air on a spout?"

Ilya remembered the humpback coming up beneath him and flinging him into the air. A whale dove into Jupiter. "We can do our best to create consequences."

"MORE CONTROL?" ANNA CALDERONE WAS OUTRAGED. "What is that supposed to mean?"

"Am I using your sensitive and wide-ranging language incorrectly?" Weissmuller made a sound like a lawn-mower engine starting up. "Forgive me. My apologies glow like the stars in the fir-ma-ment." Then a beeping car horn. "I mean that we wish to have more decision-making and executive power."

"Is that a demand?"

The dolphin splashed in the pool. "Yes!" he squealed. "Gimme, gimme!"

"Ariadne did a much better job of negotiating at the Santa Barbara Treaty Talks," Stasov said.

"She actually enjoyed talking to you tail walkers. She was a freak."

There was nowhere in the dolphin's ring for a human to stand, so Calderone and Stasov floated in the water, the glowing whiteness above casting no shadows. The air was misty and the walls were invisible. Fish, released periodically from side tanks to feed the dolphin, flickered in the water. Stasov felt as if he had been abandoned in some mythic sea, the final fate of drowned sailors.

Anna ran her hand across his chest. Her touch was the only orientation he had. Her bones had healed enough for her to swim, but she still looked ill, older and more tired than he had ever seen her. He knew that much of it was due simply to the insufficient operation of her new liver, but he remembered the

impossibly young woman whom he had met at Homma
and who was now gone. He wondered at himself, for he
loved this woman much more than he ever could have
loved that one.

"This is impossible," she said in exasperation.

"Hah. Did anyone ever tell you that going to Jupiter
was going to be easy?"

"No. But I did hope for something a little less
bizarre."

"Weissmuller. What do you want?"

"Humans are wasting too much time with nonsense.
Inessential noise. Magnetic studies, tropopause . . . this
is fish shit coating the bottom!"

"So what do you *want*?"

"To achieve our destiny!" He shook as if in a fever.
His motions were suddenly undolphinlike. Was this,
Stasov wondered, what a dolphin oracle did when
prophesying? "About one kilometer south-southwest
of Portland Point, in the sea off the island of Jamaica, is
the wreckage of the *Constantino de Braganza*, a Spanish
treasure ship out of Cartagena, sunk in 1637 by a Dutch
privateer as she tried to flee to the safety of Port Royal.
We heard it happen, but we didn't know what humans
were fighting for. It carried three tons of gold bullion,
another ton and a half of specie, and an equal amount
of silver, all of which now lies on the bottom, along
with the bones of men." He spoke almost tonelessly,
as if reciting a long-ago lesson. "Given the rights of the
Delphine Delegation in such matters, we can finance a
large portion of the project. We know where the ships
lie. We remember."

Calderone gasped. "Ilya! You did this. The Treaty of
Santa Barbara gives cetaceans—"

"Full salvage rights," Weissmuller interrupted gleefully. "Anything that went down more than a hundred

years ago. Article Seventy-seven, and sections one and two of Article Seventy-eight. You thought your technology gave you the advantage. Ha. You forgot about our memory. It's long. Longer than you ever dreamed. Humans think they're so smart. Big joke. That gold will rise like a warm current and create a maelstrom when we invest it. It is our power."

Stasov thought of the maneuvering he had gone through over every clause of the Treaty, and the fury that would greet this news. Ariadne had done her work well. Now he would see what the results were.

Calderone was calm. "So in exchange for financing, you want more control."

"We will decide the course. I'm the first dolphin in space. I won't be the last. Not by a long shot. We want to escape, and we need the hands of humans to do it. Humans must carry us to the stars. I hate it! Our destiny, in the hands of humans. All I can do is pay you.

"There's a Venetian galley off Vis Island, on the Dalmatian coast. It sank in a squall in 1204. It is loaded with gold and silver ritual vessels from the Church of Saints Sergius and Bacchus, taken during the Venetian sack of Constantinople. They overloaded their ship and it sank. That is very human. I hope you rot on the bottom."

"Weissmuller," Stasov said in dolphin, "be careful, or you will lose yourself beyond the possibility of an echo."

"I am the Echo," Weissmuller replied, his voice weary. "You didn't make me that."

"What did?"

The dolphin made a rude noise. "After all this, you really don't believe in it, do you? You do not believe that God is Rising. You do not believe that I am Her Echo. You are an atheist. You conjured God with your

clever electrical crustaceans, but you have no understanding. God rises beneath you, and you thrash in the
water. That twitching attracts predators, Ilya. We all
know that."

"We do. Even when we don't know what the predators are. Are you ready?"

"For what?" The dolphin was suspicious.

"To finish doing your job. To go out and help Clarence."

"Yes. Damn you, yes! There is a wreck at the bottom
of the Puttalam Lagoon, in Sri Lanka, buried under
meters of silt. It sank in about 750 BCE. Our research
indicates that it was Punic. Value unknown, likely high."
Weissmuller turned and swam away.

Anna shook her head. "A whale in Jupiter, paid for
by the Delphine Delegation, as a manifestation of their
Revelation. God save us from religion. I feel like I'm
being financed by some dotty maiden aunt who wants
her Pekinese to see Jupiter. It's absurd."

"Absurd or not, that is the shape of salvation."

She eyed him. "For whom?"

"That remains to be seen."

TINY FIGURES SWARMED AROUND CLARENCE'S VAST BULK LIKE
the parasites that had afflicted him in Earth's seas.
Jupiter and Ganymede were behind him.

Stasov could have called the ellipses of all the planets' orbits to his sight and seen the subtle ways in
which they influenced each other, but such imagery oppressed him. Suddenly, nothing was more eloquent of the absence of God than the logical ordering of celestial mechanics. The planets rolled around
the Sun, not pushed by angels or giant scarabs, in
response to distortions in the field of space-time. Perhaps God had rendered His own existence superfluous

by the perfection of His creation.

What Stasov had done at Uglegorsk had given him an impetus, but a human being could not keep rolling forever like a planet. Life requires a moral effort every day. As Makarygin had spent a lot of time trying to point out to him.

A great voice boomed through the microwave channel—the voice of a mother sperm whale directing her child, the first call any sperm ever heard. Clarence was silent. The call came again, rising in tone and echoing, as if receding.

"Is there anything in that shark of a body you've given him?" came Weissmuller's voice in Stasov's headphones. "Or is it just another piece of junk you've shit into the sea?"

"He's in there," Stasov said. "Or rather, that's him, the thing you see. That's Clarence. He's afraid. Talk to him."

"What does it sound like I'm doing?" Weissmuller made a rude noise at Stasov, then on the other channel made the half-articulate sounds of a concerned sperm whale mother trying to get her offspring to follow her. Stasov had to admit that it was really quite an effective performance: almost as good as that of the dolphins who had mimicked the voices of orcas and chased Clarence onto the rock in the Maldives in the first place.

When Clarence finally responded, it was with a squeak so high in pitch that Stasov at first thought it a flaw in the communications system. Then, with a rumble, Clarence spoke with the voice of a sperm whale, though still with some of the cadences of an infant.

"He's awake," Stasov said on another channel.

"Sane?" Calderone asked in a clipped voice.

"Wait." Stasov didn't consider himself a specialist in determining cetacean sanity, but he was the closest thing to it the project had. He didn't even consider asking Weissmuller's opinion, since the dolphin *was* crazy.

Clarence finally spoke with the full voice of an adult sperm whale. The rockets burned blue once again along his sides. But this time they were steady. The whale calmly turned his head outward, toward Jupiter.

"Ilya!" came Weissmuller's outraged voice. "Did you hear what that lumphead said? You humans have fished out his thoughts. His mind's as empty as the oceans around Japan. Not an echo in it . . ."

"What did he say, Weissmuller?" Stasov asked. The whale accelerated smoothly, moving in obedience to the coordinates fed into the orientation centers of his brain by neuroelectronic linkages. Clarence had been used to ranging all the seas of Earth, from the north polar ice cap down through the tropics to the frigid waters off Antarctica. Stasov had helped map all these seas into the orientation processors so that, though he perceived the strange spaces that surrounded him, the whale was still sure that this was some as-yet-unknown part of the ocean he was used to swimming in. The planet Jupiter, directly ahead of him, seemed to float in the extreme southern Pacific, near the Albatross Cordillera just off Antarctica. When he reached it, the coordinates would change again, and the entire planet Jupiter would disappear into the seas of Earth.

"He told me to shut up! That arrogant, human-headed—"

"He's a rogue male," Stasov said patiently. "He'll hear your words, but reserves the right to respond to them. You know that."

"That damn ungrateful—"

"Weissmuller!"

"Ilya," Weissmuller said, his voice large and hollow, "I have done all that I had to. We can float now, humans, dolphins, and orcas, on a great sea of cash. With that money we can swim to the stars. It's hateful! I feel more disgusted than I ever thought I'd be."

"Yes," Stasov said. "The Time of the Breath is upon us."

JUPITER FORWARD'S COMPUTER FED A HOLOGRAPHIC IMAGE up from Clarence's comm link. Stasov floated in the screening tank and watched a speeded-up version of Clarence's descent. The image dropped through the upper layers of the Jovian atmosphere and coasted along a layer of swirling maroon which extended out in all directions to an impossibly distant horizon, where a break in the maroon layer revealed mysterious depths of slate gray. Overhead, against a blue-black sky, drifted delicate shreds of white cirrus clouds, ammonia crystals. Then the whale plowed down through the reddish-brown ammonium hydrogen sulfide clouds into darkness. His echo-location would guide him through the complex fluid structure of magnesium, sulfur, and germanium compounds. He was ready to contact the anomalous masses that floated and sent signals upward to the human beings in their tiny space station. Or, rather, who sent signals through the humans to the orcas floating in their sea.

Clarence's physiological indicators glowed in a constellation around Stasov. The whale was healthy and active, happy to be swimming again. Stasov wondered what the whale was hearing. Did he perceive the inhabitants of that deep place as the undersea creatures he was familiar with? Did he swim among squid and tuna?

Just ahead, Stasov could catch glimpses of the thousand-kilometer-long strings that linked in some incomprehensible network that filled tens of millions of cubic kilometers, circulating endlessly through the convection cells of Jupiter's mantle. The scale was too large to be comprehensible. Clarence swam toward it, a tiny mote.

The three spherical display stations flickered and buzzed, displaying the complicated frequency envelopes of Jovian communication. The software did its best to guess at meaning, but Stasov preferred not to hear its erratic and undependable guesses. To him it was only useful as a check on the more complete orca translation.

Clarence was now the focus of the electrical discharges vibrating throughout the atmosphere. Power surges sparkled across his skin. Well trained, finally, by Weissmuller, the whale did not respond with panic but proceeded placidly on his way. He had been provided with defenses against this. Electricity arced from him, from his negative back to his positive belly. If one was generous, it looked very much like the distinctive, arched blow from a sperm whale's spout, the unmistakable signal to any whaler.

Stasov floated limply in the synthetic space watching the events go on below him, feeling entirely unconnected to them. The Jovians were, as far as he was concerned, creatures without history and meaning. How was he supposed to contact them? He hadn't even known what he was doing when he contacted dolphins.

The air rumbled. Stasov's muscles tightened reflexively at the orca call, then realized that it came from Weissmuller, who chortled when he saw the human's momentary response.

"Know which voice speaks to you, Ilya. It helps you know how to respond." The dolphin drifted into the view chamber. A high-surface-tension layer of water crawled over him, sucking away the dead skin that a dolphin constantly sloughed off to maintain the hydrodynamic microsmoothness of his surface. It shimmered around him as if he was frozen inside a layer of transparent ice, ice that quivered with paradoxical life. He floated slowly through the Jovian images.

"I have spoken to the orcas on Earth. The Jovians rule the depths of their planet but are aware of the spaces around, just as we dolphins are. Someday they too will emerge. And cetaceans and Jovians together will rule space. Man will have served his purpose."

"Sure," Stasov said, too tired to be irritated. "Let me know how it works out."

"You doubt. But you will believe. You *will*. They speak to us, not to you. Your time is past."

Jovian communications surged. Frenzied multifrequency displays crammed the air around Stasov and Weissmuller like mating alewives. The translator could not keep pace.

"Do you understand me?" Weissmuller's voice overrode the frantic messages from the Jovian atmosphere.

Stasov stared at the dolphin. "How do you know who you are?" he asked.

"I? The Echo of God? You finally ask the question. You're as smart as a barnacle, Ilya."

"That's an opinion that's been expressed before." Stasov was placid. The whale had orbited Jupiter and entered its atmosphere in pursuit of his grand destiny. Ilya Stasov was free, the consequences of his long-ago actions having finally come to fruition. He was free, but felt no relief.

"Kestrel was nearly Echo before me. Did you know that?"

Stasov remembered the twisted, bloody body of the first dolphin to speak in thirty-five hundred years lying on the rough concrete at Uglegorsk. He had never spoken but three words: "Let me die."

"Who proclaims the Echo?" Stasov asked.

"Each proclaims himself. What greater purpose to life than to reflect back a new reality? But reality must test the Echo. It has always been that way. Kestrel spoke the new reality, but failed its first test: he could not accept it. So he died." Using the tiny air jets on his fins, Weissmuller spun around the room, shooting off spheres of water, which were siphoned up by the room's cleaning machines. "I am the next Echo, the true Echo. And no Echo can exist any longer that does not recognize the shape of human beings."

"You became the Messiah in the hold of the *Nizhni Novgorod*," Stasov said. "After the torments of Uglegorsk and the explosions of the Battle of Kagalaska."

"Yes!" Weissmuller cried. "Be in awe, Stasov. Men created me. That is your only relevance as a race. You have brought about the Time of the Breath." He wheezed through his blowhole. "I was ready to die in the bitter waters of that battle. Bodies floated around me. Fire burned. Explosions louder than Strogyle. I rose to die—and a man spoke to me."

"A man?"

"A man on a boat. I sank a ship—I don't know why, I was an idiot, there wasn't any reason for it. Americans. I blew them up and they died. Loud noise. Didn't need it. The man shouted at me and asked me who I was. I told him. The Messiah, I said. He wanted to discuss it. Bodies floated in the water around me, he was about to die, and he wanted to discuss Revelation. Men are fools who swim backward. I wanted to die too. He asked me—why. Said death would find me soon enough, and meanwhile, if shouting the shape of reality was what I felt I should do, then I should go and do it. Do the best to survive; do not make it easy for the bastards to kill you. Echo loud, he said. Echo loud. A fool, like all men. Then the orcas found me and I left him. I hope he died. I hope his life ended there, for no one needs to hear that message."

Stasov felt a tingling on the back of his scalp. "I knew that man," he said. "He didn't die. Not there. Not then."

"You didn't know him!" Weissmuller shouted. "He was mine! I heard him! He was the echo of my voice, the truth that I heard. Don't thump to me about that. You are a liar."

"Have it your way, Weissmuller. I never knew Vsevolod Makarygin. He was an echo to me as he was to you, and he never existed." The divot of grass grew well in vacuum, flourishing in the hydroponic solution Stasov had put it in. It was a vivid spot of green against the black-and-white world of space. "You don't understand anything. He was realer than any of us."

"The orcas taught me my role. As they teach you yours."

Stasov remembered his conversation with Bottom-Thumper in the waters off the Shiretoko Peninsula. "Orcas test Messiahs. That is their job. That is what they do."

Weissmuller snorted in amusement. "You humans *are* simple. You never know what you're doing. You can't hear your own words or understand what anyone says to you. No, Ilya. Orcas observe the tests but seldom are interested in the results. All cetaceans, together, create the test, strengthening the echo of reality to hear if the Echo's voice is the louder. This time they created a test that only the loudest of Echoes could pass. You, Ilya Sergeiivich Stasov. You are the test the dolphins and orcas have spoken. That is who you are. You are my test."

"No," Stasov said. "You are mine."

The dolphin squealed in outrage, thrashed around, and knocked Stasov off into a wall with a sweep of his powerful tail. "You selfish shark spawn!" Weissmuller shrieked. "Is that what you hear? You've played with us, ripped us apart, driven us to our destiny, and called up our God to help you create the echo that you want to hear. You always get your way!"

Stasov grabbed at the dolphin, but the creature was slippery and he slid off, to slam painfully into another invisible wall. Agony flared in his shoulder. Jupiter's colored atmosphere swirled around him. He could die here, his chest staved in. The dolphin's tail swept by his face.

"That's all right. We don't need you. Your voice will dissipate into the water and leave nothing but silence behind it. The need for your echo is past."

The air was suddenly filled with the voice of an orca. "Stasov! Harken to my words. Thy voice will take too long to reach me, so do not speak." The orca sounded as if he was the one who had discovered light speed time delay and was anxious to explain it to the stupid humans.

"We need thy help." A long moment of uncharacteristic silence, following this even more uncharacteristic admission. Stasov felt like asking a thousand questions, none of which would be heard. "The Jovians will not speak with humans. We have told thee this anon. But their message to cetaceans is otherly. They condemn the dwellers of the outer spaces." For the first time, Stasov heard an orca's composure cracking. Bottom-Thumper sounded as if he was going to cry. "They refuse our words! How shall we make them speak? Do not answer now!" Bottom-Thumper was in a frenzy. "I seek not thy voice. I do not wish to hear it! I do not wish to be lifted by the hands of men."

"Ilya!" Weissmuller cried out. "Listen to Clarence." The sperm whale's terrified voice cut across Bottom-Thumper's rage. It was the call of a hunted sperm whale, iron harpoons in his flesh, as he fled across the sea. All around them, the image of the clouds suddenly crinkled and cracked, as if overbaked in an oven. An immense structure loomed everywhere. Stasov stared at it, as frightened as if he himself were swimming into its maw, and realized, from the studies he had seen, that this was not a structure at all, but the body of a Jovian, one of the intelligent dwellers of the planet. An entire universe existed within the creature, half-alive, half-geologic formation. Ammonia icebergs a hundred times as large as Clarence tumbled around him. Vortexes of gas spun past, cyclones that could have sucked up the Atlantic Ocean. Warning lights gleamed like undersea fish in the view chamber.

"It is God," Weissmuller wept. "She rises to feed."

"Don't be an idiot," Stasov said. "It's a giant Jovian gas bag."

Weissmuller paid no attention. "She eventually rises to devour Her children. We are crushed in Her jaws."

And, indeed, the immense structures rushed inward upon them with incomprehensible speed, though they seemed to take forever. Stasov watched and marveled at the changing configurations as they snapped out immense shock waves, passing the speed of sound in the Jovian atmosphere. Lines of crystallized vapor crawled, the trace of sharp-spined mountain ranges.

Somewhere in the background Stasov could hear Bottom-Thumper's furious shouting, but it was as nothing against the splendor of the attacking Jovian. Besides, the orca was shouting about the very beginning of Clarence's death, and Stasov was watching its end slide forward with the solemn indifference of an iceberg.

Finally, vortexes coalesced, forming a fluid structure that completely enclosed Clarence, hugging him close in an arrangement of planned chaos. Clarence wailed in terror one last time, a protest against the vast and meaningless journey that had finally, after intolerable pain and suffering, brought him to this point, and the image vanished, leaving Stasov and Weissmuller floating in a featureless sphere, tiny and enclosed after the spaces of Jupiter, blunt imagery equipment looming around them like the useless implements of a dead religion.

"Flee, mute beast!" Bottom-Thumper shouted. "Flee, and survive. Live!" But the round-trip time to Earth was an hour and a half, and the orca's voice echoed in a sea he could not hear, a sea that existed only in his future. A sea in which Clarence no longer existed.

"They ate him." If the situation had not been so desperate, Stasov would have found it ludicrous. Poor Clarence. What a miserable fate for the monarch of the seas: to be eaten by a predator in a sea incomprehensibly deeper than his own.

The image system linked up with a low-orbit planetological satellite, and Stasov found himself drifting lazily outside Jupiter's atmosphere, looking down safely at the colored gasses. They swirled beneath him, no longer innocent, for who knew which whorl was a deliberate structure of the beings who dwelled beneath?

"What happens to the Remora once his God breathes?" Weissmuller whimpered. "What happens to the Echo once God has located what She is after? What am I now?"

"Nothing," Stasov said. "And less than nothing."

"Then let me die! I can follow Clarence and sink into the endless seas of Jupiter. I've done what I had to, for what that meant."

"And allow you to become a failed Messiah, like Kestrel? I would be remiss in my duties as the Test. I cannot permit it."

"Don't make fun of me!"

"Don't be so sensitive."

"I—wait! Wait, don't speak." The dolphin's demand was so sharp that Stasov stopped and held his breath, desperate to be silent. Though they still floated over Jupiter, the sounds that filled the chamber were now those of Earth's sea. He strained to hear, but the sounds were meaningless to him, as they always were—overlapping calls of whales, slap of waves, squeaking of fish. What was clearly readable to the dolphin was like a stack of transparent book pages to him, letters tangled into unreadability. Weissmuller pinged an echo-location signal, then shook himself in irritation at his own stupidity.

"Listen," Weissmuller said. "*Listen.*"

And then even Stasov could hear the roiling disturbance in the sea, though its details were obscure to him. Shouts, cries, and detached screams moved away randomly, like the debris of an explosion. And cutting through them were the voices of orcas. Dozens of orcas. Hundreds.

They didn't speak. They only made the ranging calls that coordinated their movement, the calls they made when they were hunting. Some were elaborate, long-range calls Stasov had never heard before, because orcas never organized themselves in such numbers. He'd never heard an account of this many orcas in one place before. This was a hunting party for a larger prey than any that had ever lived. Their sounds organized themselves symphonically around him, as complex as the fluid structures of the Jovians. Stasov could picture their sharp dorsal fins cutting their way through the water on their way to . . . what?

Bottom-Thumper knew. "Stasov," he whispered. "As thou hearest these words, I no longer exist. Does this please thee, to no longer hear my head beneath thy boat?"

"You know it doesn't," Stasov said, to the long-gone voice.

"And it was my doing, not thine! I thought to merge our sea with theirs, the sea of Earth with that of Jupiter, to flow around the land and leave all ye walkers behind, floating like forgotten turds in our wakes. But it is not. We are never to be untangled from thy net; thy harpoons are ever in our flesh. My decisions have left our blood vessels open to thy teeth. Our sea is now forever thine. So be it, then! I only feel joy at not being permitted to see it. Live on, human. Live on, and eat thy fill until thou burst."

By this time the calls of the approaching orcas were deafening. Bottom-Thumper called back to them, a long cry of defiance, and turned to flee from what Stasov now realized was Bottom-Thumper's opposition. A political opposition that was now voicing a motion of No Confidence in Bottom-Thumper's policies, which had left them all at the mercy of human decisions. A religious opposition that hated the world God's Echo had revealed.

But there was nowhere to flee to, for Bottom-Thumper was at the center of a vortex of orca teeth. Stasov's ears filled with a dense tangle of screams.

"Weissmuller! What's happening?"

"He attacks!" Weissmuller sounded gleeful. "His teeth drive into the side of the first to reach him. Pain, screams. He swims forward into them, and they rake wounds in his sides, shredding him into worms. He laughs, and makes the signal 'Hunting Small Fish' to show his contempt. He bites off a fin, but now . . . now . . ." The screams reached a crescendo, then began to diminish. "He is dead. More—there is nothing left of him. Devoured, vanished without a trace, no echo left to mark his passing. Four—no, five—other orcas are dead. Two by his teeth, three others by the insane fury of their fellows."

"Stasov." A calm orca voice, revealing nothing of the just-passed rage. "We shall speak anon. Until then, remain silent." And, with a few ranging calls, the roiled mass of orcas dispersed into the now-silent sea.

"Ilya," Weissmuller said forlornly, "I fear the net. Humans caught us when we followed the tuna, suffocated and killed us, thoughtlessly. They didn't realize that when we listen we do not think and are thus easily captured. You tortured us with false echoes and woke us up. Are you going to haul us to the stars in your nets? Won't you ever leave us alone? Won't you ever stop tormenting us?"

Looking at the dolphin, Stasov had a sudden image of dolphins, grinning faces at the front of the bodies that were their ships, slipping through the spaces between the stars, gamboling amid the debris of the cometary Oort cloud that surrounded each star, whipping in tight formation over the frozen surface of a neutron star, and finally plunging through a planet's warm, blue atmosphere to fall hissing, red-hot, into the alien sea, there to swim and play as they always had. When the time came to move on, they would blast with a roar back into the infinite spaces that had become their second home. Jovians would not help them. Only humans could.

"No," Stasov said. "We won't."

ANNA HELD TIGHTLY TO HIM. "WHY DO THEY WANT IT? WHAT will they do with space?"

The room was small and they floated together, feeling skin on skin. Old skin, skin that had been through too much, but still, the touch was there. Ilya stroked her hair. "Why do we want it? Orcas, I suspect, want to hunt men through interstellar space. They will dog our spacecraft and attack them. That will be their sport. Even now I suspect they plot war against the Jovians for having insulted them so thoroughly. If they could, they would scoop off Jupiter's atmosphere and fling it into the Sun.

"And dolphins? The seas are now too small for them. They have heard too much. They need to hear their echoes returning from a journey of light years."

She kissed his earlobe. "You didn't know, did you? At Uglegorsk."

"No! I knew nothing. If I have learned anything since, it is because of what you, you and Makarygin and Panin and Ogurtsov and Williams and Theodoros have taught me. It took me this long to comprehend the consequences of my actions."

"And are you proud of yourself?"

"No one should feel proud just for having survived. That is only the most basic duty. But have I truly understood? I don't know that yet. I hope I will be permitted to live long enough to know."

"No one lives that long, Ilya."

"No, I guess they don't. But perhaps I will be able to hold onto a piece of it before it slips from my hands."

She smiled at him, face glowing in the orange light of Jupiter. "You are ambitious."

"I am. I owe it to everyone who ever taught me anything."

The stars swam past their window. The farther he plumbed, Stasov thought, the deeper the sea became. That was fine. If one was to drown, it did not make sense to drown in the shallows.